There can be no tyrants where there are no slaves.

*- Jose Rizal*

*About the Author*

John Pullinger is a former travel writer, English teacher and hotelier born and educated in Brisbane, Australia. He has worked in and out of Southeast Asia for over twenty years, and lives on the Sunshine Coast of Queensland, Australia.

# The Last Jeep to BaClaran

## John J PullinGer

Copyright © 2010 John J. Pullinger
Published by Vivid Publishing
Fremantle, Western Australia
www.vividpublishing.com.au

National Library of Australia Cataloguing-in-Publication data:
Author:  Pullinger, John J. (John Julian), 1939-
Title:     The last jeep to Baclaran / John J Pullinger.
Edition:  2nd ed.
ISBN:    9781921787041 (pbk.)
Dewey Number: A823.4

Disclaimer: All the characters in this book are fictitious and any resemblance to real persons living or dead is purely coincidental, except for President Ferdinand Marcos, Corazon Aquino and those involved in the actual events of the "People Power" revolution of February 1986. The information, views, opinions and visuals expressed in this publication are solely those of the author and do not reflect those of the publisher. The publisher disclaims any liabilities or responsibilities whatsoever for any damages, libel or liabilities arising directly or indirectly from the contents of this publication.

For information about the author, and to purchase more copies of this book, please visit:
www.vividpublishing.com.au/lastjeeptobaclaran

This book is dedicated to the Filipino people with love.

# 1

Steve Conway stepped from the arrival hall of Manila's international airport into a mad scramble of touts, vendors and tourists all milling around in a wall of heat and stifling humidity. A hundred brown faces surrounded him selling everything from sex toys, flick knives, knuckledusters, cigarettes and sunglasses, to the sweet smelling *sampaguita*, the national flower of the Philippines.

'Sir! Sir! You buy Sir!' they yelled and pleaded, pushing and shoving their wares under his nose. He was trying to fend off an over-eager vendor when he heard, 'Steve Conway, Mr Conway! Over here!' Conway wheeled looking for the voice. To his right waving above the crowd, was a smiling black giant.

'Jumbo Keyes I presume,' grinned Conway as they shook hands.

'The one and only sir, follow me, your carriage awaits,' said Keyes in a west coast American accent. He hefted Conway's suitcase shouldering his way through a sea of yelling touts and panhandlers out on to the concourse where a bright yellow mini van with *Down Under Hotel* emblazoned in red on either side and covered in stickers declaring, *Cory for President* stood waiting.

A Filipino driver immaculate in a crisp white shirt and black pants leapt from the front seat and held open a back door for his new boss. Keyes heaved the suitcase in behind Conway and eased his bulk into the front seat beside the driver he introduced as Mario.

'Welcome to the Philippines sir,' said Mario, with the kind of smile Filipinos are famous for.

The sun was low in the west as they moved out onto the wide palm tree-lined Roxas Boulevard which curved around the turgid waters of Manila Bay where assorted paint-streaked rust buckets, a few freighters and heavily laden container ships lay at anchor. The traffic was almost at a standstill giving Conway a chance to have his first look at Manila. It didn't look too promising.

He checked out the movements on the harbour for a few minutes then turned his attention to the right where fronting the boulevard were dreary concrete apartment blocks, nondescript hotels standing between run-down karaoke bars and eateries. The grass on the worn concrete median strip between the boulevard and a service road was overgrown and scrubby; a convenient rubbish dump for bits of plastic, soiled paper, piles of dirt and other indeterminate rubbish. The whole scene reeked of poverty and neglect.

I hope it gets better than this, he thought to himself. He was going to ask Keyes but decided against it. I shouldn't complain it's a new country, new things to see, do and experience. He relaxed and stifled a yawn. It was better than mourning back in Australia.

Holding up the traffic were vendors selling cigarettes and trinkets together with scores of locals bearing yellow flags, placards and banners, some in English, others in the native Tagalog dialect. Some messages were different but all said the same thing. *Cory for President, Marcos must go.*

They seemed cheerful enough waving and smiling to the commuters tactfully ignoring a few armed, grim-faced soldiers standing at intervals along the roadside.

Without turning around Keyes said, 'I don't like the look of this.'

Despite the perceived good-natured attitude of the protesters Conway didn't like the atmosphere either. The surly expressions of the soldiers bespoke a desire for the protestors to start something…something they would be more than willing to finish.

When Conway asked why the anxiety, what Keyes told him next only increased the tightening in his stomach.

'Not everyone wants Cory. There's been some pretty violent clashes between her supporters and those of Marcos recently and they seem to be getting worse. Shops have been trashed, vehicles burnt, a lot of injuries, even a couple of deaths. This is the first time I've seen troops out on the streets. If trouble starts my friend, we are bloody vulnerable sitting in this traffic. Come on Mario try and move it, we need to get out of here…fast!' But traffic coming out from a number of side streets slowed them further. Keyes cursed, to no avail.

They continued slowly along the boulevard leaving the Cory supporters behind. Conway settled back in his seat breathing a sigh of relief; a relief short-lived. Without warning their vehicle and those in front and behind were surrounded by a screaming, chanting mob who seem to appear from nowhere. Like the previous protestors they were waving flags, cardboard placards and shabby linen banners. This time they were all red. But unlike the former group, they were angry, very angry.

'Shit!' yelled Keyes, 'bloody Marcos supporters. They're souped up and they've seen the Cory stickers on our vehicle. Mario, you bloody idiot! I told you not to put those fucking stickers on.'

The words had hardly left his mouth when a young male protestor smashed the wooden handle of his banner across their bonnet. In front a jeepney was torched and passengers jumped out screaming onto the roadway.

'Holy Shit!' cried Conway as the young guy and others began yelling and banging on the roof. One of them had his face flattened against the window glass his face contorted with rage the glass distorting his expression into a tribal mask of hate and vengeance. In his hand he held a tree root as a weapon. Fuck, thought Conway. I'm going to be killed by a fucking tree root. Their vehicle began to rock violently as protestors grabbed it from either side. The window beside Conway suddenly smashed showering him with broken glass.

He put his hands up to shield himself but too late, he'd been cut and blood began to flow from a wound on his forehead and cheek. They were pushed to an angle of 45 degrees to the road and in imminent danger of toppling over.

Now completely surrounded, enraged hands tried to wrench open the doors. A brown arm reached in through the broken window but it quickly withdrew screaming as Conway grabbed the wrist and smashed it against the inside of the door. Another tried and reeled back his nose broken by a clubbing right from the Australian only to have his place taken by a youth, his eyes red and dilated, brandishing a pistol, which he pointed at Conway's head. The finger whitened as he squeezed the trigger. Horrified, Conway tried to throw himself sideways but there was no where to go in such a confined space.

BANG! The shot echoed through the vehicle. The youth's eyes opened wide with surprise and a fleeting look of bewilderment before he fell back into the mob behind him blood spurting from a wound at the back of his head. There were more shots and the crowd turned in confusion, screaming in panic as khaki clad soldiers with M16's and others in brown uniforms wielding batons, swarmed in shooting and clubbing indiscriminately.

'The army and riot police of Metrocom,' shouted Keyes above the din. 'Sit tight!'

Conway didn't need to be told. He sat wiping blood and glass from his face and arms and crouched looking around for something to protect himself. There was nothing.

'Sweet Jesus,' he gasped his heart thumping. He looked down to see both his hands trembling. He'd been a split second from sudden death. He tried to makes sense of what had just taken place in front of him as the riot continued to rage around them. The black hole at the end of the gun barrel and the look on the kid's face as half the back of his head was blown off would stay with him forever.

Eventually the army and police took control and cleared the area leaving broken bodies in their wake. A white-faced Mario climbed back up from the floor where he'd been crouching in terror and kicked the engine into life. They began to edge forward. Keyes directed him to the service road where the traffic was lighter. Finally recovering some composure Conway said,

'What the hell was that all about?'

Keyes half turned and Conway noticed he'd also been cut on the cheek by the flying glass. A few pieces were in his mop of fuzzy black hair. Taking a handkerchief from his shirt pocket he wiped the blood from his face and gingerly extracted the glass.

'Steve, this town is on a knife edge. These days the rule of law is almost non-existent. There's a high stakes game going on here and the prize is the nation itself. The people are pissed with the current regime and they want change. The battle for supremacy is between the Marcos forces whom you just had a taste of and those supporting Cory.'

'Tell me more about Cory.'

'Corazon Aquino. She's the widow of Benigno Aquino. He was a popular senator assassinated on his arrival here in 1983 when he returned from exile in the States. Cory won the presidential election but Marcos won't step down. The people have had enough. They want her in and Marcos out.'

'You've been here a long time, what do you think. Can the people win?' asked Conway.

Keyes paused before answering. 'I don't know. To be honest, it scares me a bit. Ever since Aquino was murdered, there's been trouble brewing. Marcos has ruled for over 20 years but he's a sick old man these days and his cronies have virtually taken over. Corruption has got completely out of hand. Anyone opposing the government has mysteriously disappeared. It would take a revolution to get rid of Ferdinand Marcos but Filipinos are not a violent people, so I can't see that happening. For sure, there will be a crackdown on these protests if they go too far, Marcos rules with an iron hand. The next few months will be very interesting and...'

He was interrupted by the high pitched scream of a female from a passenger jeepney which had come to a stop in front of them. A barefoot, shirtless teenager in torn jeans, leapt from the back of the jeep and began to sprint away through the stationary traffic. A woman of around thirty, in a tailored, dark business suit and bright yellow scarf stumbled out behind him.

'Stop him! Stop him! *Magnanakaw*,' (thief) she shrieked, 'he's got my purse!'

Two men both in white tee shirts and jeans appeared, shouting and moving at pace with drawn hand guns took off after the youth.

The thief stopped for a moment, looked around, then seeing the two gunmen, turned and set off ducking and weaving in a desperate crouching run toward a crowd which had gathered on the sidewalk. But the two pursuers were young, fast and determined.

As he reached the sidewalk the youth stumbled as his big toe hit the concrete edge, but quickly regained his balance. That split second was all his chasers needed.

Simultaneously, they dropped into a combat crouch, raised their revolvers and with both arms extended to form a vee opened fire. Crack! Crack! Crack! Crack! The staccato report of gunfire echoed with awful clarity across the evening air.

For a moment it seemed they had missed. But almost in slow motion the boy straightened up on tip toes his arms outstretched as if reaching for something. The purse in his right hand flew into the air away to his left as he took the impact of the .45 calibre bullets.

He stood frozen for a split second before falling in a twisted bloody heap his head resting in the sidewalk gutter, his arms and legs splayed out in a grotesque tableau.

Blood oozed from gaping wounds in his lower back, behind his right thigh and the back of his head. He wasn't quite dead and lay moaning until one of the shooters walked up and calmly finished him off with one shot to the base of the neck. The body jerked once and then lay still.

His killer looked at the boy expressionless for a moment, tucked the revolver into his jeans beneath his tee shirt, turned to his companion and said something before they casually strolled away, one offering the other a cigarette.

The woman whose purse had been stolen had reached the boy and knelt beside him her face distraught, tears streaming down her cheeks. Ashen-faced, she turned screaming and shaking a clenched fist at the departing killers. Then taking her scarf, she carefully covered the dead youth's head. A scarlet stain almost immediately started to spread across the bright yellow material. Still sobbing, she regained her feet and with head bowed made the sign of a cross, then slowly pushed her way through the jabbering crowd which had gathered around the body.

It had all happened so quickly Conway took a few moments to realise what he had just witnessed. After nearly being shot himself he had now seen a kid picked off like a duck in a shooting gallery. Two deaths in twenty minutes; it left him stunned and almost speechless.

'Secret Marshals,' said Keyes grimly. 'As I said, the town has become lawless so Marcos put them on passenger jeepneys to reduce the number of robberies.' He took a deep breath. 'It's been getting out of hand, something had to be done but these assholes are dangerous! They shoot first and ask questions later.'

Conway finally found his voice. 'Summary justice alright,' he said shakily. 'You ok Jumbo?'

'Yeah, I'm ok, let's get outta here.'

'Just a minute, what happens now?' Conway pointed across to the mob gathered around the body. 'How long are they going to let the kid lie there and what was the woman actually shouting to those two guys?'

Keyes shrugged. 'The cops will come and have a look then get a meat wagon to take him away. They'll probably dig a hole and bury him in a dump somewhere…here they are now.' Several police emerged from a white patrol car and while one examined the body, the others spoke to bystanders.

'As for the woman,' he continued, 'believe it or not, she was asking why they had to kill such a young kid. But…that's what happens to thieves here; life's cheap.'

'Did you see what happened to the woman's purse?'

Keyes looked at Conway, his expression a cross between cynicism and despair. 'Yeah, the purse flew out of the kid's hand when he was shot right? The instant it hit the road, another kid swooped on it and took off through the crowd…you can't drop your guard in this town buddy.'

'I'll remember that,' Conway said as the traffic began to move again. 'I think this is going to be a very interesting job. That's if I live long enough.'

Keyes smiled ruefully and patted Conway on the shoulder. 'Hey man, it's not always like this.'

'Shit I hope not! Two murders in twenty minutes I'm beginning to realise why my predecessor quit. Maybe he was bumped off too!'

Keyes shook his head. 'Steve, like any big city it's got its good and bad points. The good points I'll show you when we go out on the town tonight. I promise you, you're gonna love it, and oh, by the way, there's something I forgot to say.'

'What's that?'

The big American's face lit up in a huge, crooked smile.

'Welcome to Manila man!'

# 2

Mabini Street bisects Ermita, Manila's 'Tourist Belt,' a squalid rectangular strip of poverty on the shores of Manila Bay. By day it is an overcrowded, concrete ribbon of despair, home to dusty antique shops, tiny art galleries, scores of run-down Go-Go bars, and shabby cocktail lounges. Massage parlours adjacent to VD clinics offer a none-too-subtle warning to the tourist in search of cheap sex. Beggars sprawl against shopfronts, hands outstretched in silent expectation, while on cracked and broken sidewalks naked babies suckle at their mother's breast beside putrid open drains and piles of rotting rubbish. Through this urban jungle pimps, prostitutes and panhandlers prowl plying their trade on gullible tourists and naive foreign business types.

By night, Ermita sheds her cloak of poverty and becomes a seductive jezebel. She is transformed into a pulsating, dazzling, neon-lit paradise of prurient pleasures for wide-eyed tourists, jaded expats and lost souls from every part of the globe. Bars and discos overflow with roistering patrons. Rock music blares from a hundred doorways outside which, spruikers shout beside scantily clad young women with flashing smiles urge the passing throng to, 'Come inside Sir.'

To Steve Conway on that steamy afternoon none of this was evident. Prior to arrival, his research on Ermita told him that during World War II, Manila had been liberated from the Japanese and literally flattened by the Allies. Ermita, once an affluent residential district of rich Spanish families had born the brunt of the fighting. Years of neglect and endemic corruption had done little to restore the area.

'Hasn't this country heard of noise pollution?' he shouted to Jumbo Keyes above the cacophony of blaring horns and the ear-splitting roar of diesel-fed passenger jeepneys and overloaded 16 wheelers.

The American grinned. 'You've only been here two days man, you'll get used to it!'

'Hey come on, is it always this crowded and noisy?'

'Yeah it's usually like this, except on Sunday, then they're all in church and we heathens have the streets to ourselves,' chuckled Keyes.

'It's a bit different from Christmas Creek in Queensland where I come from. More than three cars coming down the main street at the one time and they think they're being invaded.'

Jumbo smiled at his companion. He'd been concerned about the kind of guy Australia was sending as a new manager. This guy was friendly, had a good sense of humour and yet beneath the easy going manner he sensed hidden strength. Yeah, he said to himself. I think I'm going to like working with Steve Conway.

He'd probably be late thirties, a little under six feet, well muscled, wasn't a bad looking guy except for a slightly broken nose. Dark brown hair cut short, army style, sat above an open friendly face. A face which crinkled when he smiled, which was often. He was wearing a light blue knit shirt, white cotton slacks and moved with an easy athletic grace through the crowded sidewalk. Although his eyes swept almost casually around the scene, Keyes had the feeling he missed nothing.

'If you think this is noisy, wait till I take you to a few bars in Del Pilar tonight, man, that's noise!'

Conway grinned. 'I've heard Manila night life is…interesting.'

'Better believe it buddy. There ain't no place on earth like it.'

They moved on with Keyes pointing out places of interest. As the new manager of the Down Under Hotel, Conway had asked for a tour of the neighbourhood and if possible meet some of the locals.

Keyes had smiled to himself. 'I am only too happy to oblige Steve.'

Jumbo Keyes had retired from the United States Air Force after twenty years, the last five of which had been spent at Clark Base the largest facility of its kind outside mainland America, located in Angeles city, 50 miles north of Manila. During this time, he'd grown to love the Philippines and its people.

Calling it quits at the end of 1984 he decided he didn't want to return to the mean streets of East L.A. so had sought and received Philippine residency. Eighteen months before, he'd married a Filipina named Angie. Angie was short and rotund, no Miss World, but wore a perpetual smile and was loved by all. She had recently presented Jumbo with a little boy they called Joey. A cute little bundle as all Filipino children are, with huge round brown eyes and his mother's happy disposition. Keyes changed overnight from a confirmed bachelor to a devoted family man.

An application for a job at the 'Down Under' prior to his retirement had been successful. He moved the family to Manila and set them up in a comfortable apartment within walking distance of the Down Under Hotel. Jumbo Keyes was a happy man. He had his beloved Angie, little Joey and a good job; what more could a man want?

They moved on through the crowd with the American explaining the geography of the area in relation to the hotel, while ignoring persistent vendors. One in particular, a ragged individual, would not give up.

'Sir! Sir! you buy sunglasses, you want shoe shine? You want girl? She very young, very clean, what about my sister?' He continued to follow them, holding out his wares.

Keyes finally ran out of patience. He stopped and looked down at the pimp and then lowered his face almost eyeball to eyeball. His voice began quietly but increased in tempo, ending in a roar. 'This man is the new manager of the Down Under Hotel, spread the word among your buddies. LEAVE HIM ALONE, PISS OFF!. *ALIS! ALIS!*'

Jumbo Keyes had a raging hangover, a legacy of a big night in the bars the previous night and he was in a fragile mood. The pimp's eyes widened in fright; he dropped everything and took off backwards nearly turning himself inside out in a frantic effort to get away from this awesome black giant with the huge white teeth and frightening, dilated red-rimmed eyes.

Steve had watched this with a mixture of amusement and amazement. Placid, softly spoken Jumbo Keyes in an instant had turned into this huge fearsome monster, all six foot five inches of him. He'd only raged at the little low-life for a moment but it was enough for Steve to realise that this seemingly gentle man was not to be trifled with. I'm glad he's on my side he thought.

They both watched for a moment as the pimp scurried away through the crowd.

'Like a beer boss?' grinned Jumbo, 'you look like you could use one and I sure need a "hair of the dog".'

'Great idea, my shirt's saturated, this humidity is a killer! Was that the local lingo you said to that guy?'

'Yeah. Tagalog, it's the local dialect here on Luzon. Within a day everyone in the area will know who you are and I don't think you'll have any problems. If you tell them firmly, they will leave you alone, but for God's sake... *don't* touch them!'

'Oh?' Steve's eyebrows rose quizzically.

Keyes paused in his long loping stride.

'Steve, you're a nice guy, but there's a lot to learn about this place, in particular, how you handle the locals. Basically they are a simple, friendly and kindly bunch, but buddy, like all races they have their bad sonofabitches so try not to upset them because they can be nasty, I mean like *very* nasty, and, they have *very* long memories.'

'Thanks for the tip. I must admit those I've met in the short time I've been here have been great; very friendly, eager to please and the women... I've never seen such beautiful smiles!'

Keyes looked away and then back at Steve with both huge hands outstretched palms up, like a politician desperate to make an important point.

'Yeah, as I said, most are great and easy to get along with but, they have their pride too and they're not silly. 'Face' here is a big, big, thing; whatever you do don't let them lose face. If you do...you could make a bad enemy, and as I said before, these guys have got long memories!'

Conway nodded. His expression for a moment seemed far away as if he was remembering something he'd rather forget.

'Yeah, I'll try to remember that,' he said quietly.

'Come on Steve, let's cross over here and we'll have a drink in *The Black Jack* Club.'

The lights at the United Nations Avenue intersection had stopped everything on Mabini Street allowing them to thread their way between the stationary traffic and head down a narrow garbage littered side street to a closed red door above which an unlit flouro heralded, *The Black Jack Club*. As they were about to enter Keyes stopped and placed his hand on Conway's chest.

'Now remember man, I'm your official guide and it's my duty to keep an eye on you, introduce you to the local gents and make sure you don't get into trouble, ok?'

Conway frowned, 'Just a moment, sure, you're the guide and I appreciate it, but what makes you think I'm likely to get into any strife?'

'Steve, some of the characters you'll be meeting are your own countrymen and just *some* of them, have inflated egos and don't mind trying to give a new guy a hard time, just play it cool, ignore them if they try to bring you on, ok?'

'Thanks again for the advice, but I'll play it my way.'

'Right, just so long as you know... follow me.' Keyes nodded to the shotgun toting guard who held open a worn, dark curtain.

Conway blinked a couple of times trying to become accustomed to the gloom after the bright sunshine outside. *The Black Jack* bar dimly lit by red wall lamps was small, smoky and smelled of stale beer. On the left an upraised stage with floor to ceiling mirrors occupied the entire length.

A well-built young dancer in a tiny white g-string bikini writhed unconvincingly to Springsteen's *My Home Town* around a chrome pole. Either side of her two girls in similar attire shuffled slowly. One chewed gum, the other with her back to the bar, gazed fixedly at her image in the mirror. It was early, trade was slow and the atmosphere one of bored detachment.

Keyes motioned to the only other people in the place, three middle-aged men at the end of the bar. 'These three heroes you're better off meeting later rather than sooner, but I'll introduce you anyway,' said Keyes.

Two of them looked around at the newcomers but it was the third at the end who took Conway's eye. He was a huge, gross individual unshaven, with black, close-cropped hair who looked like he'd slept in a grubby white cotton tee shirt which seemed ready to burst over the rolls of fat around his waist. His tatty, navy blue shorts could hardly be seen beneath his huge belly. His was the appearance of a bloated toad but it was the jewellery that set him apart.

Around his neck hung four, thick gold chains which gleamed in the dim light. On the fingers of each hand were gold and black onyx rings, and each thick, hairy wrist was adorned with several gold and copper bracelets.

As they approached the fat man slowly lifted his head back and took a long swallow of his bottle of San Miguel beer, then belched loudly.

'G'day,' he said, peering at them out of piggy, bloodshot eyes. He wiped beer which had dribbled down his chin, with the back of one huge paw and sneered, 'who've we got here, the Black Batman and who's his mate? Fuckin' Robin! ha, ha, ha.'

'Meet Bert Groyne, bar owner, petty crim and nobody's friend,' smiled Keyes, ignoring the jibe.

'Guys, this is Steve Conway, the new manager of the Down Under Hotel, new to the Philippine islands.' Conway leant across and shook Groyne's hand; a hand that had neither strength, nor warmth.

'Steve, now these other two gentlemen, and I use the term loosely are, Dick Watson, known as 'Biro'.' A skinny guy, fifty-ish, completely bald, with a booze-poisoned complexion, extended a thin arm and a hand which was swallowed in Conway's firm grasp.

The little man blinked a couple of times. 'G..g..g.'day...Steve,' he stuttered.

'And...Completing this erstwhile trio,' grinned Keyes is, 'William Fish, 'Mullet' to his friends, unfortunately he hasn't got many, that's why he hangs around with these two deadbeats.'

Mullet's age was hard to guess. The grog had got him early. He was anywhere between forty-five and sixty-five, just over five feet with straight, reddish blonde hair. Meaty features were dominated by a bulbous nose suffused with bumps and crimson veins. He'd been solid once, but years of propping up bars had left him overweight and sloppy. A huge gut fell over the front of his jeans. He reminded Conway of Humpty Dumpty.

'G'day Mullet, how are you?' smiled Conway, holding out his hand.

Mullet took it, gave a perfunctory shake and mumbled, 'Ok, pleased t' meetcha,' then returned to his Scotch with a speed that suggested he was afraid it might evaporate in the interim.

These guys wouldn't look out of place in any line-up. I'll bet they've been in a few, particularly Groyne, thought Conway. I see what Keyes meant about *some of my countrymen.*

Groyne's baleful eyes fixed on Conway. His philosophy was any newcomer to his bar had to buy everyone a drink, whether they liked it or not.

'Ah, just in time for a shout,' he sneered, 'mine's a San Mig, Biro'll have one too and give Mullet a double Johnnie Walker. He's pretty thirsty today aren't yuh Mullet?'

Conway looked at Keyes who winked and said quietly, 'I'll get 'em.'

'Sally,' he said to an attractive bar attendant waiting patiently for their order. 'We'll have four 'San Migs,' and a single Scotch for Mullet.'

'Bloody cheap Charlie Yank!' grunted Groyne. 'Hope your mate's got longer pockets.'

Groyne continued to eye Conway who stood quietly saying nothing. It was time for a put down. Groyne often impressed himself with the power of his sarcasm and he wasn't going to let this guy escape without receiving some of his sensational wit.

'Sooo...this is Perc Prickett's new bum-boy,' he jeered, taking a huge gulp of his beer. 'You won't last long son. I've seen 'em come and go. Perc sucks 'em in and then spits 'em out and I can tell, you'll soon be history like the previous dickhead manager!'

Keyes felt Conway stiffen beside him. Conway looked the bloated bar-owner straight in the eye and then reached over to the bar as if to pick up his drink. At the last moment he wheeled and stepping in close to Groyne, with one hand grabbed a handful of gold chain, twisted it savagely and lifted the fat man out of his seat.

'Aaaaah!' yelled Groyne, his face contorted in pain as the chains threatened to choke him.

'Listen Mudguts,' grated Conway, 'didn't you hear him?' he motioned to Keyes, who, like the others, stood mouth agape.

'The name's Conway, Steve Conway! Got it! And,' lowering his voice to just above a whisper, he hissed, 'Let's get the rules of the game straight right from the start. First of all old *mate*! I'm *no one's* bum boy! Secondly; I'm going to be around here a long time!' He gripped the chains even tighter and the fat man's eyes began to bulge and spittle started to dribble down his chin.

'Thirdly, you keep a civil tongue in your head when you speak to me or I'll rip it out and ram it down your fucking throat! And fourthly, I have heard you bring your 'girls' into the hotel to fraternize with the guests, is that right?'

Groyne's tongue was protruding from his mouth and Conway's iron grip prevented him from making any intelligible sound. All he could do was nod.

'Well old *mate*! You and *they!*, had better behave. You step out of line for one second and you and your motley crew will be banned permanently...got it?' Conway released his grip and Groyne slumped back against the bar.

'Now, I think it's *your* shout pal.'

The bar had gone quiet as everyone waited for Groyne's reaction. Springsteen had stopped warbling and the dancers stood looking down, open-mouthed.

The fat bar-owner was shaken. His face was flushed, both with embarrassment and the effect of Conway's stranglehold. Taking a couple of deep wheezing breaths he got back on his stool and glared at Conway, his face a picture of pure hate.

He turned to Sally, whose eyes were like saucers.

'Another round here,' he snarled, then looking back at Conway he said, 'that wasn't fuckin' necessary, I was just sizin' you up, where do you think you are, the Wild West?'

Conway said nothing for a moment as Sally handed him a beer.

'Just letting you know the ground rules fella. You behave and we'll get on just fine. I might even come to this flea-bitten hole again some time because despite you, the beers cold and,' he smiled at Sally; 'your staff seem quite efficient.'

'Yeah, alright, but no more of that bloody rough stuff or...'

'Just drink up and shut up Bert you asked for it,' growled Keyes. With the prospect of no blood being spilt the dancers reluctantly went back to their gyrating and the atmosphere returned to normal.

'Now,' asked Keyes, 'what's doin with you guys?'

Biro, swished at any imaginary fly from his face. 'Nothin' much Jumbo,' he said in a reedy voice. 'Apart from this country about to start a civil war, there's talk that Aussie TV might be payin' a visit to do a story on the bars.'

'Is that right?' replied Keyes trying to keep a straight face. 'Not another great *expose* about all you God-awful diggers here exploiting and corrupting these poor innocent Filipinos?'

'Yeah, pretty crook isn't it,' wailed Mullet, 'A bloke just wants to come up here and live in peace... away from all that bullshit that's goin' on in Oz, and the bastards are gonna come here and do a nice old one-sided bit on us, making us out to be depraved old bastards.'

'Well, you are a depraved old bastard Mullet,' scowled Groyne, displaying a mouthful of tobacco blackened teeth, 'the sooner they weed out dirty old pricks like you, the better.'

'Christ Bert,' moaned Mullet loudly trying to make himself heard above Cindy Lauper's *Girls Just Wanna Have Fun.* 'If the bloody TV cameras get a shot of you and play it in Australia, you'll have the Tax men, the AFP, a heap of women and more than a few husbands up here in a flash, you'll be in what's commonly known as *Deep Shit!*'

'Look who's talking!' exploded Groyne, 'What about those land *Deals* you did in Queensland. You know, the Bay islands, near Brisbane. *Waterside allotments* you called 'em, they sure were, the only problem was, that when the tide came in they were *Underwater* allotments ha, ha ha, ha! I know who'd be in deep shit if they find you up here...old pal!'

Groyne had now recovered his composure. He rubbed his stubbly fat chin between his thumb and forefinger and looked across at Watson as if something else had just occurred to him. Turning to Biro, and then back to Conway and Keyes he pointed to his bald companion.

'And while we're on the subject, what about this guy!' he said pointing to Biro.

'Look at him, there's more hair on a ping-pong ball than on his head. If he goes out driving at night he has to turn his head down to dim!'

Groyne took another great slurp of his beer, wiped his chin. He was having trouble getting his words out without laughing.

'Ha! Ha! Ha! This bloke,' he spluttered, 'made a small fortune selling of all things would you believe...*a baldness cure, by mail-order!*'

'He put ads in the fuckin' newspapers and magazines telling what an amazing potion he had. A secret mixture he'd found when he'd lived with get this...a *stone-age* tribe of Indians in the Amazon! The closest he's been to the Amazon was when he opened the *Jacaranda Atlas of the World.* He even had two photos in the ad; one *Before,* and one, *After.* The only problem was, the *Before* picture was his natural self; bald as a coot! The one *After* was him with a fuckin' wig on!' he cackled.

'Fair dinkum, he got 'em in. The ad had all the right words with testimonials; you know *J.B. of Warrnambool* says, *I noticed a dramatic improvement in six months.* etc, etc. You'd be amazed how many punters fell for it. The ad said that it would take at least six months under normal circumstances for the potion to have any real effect...he cleaned up a lot in that time, didn't you mate?' Biro just smirked and took another mouthful of beer.

'And,' Groyne went on, 'I nearly forgot the best bit! Biro's strollin' down Collins Street in Melbourne one day done up like a pox doctor's clerk and resplendent in his wig and... Suddenly he hears the pitter patter of running feet behind him. Next thing, he feels someone grabbing his wig...they rip it off and keep runnin' without breakin' stride...guess what...Ha, ha ha ha!...*they'd repossessed his fuckin' wig*! He'd fallen behind in the payments!'

Despite himself Conway couldn't suppress a grin, he could imagine the scene, but he found it hard to imagine this hapless little guy in front of him as a master con-man.

Sally had been hovering near the group. She'd heard it all before. A Chinese-Filipino with an exotic, high-cheek boned face set off by a page boy bob, she was just over 5 feet tall and had an unusually full figure for a Filipino female. The glow from the red wall lamps cast a smooth sheen over the brown satin of her naked shoulders, shown to advantage in a white peasant blouse, and a black mini-skirt revealed a pair of very shapely legs, the equal of any of the dancers on stage.

Her English was good having graduated from college with honours. She had harboured dreams of becoming a nurse and taking a magic carpet to the USA with her lover, a Marine based at Subic Bay. Unfortunately, the Marine had another girl in Subic who became pregnant so he requested a rapid transfer back to the States, and got it. Now, nearly thirty years old, Sally was resigned to serving drinks in a run-down bar in Ermita, listening to the tales of drunken expats and hoping one day 'Mr Right' would walk in that door and take her away.

'Sally,' smiled Conway, 'we're going, but would you get these guys a drink on me,' he threw a 100 Peso note on the bar.

'Will that cover it?'

She beamed and a pair of full red lips opened revealing a perfect set of white teeth. 'Thank you sir...that will cover it ok... May I have your name sir?'

'Steve Conway. I'm the new manager at the Down Under Hotel.'

Sally's sloe eyes widened and she felt a sudden thrill run through her body. This new man was very good looking, and he had an important position in the area. It would be nice to become friendly with him. Plus, she was secretly pleased the way he had handled Groyne.

'I am very pleased to meet you sir and I hope you will come in again soon sir,' she said brightly, extending her hand in greeting.

'I certainly will, particularly if you're here Sally,' he grinned, looking her straight in the eye taking her hand. She lowered her eyes and blushed but he felt a gentle squeeze as she withdrew and went to serve another customer who had come in at the far end of the bar. Conway watched her swaying hips for a moment then turning to Keyes he gestured to the door.

'Let's go, we'd better get back. I've got a few things to do. See you guys later.'

'Yeah, righto Steve,' said Biro.

'Huy, ah yeah see y' later,' Mullet muttered taking a sip of his Scotch. Groyne had turned back to his beer and didn't bother to acknowledge their departure. His ignorance wasn't lost on Conway. You'll keep sport he thought following Keyes to the door.

# 3

The Down Under Hotel was an unpretentious, three storey white stucco building facing onto the tumultuous traffic of United Nations avenue in Ermita. It held 100 basic tourist class rooms popular with short-term holiday makers and tourists; a popularity stemming from its location in the heart of Manila's legendary night club district.

Guests arrived through a black and white tiled foyer decorated with pot plants of pink and purple blooms to a front desk staffed by bright-faced Filipinas. The fragrance of *sampaguitas* and hibiscus together with the polite, softly-spoken Filipino staff created a serene counterpoint to the noise of the choking traffic and crowded sidewalks outside.

To the right of reception, red carpeted stairs led to the main bar and coffee shop on the first floor. The L-shaped bar ran along one side of a rectangular room and right-angled at the far end past large stained glass windows finishing at the opposite wall. Along this wall were a number of cosy nooks where customers could sit away from the bar and whisper sweet nothings to their lady friends.

The Australian ambience was evident from the walls adorned with advertising material including Qantas airways and Fosters beer posters. Intermingled with these were a few black and white sepia photos of Aussie boxers, footballers and swimmers of yesteryear. In order to put his own stamp on the place, Keyes had cheekily brought in a slice of Americana. He'd somehow acquired a large oil painting of General Douglas Macarthur, which he claimed had hung in the famous general's old residence at the Manila Hotel. This had been placed above one end of the bar flanked on one side by the Stars and Stripes flag and a Confederate banner on the other.

'We don't mind havin' any Yank paraphernalia here,' one old Aussie degenerate told Keyes. 'But don't foist any of that weak Yank piss on us will ya.' But, when like magic Keyes produced an ice-cold can of Budweiser, the old-timer leapt on it as if it was the last beer on earth.

The bar of the Down Under Hotel was regarded as the friendliest and most convivial in the area. It exuded an air of excitement and activity and had become a meeting place for tourists, local and Western businessmen and expats alike. The attractive, vivacious female staff wore uniforms of mint green, short-sleeved blouses with bright yellow maps of Australia embroidered on the left breast pocket. Mini skirts of sparkling white showed plenty of brown, shapely legs and the outfit was complete with white shoes and gold, silk bandanas which swirled as they swayed up and down laughing and exchanging saucy banter with their customers.

The bar on that Saturday night was crowded, smoke-filled and noisy. Groups of men, mainly Australian, a few Americans and Brits were either guffawing at some bawdy joke or arguing about an obscure point of politics, religion or sport.

Others however, bore an air of melancholy. They were the guests returning home. Their holiday finished; fantasy over and cold hard reality beckoned just an eight hour flight away. On Monday they would be back in their factories and offices, or on building sites and mines in the outback reliving with their mates, the real and imagined sexual exploits of their Asian adventure. The one thing this group shared was the reluctance to board the hotel bus for the airport.

Conway eyed this scene for a few minutes a slight smile hovering on his lips. Around him, men of varying ages were propped against the bar leaning in to their girlfriends whispering final farewells.

Some of the girls were sobbing, promising undying love and chastity. Others simply sat with vacant expressions occasionally checking their watches. The next plane load of guests was due in about an hour; approximately 30 minutes after this lot had left. Soon, someone else would have his arm around them breathing duty-free liquor and offering lascivious suggestions as to how they would spend the rest of the evening.

Conway noticed Keyes in the far corner of the bar reading, seemingly oblivious to the din around him. As he pushed his way through the crowd, Tess, one of the bar staff caught his eye and flashed a smile; one must not keep the boss waiting.

'What would you like to drink sir?' she called over the crowd.

'Just a San Miguel beer Tess, you want one mate?' he asked, finding a space beside Keyes.

'Hi Steve,' Jumbo grinned, looking up from the *Stars and Stripes* an American military newspaper. 'Sure, make mine a *Tanduay* rum and coke.'

'Well Steve,' said Keyes, turning to survey the bar. 'Here's your first Saturday night man, chaotic isn't it?' he chuckled. 'We get rid of one lot and another posse rides into town to take up where this crowd left off.'

Conway nodded as Tess leaned across the bar between two customers and handed him a bottle of San Miguel and the rum and coke for Keyes. 'Yes, it's great to see we have a regular clientele who keep turning over the till.'

The American sipped his rum. 'Buddy, this joint is *the* hub of Ermita. This is where it *all* happens my friend; romance, shady deals, bullshit stories, yeah, if I could bottle the bullshit I've heard in this place and sell it, I'd be a very rich man.' His big belly shook as he laughed at his own joke. 'Speaking of bullshit, the personification of it just walked in.'

Bert Groyne with Biro and Mullet in tow, accompanied by two of the dancers Conway had seen in *The Black Jack* and two others he hadn't, swaggered in as if he owned the place. At a nook near the toilet he pushed a couple of hookers off their stools and made space for himself and his entourage.

He crooked his finger to one of the bar staff then with an imperious circular motion pointed back to his group indicating he wanted service. As a regular, the staff knew the order and it wasn't necessary for the theatrics, but the egomaniac in Groyne couldn't resist the opportunity to show off in front of his cohorts.

Conway watched this little circus; Groyne's arrogance raised his hackles.

'Have you seen Perc today?' he asked Keyes. 'I need to discuss a couple of things with him.'

'Our fearless leader? Man, didn't you notice him? There he is over at the other end of the bar.'

The object of their attention was a short, fat, individual wearing a light blue short-sleeved shirt undone at the neck, leaving his garish, multi-coloured tie hanging loosely at an untidy angle. He was trying unsuccessfully to negotiate a spoonful of tomato soup to his mouth. He'd missed a few times and the front of his shirt and tie was splattered with pale red stains.

Percival Reginald Prickett, the major shareholder and self-styled president of the Down Under Hotel was drunk, very drunk. Mid fifties, Perc fancied himself as a ladies man and bon vivant. He had no neck and a head like a bowling ball except for two tufts of iron grey hair which stood out from either side of his head ala "Dagwood".

Small, shifty eyes squinted from pallid cheeks and a heavily red-veined nose bespoke too many nights in the gin mills of Asia. The fleshy lips wore a perpetual sneer and several chins rounded off a picture of an individual who would have made a perfect extra in a Fellini film. But those who knew him were aware that his lack of looks and stature were more than made up by a huge ego and a cunning, devious brain.

'Probably not a good idea to try and speak to him right now, the condition he's in.' offered Keyes.

'Does a good job on himself doesn't he?' smiled Conway. 'Oh, oh, I think he could be in trouble, here's his good wife.'

A slim, smartly dressed, sharp-featured Filipina in her early thirties had joined Prickett and although they couldn't hear her, it was obvious from her expression and finger-waving, she was giving her husband a going over. It was a waste of time because "the president" was too far gone to notice his wife's ranting.

'You know Steve old buddy, Imelda has a snowball's chance in hell of getting ole Perc to take notice. She'll probably either belt him in the ear, storm out or both. Either way, it'll be ugly.'

Before Conway could reply, the hand holding his beer was bumped by a thin, grey haired guy in shorts and tee shirt trying to get to the bar.

'Sorry mate,' said grey-hair trying to wipe the beer off Conway's shirt. 'Some silly bastard pushed me. I really am sorry. Can I get you another one?'

'Don't worry about it, no harm done, there wasn't much left anyway.'

'Thanks mate. Jeez, your're a fit lookin; bugger, I wouldn't want to upset you. Me name's Stan Connell, goin' back to Oz tonight.'

'Steve Conway. You been coming to this part of the world long Stan?'

'Yeah, been comin' here since the Seventies. I've had a good time as usual; bar hoppin' in Del Pilar and up to Angeles City, jeez that joint swings, been there? Thanks love,' he said as his beer arrived.

'No, not yet but hope to make it soon. So you're happy with the service here? Everything Ok?'

Connell turned and glared in the direction of Perc. 'Yeah, this place is great the only thing I'm crooked on is that little prick over there.'

'Perc Prickett? Why?' Conway followed Stan's glare to his boss who had given up on the soup and now stood slumped at the bar oblivious to the ear bashing he was copping from his wife.

'Well, as I said, I like this pub; the staff are friendly, the joint is reasonably clean, rates aren't bad but I wouldn't trust that little bugger and his missus as far as I could spit.'

'Why's that Stan?'

'Take a look at him. He's a shifty little bastard and the word is he's been in more shady deals than you can poke a stick at. He'll lie, cheat, steal, do anything to get a buck and his taste in women is about as good as her taste in men, but mate,' he paused and moved closer to Conway lowering is voice to barely above a whisper. 'She's the dangerous one. Cross her and you could find yourself fitted with a pair of cement slippers and tossed in the Pasig.'

'The Pasig?'

'Yeah Steve, it's a polluted, dung coloured piece of shit they call a river.' He paused to take a long swallow of San Miguel. Wiping his lips with the back of his hand he squinted up at Conway.

'Yeah, they dudded George Coleman, he was the previous manager y'know?'

Conway nodded, his eyes still on Groyne and his crew.

'Yeah, well they promised him the world; good money, flash apartment, the works but...'

'Go on,' said Conway. Now Stan had his full attention.

'Poor old George, not a bad poor bastard; tried his best, copped it for a year or so but they fucked him around so much and broke their promises. Put him in a flea pit apartment 'n paid him a pittance; told him he'd get a bonus at the end of the year. Imelda kept overriding every decision he tried to make and kept him in the dark about what they were up to which from all accounts, was no good.'

Conway looked around at Keyes who had gone back to reading his paper. He bent his head closer to Stan. The bar was noisy but walls have ears.

'Keep your voice down, what do you mean "no good"?'

Connell glanced around nervously, as if he wished he hadn't opened his mouth.

'Ah, well, he didn't say much, he seemed a bit scared but kinda indicated that he thought the Pricketts were involved in something, he didn't know what...'

'Stan from what I can gather he just disappeared and nobody seems to know what happened. You seem to know the scene here, got any ideas?'

Connell shook his head vigorously. 'No sorry, you hear stories but I dunno anything about it. That's all I can tell ya, sorry.' He took another gulp of his beer, his voice was now barely above a whisper. His agitation increased.

'Look, mate, forget I said anything, ole George, probably took up with a woman and headed for the province, who knows...I don't care.' Connell then changed the subject.

'Anyway, I've heard they've hired another bloke, some bushie I believe. Hope he's more on the ball than Coleman...watcha name again son?'

'Steve, Steve Conway. I'm the *bushie* they hired.'

Stan nearly swallowed the bottle at his lips. 'Shit mate,' he spluttered, narrowly avoiding showering Conway with beer. 'I'm sorry, I didn't know.'

'Don't worry about it,' grinned Conway. He waved to Tess. 'Get Stan another beer on me.'

'Thanks mate, but I gotta go, want to see someone before I leave, nice meeting ya,' said Connell reaching out to give Conway a quick handshake before pushing his way back through the crowd. Conway turned to Keyes.

'You hear all that? What do you think?'

Keyes looked up and yawned, 'yeah, you hear these stories. I never got to know Coleman. He kept to himself, used to drink away from here. One day he just didn't turn up for work. There were rumours...'

'What rumours?'

'The scuttlebutt was he'd been salvaged.'

'Salvaged?'

'Bumped off, murdered, it's the local term in Manila.'

'Do you think there was any truth in it? Why would anyone want to kill him?'

Keyes took a sip of his rum and placed it back on the bar. 'As I said, I didn't get to know him very well, quiet sort of a guy, didn't seem the sort to get involved in any funny business, but you never know in this part of the world. I know he wasn't happy and used to complain about Perc and Imelda...'

'What about?'

Now Keyes appeared to be reluctant to canvas the subject. He seemed to be choosing his words carefully.

'Coleman apparently had a five star Hotel background and this ain't a five star establishment. He didn't like the way things were run here. Thought the Pricketts were unprofessional, he hated their nepotism.'

'That's all? Nepotism's a common beef among employees about their bosses. I know Imelda has a few of her relatives here but as long as they do their job I can't see a problem. What's this "no good" that Stan was referring to?'

'I agree with you about the nepotism as for the "no good" reference, again, you hear stories but in Ermita Steve, you'll find, it pays to keep your nose clean. Hear all, see all, say nowt.'

Conway nodded. Keyes clearly didn't want to discuss this subject. He drained his beer and was about to order another when he noticed at the far end of the bar one of the customers staggering from the toilet.

Willie Henry was part of the furniture around the hotel. He'd retired from Qantas a few years ago and had apparently in his time been a gun air-frame fitter. A couple of broken marriages and a life-long love affair with the booze had got him into so much strife in Australia he'd decided to seek a quieter life in the Philippines. Willie discovered Ermita and knew he'd found home. The booze and the women were cheap, he could live off his Qantas pension and best of all; he didn't have to get married.

Willie did have one problem though. Occasionally when drunk, he'd forget where the toilet was and in a daze, would urinate in one of the planter boxes placed around the bar. The staff well aware of Willie's little foibles and usually intercepted him if they thought he was going to water the plants. But because he was coming *from* the toilet, they thought all was well.

A big mistake.

Willie staggered over to a luxuriant hibiscus next to where Bert Groyne was boasting to his cronies about a shady deal he'd just pulled off. He stood wobbling over the plant beside Groyne and unzipped his pants. Tess glanced over and saw what was about to happen and screamed

'Willie no! no!'

Too late. Willie slowly turned around at the sound of her voice and directed a powerful stream into the back of Groyne's neck.

Groyne leapt up from his chair. 'What the fuck!' he screamed, throwing his arms in the air and accidentally upending the table and everything and everyone on it; bottles of beer, glasses, purses, cigarettes and lighters all hit the deck. Biro, Mullet and the dancers crashed onto their backs in a tangle of white and brown legs, one pair of the latter revealing coloured silk knickers, the others not having bothered.

'You stupid sonnavabitch!' he yelled stumbling away from Willie, desperately trying to wipe the urine from his head and shoulders.

Staff rushed over to grab Willie and clean up the mess while Groyne, cursing and shouting made a lunge for Willie but slipped on the beer, urine and broken glass. Trying to remain upright he made a grab for a big oil worker who had been watching the havoc with amusement.

The oiley's amusement quickly turned to a howl of rage as Groyne knocked a full glass of *Johnny Walker black label* down the front of his *Ralph Lauren* shirt on to his Levis, both bought that very morning.

'Hey! You clumsy mother-fucker, look what you've done to my threads?' With that he hauled Groyne up off the floor and belted him with a booming right. It sent the big bar owner staggering back onto his girls who had just climbed from the floor holding each other trying not to slip in the slippery mess. They tried to hold their boss but he was too big, too heavy. They let out ear piercing screams as they all crashed to the floor again adding to the growing pandemonium.

'Hey you, leave my mate…' spluttered Biro a split second before a powerful uppercut lifted him off his feet and dumped him in a graceful arc on to the squirming heap of Groyne and his girls. Suddenly the bar was in uproar. Small fights began to break out and the melee escalated. Conway and Keyes moved in to try and restore order and became targets of ill-directed mainly harmless, punches.

Prickett seemed oblivious to chaos around him and attempting to direct another Scotch to his mouth was bumped, spilling the contents over Imelda's white silk Dior creation.

'Aaaaagh!' she shrieked frantically trying to wipe the large dark stain from her now ruined dress. Unfortunately for Imelda, she stumbled back into Ruby, one of the waitresses fighting her way back to the bar.

Ruby hated Imelda. She had fired her brother Efren. He had been a driver, hard working, conscientious and liked by all. There seemed to be no good reason for his termination. Shortly afterwards he disappeared in circumstances, some said had the hallmarks of Imelda although it could not be proved it simply increased Ruby's simmering hatred for the haughty Filipina.

When Imelda stepped back, one of her stiletto heels dug deeply into Ruby's instep. The little waitress snapped. Howling with a mixture of rage and pain she grabbed Imelda's expensively coiffed head with both hands and yanked… hard.

Imelda let out an ear-piercing scream as she felt a tuft of her thickly lacquered black hair leave her head. She forgot about Perc and turned to her furious adversary. She made a grab for Ruby's hair and both women went down pulling, kicking and screaming under a seething mass of bodies.

Someone had picked up Willie and put him on the bar where he looked stupefied over the brawling mob. Amazingly, he had acquired another beer and just as he raised it to his lips an empty bottle came flying out of the blue and belted him on the temple. Without a sound, arms outstretched, skinny legs in the air, Willie dropped out of sight behind the bar.

Meanwhile, Conway and Keyes were struggling to restore order. Ducking punches, flying bottles and abuse they tried desperately to pull the protagonists apart. As he stepped in to break up a group of four Conway copped a vicious back-hander across the nose. For a moment his eyes watered and for a few seconds all he could see was a red haze but it had nothing to do with the blow. Gritting his teeth he pulled the guy who'd done it forward by the collar and drew a clenched fist back. As he did, he felt his elbow strike a soft wall of flesh followed by a choking moan.

Groyne had been sneaking up behind Conway with a bottle. This was "get square" time. Unfortunately as he lifted the bottle he ran straight into

Conway's elbow. He grabbed his throat gasping for air and slowly slumped back for another visit to the floor, this time losing all interest in proceedings.

Conway glanced around, seeing it was Groyne, ignored him. Then his protagonist grabbed him in a bear hug. Conway dropped his shoulder and drove a sharp left into the guy's substantial belly. The air rushed out of him and he crumpled to the floor beside a still gasping Groyne.

All thought of managerial control went out the window but suddenly he had an idea. He went into a boxer's crouch and started cutting a swathe through the mob. Vicious left hooks, rips and rights dropped man after man as he bobbed, weaved and battled his way through to the bar. This wasn't in the bloody job specification. How many Hotel managers have to knock out half their guests to restore order?

Keyes at the other end had his own problems. He'd been king hit with a bottle from behind, his shirt was ripped and blood was flowing from his nose. Another blow to the back of the head buckled his knees and he staggered forward barely able to stand. Another few seconds and he would be on the floor at the mercy of a mob now almost out of control; almost but not quite.

Suddenly above the bedlam came the furious clanging of a bell.

The fight stopped instantly.

Ringing of the bell meant someone was shouting everyone in the bar a drink. A good brawl might be fun but no one was going to miss out on free booze. A bruised and bloody Conway stood beside the bar holding the bell pull. Naked to the waist, blood dripping from a cut above his left eye and nasty two inch gash beneath his right ear, he climbed on to the bar and shouted over a now silent crowd.

'OK! Ok boys the show's over! All those for the airport the bus is waiting downstairs and you are now *very much overdue!* Get down there now or you can bloody well walk to the airport and if I see any of you guys step out of line in this place again, you're barred, permanently! Now piss off!'

Then grinning from ear to ear he accepted a beer from a hovering, smiling Tess. He wasn't going to tell anyone, but he'd enjoyed the fracas. The mob never knew that it had allowed him to let off a bit of pent up steam also.

'I think I need this,' he said taking a long swallow.

There was a brief pause then, to Conway's amazement the bar erupted again. This time differently.

'Three cheers for the new guy, he's a bloody beauty,' roared the big oily.

'Good on yer mate,' yelled a skinny, bearded guy in a blood spattered tee-shirt with *Peace and Love* across the front. 'Yeah, welcome to the Down Under,' chorused a drunken foursome who only seconds before had been trying to belt hell out of each other, now had linked arms like long lost friends.

The bar had almost instantly been transformed from mayhem into a brotherhood of friendship and bonhomie with many helping each other from the floor, brushing them down and apologizing profusely. More amazingly was their enthusiasm as they surged around Conway shaking his hand and clapping him on the back.

Ignoring his new-found adulation Conway pushed his way over to Keyes who was similarly being treated as a hero.

'You ok mate?' he asked putting his hand on the big man's shoulder.

'Sure man, just a few scratches, nothing a few drinks won't fix,' Keyes grinned ruefully attempting to put back on the remnants of his shirt.

'You sure are one tough Aussie sonofa, glad you're on my side,' said Keyes, wiping blood and sweat from his eyes.

'They'd have murdered me without you Jumbo, thanks mate,' said Conway gripping the American's hand. They looked at each other for a moment. An unspoken bond had been formed.

'Ok, let's clean up this place,' Conway said to the staff gathered around. Frowning, he turned to Keyes. 'Hey, what happened to Perc? And…where the hell was our guard when all this was going on?'

Keyes threw back his head and roared with laughter. Wiping tears from his eyes he told how he'd seen Prickett crawling behind the bar to escape the brawl. One of the cooks who had come out to see what was happening saw Prickett's big backside as a perfect target to release some long held animosity he had over the poor wages and working conditions. Checking to see no one was looking, he delivered a kick any footballer would have been proud of, sending Perc face first into a pile of cartons of rubbish and empty bottles, where he remained inert.

'As for the guard, well man, he's come in and had a look at all these big mothers fighting and said to himself, 'fuck this! I'm not getting my head kicked in for 80 pesos a day and promptly backpedalled down the stairs.'

'Some protection we've got in this hotel Jumbo. What about Imelda? The last I saw of her, she and Ruby were having a donnybrook on the floor.'

'Romy, Imelda's driver came in and rescued her and took both Pricketts away. I think Ruby can kiss her career goodbye.'

'Well, assaulting the boss's wife is not exactly a good career move is it?'

'Y' know Steve I don't think Ruby'll mind. She got her licks in and some revenge for her brother even though there are still questions to be asked about his disappearance. Frankly, I think she was only hanging around to get her own back. Remember what I said about their long memories?'

The bar emptied as most left unaided to board the airport bus or return to their rooms. A few like Groyne had to be assisted off the premises. With peace restored staff started cleaning up the mess and repairing the surprisingly small amount of damage.

The floor was littered with empty beer bottles, portions of pies, pizzas, bowls of half-eaten noodles and rice, remnants of meals abandoned in the melee. More serious were the chunks and slivers of glass here and there. One of the mirrors behind the bar had been smashed but most of the damage had been done to the combatants, some of whom would be carrying home black eyes, bruises and fractures legacy of their holiday *Where Asia wears a smile*.

Around midnight when they had the place cleaned up and almost back to normal Conway gathered the staff around him.

'First of all,' he said, 'I wish to apologise to you for the incident that happened tonight and thank you for the manner in which you conducted yourselves. It was very unfortunate and I will be taking steps to see it doesn't happen again and Willie Henry,' he couldn't suppress a small grin, 'will be first on the agenda. Before you go, cashiers, don't forget to balance the registers and check the stock. The rest of you go home, and thanks again.'

The female bar staff stood around him with shining eyes. He was still shirtless and his muscular torso gleamed with sweat and a mixture of dried blood. To them he cut a heroic and *very* desirable figure.

'Oh sir,' cooed Tess as she gently ran her fingers over an angry red weal on his ribs and the cut beneath his ear. 'You are hurt sir, let me help you.'

'Yes sir, oh sir, you are so macho,' purred Mindy gazing up adoringly into his face and taking hold of his left hand.

'You are our hero sir,' murmured Jackie, encircling his right arm with hers and pressing her slim, shapely body close.

'Er, yes, thanks girls, thanks very much,' Conway stammered, unable to hide his embarrassment. Keyes had patched up his wounds and stood watching this little scene with a grin from ear to ear.

A bowl of warm water and sponges appeared and several pairs of willing female hands administered a soothing balm to numerous wounds on his body. Jackie in particular took her time wiping the blood from across his chest all the while looking lovingly up into his eyes. Conway was beginning to feel more than a little uncomfortable from this attention and was relieved when finally someone produced another shirt.

With order again restored Conway felt he'd had enough excitement for one night; time to return to his apartment. 'See you in the morning,' he called to Jumbo who was on the phone talking to Angie.

'Ok man,' replied Keyes giving him the thumbs up. 'Watch how you go.'

Conway had been provided with a furnished apartment a few blocks west of the hotel and within walking distance but the mean, ill-lit streets of Ermita at night can be dangerous. The shadows conceal muggers, pickpockets, drug addicts and worse. Only a fool takes chances, so Conway with his wits about him, took off at a brisk pace. As he approached the intersection near *The Black Jack*, a female rounded the corner towards him. It was Sally, who had finished her shift and was also heading home.

An unusually cool breeze had come in from the bay and she walked with her shoulders hunched and head down not noticing him. As he was about to pass he put out his hand.

'Hey there Sally, have you finished for the night?'

She stopped abruptly looking up, fear in her eyes. When she saw who it was, she sighed with relief and her face broke into a wide smile.

'Oh hello sir, yes I have. I'm going home now, how about you?'

'Yes, I'm on my way home too. Where do you live?'

'Sampaloc.'

'Is that far?'

'Only two rides sir.'

Filipinos describe their journeys in terms of the number of jeepney rides. It was dark, it was late and she had a reasonably long trip in front of her. He suddenly remembered what Keyes had told him about the recent escalation in robberies on jeepneys. A thought flashed into his head. At this time of night the Hotel vehicles were rarely used and since all guests had left a few hours earlier, one would be available.

'Sally…would you like a ride home…with me?'

Sally's radiant smile gave him her answer. 'Oh sir, you are very kind, thank you.'

They returned to the Down Under and knocked on the window of one of the land cruisers parked out the front. The duty driver was asleep on the front seat. He woke with a jerk and his eyes widened with embarrassment when he saw who it was.

'Give him the directions Sally,' Conway said, helping her into the back seat. She exchanged a few words in Tagalog with the driver. He nodded, threw the vehicle into gear and they headed off through the darkened streets for Sampaloc.

Conway turned to look at Sally snuggled up beside him. It had been a pretty eventful evening, and it wasn't over yet.

4

Light rain was falling as the land cruiser moved slowly down a dark, pot-holed street. Its headlights cast weird shadows that danced off a festering slum of small, shabby dwellings of plywood, cardboard and sheets of rusty corrugated iron; shanties without electricity or running water.

Families lit by the faint glow of kerosene lamps huddled from the rain in these makeshift shelters talking, laughing and eating while red-eyed rats scurried in and out of the shadows from piles of rotting rubbish where sidewalks should have been. Conway gagged as through the open window the putrid stench of urine an untreated sewage hit his nostrils.

'Wind the window up quick!' he shouted to the driver.

'Squatters,' murmured Sally, reading Conway's thoughts. 'They have nothing, but they have to live somewhere.'

Conway shook his head. 'Poor devils.' What he'd seen of the city so far resembled a huge rubbish dump and yet he remembered reading that prior to World War II, Manila had been a thriving city and the Philippines one of the most dynamic countries in Asia. What the hell had brought it to this level? If he had any doubts about the debilitating effect of the Marcos dictatorship and its endemic corruption, the evidence was outside the window of his vehicle.

Didn't anyone care? If the newspapers were to be believed, and the riots were an indication, the answer was a resounding "Yes".

A few minutes later they rolled to a stop outside a white two-storey apartment block enclosed by a six foot high, colonial wrought iron fence and a formidable steel gate. It looked out of place in such a poor area.

'Ok, I'll see you to the door Sally, I don't want you to stand out here in the dark,' he said helping her from the vehicle.

The gate was closed and unattended.

'My God! Where is the guard,' she cried, 'he's so unreliable.' She banged in frustration on the gate. After an eternity and more banging it was opened by a teenager in a white *Cagers* singlet and black satin basketball shorts. They followed him along a brick path to a steel-framed door over which a single bulb flickered. The boy opened the door and stood back allowing them to enter passing a snoring, blue uniformed guard with a shotgun across his lap.

Sally stopped to say something but thought better of it. She put a finger to her lips and they stepped past him and climbed stairs to the first floor turning right along a dim corridor to her apartment where a "7" was crudely painted on the door. Conway glanced around at the moth-eaten carpet and paint peeling from the walls. It was no palace.

She hunted in her handbag for the key in the semi-darkness and unlocked the door. He turned to leave but she gently placed a hand on his arm.

'Please sir,' she said softly, 'would you come inside? I would like to show you my place.' He looked at her for a moment then grinned broadly.

'Ok, but hey, I can tell you are a respectable girl and I don't want to damage your reputation. You know, being seen inviting strange men into your apartment late at night, and a foreigner at that.'

'It will be ok sir,' she assured him, missing his weak attempt at humour.

'Please come in.'

He followed her in and stood looking around at a modest studio apartment with a kitchen nook on the right accommodating a small refrigerator and two burner gas stove. Light green painted cupboards sat above a stainless steel sink and laminated bench top.

Beside a tiny white-tiled bathroom, a double bed occupied most of the bedroom cum lounge/dining area; a polished parquet floor led out through pink, floor to ceiling drapes, to a sliding glass door onto a balcony where a line was strung with washing.

Facing the bed in the far corner a small dressing table stood next to an ancient television sitting on a bamboo storage unit whose shelves where piled with newspapers and women's magazines. The cream stippled walls were adorned with several prints of Filipino village scenes and landscapes. A picture of the Virgin Mary occupied pride of place above the bed. Even in the poor light of a single overhead bulb, he could see that the place was spotless.

Sally took pride in her little abode.

'Your family?' He said pointing to a photo on her dresser of a handsome, middle-aged couple who sat stiffly flanked by two attractive, smiling girls. One of whom was a much younger Sally. Two good-looking teenage boys completed the picture.

'Yes sir, my dad, mom, younger sister Alma and my twin brothers Romy and Raffie.'

'Where are they now?'

'In the province of Cavite sir, not too far away,' she replied happily.

'And…who is this?' he asked, pointing to a photo of a square-jawed man in his late twenties in the uniform of the United States Marine Corps.

'Oh, oh,' she said, shaking her head. Embarrassment and dismay washed the happiness from her face. She looked down at the photo for a moment then turned it to face the wall.

'He was a friend I once knew,' she murmured biting her bottom lip.

'What happened?'

'He went away.'

'Ok, sorry.' He was obviously a former boyfriend for whom she still carried a torch. No point in pursuing it and upsetting her further.

'Sir, I want to tell you about it if you don't mind.' Her tone had an air of desperation, as if it was something eating at her that she needed to share with someone.

'He was my lover and in my life, the only one so far I have ever felt deeply for.' Her voice faltered.

'It's ok Sally,' he said putting an arm around her shoulders. 'You don't have to tell me, if it's going to hurt that much.'

'No, no, please, I want to tell you, I need to.' She described how they had met in *The Black Jack* when the Marine was on leave from the American naval base at Subic Bay several hours north of Manila. A relationship had developed over a few months; they became lovers and there had even been talk of a future together in the US. Then one day he went away and all communication stopped. Letters went unanswered, phone calls not returned. In desperation she went to Subic and found a gruff master sergeant who knew him. The tough 20 year man looked down into the large brown, expectant eyes of the beautiful young Filipina and his heart melted.

It was times like this he hated his fellow man. He gritted his teeth and explained the reason for the Marine's silence. There was another woman. The bottom fell out of her life. She couldn't sleep or eat and cried for weeks, but despite her sorrow, she couldn't bring herself to destroy his photo.

He hugged her gently. 'I'm sorry Sally. Come on, I know it was terrible for you and I know these are only words but, life does go on. You are a lovely girl, there's a million men would give their right arm to have you.'

She looked up at him, her eyes hardening for an instant.

'It's very hard to meet a good man working in *The Black Jack*.'

'Perhaps you should look for better employment?'

'Good jobs are hard to find in Manila these days sir,' she sighed.

'Sally,' he said putting both hands on her shoulders.

'Yes sir?'

'Please stop calling me *Sir*. My name is Steve.'

'I'm sorry si...uh, Steve. It's force of habit, a sign of respect. We learned it from the Americans.'

'No worries, I didn't mean to embarrass you but where I come from we don't call people Sir unless it's some very, very important person. Anyway I guess it's something I'll just have to get used to. He glanced at his watch. It's late, you're home safe, so I had better be on my way.'

Her face fell. 'Can I get you a drink before you go,' her fingers lightly traced a pattern on his arm. 'Coffee, or maybe a soft drink? I have some pineapple juice in my ref.'

Conway looked down at her upturned face; the beautiful sloe eyes, luminous in the dim light. Small beads of perspiration had formed above her lips and her breathing had become ragged; her tempting breasts heaved beneath a white muslin blouse.

This was one very desirable woman and he could feel his testosterone and other things rising. But hell, he'd not been in town a week and as gorgeous as she was; to become involved so early was definitely *not* on his agenda.

He tenderly cupped her face in his hands. 'Sally, you are very, very lovely and I would love to stay, but it's been a rough night and I've got an early call for a meeting with my boss in the morning and hey...it's ok.' He pulled her gently to him again as her shoulders slumped. She buried her face in his chest and burst into tears.

'I, I, I, sorry sir, I mean Steve,' she sobbed, 'I am so embarrassed, I should not have asked you to come in. You will think I am like those girls in the bar.' She looked up tears streaming down her face. 'Please believe me I am *not* like that!...I am not! Oh my God!' She fell onto her bed and hid her face in her hands, her shoulders convulsing with emotion.

He sat down beside her and placed his hand lightly on her back.

'Sally,' he said quietly, 'I know you are a decent, hard working girl and I know that's *not* why you're crying. It's got nothing to do with you asking me to come into your apartment.'

She pushed herself up and wiped her eyes with a handkerchief he handed her.

'You know... then what is it?'

He looked away for a moment then said. 'It's all about your lost love. I know the kind of pain still inside you. I've been there and know how hard it is to forget,' his voice trailed away.

'You? You do?' she said brokenly. 'What do you mean? Who did you lose?' She reached out intertwining her fingers with his. 'How? When?'

He disengaged his fingers and stood up. 'Forget it, I have to go now,' his tone brusque.

His sudden change of mood surprised her and she remained on the bed open-mouthed.

'Look I,' he got no further as the room shook from someone pounding on the door. A male voice shouted, urgent, frightened.

'Open up! Open up ma'am! Quick!'

Conway ran to the door and looked through a peep hole to see it was the guard. He almost fell on his face as Conway yanked open the door.

Conway grabbed him by the shirt and hauled him upright.

'What the hell is this all about, what do you want?'

'Sir! Sir! Please, don't go near the window. Keep your door closed, the police and NPA are down in the street, there's going to be a shoot out – Aaaeeii!' He screamed as a loud bang was followed by the glass sliding door to the balcony shattering. The shootout had started! The guard raced from the room slamming the door behind him. Conway quickly switched off the light and pulled a terror-stricken Sally to the floor.

'What or who the hell are the NPA?' He yelled as more shots shattered the still night air.

'They're the Communist party of the Philippines, they want to take over the government, they have killed a lot of innocent people in recent years and assassinated politicians and journalists in the south but now they have moved into the cities, especially Manila, oh my God, listen to that shooting,' she moaned, pulling him in close.

'Stay still and keep quiet and we'll be ok,' he said with a conviction he didn't feel.

'Y, yes, please don't leave me, I'm so scared.' The firefight outside now intensified and the staccato barking of what he knew to be M16's was occasionally broken by shouts and screams as someone was hit. There was an explosion followed by another…grenades…they were too close for comfort.

Conway lay there pondering his situation as another grenade rocked their building rattling the windows.What the hell have I got myself into? Cold blooded murder in the streets; riots; a country on the verge of revolution and now there's a murderous bunch of Commo rebels trying to take over as well. He felt Sally flinch as another furious burst of gunfire erupted below their balcony. And here I am, face down in a darkened room somewhere in Manila, with a terrified woman who's got me in a vice-like grip while world war three is being fought a few metres away!

They lay huddled as the battle raged on, then silence. Slowly, quietly he eased her away and slithered across the floor toward the sliding door. A sharp, agonizing pain erupted across his belly and he realized his stupidity. He had slid over a shard of broken glass from the shattered door. He felt warm blood seeping through his shirt.

'Sally,' he whispered hoarsely, 'get me a towel or something, I'm cut.' Holding his shirt across the wound he eased himself up into a half crouch and peered out down into the street. In the glow of the streetlight he could see several open-sided vans and about ten to fifteen men in the brown uniforms of Metrocom and another group in white tee shirts and flack jackets. All were heavily armed, most carrying automatic weapons. They were standing around some smoking, others talking and joking. It seemed the battle was over but where were the bodies?   Maybe the NPA had escaped?

In the dark, half crouched they moved carefully across to the bathroom. She closed the door and turned on the light. It was unlikely that the 25 watt bulb would be seen from outside. He took off his shirt and sat on the toilet while Sally bathed a gash nearly four inches long. It looked nasty but once cleaned up proved to be quite shallow.

He looked down as Sally's bent head, tenderly bathing the wound. She looked up occasionally, her face a mask of concern.

'Oh, Sir Steve, you will be alright. I will look after you,' she said almost to herself. She stopped the bleeding and reached up to a cabinet above the basin taking a small bandage from a first aid box and taping it over the wound.

He grinned. 'You should have been a nurse. Bloody hell!' He stood up so quickly she nearly overbalanced backwards.

'Oh my God! Did I hurt you, I'm so sorry!'

'No, no, I just remembered, my vehicle! I wonder what happened to it?'

Forgetting his wound he tore out the door and flew downstairs to find the guard talking to two uniformed policemen. They wheeled around as Conway shirtless and bloody, charged down the stairs toward them. The guard momentarily startled then smiled in recognition but the two lawmen looked tense and the younger of the two reached for his holstered .45 Smith and Wesson.

Ignoring the hard stares of the cops Conway grabbed the guard by the shoulders.

'Mate! Where is my vehicle? Do you know where it is?'

'It's ok sir,' replied the still smiling guard. 'When the police arrived, your driver said to tell you he was going back to the hotel.' His smile widened. 'He left very quickly sir.'

A relieved Conway was about to return upstairs when one of the policemen stopped him. They were now more relaxed; their expressions friendlier.

'Sir, what happened to your stomach?' asked the older cop pointing to Sally's dressing.

Conway quickly explained who he was and the circumstances of the wound and how he had been injured trying to protect a respectable young lady during the gunfight. He emphasized the word *respectable*. They accepted his story and were now all smiles, even offering to send for a doctor but Conway declined asking instead for the guard to find a taxi.

'We can do better than that,' said the older, more senior officer expansively.

'We will take you to your hotel in one of our cars.' It had been a successful operation. A dozen NPA lay dead in the house opposite and he knew his chance of promotion would soar after tonight.

Conway thanked them and asked the guard to arrange for repairs to Sally's apartment and send him the bill. A one hundred peso note clinched the deal and he assured Conway, 'it will be my pleasure sir, I will supervise it personally.'

'Do you wish to come with us now sir?' asked the younger officer.

'Give me a few minutes and I'll be right with you.'

Conway explained to Sally what he had arranged.

'I know you have to go, but thank you for staying,' she said resignedly. He stood for a moment, not sure what to say or how to console her but one thing was certain. He had to leave, immediately! He took her hand and squeezed it gently.

'Goodbye Sally.'

She reached up and gave him a quick peck on the cheek. 'Thank you sir… Steve, I…I,' her voice cracked as he bent and softly returned her kiss.

'Ok Sally but now, I really *must* go,' he said glancing at his watch.

'Holy hell, it's nearly 4 am! Bye.' And then he was gone.

She heard his hurried footsteps fade, then stepping carefully over broken glass she went out onto the balcony in time to see him get into the back of a white police car. She watched it disappear into the darkness then went inside and fell on her bed. She lay staring up at the ceiling. Sleep now seemed beyond her. Dawn was breaking in pale yellow streaks on the horizon before she drifted off into the warm welcoming blanket of slumber.

# 5

Perc Prickett was miserable. He sat slumped in a plush executive chair in his first floor office of the Down Under Hotel. He had a huge hangover and a very sore backside. He could figure out the hangover because he vaguely remembered he'd attended a boozy business meeting the day before but his sore bum was a mystery. Must have fallen over somewhere he thought, rubbing the tender spot near his tailbone.

But worse still was the shellacking he'd copped from Imelda this morning. She'd given him a nice old towelling about appearing drunk in front of the guests. So what's new? He'd done it before and most of them were in the same condition. It's good PR to let them see he was one of them.

What did puzzle him though was Imelda. He couldn't help noticing she was ranting and raving through a split bottom lip and oodles of makeup couldn't hide the black eye and the puffy, bruised face. Someone had given her a going over but he wasn't game to comment. He thought he'd heard vaguely someone mention something about a fight in the bar and how the new bloke Conway had sorted it out; must remember to ask him about it. His reverie was broken by a knock on his door.

'Yeah, come in ...Oh it's you Steve, how are you mate? Take a seat,' said Perc, trying a friendly smile which didn't quite come off. The last thing he felt like doing was discussing business and just looking at this clear-eyed, fit looking bastard made him feel tired.

'Good Perc,' replied Conway. He didn't bother to ask the little fat owner how he felt. One look at the half-open blood-red orbs squinting at him was enough.

'Settling in alright son?' inquired Perc, wishing he would go away.

'Fine Perc, but there's still a lot I have to learn about this place yet....I mean both the Down Under Hotel and this town.'

'Yeah, yeah, take your time. Anything you want to know, just ask me. I've been here ten years y' know and there's not much I don't know about this joint,' boasted Perc with a self-satisfied little smirk.

Typical of his ilk, Prickett's ego got in the way, especially when drunk. Then he became particularly obnoxious. He couldn't help bragging about any business, drinking or sexual exploit but his loud mouth and shifty smart-arse manner turned most people off. He had a small coterie of sycophants, mainly no-hoper expats and a few locals who were prepared to wear his bullshit for the occasional free drink. This was one way Perc found he could entice someone to drink with him and there was usually one or two desperates around who would put up with anything, or anyone, for a freebie.

Yes, I'll bet you do, and for sure it's not all kosher, thought Conway, remembering what Stan had told him. I think I'll have to be careful around you Perc old mate.

'Anyway, how are yer findin' us? I believe you sorted out a bit of trouble in the bar last night,' said Perc trying to sound as if he cared. He then leant back in his chair and clasped his hands behind his head. Perc always felt this gave him the 'relaxed, all-knowing executive look'.

Conway grinned to himself. Perc was definitely in La La land last night and wouldn't have known if the roof had fallen on him. I wonder how his backside is this morning?

'So far, so good,' smiled Conway. 'Last night? No big deal. A few of the boys got a bit excited, but nothing to worry about.'

'Yeah, well thanks,' said Perc yawning and then with a crooked little grin. 'But I guess that's what I pay you for eh?'

'Is it? Well then what do we pay our guards for Perc? They were no where to be seen when the trouble started,' snapped Conway, becoming a bit tired of his boss's smugness. If this sawn-off little drunk thinks I'm going to be a bloody bouncer, he can think again.

'Eh, er, well, er.. Where the fuck were they? Was he? I'll bloody fix this, leave it with me,' spluttered Perc, his breath coming in short gasps. Sweat beaded his brow and his flabby cheeks resembled the shade of a bad tomato. He pulled a soiled white handkerchief from his pocket and wiped his forehead and face.

'No, if you don't mind, I'm the manager I'll speak to them later. In the meantime, I'd like to look at the books and check on the operational procedures so I can get a proper picture of how this hotel functions. Ok by you?'

Perc's drink sodden face became at once blank, then anxious. He wasn't too keen on anyone having a close look at the books and *operational procedures?* What the fuck's he talking about? You kept the fridges full of piss for the drunks, changed the sheets occasionally, paid off the cops on Saturdays when you ran the illegal gambling and ripped off the punters for their foreign exchange. These were the only *procedures* Perc knew but so long as he didn't delve too deep it mightn't hurt to let this joker to have a look. Who knows he might find a scam I don't know about and could use meself.

'Ah, yeah, well, I suppose that'll be alright,' he said hesitantly.

'Go and see Susan Santos, you've met her haven't you? She's our chief accountant.'

Conway nodded, 'yes I have, was there anything else?' Perc looked for a moment as if he was about to say something but changed his mind. 'Nah, that's it for the moment Steve, I was going to talk to you about something but...some other time.'

'Right, I'll talk to Susan now, thanks Perc.' As Conway reached the door he turned and there was Perc, eyes closed, chin on chest and mouth open. Not a pretty sight. Conway shook his head and closed the door.

Susan Santos sat at the top of her office like a little queen in front of her eight subjects. Quiet in speech, gentle and shy in manner, her delicate china doll appearance belied the fact that she was a very bright and accomplished accountant.

Late twenties, petite, pretty and small even by Filipino standards she had graduated with honours from the Philippine National University and spent most of her time when not working or studying, caring for her family. Although not married, as the brightest and best educated of a large provincial family, she, like many women in the Filipino matriarchal society, felt duty-bound to provide for those less fortunate of her kin.

Her benevolence was not restricted to her family. Friends and colleagues in financial strife, who had come to her for help, had never been refused; and not one had been asked to repay. Some did, many didn't. If she was disappointed in those who reneged, she never mentioned it. It had been said more than once that Susan Santos should have been a nun or in one of the other caring professions. Her family's poverty and her desire to relieve it had dictated Susan's course in life.

'Hi, Susan,' Conway said standing at her door. 'I hope I'm not interrupting but could you spare a moment to discuss a few things about the accounting system, your reporting, and any problems you have?'

Susan smiled briefly. She had little experience in dealing with foreigners, particularly Australians. She found their accent hard to understand and the few she had met were loud and often drunk.

'Yes sir, what can I do for you,' she asked with just a trace of nervousness. Conway sensed her unease and put on what he hoped was his friendliest smile.

'Firstly, I'd like to have a look at the financial reports for the past three years and then the operating procedures for all departments. I believe you may have them?'

Susan called one of her clerks and spoke rapidly in Tagalog. She turned to Conway with a puzzled look. 'Operating procedures sir?' she said. 'I don't know if we have any. I think maybe Mr. Prickett or Mr Keyes would have them; I only have a few financial records. These are what I have,' she said as the clerk returned with a dark brown cardboard folder.

He quickly scanned through sheafs of paper which seemed to be nothing more than scribbled notes of expenses and memos until he came to an Income Statement dated six months previously. He frowned. 'Where's the rest?'

'I am sorry sir, that's all I have,' she repeated quietly her face expressionless but her eyes betrayed the embarrassment at having so little to show him.

'How long have you been here Susan?' he said grimly, placing the file back on her desk.

'I started here two weeks ago sir.'

'Oh, so you're new also,' his face softened. 'Looks like we both have the job in front of us.' He half smiled in an effort to draw a response but she continued to look at him impassively.

'Well, do you know what happened to the previous reports?'

'No sir.'

'Do you have *any* idea where they *might* be?' he said with growing impatience.

'Well,' she paused, 'they could be with Mr Coleman'

'Are you aware that no one knows where he is?'

'No sir.'

'Who prepared *these* reports Susan? And give me an answer that contains more than two words please,' he said sharply. She grimaced and ran her fingers through her thick black hair. It was a habit he was to notice that surfaced whenever she felt under pressure.

'I'm sorry sir. These reports were prepared by Mr Salazar.'

'Oh, and who's he? And more importantly, where is he?'

'Sir, he's our auditor.' Then pausing she said softly, 'I think he's in the States...sir.'

'When is he coming back?'

'I don't know, I don't think he is coming...'  Her voice was almost inaudible.

'What!  Then you can't verify these reports?'

'No sir.'

'Do you think they reflect the accurate trading of this hotel at that time?'

She took a deep breath.  'I can't say, I will know when I have reconstructed the accounts sir, but it may take some time.'

A disturbing picture began to emerge.  The previous manager had disappeared with or without the other documentation possibly because it could incriminate him but had missed this report in his haste.  The auditor was nowhere to be seen so he and Colman were probably in cahoots in some sort of scam.  Now this lady had been left a mess of incomplete accounts, reports and documents.  Judging by the pile of bank statements spreadsheets, journals and other bits and pieces on her desk, she was in the process of attempting to make some sense of it all.  The one thing he was sure of was that the redoubtable Percy Prickett would have been no help to her at all.

'Susan, I have to have an accurate updated set of accounts as soon as possible, I repeat like yesterday.  Do you understand?'

'Yes sir.'

'And Susan.'

'Yes sir.'

'Oh, forget it!  I'll get back to you later.'  He was out the door so quickly he didn't here her final, 'yes sir.'

\* \* \*

'Hey man, how goes it?'

Conway looked up from the desk in his second floor office desk to see the large, smiling frame of Jumbo Keyes filling the doorway.

'Good mate.  Hey Jumbo, have we got any operating procedures for this hotel.'

The big American's smile got wider.  'Funny you should ask that man, I asked the same question when I got here and I'll give you the answer I got old buddy.'

'And that is... as if I didn't know,' grinned Conway leaning back in his chair.

'You guessed it, but all is not lost, because, I, yes I, Jumbo Keyes have been preparing same documents.'

'Thank God for that, but how has this place been operating? How have the staff functioned if there's been no guidelines?'

'Well, it's not that bad Steve because apparently over the years they've had some good department heads who have been pretty competent and followed standard hotel work practices.. But I agree, there should be something laid out in writing and that's what I'm putting down at the moment. I should have it finished by the end of the month, provided of course, there's no more dramas,' he chuckled.

'Ok thanks Jumbo, give me a look at what you've done when you get a chance eh?'

'Sure. What've you got there?' asked Keyes, leaning over the desk.

'The only financial accounts available, would you believe, and they don't look too authentic to me.'

'Why?' Keyes jovial manner suddenly became serious. Conway leant one elbow on the desk his fist supporting his chin, his brow furrowed.

'Well, for a start, these are the only accounts available and they're out of date. They were prepared by a Mr Salazar who is now in the States and it seems will not be frequenting these shores again. And I suspect the recently departed Mr Colman has all the other accounting reports and God knows what other files oh, and by the way, this afternoon I tried to contact a Mr Marquez, who was the company's lawyer. Guess where he is?'

'The States?'

'You got it in one my friend. The thing is, these accounts show a very modest profit and therefore little return to the shareholders on their investment. Considering what I have seen since I've been here and what I was told by some of the company's shareholders in Australia the place is usually 100% occupied, all the time. I know the bar and restaurant are always full and we do most of the foreign exchange trading in the area, and that as you know, is a big earner.'

Conway looked up at Keyes. 'One would expect a better trading result than what I see here? The shareholders in Australia are worried that there are scams going on here that are reducing the profits. They are very unhappy with the dividends they've been receiving in recent times. That's basically why I'm here; to overhaul the operation and turn it around. Look at this turnover for a start!' He stabbed at a figure on the white sheet in front of him.

'The Sales! These figures have to be bullshit. They're way too low for the size of this operation and the expenses ratio is far too high. Running his finger down a column he looked back up at Keyes and shook his head. The advances to shareholders are ridiculous and these 'other advances,' I wonder who these

'Others' are? Sundry debtors are a joke. I think I shall have to spend time with little Miss Santos on these figures.'

Keyes nodded, 'Yeah man. Look I hope you don't think I've been slack but to be honest I just hadn't got around to checking out things like the accounts,' he said apologetically. 'There were so many other things that have needed attention when I took this job. There was no discipline among the staff, no control of the inventory and suppliers were ripping us off and giving kickbacks, mainly to people here who just happen to be relatives of Imelda.'

'What did you do about it?'

'I fired two of them but a week later they were back on the staff in another job. I raised hell with Imelda but to no avail.' He closed his eyes for a moment and gritted his teeth.

'It's bloody frustrating man, but I'm a foreigner, they're Filipinos, and it's their call.'

'And,' he continued with an air of resignation, 'unfortunately I need the job right now.'

Conway nodded, 'yes, you've got a family to think of. Let's work together on this, it can't be that hard to sort this place out but, I'm the manager, it's really my problem.' Conway leant back in his chair and looked out the window then back at Keyes.

'Did you spend much time with Colman before he left?'

'No,' frowned Keyes, 'he was a strange sort of guy, as I mentioned, kept to himself a lot. I was surprised because I've always found you Aussies a friendly bunch.'

'Well, he may have had good reason.' Conway went on to explain his suspicions about the bashful Mr Colman and related his conversation with Susan.

'Yeah man there's been admin problems for sure but, that's only part of it; there are other reasons. For example, most of the staff, apart from Imelda's relations are paid well below the minimum level. But, it's the old story. They need their job and aren't game to complain.'

'Yes I know.' Conway's face hardened. 'Perc drives around in a gold Mercedes, Imelda dresses like a Paris model and drips with diamond rings and gold bracelets. Do you know that Susan Santos, our chief accountant is paid the princely sum of US$6.00! a day! She's here before eight in the morning and I've seen her still in her office after eight at night.'

Keyes nodded. 'Yes I've noticed her still here late at night and I've never heard her complain. For that matter, I've never heard any of them complain. Workers in Western society don't know how well off they are.'

'Look mate,' Conway said angrily, 'a proportion of the staff in this place are being shit on and we've got to do something about it. I'm beginning to see the basis of the problems in this operation but, it's going to take more than just updating a set of accounts and procedures to fix it. The problems go deeper than that and I'm going to need all the help I can get and *you* Jumbo, are the one I'm going to need most...you in?'

Keyes leaned down and stuck out a huge paw. 'I'm in buddy! Shake!'

'Thanks,' said Conway taking his hand.

The Australian glanced at his watch. 'It's been a long day. How about a drink away from here, is Angie expecting you early?'

'Ang expects me when she sees me. That's why I love her,' grinned Keyes.

'Well, you know the town better than I; where to tonight?'

'I'll give Ang a quick call, and then how about a nice Chinese meal at Mrs Li's Tea House followed by a bar-hop along the strip?'

'You've got me, let's go.'

Half an hour later they were seated at a window table in Mrs Li's Tea House, a Chinese restaurant regarded as one of the best in Manila. Situated in a side street off United Nations Avenue, it was large and airy, tastefully decorated with cream walls, adorned with gold dragons and other motifs denoting scenes from Chinese folk-lore.

Crystal chandeliers hung from the high ceiling above the many tables most of which were occupied by chattering families, small groups of well-dressed Filipino businessmen and a sprinkling of foreign couples either expats or tourists. In a far corner there were several alcoves tucked away for more discreet dining, and more than one was occupied by couples gazing longingly into each others eyes in the eternal unspoken language of love.

Some of the diners recognising Keyes waved and smiled.

'You're well known here mate,' said Conway.

'I come here a lot. It's the best Chinese in Manila, well priced, and best of all, they don't stint on the servings.'

He was right. The chicken soup with quail's eggs alone was nearly a meal in itself. Served in a bowl that was almost a tureen, it was thick, delicious and quite filling. They were halfway through a course of pork and black bean sauce when Conway noticed an exotic Eurasian woman gliding across the lime green carpeted floor in their direction.

She was an absolute knockout!

As she came to their table Keyes stood up and bowed slightly. 'Good evening Mrs Li.'

'Nice to see you again Mr Keyes,' her voice was soft and sensual. She seemed to caress each word. It was one of the sexiest voices Conway had ever heard.

'Mrs Li, may I introduce you to Mr Steve Conway, the new manager of the Down Under Hotel.'

'Delighted to meet you Mr Conway,' she purred, extending a delicate bejewelled hand as he rose to greet her. The subtle fragrance of her perfume enveloped him as they lightly touched hands. The gesture may have appeared to be perfunctory but she seemed genuinely pleased to meet him. Her eyes crinkled in a merry smile revealing perfect white teeth. She wasn't young. He guessed, probably mid-forties, but who knows, Asian women, seemed to age a little better than their western counterparts and he'd read somewhere that Eurasian women even more so.

Up close, she was exquisite. Her lustrous coal black hair was pinned back with an ornate silver comb and caught up in a chignon which emphasised her high cheekbones and the flawless golden skin of an unlined face. Huge turquoise, almond shaped eyes were dusted with pink kohl and her lusciously full lips had been sculptured with a deep crimson lip gloss. She was dressed in a sleeveless salmon and gold silk Cheong San, split to mid-thigh, allowing a tantalising glimpse of a shapely leg. The fine silk moulded the bold curves and valleys of her disturbingly statuesque body.

'The feeling is mutual Mrs Li. I must say I am enjoying your restaurant and your food immensely,' he said gallantly.

Mrs Li was impressed. This was a nice man, with manners and good looking as well. She had been a widow for many years now and meeting a gentleman of this calibre, suddenly brought on an urge which she had purposely kept dormant for far too long. They chatted for a few minutes then Mrs Li left to attend to other matters. Conway and Keyes watched approvingly as she made her way across the room stopping occasionally to smile and offer a word to other diners.

'That's all woman,' Conway said, still eyeing Mrs Li now with head thrown back emitting peals of laughter at some remark by one of the customers.

'Like's a joke too,' observed Keyes helping himself to a generous portion of Chow Mien. Later, had Conway not been so busy attacking the superb Peking duck he would have noticed Mrs Li often glancing in his direction from behind her position at the cash desk.

Their meal finished they paid the waiter leaving a generous tip. Reaching the door Conway paused and looked around. Across the restaurant, Mrs Li waved, flashing that megawatt smile. Conway returned the smile. The interaction was not lost on Keyes who smiled quietly to himself as they stepped into the street and headed back down toward MH Del Pilar Street, the bar Strip.

It was Friday night and the Strip was more noisy and crowded than usual. Touts and painted girls waved and shouted to them from the bars as they wandered slowly through the throng until they came to the largest and brightest of them all. *Nightbirds.*

# 6

A burly, unsmiling doorman in a white short-sleeved *Barong* and black pants ushered them in through a curtain where their senses were immediately assaulted by the thunder of ear-splitting heavy metal rock, and the sour stench of stale beer and tobacco. They had entered a large rectangular room, smoky and dimly lit with pink fluorescents and the obligatory floor to ceiling mirrors running the length of the room on opposite walls.

Along each wall was an upraised stage on which ten, red bikini-clad dancers writhed and gyrated seemingly oblivious to the jibes and yells of the raucous male audience. Some danced side by side, two had their back to the throng obviously transfixed by their image in the mirror, others smiled hopefully down at the customers while several of the more energetic snaked themselves sinuously around several ceiling-high chromed poles which like the mirrors, appeared to be an essential prop for dancers.

At the far end in a corner was a small bright pink fluorescent sign which proclaimed, *Comfort room*, the elegant Filipino expression for toilet. The decor was plush red carpet, black plastic and chrome furniture. The whole place had an ambience of noisy, decadent opulence. A lot of money and been spent fitting out *Nightbirds*.

They found a couple of spare stools at the nearest stage and Keyes ordered two San Miguels. The drinks arrived and they had barely taken their first sip when from over Jumbo's left shoulder came a loud, squeaky voice.

'Hey Jumbo, you bloody old reprobate how are you?' Both turned to see a large individual, well over six feet, in an open-necked red and white, short sleeved shirt and jeans, probably late forties. He was solidly built except for a slight beer belly. A friendly moon face smiled at Conway the light glinting off the gold in several of his front teeth.

'Barney Lawson,' he said in a broad Australian accent, extending his hand to Conway, 'but my friends call me 'Henry'. I'm the owner of this salubrious establishment.'

Conway had to stop himself from laughing. Lawson's high-pitched voice was completely out of character with his ample, rugged appearance.

'Steve Conway, Henry,'

'Steve's the new manager of the Down Under Hotel,' said Keyes perfunctorily acknowledging Lawson's greeting. Conway sensed Jumbo wasn't all that keen on the gregarious bar owner.

'Ah ha, so this is him! I've heard about you Steve. The word is you can handle yourself. I believe you sorted out a stoush in the Down Under the other night?'

'Nothing to write home about Henry, nice place you've got here. Must have cost you a shilling or two?' said Conway, taking a sip of his ice-cold San Mig.

'Better believe it Steve, but,' his grin widened revealing yet more gold. 'We make the odd dollar out of it,' replied Lawson smugly. Then waving to a barmaid, he gestured to Conway and Keyes with the air of someone who knows his every order will be executed without question.

'Two more here.'

'Where y' from Steve?'

'Queensland, you Henry?'

'Sydney m'self. Long time ago though. Just love it here mate, and why wouldn't yer,' he said, waving his hand to embrace the scene. 'Came here, set up this joint and haven't looked back. Imagine tryin' to do something like this in Australia. Two minutes later some wowser or do-gooder prick would scream his head off to the papers or TV and you'd be fucked in a stride. Doesn't matter that 99% of the male population would love it. Only the minority rules where you and I come from Steve old mate.'

'No thoughts about going back then Henry?'

'Well to be honest mate,' he said lowering his voice, 'I can't. Unfortunately, I left a few little problems back there and the 'wallopers' and the three letter men would like to have a word with me.'

'*The three-letter-men?*'

'Yeah, you know. The T-A-X men, the bloody Australian taxation department. Yeah, I've never put a tax return in, in me life and the mongrels want to know how I got the mansion in St Ives, the Rolls Royce and the 40 foot cruiser at Pittwater. Fuck 'em, they're not gunna find out either huh?' His little outburst was cut short by an attractive, female in a tailored red jacket and black mini-skirt who whispered something into his ear.

'Yeah... O.K....I'll be right there. Sorry, duty calls, give the boys here another beer on me,' he ordered a hovering waitress, then flashing a cheesy grin and a wink, lumbered after red jacket to a far corner of the bar, where with bent head he listened intently as she waved her arms in an animated fashion.

'That woman's a supervisor, seems to be some trouble afoot. It's not all plain sailing running a place like this buddy,' remarked Keyes dryly. 'Let's just enjoy the scenery.'

His suggestion was not necessary as Conway was already gazing up on stage at a tall stately dancer in a tiny g-string bikini. She was bumping and grinding in front of him with the mother of all 'come hither' smiles. Conway grinned at her and turned to Keyes.

'I wonder what a nice girl like her is doing in a joint like this?' The American look up at her and smiled. 'Man,' he said shaking his head in mock bewilderment, 'I guess she's just a simple music lover who's hooked on dancing.'

His tone then became serious. He put his beer back on the bar, looked at it for few seconds and turned to Conway. 'Steve, a lot of these kids have little or no education and come from dirt-poor families in the province. Unemployment is over forty percent here, and this is the only way some of them can find to make a dollar.'

'Not a real nice way to make a living but most seem to be enjoying what they're doing,' replied Conway.

'They've got to eat man, and you know what? There's a kind of sisterhood among them.'

'What about government assistance?'

'*Government assistance!*' Keyes nearly choked on his beer. 'You've go to be kiddin' man. There's no such thing in this burg! The government here assists *itself!* Not these poor mothers. Shit man, where you and I come from, for all the faults, there is some sort of social conscience...not here! This place is run by a group of families as their own private fiefdom and our old mate Ferdinand, man, he's top of the heap, and I mean *real,* top of the goddam. Man, these people are O.K. but there are some real, rotten apples at the top of the tree here!'

Conway nodded and took a sip of his beer. 'I've read some of the history of the Philippines, and it seems they had a good president in Magsaysay, but unfortunately he was killed in a plane crash. Since Marcos got his hands on the presidency things seem to start off well but these days the place is going down hill…fast.'

'Yeah, that's true, but you know the old saying about 'power corrupts and absolute power, etc, etc.'

'But the people have had enough haven't they? I've read that things here have been hotting up since Benigno Aquino was murdered.'

'You're right, and even though I don't think there will be a revolution, you never know. To be honest I wouldn't really be surprised the lid doesn't blow right off this whole trash can soon. You can feel it man, and see it in the faces of the people.'

'You mean a Communist takeover?' said Conway sipping his beer. The incident at Sally's apartment had spiked his interest in the extent of the NPA involvement in Manila and how much of the local unrest was fomented by the insurgents.

'No, not the NPA, they're strong in the south but not so much here, too much military and police but they do have their *'sparrow units','*

'Sparrow units, what are they?'

'NPA hit teams of usually just two who go around shooting the local cops. They walk up behind usually a uniformed man and bang! You're dead! If they get caught, the same thing happens to them. Something has to be done to help these poor bastards, as I said, they are *good* people and they deserve a better hand than what they're being dealt now. But the NPA are definitely not the answer!'

Talking about the plight of the Filipino people obviously ignited a passion in the big man, a passion surprising in such an outwardly placid individual. It made him thirsty too. Draining his beer in one huge gulp, he motioned sharply for yet another two. After their initial round, and the booze Lawson had bought, the session was developing; it looked like being a long night.

A new set of dancers had come on stage and the object of Conway's pretended desire seemed to have disappeared. Keyes was still on about the local political scene when Conway felt a tap on his shoulder, and there she was; the tall dancer. She now wore a thigh-length light cotton jacket over her bikini. It was loosely tied at the front so as not to restrict his view of her burgeoning brown breasts, barely contained by the tiny bra.

'Hello Sir,' she breathed, 'what is your name? Where do you come from?' Up close and away from the deceptive lighting, she was much older than she appeared on stage. The heavy make-up couldn't hide the acne scars and the crow's feet running away from the eyes; this lady had been up a few dry gullies.

'Hi, Steve from Australia,' he said politely taking the extended hand. 'What is your name?'

'Baby, sir.' Her smile revealed an urgent need for orthodontic work. 'May I join you sir?' she murmured, moving in close, placing a hand on his thigh.

'I don't think so Baby,' Conway said, taking her hand off his leg. 'I'll be leaving soon.'

'Sir, you buy me a drink,' she pouted, returning her hand to his leg.

'Sorry sweetheart, not tonight, maybe some other time,' Conway said removing her hand again. The smile vanished as quickly as a politician's promise and she flounced off to another target. Keyes polished off his beer and stood up. 'I'm off to the comfort room man. We might head off after this what say you?'

'Sure, but let's have a nightcap at the *Black Jack* on the way home, I'd like to see Sally again.' Conway had told him about the episode at her apartment and wanted to know if the repairs had been done.

'Ah hah, is that all?' grinned Keyes, lumbering off to the toilet.

Conway sat staring at his beer oblivious of the dancers writhing above him. His mind was turning over the problems in the Down Under. Perc and his wife were a worry. Something was amiss: he'd better tread carefully.

Keyes returned and they were about to leave when ear-splitting screams from behind made both men wheel around. A few feet away two dancers stood with clenched fists shouting at each other in Tagalog. One of them was Baby.

'They're fighting over a man. The usual problem…it'll blow over,' Keyes said with the resigned air of one who'd seen it all before.

Conway frowned. 'You think so? They look pretty serious to me.'

The screeching reached a crescendo as both women tore into each other grabbing hair and any other part of the other's anatomy that was available. Nearby the guy whose favours they desired, watched on with a smirk. To Conway's surprise, no one seemed interested in intervening except a waiter who was immediately pushed back by a brawny onlooker.

'Let 'em go,' he yelled above the hubbub. 'Good fun!' Both women were now rolling around the floor, punching scratching, pulling and screaming like banshees.

Baby's jacket was lying in shreds on the beer-soaked floor and her large dark-nippled breasts lay exposed from a torn bra. Her g-string had been ripped off but her rage made her oblivious to her nudity. From the urging of the crowd it seemed her opponent's name was Lisa. She was slightly smaller but no less energetic. Lisa had also lost her bra and was in imminent danger of losing her bikini bottom too, but she also seemed not to notice, so intent was she on belting Baby. Both women rolled away from each other, regained their feet and glared at each other, panting, eyes dilated: Lisa, now naked, rushed at Baby who took a wild swing, missed, and found herself pinned against the bar.

Drawing back her right fist Lisa crashed it to the side of Baby's jaw and the taller girl wobbled, her eyes rolled back and she staggered forward, dropping her hands, straight into another big crunching right which broke her nose.

The fight had gone out of Baby. Lisa stepped in and buried a vicious left into her unprotected belly. Baby let out a long moan and crumpled to the floor where she lay, writhing and gasping for breath. The fight was over. The smaller girl stood over her beaten foe, dark eyes flashing. Sweat trickled between her breasts down over her belly into a small patch of black pubic hair. A laughing dancer grabbed her fist and held it aloft shouting, "the winner by knockout!" The crowd cheered. Lisa stood for a few seconds, arms in the air savouring her victory, then realising her nakedness, let out an embarrassed scream and hurried off through the crowd.

Conway shook his head at Keyes. 'Let's go,' and headed for the door. The last they saw of Baby was her limp form being dragged away, by which time, the mob had turned their attention back to the stage as if nothing had happened,

'Never a dull moment in this town eh man, *Black Jack?*' laughed Keyes slapping Conway on the back as they stepped out into the humid Manila night.

Although it was nearly midnight the sidewalks were still crowded and most of the clubs were still doing a roaring trade. They were about to take a short cut down a side street when a large black limousine cruised slowly beside them and from the back passenger window a familiar female voice called out.

'Mr Conway, Mr Keyes, just a moment!' They turned to see, her painted red lips flashing a wide smile, the exotic Lily Li.

# 7

Mrs Li usually stayed at her restaurant until closing time in the early hours. It was often busy after midnight when she caught the late night trade from the Strip but tonight she decided to go home a little earlier. She had seen the boys and pulled up to offer them a lift home. At least that's what she told herself.

'Your very kind Mrs Li but I live nearby and my wife is waiting, I can walk from here,' said Keyes politely. Conway turned sharply mouth half-open in surprise.

'Hey, I thought you wanted to...'

'Steve, as you said earlier, it's been a long day. I think I might turn in, hope you don't mind?' His smile was wide and he attempted a yawn, which didn't fool Conway for a moment.

'Alright, I'll see you in the morning...*early*!'

'Sure thing boss,' Keyes said, stifling a laugh.

'Where do you live Mr Conway?' asked Mrs Li in that low, seductive voice.

'Well, actually, not far from here either Mrs Li, I can walk...'

'Please,' she interrupted him smoothly, 'please allow me to give you a lift. That is,' she said arching beautifully drawn eyebrows, 'unless you have, someone else to meet?'

'No, I haven't, that's very kind of you. I'm in the Silver Diamond apartments on U.N Avenue. I hope that's not out of your way?'

'No, it's not,' she said opening her door, 'please get in.'

In the darkness of Mrs Li's limousine Conway was almost overwhelmed by the headiness of the perfume. He was only too well aware of her closeness and the heat of her thigh through the silken Cheong Sam. He looked out the window and started to wonder what he had let himself in for. As the big vehicle rolled out onto Roxas Boulevard and back down toward United Nations Avenue he yawned, and pretended to doze.

He opened his eyes as the vehicle came to a halt and to his surprise they weren't outside his apartment but had pulled up in front of a set of imposing wrought iron gates. Mrs Li placed a hand lightly on his thigh. He glanced down at her hand; must be a thing in this part of the world: Baby, now Mrs Li.

'Mr Conway, like me, I am sure you have had a long day,' she said, leaning even closer.

'You must be tired, and I have a special Chinese green tea that will help revive you, but at the same time, ensure you have a good night's sleep. Would you care to come in for a moment and I'll make you some? I promise I won't keep you long.'

Her tone indicated that it was an invitation that offered more than just a cup of tea. He knew he should refuse. But the nearness of this beautiful, exotic creature and the San Miguel beer he'd consumed lent flight to better judgment. A cup of green tea can't hurt, he told himself, and I can't be far from my apartment. I guess I can be polite and still make it out of here and be home at a respectable hour.

'That's very kind, thank you Mrs Li.'

'Please call me Lily,' she said softly looking him straight in the eye.

'Then you must call me Steve.'

Half of him wanted the familiarity but the other half was telling him it was not a good idea. In the circumstances, the latter half was fighting a losing battle.

They drove in through the gates and a uniformed guard opened Mrs Li's door with a smile as they alighted in front of an imposing white, Spanish-style hacienda.

Conway followed her up several steps through a white archway and across a black and white tiled portico to a broad mahogany door with a huge gold knocker where they stood for a moment breathing in the sweet fragrance of hibiscus. Mrs Li was about to knock when the door was opened by a pretty, smiling young maid.

'Good evening ma'am, sir,' she said brightly as she ushered them into a spacious, tastefully furnished morning room. Conway looked around and whistled softly. It was the size of a small ballroom. Two large crystal chandeliers lit a room the floor of which was tiled in white marble. The chandeliers were dimmed creating an atmosphere of intimacy. Expensive gold and silver objet d'art, and pottery which Mrs Li said proudly was Ming dynasty and priceless, decorated a room upon the walls of which, hung several large gilt-framed Philippine land and seascapes. The centrepiece was an exquisitely carved dining table and eight chairs of dark mahogany. Conway took in all this opulence and thought about the slums he'd seen on the way to Sally's apartment...

She led him through an archway into a smaller carpeted room where by a French window stood a round mahogany coffee table and two Brentwood chairs. On his left was a maroon velvet settee, and in front of him, of all things, a white marbled fire-place. He was looking askance at the fire-place when she took his hand and said with a knowing smile.

'An indulgence of mine I'm afraid and of course we never light it. When I was in France my late husband and I fell in love with fire-places; they give a house so much style, don't you think?'

'Ah, yes, Mrs Li, er...I mean Lily, it's just that I didn't expect to see a fireplace in a tropical country like the Philippines. You're right though, it does give this place style, and I get the feeling I could be in Madrid and it gets cold there sometimes.'

She nodded appreciating his graciousness and picked up a small crystal bell from the coffee table. She rang it lightly and a few moments later the pretty maid appeared.

'Yes ma'am?'

'Binky, would you bring us some of my special Chinese green tea please.'

Mrs Li gestured to the settee.

'Please Mr Conway,' she said patting a place beside her. He sat wondering what was coming next.

'So, you are Australian, can you tell me more about yourself. For example, are you married?' she asked with twinkling eyes.

'No.'

'Then you must have a girlfriend? I mean in Australia...or here?'

'No, I haven't Mrs Li, neither there, or here. I have only recently arrived and I have been too busy in my new job, getting to know this city, I am sure you understand.'

She pursed her lips as if determined to press the point.

'Well, yes I do of course but there is a question I have to ask.' Her eyes never left his as she asked the question. 'What do you think of our women,' she paused for effect, 'in the short time you've been here?'

'Very attractive, present company included,' he said quickly.

This pleased her. 'I'm sure you'll get to like our city...and our women. I also hope you will visit my restaurant...often,' she giggled almost girlishly.

Conway began to sweat. He wanted out but didn't want to offend her. She rose and placed a hand lightly on his chest as he went to get up.

'No, please stay there, I won't be long. I promise,' she said coquettishly, leaving with a roll of shapely hips.

He sat there pondering his next move. He doubted very much that Mrs Li had invited him for a quick cup of tea. A quick 'something else' was more like it. He shook his head and smiled to himself, Christ, Conway, you get yourself into some situations at times. I shouldn't have accepted her invitation, but I just can't leave now without insulting her. Ah well, she's a terrific looking woman, so what am I complaining about? Soft music from another room interrupted his thoughts. It was Mcdowells '*To a Wild Rose.*' He grinned. How appropriate.

A few minutes later Binky returned with a silver tray holding a white, fine china teapot and two small delicate, gold-rimmed white cups. She set them down on the coffee table and looked about her with a puzzled expression.

'Sir, where is ma'am?'

Conway shook his head. 'I don't know Binky but she said she'd be back in a moment.'

'Ok sir.' Binky flashed yet another blinding smile and retreated.

May as well try this he thought and was about to pour himself a cup when Mrs Li appeared. He looked up and nearly dropped the teapot!

She had changed...and how! Gone was the cheong sam and in its place was a diaphanous white silk number. It left nothing to the imagination and for all it covered she may as well have been naked. It dipped low across full, tempting breasts, revealing a deep cleavage and clearly outlined were the dark circles of her large nipples. It finished at mid thigh, proving that the legs glimpsed so tantalisingly in her Cheong San, were just as good all the way up.

She had let down her thick coal black hair, and it now tumbled carelessly over bronze shoulders which gleamed in the soft light. She looked younger and the slight smile playing around her lips was wanton, challenging and full of promise. Her feet were shod in elegant Mediterranean sandals and she could have been a Greek goddess. Conway sat stunned, his mouth half open.

She glided to the centre of the room, pirouetted slowly before him hands on hips. 'You like?' she murmured, her voice thick with lust.

'Er, ah, yes,' stammered Conway. For a few seconds his cool was off somewhere else. Here he was in a dimly lit room with a nearly naked woman parading in front of him asking him if he was enjoying himself. Was he what! She lowered herself down beside him, her perfume almost overpowering.

'That's, er, lovely perfume you have,' he said, trying to think of something appropriate to say and fast forgetting about an early start in the morning.

'It's called *Bold Desire,* I thought you might like it,' she breathed moving closer so that her bare thigh now touched his.

'Have some tea Mr Conway.' She took a cup, filled it with the steaming liquid and handed it to him, her eyes glowing. He took a sip and closed his eyes trying not to choke.

'Mmmm, it's different, what is it?' His mind was racing. This is like a scene out of a B movie but what the hell! *I like B movies.*

'Oh, a special blend, my late husband was given from an old Chinese friend. It is supposed to do many things for you,' she said looking at him over the rim of her cup.

'Such as?'

'Well apart from promoting inner health, and sound sleep, it's supposed to be a very potent aphrodisiac,' she said raising her eyebrows.

'Very interesting Mrs Li, and no doubt appreciated by those who need it,' he said entering into the spirit of the game.

'What do you mean Mr Conway?'

'An aphrodisiac.'

'Oh, you don't need one?' Her breath quickened, causing her breasts to rise and fall disturbingly against the thin fabric.

'Never had the need for one in the past,' grinned Conway sipping his tea.

'No, I don't suppose a healthy, good-looking man like you would have had to resort to such assistance, and, neither have I,' she chuckled throatily taking his cup and gently placing it on the coffee table.

'Come,' she said taking his hand, 'I'll show you more of my home.'

For the next few minutes she showed him with obvious pride, the various areas downstairs of what was a palatial mansion complete with a large kidney-shaped swimming pool lit underwater by a series of inset lamps. The pool deck was tiled with the same white marble he'd seen inside. There were two lazy boy lounges and in one corner was a small open bar and dressing room.

'Some pool,' he whistled.

'You like to swim now Mr Conway?'

'Well, yes, but?'

'You have no costume? Never mind, come, you don't need one,' and in an instant she shed her clothes and stood proudly naked in front of him. Shoulders back slightly, her full breasts heaving, their large pink nipples distended.

He stood there for a moment open-mouthed. If her body looked good in clothes, it was sensational without them. Her skin was flawless and for her age, the large breasts were still firm with only a hint of sag and sat proudly above rounded hips which curved down to strong toned legs. It was a body which had been well looked after.

'How do I compare with your, er, showgirls on Del Pilar?' she smiled, cupping her palms lightly over her breasts, then slowly placing her hands behind her head, posing for his inspection.

He stood dumbfounded.

'Could I compete?'

'No…contest.' He didn't recognize his voice. It was more of a gasp than a statement and came out of a suddenly dry throat. Trying to keep his cool he added, 'You win.' A small voice from inside his head said, 'fuck the early night!'

She undid a couple of buttons on his shirt and ran her hands underneath over his chest. 'So macho,' she said dreamily, closing her eyes then quickly undoing the rest of the buttons.

He ripped off his shirt while she unzipped his trousers. A few seconds later, he was as naked as she. He pulled her to him and smashed his lips on hers. He didn't realise how close they were to the side of the pool and the ferocity of their embrace caused him to lose his balance. They tottered on the edge then fell in with a loud splash.

The water wasn't cold but it was enough to clear his head. Gasping he came to the surface and for a moment he couldn't see her. Then he jerked as he felt a soft hand encircle his cock and squeeze lightly. She broke surface like a frolicking porpoise, emerging with a triumphant smile on her face. He pulled her in close and felt the velvet smoothness of her back as their lips met. Her tongue attacked his with an almost frantic urgency. He responded hungrily. It was a long time since he'd been with a woman.

And he was with a *real* woman now!

He lost track of how long they stayed kissing, fondling and splashing each other like a couple of kids, but finally he helped her from the pool and was surprised to find on one of the lazy-boys, a couple of towels and two white thick terry towelling robes. Binky unnoticed, had brought them out while her boss cavorted merrily a few feet away.

They quickly towelled each other dry and donned the robes. With her hair damp and hanging loosely she looked years younger, almost childlike. Her eyes sparkled as she reached up on tip toes and pecked him on the lips.

'You are very handsome Steve.'

He cradled her cheeks in his hands and kissed her at first softly then with increasing passion, feeling her soft smooth body melt into him. Long minutes later he stepped back his chest heaving.

'You are something else Lily,' he said thickly.

Taking his hand she led him up the stairs to the next level where outside a door she turned and smiled impishly. 'Come into my parlour sir.'

He smiled to himself. I think I know who is the spider and who is the fly here.

Her bedroom was large, opulent in keeping with the rest of the house. It was lit softly by hidden wall lamps. The centrepiece was a huge round bed covered with a pink satin doona and two snow-white pillows. What a playground, thought Conway glancing at the floor to ceiling pink velvet drapes.

He watched as she went to the other side of the bed and plumped a pillow.

'I hope you will be comfortable dear,' she said, then opened her robe and shrugged it from her body, her big breasts bobbing ripely as it fell silently to the floor. She fell onto the bed with a giggle and rolled onto her back her arms clasped back behind her head arched her body and uttered the most unnecessary words he had ever heard.

'Care to join me?'

He was already naked and straddled her as she came up to meet him wrapping her legs around him. Gone was the cool sophisticated exterior, now she was a sexual tigress…and a very hungry one.

Their mouths mashed savagely. This was not the sweet sensual embrace of two lovers. It was one of passion; of two people eager to fulfil a long overdue need. It was not lovemaking. It was simply …fucking.

Like two wild animals they thrashed around on the bed his lips moving over her body, licking her breasts and the large pink aureoles, his cock hard and thrusting between her open, waiting legs. He felt her teeth biting his cheek, her lips kissing his neck. Her arms held him as if never to let go. 'Fuck me! Fuck me PLEASSEEEEE,' she moaned. 'I have wanted it for so long! PLEASSEEEEE! OH GOD! OH GOD! OH GOD!' She screamed. 'DO IT TO ME…NOWWWWWWW!!!' He entered her easily, inch by throbbing inch. She moaned and writhed and rolled across the bed with him hanging on for grim death.

He didn't know how long it lasted. It was just a wild whirl of moaning, groaning and thrusting. She met him thrust for thrust until finally with a loud moan she collapsed at the same second he did. They both lay there, exhausted. Sleep came quickly.

He woke and sat bolt upright wondering for a moment where he was. 'Shit!'

He jumped out of bed, grabbed his clothes and dressed frantically, tripping over the cuffs of his pants in his haste.

'Darling,' she murmured sleepily, 'where are you going?'

'I've got to go, it's 3 am!' he yelled over his shoulder as he pulled up his pants and stumbled to the door.

Out in the street he was in luck. A passing taxi screeched to a halt and a short time later, he was back in his apartment where without undressing, he collapsed onto the bed.

# 8

Conway sat in his office trying to check daily stock usage sheets but his mind kept drifting back to the previous night's encounter with Lily Li. I better not get too involved there, she's a man-eater. His reverie was interrupted by a quiet knock on his door.

'May I come in sir?' Steve looked up to see Susan Santos standing at his office door with a bundle of dark brown files in her left hand, her right poised to knock again. She looked nervous.

'Of course Susan,' he smiled, trying to put her at ease. 'What can I do for you?'

She was wearing a tailored grey suit and red shoes on her tiny feet. A crisp white blouse, coupled with a bright yellow scarf and expensive looking ruby earrings completed the outfit. Her small, pretty face was framed by an urchin cut giving her a girlish appearance.

She stood there for a moment, hesitant as if waiting for more instructions. Suddenly it was if he was seeing her for the first time. She was lovely; the essence of a beautiful, fragile Filipina. A Filipina who seemed unaware of her innate beauty.

'Sir, I have constructed the financials for the three month period to March before you arrived, and reconciled the banks statements,' she said placing the files on the desk in front of him. He opened the files and frowned.

'Nothing more current than this?'

'I'm working on an update now,' she said quietly, avoiding his gaze.

He flicked through the files still frowning.

'Where's the Balance Sheet Susan?'

She grimaced.

'Sorry sir, there is no asset register and we are still trying to value them and list the liabilities that we know of,' she explained. 'I was left with nothing much to work on when I arrived here.'

'How long is that going to take?'

'I am not sure, it could take a few weeks. We have to start from scratch and it is a big job identifying, counting, valuing…'

I thought he would be better, but he's just like all the other foreigners, they don't want to understand our problems; they think they can snap their fingers and the job will be done.

Conway drew a deep breath.

'Ok Susan, sorry, I know you have a big job but please make it a priority. Let's have a look at what you have there.'

Susan blushed. His tone suggested he doubted her professional ability. Usually a quiet, placid personality she now seethed inwardly. He showed no sympathy or understanding of the massive job she faced.

For the next forty-five minutes they poured over the financials and bank statements with Conway asking many questions about various balances and individual items in the expenses and the ratios of them to the income. The bottom line again did not reflect results that he would have expected having seen the daily turnover of the hotel. She grudgingly admitted to herself that at least he did seem to know what he was talking about. He closed the files and looked hard at her. The funds bore no relation to the statements of account. He leaned back in his chair, and asked the 64 dollar questions.

'Where's the money?'

Susan's pretty face flamed.

'Sir, I have to prove it but I think a lot of it has gone in advances to shareholders and other people.'

'*What other people?*'

'Sir,' her voice was almost inaudible. She was struggling to keep her emotions under control. 'There are others, friends I think of management here who have been able to take advances.'

'On whose authority?'

'I am not sure sir. I will find out and let you know.'

'Please do. These figures are ridiculous,' he said, unable to contain his anger. 'What are we running here, a bloody bank?'

'Sir, this is what I have found,' she replied, her voice rising. 'I was not here when these transactions took place. I do not have the authority to allow such advances. I just do my job and produce the figures for management from the information I have…sir.' Now she was unable to contain *her* exasperation.

Conway looked at her with raised eyebrows. Gentle little Susan had a temper after all.

'Ok. Please make your investigation and the Balance Sheet a priority... and a Funds Statement would be handy for us to track the cash movements, ok?'

'Yes sir.' She stood for a moment then realizing the meeting was over, headed for the door.

'Susan, wait a moment.'

'Sir?'

'You are doing a good job,' he said trying to smile. He knew he had gone too far and offended her. He needed to make amends. 'I know what you are thinking but believe me, I *do* appreciate your difficulties and if you need any help, my door is always open, ok?'

'Yes sir,' she replied, her face expressionless. 'Thank you.' She turned abruptly and left, leaving him in no doubt his attempt at appeasement had not worked.

He continued to study the figures, his frown becoming deeper.

What's going on here? This hotel is a goldmine. Someone is ripping the joint off and I better find out who and how...and quickly.

'How is Mr Conway today, you look a little tired buddy?'

Conway looked up to see a grinning Jumbo Keyes. The big American was right but Conway was in no mood for admissions.

'I'm fine and why shouldn't I be Mr Keyes?' replied Conway, poker faced.

'Well Mrs Li looked like she was ready to perhaps, er, show you her etchings.' The big man couldn't help himself and started to laugh helplessly.

'What gives you that idea?'

'The look in her eye for starters; come on man, what happened, did she take you home?'

Conway tried to keep a straight face.

'We went to her place and had a cup of Chinese tea.'

'Chinese tea...Bullshit!' Keyes great belly shook with laughter. 'This is Jumbo Keyes you're talking to buddy.'

'A gentleman does not discuss his nocturnal activities with underlings,' grinned Conway.

'Ok, if you don't want to liven up poor old Jumbo's boring life with your sexual escapades so be it. Hey I saw little Susan just coming from here how are things there?'

'Fine. She seems very efficient. What do you think?'

'She's as sharp as a tack; a good girl. The place is better since she came.'

Conway nodded, 'Yes I've got her working on bringing the financials up to date. They are well behind. It's a big job but I need these figures as soon as possible. From what I've seen so far, something's not right.'

'You mean the figures don't add up?' said Keyes quizzically. 'To be honest Steve it wouldn't surprise me. Perc and Imelda are very cagey when you bring up the state of the finances here. All of a sudden, loquacious Perc becomes rather vague.'

'Have you ever tried to quiz him when he's full of soup? That's the time they usually give things away.'

The American shrugged. 'Yeah, sometimes in the bar but he just gives a silly grin and ignores you and turns to his cronies. He's usually got a few hanging around him.'

'I'd like to meet them. Who are they?'

'You will man but you won't get much out of them they're a strange bunch, mostly expats and a few Filipinos. I try to stay away from them; there's too much verbal masturbation when they get together with Perc. They know everything, or think they do; small dicks 'n big egos.'

Conway's antiquated phone jangled. Prickett.

'Busy?' rasped Perc.

'Got a bit on, why?'

'Come to my office I've got someone I want you to meet.'

'Ok, be right there,' said Conway winking at Keyes. 'The Master calls.'

Perc offered a twisted smile when Conway arrived.

'Wancha to meet a good friend of mine,' he said, motioning to a thickset, sallow-faced middle-aged individual, all khaki and epaulettes.

'Steve, meet Colonel Ramon Sanchez, Chief of Police for the Western district. Ramon, Steve Conway my new manager.' Conway smiled offering his hand but it was ignored. Instead, the police chief looked Conway up and down and said abruptly, 'Australian?'

Taken aback for a moment by the unfriendly tone and stony face, Conway dropped his hand and simply nodded. Prickett tried to cover up Sanchez's rudeness.

'Yeah Ramon, Steve comes highly recommended, he's already sorted out a few things here I'm sure he'll keep things in order. Woncha mate?'

'Yes…I most certainly will,' said Conway slowly, not taking his eyes off Sanchez.

'Yeah,' continued Perc, 'Ramon here's a real crime buster. He don't take shit from anybody and he's real down on drugs. The papers are always talking about him and how he's cleaned the local area of the bad guys. He's a real local hero.'

Sanchez remained stone-faced. He and Conway continued to stare at each other. The instant dislike was mutual. The air could be cut with a knife. Perc hurriedly brought the meeting to a close.

'Thanks Steve, I'll let you get back to it.'

'Ok Perc,' Conway said, ignoring Sanchez, and leaving without another word. 'I won't be sending you Christmas cards pal', he said to himself as he walked back downstairs, just in time to see Keyes coming up.

'Hey Jumbo, come with me I want to talk to you about something. It's lunch time let's go somewhere quiet.' Keyes suggested *La Boheme*, a French restaurant tucked away in a small side street off United Nations Avenue where they quickly found a table well away from the other diners.

'What is it Buddy? What's eating you, you look pissed?'

'I just met Ramon Sanchez the local police chief; you know him?'

Keyes grimaced. 'Yeah I know him, met him once or twice, unpleasant son of a...'

'I have the same impression. What's his problem? Most of the Filipinos I've met have been charming and easy to get along with.'

'I don't really know Steve,' said Keyes shaking his head. 'His attitude has been a talking point among expats in this town for a while now. For some reason he seems to dislike foreigners; Americans and Australians in particular. It's known he's not averse to a little payola so maybe a few Australian and American bar owners haven't coughed up their share of "protection" but I really don't know.'

'Like as in Mafia type protection?'

'You got it man.' Keyes nodded to a pretty young waitress waiting expectantly.

She handed them each a menu, with a smile which brightened the room. Keyes winked in appreciation. Conway looked on in amusement as she blew Keyes a silent kiss.

They sat in silence for a few moments perusing their menus. Conway wasn't hungry so he ordered a *croque madame*, cheese and coffee. The big man pored over his menu for some time, finally deciding on an entrée of *terrine rustiqu* then *Pork filet mignon with onions,* coffee to follow.

'If Sanchez doesn't like Australians what's he doing hanging around with Prickett? They seem very friendly?'

'They are. I don't know what the connection is but they're often seen huddled together in shall we say, "furtive conversation".'

'What do you know about Sanchez?'

'Only what I read in the papers. He's supposed to be some kind of super cop; a drug crusader who's feared by the bad guys. The media here love him; they've made him into some kind of folk hero but between you and me, I think he's dirty.'

'Why?'

'Just word you hear around town. He's also supposed to be some sort of moral crusader and wants to close the bars. What crap! In my experience moral crusaders are usually suspect. The scuttlebutt is he has his own bars in Quezon City. Steve, be careful in your dealings with him. He's dangerous man; he makes people disappear…'

'Yeah, he's got the eyes of a dead fish, reminds me of the *white mice*, remember them?' said Conway referring to the feared Saigon police during the Vietnam War, whose all-white uniforms and brutal behaviour earned them the scornful epithet.

'Only too well buddy,' replied Keyes sipping his water. 'They were hated more by our guys than the VC.'

Their meals arrived and they ate in silence for a few minutes.

'You know Steve the word is around town that Sanchez is a millionaire… on a cop's pay? Makes you wonder doesn't it?'

Conway nodded and took a sip of his ice water. 'For sure he's got skeletons in the cupboard. I've only met him briefly and there's no doubt, he's a nasty piece of work. I wouldn't put anything past a character like that. Corruption, murder, you name it. I'll give him a wide berth but his connection with Prickett is a worry.'

They finished their coffee and Conway paid the bill leaving a good tip.

'That's good French food, must go there again,' mused Conway to Jumbo's grinning satisfaction. It was nice to have a free meal on the boss.

As they stepped out from the air-conditioned restaurant into the burning heat of early afternoon Keyes said Angie had not been feeling well and asked leave to slip home to see her. Conway waved him away and walked back along the always crowded Mabini Street to his office still deep in thought. Back in the hotel he stopped in the bar for a moment to check on the lunchtime scene.

It was crowded. It appeared his little effort stopping the fight had got around the area and guys from other bars had come to make the acquaintance of the new manager. He was about to leave when he noticed three die hard regulars engaged in animated conversation. On closer inspection it seemed the conversation was one-sided. Two looked as if they were trying to ignore the third guy.

The three consisted of two large individuals and a third; a weedy little fellow known to all and sundry as "Weasel". Weasel was noted for the outlandish stories of his sexual and other exploits in Australia and the Philippines. No one believed him and he was generally considered a pain in the arse. To make matters worse he was known to have a "death adder" in his pocket.

"Wouldn't shout if a shark bit him", was the general opinion. He stood between his two companions and was in full flight to the bored looking drinker on his left.

The big guy copping the non stop barrage looked over Weasel's head at his mate who nodded. Then, in unison, they grabbed the little guy under each arm and using his head as a battering ram hoisted him upwards. *Boing!* his head smashed into the bell above him and pandemonium reigned as everyone hollered for their free drink. Weasel began spluttering and yelling frantically.

'No! Fuck No! Fuck! You bastards! Stop it! I didn't…Oh fuck!' No one took any notice, least of all the bar staff, who had their hands full coping with the sudden rush. They all laughed and cheered the unhappy Weasel. It was going to cost him a packet. No one laughed louder than Conway at the unique way the two guys had got their free drink. He continued on to his office arriving as his phone rang. It was Prickett and he was angry…very angry.

'Where the fuck've you been? There's trouble in Angeles. Get up to the fuckin' Billabong and take Susan with you!'

The Billabong was their sister hotel in Angeles City. Conway had spoken to the manager "Snow" Burgess another Australian, a couple of times on the phone.

'What's up Perc, what's the problem?' asked Conway calmly, holding the phone away from his ear as Perc's expletives crackled down the line.

'We think some bitch in accounting has fucked with the payroll. Zeny Diaz the new accountant there just phoned. Grab a driver and go, immediately!'

Thirty minutes later Steve and Susan were in Quezon City heading for the northern freeway to Angeles. They reckoned on about two hours to Angeles and once through the squalor of Quezon City it would be a straightforward drive on a good highway, which Keyes had proudly mentioned, been built by the Americans.

It was a pleasant evening without much traffic apart from a convoy of military vehicles full of troops and armoured personnel carriers moving into the city. Conway glanced sideways at Susan for a reaction but she sat quietly, relaxed and seemingly enjoying the chance to get away from her desk.

'Do you know the new accountant Zeny in Angeles Susan?'

'I have spoken to her on the phone a couple of times sir, she seems quite capable.'

'Have you asked her about the payroll problem?'

'No sir, I did not know about it until you told me…'

They lapsed into silence. Seeing it was going to be a one-way conversation he let the matter drop and looked around at the passing countryside.

It was flat to the horizon on the left but broken by distant hills on the right. The brown scrubby grasslands with patches of green were dissected by a number of small rivers, most barely more than a creek. One river bed so dry, it was nothing more than an expanse of rocks and sand. They continued on past rice paddies, a few small *sari sari* stalls and frail *Nipa* huts on stilts until just under two hours they rolled into Macarthur Highway, the main thoroughfare of Angeles City.

Night had fallen as they turned off Macarthur Highway into a street signposted, Fields Avenue. If the drive to Angeles had been mostly boring, first impressions of Angeles after dark certainly were not!

Conway couldn't believe his eyes.

The streets of Angeles city resembled a scene of bacchanalia! Fields Avenue and its precinct were the focal point of the night life and action. And what action it was!

The traffic was heavy and slow allowing Conway to gaze incredulously at a spectacle, the like of which was not surpassed in the wild days of Saigon. The street lighting was poor but more than made up for by the blazing kaleidoscopic neon lights from scores of bars with salubrious names like *Welcome Inn, Superhead, Muffdivers, Love Shack,* outside of which spruikers in flashy clothes and bikini clad girls urged passers by to come in and sample their dubious "wares".

Both narrow sidewalks were choked with foreigners many with Filipino women on their arm. Groups of men young, middle-aged and older, some obviously drunk, laughed, pushed and shoved each other as they wobbled out onto the almost unpaved, potholed roadway where muddy puddles of water from recent showers reflected psychedelic colours from the lights of the bars.

Conway wound down the window and was immediately almost deafened by blaring rock music accompanying the shouts of the touts and their dark-eyed girlfriends. Dimly lit alleys revealed more bars and revellers. He looked at Susan to see what she made of all this. She sat there as impassive as ever.

They left Fields Avenue behind and came upon Don Juico Avenue which was more badly paved than Fields. It was yet another mile of muddy pot holes running parallel to the huge American Clark Air base, said to be the largest outside mainland America. The drive was torturous. They were constantly thrown against each other as their vehicle rocked and rolled finally coming to a halt in front of *The Billabong Hotel,* where a huge red fluorescent declared, *Leave your Troubles Behind.*

Snow Burgess, wearing a white tee shirt with *Billabong Hotel* on the pocket, navy blue shorts and sandals stood at the front waiting. He was of medium build with a thatch of grey hair above a weather beaten face, wary, but not unfriendly.

'Nice to meet you Snow,' smiled Conway as they shook hands. 'Do you know Susan?' he asked indicating the little accountant who stood further back.

'No, but I've heard good things about her from Zeny. *Kumusta* Susan,' he said, giving the usual Filipino greeting and receiving a quiet *Kumusta* in return.

Snow showed them to separate rooms and said he would see them in the restaurant for dinner after they had settled in. Thirty minutes later, the three of them sat outside under the stars by the hotel pool where they were joined by Zeny Diaz, a bright-eyed Filipina in her mid twenties.

Conway understood Snow's wariness and hastened to reassure him.

'Snow, I am only here to add support to Susan and help in any way I can.'

'Ok Steve.' Burgess sounded relieved. 'It's just that Perc sometimes is a pain in the butt when it comes to this place. He often comes up here and always wants to change things; and Imelda is always ready to poke her nose in where it's not wanted. To be honest, the less I see of the Manila gang, the better I like it.'

'This is your ship Snow but if you need any help or advice I'm only a phone call away.'

'Thanks Steve, I appreciate that.'

Snow ordered drinks for the four of them; beers for he and Conway and soft drinks for the girls. They all nodded when he suggested a seafood platter and as they sat eating, Zeny outlined what she had discovered.

Apparently Mayet the payroll clerk had been away sick and Zeny prepared the payroll. To her surprise she found a few names listed not on the personnel records. Suspicions aroused she conducted an audit. A retrospective check revealed the salary and wage calculations to be overstated and didn't match the records. In one of Mayet's desk drawers she found a bank account with a substantial amount of money in it; very unusual for someone on a payroll clerk's salary. She reported her findings to Snow. They discussed it and realized they had no choice but to advise Manila.

It was decided that Mayet would be suspended while Susan and Zeny carried out a thorough investigation going back through payroll records for the previous six months since Mayet started in the position. A report would be given to Snow, Steve and Prickett before any further action would be taken.

Conway and Burgess sat drinking and yarning about their backgrounds until bored with male talk, Susan and Zeny politely excused themselves and moved to a table nearer the pool where they began to laugh and chat animatedly as if they'd known each other for years. Conway stared at Susan for a moment. It was the first time he had seen her relax completely. With her own ilk she was a different woman.

Snow had been a merchant seaman and ship's cook.

'I cooked all round the world mate, never lost a man though I've come close a few times,' he laughed.

'How did you come to finish up here Snow?'

'Bit of a long story really, but basically I decided to give the sea away and came to the Philippines on holidays a few years ago. Had a week in Angeles, liked it and came back a few times over the years. Earlier this year decided to settle here and looked around for a job. Luckily there was a vacancy here at the Billabong. I applied and it so happened they wanted to improve their kitchen. To cut a long story short, I sorted it out and they made me manager. I was in the right place at the right time.'

'How do you get on with Perc?'

'Ok...if he leaves me alone, which is not often,' grinned Snow, 'but I've met worse.'

'What about you Steve, I know you haven't been in the job long either. How is it with Perc?'

Conway thought about this for a moment. He had his suspicions about Prickett but he wasn't going to show his hand to Snow.

'He's ok, no problems.'

Snow glanced across at Zeny and Susan still deep in discussion.

'They're good ladies those two, they'll sort out this payroll thing. I'll get them working on it first thing in the morning.' He looked at his watch.

'Would you like to check out the town Steve? If you've never been I can assure you there's plenty to raise your eyebrows,' he laughed.

'Sure, I got a glimpse coming in, looked pretty interesting.'

Burgess got up and stretched. 'That's an understatement. Just a minute mate.' He went over to the girls and had a brief chat then motioned to Conway to follow him.

Zeny waved and flashed her toothpaste smile as they left and although Conway smiled in her direction, Susan remained cool and aloof. Was that a hint of reproach in her eyes? He shook his head and followed Snow to a garage at the back of the hotel where a dark blue Dodge sedan in immaculate condition was parked.

'My pride and joy,' said Burgess proudly. 'Get in mate.'

Conway whistled. 'Wow, what year? She's a beauty,' he said running his hand over the wide bonnet.

'She sure is. She's a 1955 model. I bought it off a yank on the airbase who was going back to the States after his tour here. He needed to get rid of it in a hurry so I got it for a song.' He fired up the eight cylinders and the big vehicle rolled smoothly to the front gate and out on to Don Juico Avenue.

They bumped their way up to town and stopped in Fields Avenue where Burgess gave a boy a few pesos to keep an eye on the Dodge.

'Here we are my friend; we're now in the heart of the action.'

They made their way along the crowded sidewalk stopping outside a bar with the unlikely name of '*Heaven's Gate*'. Burgess received a smile of recognition from the doorman.

'There's heaps of bars in this town Steve, but this one is better than most, cold beer, nice girls and you don't get hassled.'

Their backsides had barely settled when two bikini-clad girls pounced.

'What's your name? Where you from? You buy me a drink?' They chorused.

'No hassles Snow?' grinned Conway.

Burgess smiled ruefully. 'Welcome to Angeles City Steve.'

Something told Conway his first night in Angeles City was going to be interesting indeed.

# 9

They resisted the overtures of the eager young ladies until Snow finally relented and bought a drink for one lissome young dancer in a yellow bikini.

'Gina's a good kid, doesn't go out with the customers and helps her mum in a *sari sari* stall during the day. Hey!' he laughed, nearly falling from his stool as she jumped up onto his lap and smothered him with kisses.

'He good man, not too much drunk,' said Gina happily, sipping her watered down coke between kisses.

The bar was long, narrow and badly in need of an air freshener. It was furnished with dull red upholstered stools at the bar and banquettes which lined the right hand side. Lighting designed to create an atmosphere of intimacy failed to hide the worn, shabby interior nor birth marks and battle scars of a motley collection of obviously bored dancers. And this was one of the "better" places?

Conway sipped his beer and checked out the scene while Gina smooched with Snow. They were the only customers until in lurched a heavily built, unshaven individual wearing a black baseball cap on backwards from which a pony tail extended half way down his back. A black tee shirt with *Swine* emblazoned in yellow on the front and black jeans added an aura of menace. He scowled at all and sundry then slumped down in empty stool beside Snow.

'Oh no,' whispered Gina hugging Snow a little more tightly. 'He been here before, bad man, he cause trouble.'

The object of her anxiety glared up and down the bar. "Giss a fuckin' beer and make it fuckin' *malamig,*' (cold), he snarled. The young girl behind the bar knew him and her face betrayed her anxiety as she nervously handed him a beer. He took a sip and immediately spat it out showering her with spittle.

'This shit is hot! I said give me a fuckin' cold one you stupid bitch!'

The poor girl blanched and with trembling hands brought him another. He took a swig and glared at Conway and Burgess, daring them to challenge him.

They said nothing.

Satisfied he had the bar cowed, he began making lewd remarks to the bar staff with every second word beginning with "F". Finally Snow could take no more. He turned and tapped the guy on the shoulder.

'Hey! Give it a break mate; these girls don't need that sort of language!'

Black cap turned slowly to Snow.

'Who the fuck are you? Mind your own fucking business,' and with that he backhanded Snow knocking him from the stool to the floor taking a screaming Gina with him. The whole bar became silent. Conway stooped down and helped Snow and Gina to their feet. Burgess was shaken and had a trickle of blood coming from his mouth, but was otherwise unhurt.

'Now fuck off or you'll get more,' sneered Black cap taking a long swig of his beer.

'Excuse me.' Conway reached over and took the bottle from his mouth and placed it on the bar. 'Hey, what the fuck!' yelled Black Cap. That was the last thing he said before a fist crashed into his jaw breaking it. He didn't see the next punch which Conway brought from the floor. It blasted loudmouth backwards from his stool onto the floor where he lay sprawled on his back, out cold!

While everyone looked on open-mouthed, Conway grabbed a fistful of black, greasy pony tail and dragged the limp body along the floor to the door. He heaved him to a half standing position then turned to a still groggy Snow and sobbing Gina.

'What was that you were saying about no hassles in this joint mate?' He pushed open the curtain with one hand then heaved the ex troublemaker out onto the street where he lay unconscious on his back until a mangy dog scratching through some rubbish came over and pissed on him, by which time Burgess had driven Conway to another bar called *The Eagles Nest* out on Macarthur Highway.

Snow had recovered his dignity and was still thanking Conway for his intrusion as they walked up a flight of stairs to the entrance of *The Eagles Nest*.

'After what you did back there mate, I'm sure you're a man who's got a strong stomach so I reckon you'll handle this next place ok. It's a bit depraved and it's not a joint I frequent, but if you come to Angeles you should see it, at least once.'

*The Eagles Nest* was big, square, and semi-dark. This night it was half-filled with drinkers including a noisy group of Japanese tourists who had taken up prime position in front of a small upraised half moon stage.

Above them four bored, tired looking dancers went through the motions to ear-splitting rock music. Conway and Burgess took a banquette on the left side not far from the stage. Steve ordered a San Mig and a *Tanduay* rum and coke for Snow and waited for the promised "action".

A few minutes later to Conway's relief, the music stopped and the dancers departed. From a door at the side of the stage appeared another female covered from head to toe in a cloak which was probably once white.

She stood legs wide apart in the middle of the stage and whipped off the cloak. The Japanese tourist screeched. She was naked; much older than the dancers, overweight and rather motherly in appearance. What she did next was most unmotherly.

On several tables stood coke bottles on top of which were balanced piles of one peso coins. Bouncing off the stage she approached the first table where three guys sat waiting with eager eyes. She straddled the coins, sucked them into her vagina and returned to the stage. She then sat on the small stool raised both legs high above her head and using incredibly powerful pelvic muscles proceeded to spit the coins out one by one. "Ker ching! Ker ching! Ker ching! The mob roared their approval.

She repeated the performance at two other tables while the Japanese almost wore out their fingers taking photographs. One deviate wanting a bird's eye view moved to within a few inches of her and produced a flashlight. He began to shine it on the lady's intimate region as she spat out the coins.

Bad move!

She must have decided this guy was getting more than his money's worth so manipulating another muscle she shot a stream of urine straight into his upturned, grinning face. The Jap let out an ear piercing shriek, dropped the flashlight, turned and stumbled through tables of laughing, jeering drinkers toward the door desperately trying to wipe his eyes mouth and hair.

'I told you this place was different Steve,' laughed Snow wiping the tears from his eyes. Conway shook his head and smiled. What a country! Shoot outs, fights, women spitting coins from their fannies. What next? What was that Groyne had said about the Wild West?

Snow finished his drink and looked at his watch. 'It's getting late mate so I better get you home,' said Burgess. 'Next time I'll take you to *Blow Road.*'

'Blow road! Where is it? And what is it?'

'Shitty little pot-holed street with shitty little bars; runs parallel to Fields. There you can have a blow job while you have a drink. Great way to spend a Sunday evening,' grinned Snow as they headed for the door.

"Yeah, sounds like it,' said Conway without enthusiasm. 'I think I've seen enough. Let's go.'

Twenty minutes later Conway was back in his room at the Billabong. After a quick shower he went out to the balcony to get a breath of fresh air before retiring. His room overlooked the pool and down beside it to his surprise sitting alone, was the small figure of Susan Santos.

'Hi Susan, it's late shouldn't you be in bed?'

'Huh! Oh, hello sir,' Susan was startled. She'd obviously been deep in thought and hadn't heard him come up behind her.

'I couldn't sleep so I thought I would come down to the pool for a while.' Conway took a seat beside, stretched his legs and yawned.

'I was about to hit the hay and I saw you down here. What's the matter, anything I can help you with?'

'No sir, thank you sir, I was just thinking about a few things.'

'About the job Susan? Look, I know you think I am a bit of an ogre at times but I'm not really, I am sorry for coming over a bit…ah well, you know,' he said gently.

She smiled at him for the very first time. It lit up her face in the moonlight. She looked beautiful.

'Sir, I don't think you're an ogre. Far from it…the staff at the Down Under all like you and respect you. And I do too,' she said shyly looking down at her hands which held a crumpled handkerchief. Had she been crying? This was a different Susan.

'I don't want to press you Susan but if you have a problem about the work, please tell me, I promise I will help you.'

'Thank you sir, you are very kind, but it's…'

He took her gently by the shoulders and turned her to face him. 'But what?'

'I'm worried about the accounting, it's a real mess. There is something wrong, it should not have been left like that, and …I feel I am not good enough in your eyes.'

He let go of her shoulders and gently lifted her chin so she was looking straight into his eyes. 'Susan, you have my complete confidence, not only me, but Mr. Keyes as well. We're right behind you and we'll back you. If you find something amiss, and I think you will, you have nothing to fear believe me, ok?'

'Thank you sir, thank you very much. Oh…but what about Mr Prickett?'

'Don't worry about Mr Prickett, I will take any report of yours to him. He will want to know everything.' I can't tell her my suspicions. Better to let her find things without any prejudice.

'Sir, I am also worried about my country,' she said quietly.

'Oh really?' Another surprise. The last thing he expected was her views on the current situation in the Philippines.

'Would you care to tell me why?'

She did, telling him how she and her friends were concerned about the direction of the country since Senator Aquino had been shot.

'Mr Marcos has been good but now I think he's going too far. His administration is very corrupt and the people are suffering. He promised so much but these days his cronies are the only ones who are doing well. They are growing richer and our people, the farmers of which my father is one, and the man in the street, are becoming poorer. We badly need land reform.'

He listened in growing admiration at the passion in the voice of this quiet, gentle woman.

'I am a Filipino and I love my country but these people who govern our country are destroying it! We need a change but I don't know how it will happen.' Her voice trailed away as her small hands continued to screw up her handkerchief..

He was at a loss what to say. Like everyone else, he was aware of the discontent within the populace but felt uncomfortable. He didn't know enough about the political situation and was not in a position to offer any informed comment. He certainly didn't want to be discussing politics with his accountant.

'Come on Susan, I think it's time for some sleep ok?'

'Yes, sir, sorry sir, I did not mean to speak about such things to you. You are my boss, it just slipped out,' she murmured with that familiar gesture of running her fingers through her hair.

'Hey, no worries,' he grinned trying to lift her spirits. 'I think I can learn a lot about Philippine politics from you Miss Santos, and I hope you will tell me more. If I am to live and work in your country I need to understand it at every level so I hope we can have this conversation again and I look forward to hearing more from you but Susan, it's late so you better get to bed.'

'Yes sir,' she said with a brief smile and for a moment looked as if she wanted to say something else but thought better of it. He watched as she slowly walked across the lawn and up the stairs to her room. He then retired and was asleep almost as soon as his head hit the pillow.

It was the usual steamy Philippines morning. After a few laps of the pool to freshen up, he showered and joined Snow for breakfast of orange juice, scrambled eggs, toast and coffee.

'Where are the girls, have they had breakfast?' asked Conway, munching on a piece of toast.

'They had theirs half and hour ago and are hard at it.'

'Excuse me sir,' called a waitress from the bar holding up a phone. Wiping his mouth with a napkin Burgess rose and walked across to take the phone call. Conway finished his breakfast and joined Susan in the accounting office where she and Zeny were working through the payroll records.

It appeared that there were two sets of payroll sheets so it was not difficult for Mayet to include names that did not exist and also record former staff who had long since left the employ of the hotel. Sooner or later her scam would be discovered but with an impending departure to America with her boyfriend she was making the most of her opportunity before Snow and Zeny both newcomers, discovered what was going on. Conway discussed the legal ramifications with Susan then left for Manila asking for a full report when she returned at the end of the week.

* * *

The phone in Conway's office rang. He picked it up to hear a voice with a broad Australian voice.

'Is this Steve Conway, manager of the Down Under?' Not waiting for a reply the voice went on, 'my name is Roberts, Jack Roberts of the Australian Federal Police. I'm the liaison officer between the Australian Embassy, the Philippine National Police and the Philippine National Bureau of Investigation here in Manila.'

'Yes I'm Conway. What can I do for you Mr Roberts?'

'I'd like to come and have a chat with you if you can spare me a few minutes, soon as possible.' It was more a demand than a request.

'Sure. Where and when?'

'3.00 pm, the Aurelio Hotel. You know it?'

Conway knew the Aurelio. It was five minutes walking distance from his office.

'How will I know you?' asked Conway.

'No need, I know you,' said the policeman hanging up.

Of course he would know me. The Australian feds in Manila have a file on all the Australians here whether they like it or not, according to guys I've spoken to. I wonder what's on his mind?

At three o'clock on the dot, Conway strode through the doors of the Aurelio Hotel into a spacious lobby. He glanced about but apart from a Filipino couple enjoying a drink and a few more lounging around there was no foreigner to be seen.

'Steve Conway?' said the voice with the Australian accent. He turned to see a tall, tanned, heavily built man, early forties in a dark blue suit, white shirt and tie.

'Yes, and you must be Jack Roberts, how are you?' smiled Conway as they shook hands.

Roberts motioned him to a table behind a pillar in the corner. It had a view of all incomers but could not be seen from the front door.

'Coffee?' asked Roberts lowering his bulk into a cane chair.

'No thanks. What did you want to see me about?' Conway was irritated. He didn't like the summons or the attitude of this guy.

The Federal policeman looked at the Queenslander for a long moment saying nothing. Then he reached into the inside pocket of his coat and produced a packet of *Marlboros*.

'You indulge?' he said offering one. When it was declined he lit up, then leaned back and inhaled deeply.

'For a start, relax Steve, we know you're clean. We know all about you,' the tone was still a little condescending, increasing Conway's irritation. 'But we are a bit concerned about the mob you're involved with,' said Roberts.

'Why's that?'

Roberts took another drag on his cigarette, looked at Conway shrewdly. When he spoke the tone was careful, confidential. He was weighing his words.

'My job,' he began, 'is to help the local authorities keep an eye on any suspicious characters from our part of the world, and, this area attracts more than its fair share.' He paused again blowing a ring of smoke into the air.

'You haven't been here long and wouldn't know but, the Down Under Hotel has been, and is, a haven for some of these gentlemen. It may not be obvious on the surface, but there is quite a drug trade going on in this town together with credit card scams and a few other little rorts. It probably won't surprise you to know that some of our countrymen are mixed up in more than their fair share of these deals.'

Conway sat expressionless. 'You know more than I do,' he said. 'I haven't been there long enough to know any of these guys but I have had my suspicions about one or two.' Conway said, also carefully choosing his words.

'Let me know if you see anything please Steve, I'd appreciate it mate,' said the cop, his tone warmer. Now they were "mates".

'Ok, is that all?'

'Yes mate, I just wanted to have a look at you and get to know you and let you know who I am. I'll call in and have a beer there one night, and the name's Jack,' said Roberts, smiling for the first time.

'Do that Jack, be happy to see you.'

'Yes...and Steve.'

'Yes.'

'Watch some of these white men here. They'll pull a fast one quicker than you can pull a beer.'

Conway grinned getting up and extending his hand. 'I'll remember that, thanks for the tip.'

Roberts stubbed out his cigarette and looked at Conway with that questioning look that policemen have. 'We better get back to the salt mines eh Steve?'

'Something like that.'

Both men left the hotel together. On the street they went their separate ways. The last Conway saw of Roberts he was getting into a black limousine, no doubt supplied by the Australian Embassy. What he didn't see, was a set of eyes watching him from inside a white shaded corvette stationed fifty metres up the street from the front of the Aurelio Hotel.

* * *

Percy Prickett dialed a number. 'Hey, could be trouble, he's been with a federal cop from the Oz Embassy. Oh, you know, good! Now look, I don't bloody like it. Yeah! Yeah! I know, but on top of what you told me yesterday something's gotta be done. This guy is a snooper. I can't just fuckin' sack him he's got the bloody shareholders in Australia onside, they'll smell a rat. Ok, I'll leave it to you...'

Prickett replaced the phone and sat for a few moments frowning then he picked it up again and dialed another number.

# 10

Conway walked along Mabini Street deep in thought about a phone call that morning from Susan who was still in Angeles City. She advised that Mayet had been charged with *Estafa* (theft) and the hearing would be held in a few days and she was required to be a witness. Would it be ok for her to stay and help Zeny? He agreed, but asked her to return as soon as possible.

'There's pressure from the Australian shareholders to see current accounts, it's very urgent Susan.'

'Ok sir, it's Tuesday now, I should be back by next Saturday at the latest,' she had said hopefully.

As he crossed Padre Faura he heard a familiar female voice.

'Hello sir, where are you going?' He turned to see a smiling Sally looking lovely in a white, low-cut sleeveless dress coming toward him.

'Hi Sally, I'm just going to Robinson's department store to pick up a couple of things for my apartment and maybe some clothes, what about you, where are you off to?'

'I have to go there too sir, do you mind if I accompany you?'

'Of course not, how've you been, how is that boss of yours?' he asked, guiding her between a car and an overloaded jeepney. She gave a wry grin.

'Oh he is ok sir…some times good…sometimes not so good.' A few minutes later they were about to enter Robinsons when who should appear from within, a bodyguard in tow loaded down with shopping bags, but Lily Li looking exotic and glamorous as usual in tight fitting designer jeans, calf skin boots and a white, silk top. Racier than the average Filipina and ever the exhibitionist, Lily was always ready to flaunt her assets. It was obvious she wore no bra.

Her painted cherry red lips formed an 'O' and the manicured eyebrows lifted in pleasant surprise when she saw Conway. Ignoring Sally she rushed up to Conway, embracing him and planting a passionate kiss full on his lips then stepped back smiling, arms outstretched to gauge the effect.

Taken by surprise, a startled Conway half stumbled backward off balance. For a moment he was lost for words then quickly recovering he introduced Sally who was barely acknowledged.

'When are you coming to see me again darling?' gushed Lily, 'we had so much fun last time didn't we?' she said smiling archly, knowing full well the effect it would have on the silent, glowering woman beside him.

'Er, well, I've been a bit busy lately Lily, but will try to see you again soon in your restaurant,' he said emphasizing the "your", hoping that Sally would think Lily's restaurant was where they had their "fun".

'I hope so darling,' said Lily her eyes flickering for a second to his bosomy, sloe-eyed companion checking her out, then back to Conway.

'Do you like my outfit darling?' she cooed, then with one hand she began lightly stroking the well-coiffured hair at the back of her head an action which thrust her big boobs outward in an unspoken challenge to Sally. The immediate rivalry was all too obvious. Conway pretended not to notice, told her the outfit was lovely and continued to smile and make small talk. Sally looked daggers at Lily.

Well aware of the tension between the two women, he began to move past Lily, anxious to escape from what had become an uncomfortable situation. Giving him a peck on the cheek and a smile full of lusty promise, Lily waved goodbye and left with a rolling of hips, the bodyguard staggering along in her wake.

Sally remained silent as they walked around inside looking at the large racks of clothing featuring mainly imported gear from America and Europe. On the elevator to the second floor she could contain herself no longer.

'Sexy isn't she?'

'Yes, I guess she is,' replied Conway in what he hoped was a disinterested tone.

'She has big *su sus*'.

He didn't need an interpreter to know what she meant.

'Yes, you noticed?' he couldn't suppress a grin.

'Is she your lover? When did you meet her? How long have you known her?' the questions spilled from her lips. Conway stopped as they stepped onto the next level and looked down at a downcast Sally. He had no desire to get involved in a question and answer session about Lily.

'Come with me, it's lunchtime,' he said firmly, suddenly deciding he didn't want to look at clothes. Taking her hand he marched her back downstairs out into Adriatico Street to a newly opened *Jollibee* restaurant. They ordered a hamburger, coke, a side of French fries and took a table by the window. The Australian was hungry and literally devoured his but Sally just sat there miserably, leaving hers untouched.

'Come on Sally,' he said kindly reaching over and touching her hand. 'I know what you are thinking, but she is just an acquaintance. I know her from the restaurant she owns on U.N. Avenue.'

Sally looked up her eyes brimming with tears. 'You had *fun* last time, what does that mean? Of course you are lovers,' she mumbled unhappily. Sally was a nice lady. She'd been hurt badly in the past; he didn't want to add to her pain. Clearly she had strong feelings for him which added to his unease.

'No we aren't lovers, we had fun at a birthday party in her restaurant put on for one of my staff,' he lied. 'It was a very happy occasion we had cake, there was dancing and singing; you know how you Filipinos love to party right?' he smiled handing her a handkerchief to dry her eyes.

Somewhat mollified she wiped away her tears and began to pick at her hamburger.

'Please forgive me sir, I am a silly woman' she sighed looking down at the table top.

Then she brightened. 'Sir, you are very kind, thank you so much for being my friend, it's just that I have found it so hard to relate to a man these days and I just feel good in your company, so many foreigners treat us so badly.' The words came out in a torrent as if there was some cathartic need to get it out of her system.

'I have seen how Filipinos have been treated by some foreigners Sally and thank you for your kind words. I will always be your friend and if you ever need help you know where to find me, ok? And now Miss Sally,' he said getting up from the table, 'you are lovely company but, I have to be getting back to work.' He paid the bill and returned to his office where almost immediately the phone rang. He picked it up to hear the silky tones of Lily Li. She came straight to the point.

'Your friend is very sexy darling,' she purred.

'That's what she said about you Lily.'

'Uh huh, and she has big *su sus.*'

'Well, again, she said the same thing about you,' he found it hard to keep the smile out of his voice.

'Are you lovers?' there was now an edge to her tone.

'No, we aren't,' he replied wearily.

'Lily,' he continued, 'she is a friend. I met her on the way to Robinsons and I am sorry... but I have a mountain of paperwork I must finish.'

'When are you coming to see me darling, I miss you?'

'I'll try and make dinner one night this week. Please Lily, I must go now.'

'I know you are going to your girlfriend!' In an instant her tone had changed and was now spiteful. 'Please yourself *Mr* Conway, I don't care if you come to my restaurant or not! And, *Mr* Conway, (where had darling gone?) don't mess with me! I have powerful friends in this town. They could make life difficult for you!'

Before he could answer, the phone was slammed in his ear. Shaking his head he was about to start on the pile of paperwork when he heard a commotion coming from downstairs in the foyer.

\* \* \*

Ramon Sanchez leaned back in the chair in his office at the Western Police District in United Nations Avenue. *'Tuloy Ka'* (enter) he said to the knock on his door. Lieutenant Danny Roque a short stocky man in his early forties wearing a white tee shirt stretched across a beer gut strolled in as if he owned the place and took a seat in front of his boss. He crossed his legs and sat back nonchalantly and without offering, opened a packet of *Marlboros*, lit one and waited for Sanchez to speak.

The police chief glared at Roque. Why do I put up with him? One day I won't tolerate his insolent manner but now is not the time. Sanchez was only too well aware Roque knew all about his 'activities' over the years and in fact had been responsible for implementing most of the illegal ones including debt collector and "hit man". The truth was, as much as Sanchez hated it, he had to keep Roque onside because he knew his fat little lieutenant wouldn't hesitate to blow the whistle on him if it meant saving his own skin.

'What is Conway doing; what are his activities?' snapped Sanchez. Roque leaned back and blew a smoke ring. 'Nothing apart from the meeting with the Australian policeman and a visit to Robinsons, then food with a Filipina, he hasn't done anything we can get him on.'

'You don't have to *get* him on anything lieutenant!' grated Sanchez. 'Our friends are worried that he's been looking at things he shouldn't and they are NOT happy.'

Roque squirmed on his seat. He didn't like the tone of his boss. The look in Sanchez' eyes spelt trouble for someone. He'd known Ramon Sanchez for over twenty years and knew him to be a totally ruthless and merciless individual. It was common knowledge that the police chief was a millionaire and you didn't become that wealthy on a cop's pay. He had politicians in his pocket and had destroyed the careers of more than one in the past with a few well chosen words dropped into the ears of local newspaper editors, always eager to dish the dirt on anyone.

He also knew the relentless self promotion of his 'crusader cop' image was fraudulent. Especially when it came to closing bars he called 'houses of prostitution'. His so-called "protection of the morals of Filipino women" was phony because he operated his own bars full of girls in other areas run by cohorts and set up under false names. Ramon Sanchez had more than a few skeletons in *his* cupboard.

'What do you want me to do?' asked Roque, dragging on his cigarette. He had an idea what was coming. Sanchez uttered one word. *Salvage.* Roque nodded, stubbed out his cigarette, got up and left.

\* \* \*

Conway raced out of his office and took the stairs down two at a time to see what all the noise was about down in the foyer. There he saw a sight which stopped him in his tracks. At the hotel entrance the security guard was waving his hand wildly and gesticulating to a large pot-bellied guy in black shorts and white singlet with *"I LOVE BEER"* in large red letters across the front. He was holding a wheelbarrow in which another extremely overweight individual lay sprawled, head rolled back, arms and legs draped over either side. He was either unconscious or dead. Either way, he was not moving. The guard was trying to tell the big guy he could not enter the premises with the wheelbarrow and its contents.

'I'm a bloody guest here you dill,' shouted pot belly who Conway recognized as Boof (short for Boofhead) Jones. 'Me mate is just sleepin' it off. I just wanna get him up to bed.' Closer inspection of the wheelbarrow revealed it was Boof's best mate, Keghead *'any man who won't fight on rum is a coward,'* Smith. They were miners from Western Australia over for a couple of week's fun and frolic.

It seemed that Boof and Keghead had been on an "all-nighter" at the bars on MH Del Pilar and Keghead had consumed one too many double vodkas with brandy chasers and had collapsed on the sidewalk as they staggered out of a bar called *Firehouse.*

Too drunk to lift his 118kg mate Boof had enlisted the help of the locals and someone produced a wheelbarrow into which they dumped the non compos Keghead. With the sidewalks crowded Boof had taken to the street and a gleeful crowd of locals and revellers had watched as he staggered up against the oncoming traffic pushing his large limp cargo.

'Geez they gigged me mate,' he moaned to Conway. 'You'd ah thought we were the headline act in a royal command performance. We came close to getting' skittled by jeepneys and he's so bloody heavy I nearly tipped him over a few times. But mate, I think Keghead's in love. He met a cute little girl in *Firehouse*. She was all over him like a cheap suit, says she's a virgin so he reckons he's gunna take her back to Oz but I think it might've been booze talking. Do yer think she'd be a virgin mate?'

Conway rolled his eyes and stifled a grin. He organized a few of the male staff to lift Keghead out of the wheelbarrow which they did with some difficulty and had even greater difficulty trying keeping him upright. They then struggled with him to the elevator and took the happy pair to their rooms. Back in his office the phone rang again this time with a chastened Lily Li on the other end.

'Please Steve will you forgive me?' she said. 'I am very sorry. I acted like a stupid, jealous schoolgirl. I feel so foolish.'

'Hey Lily, no worries, I could have been more gracious. You don't have to apologise.'

'Thank you so much, that is very kind of you, I knew you were a good man and I don't want to lose your friendship,' she said, her voice full of genuine contrition.

'I have decided to have a small party tonight and I would be honoured if you would come please? There are a few people I would like you to meet?'

He smiled to himself, must be some of the *powerful people* she was talking about. I don't suppose it will hurt to meet a few of the local glitterati.

'Thank you Lily, I would like that very much, where and what time?'

'Eight pm at my house. Is that convenient?'

'I'll be there, thank you for the invitation.'

She sent him a kiss and hung up. He sat there for a few minutes staring into space his mind a whirl of conflicting thoughts about the updating of the accounts, Lily, Sally, and most worrying of all, suspicions about Perc. He shook his head and commenced to plough through the paperwork which seemed to have grown legs.

Just after 8.00 pm Conway was welcomed into Lily Li's sumptuous abode by the ever smiling Binky. The morning room come mini-ballroom was crowded with groups of well-dressed Filipino men and women, chatting and laughing while being served a variety of drinks on silver trays by young waiters immaculate in starched white shirts and tapered black trousers.

Conway stood looking around feeling slightly self-conscious as the murmur of conversation seemed to cease and many eyes turned to look in his direction. He seemed to have become the centre of attention; probably because he was the only foreigner in the room.

Then Lily, dazzling in a low-cut, white silk number, emerged from a group and sashayed over to him, champagne in hand.

'*Mabuhay* (welcome) darling, thank you soooo much for coming,' she gushed.

'Come and meet some of my friends.' Leading him by the hand she took him back to where she had been chatting with a group of middle-aged Filipinos. There were four men, two in *Barongs*, the formal traditional dress for Filipino males, another in a dark lounge suit and the fourth, a short stocky individual in the uniform of the Philippines army. From the pips on his shoulders obviously someone of high rank. Making up the group were two stylishly dressed, bejewelled women.

'May I introduce my good friend Mr Steven Conway,' said Lily grandly, as if she was introducing the Maharajah of Makadore. Conway returned the warm smiles, shook hands with the men and nodded to the women. Lily told them who he was and what he was doing in Manila to the approving looks of individuals who were obviously in the top echelon of Manila society.

Lily had been telling the truth when she said she knew "powerful people". The guy in the uniform was Lt. General Fidel Ramos Vice Chief of the Philippine Army and one of the men in the *Barong* was Juan Ponce Enrile the Philippine Minister of Defence. High flying company indeed!

'I am very pleased to meet you,' said Fidel Ramos smoothly. And the inevitable question one gets when meeting a Filipino for the first time. 'What do you think of our country Mr Conway?'

'I haven't seen a lot of it Mr Ramos but the word that springs to mind is, "interesting",' replied Conway.

'Oh, and what do you find interesting, our women or course?' asked Ramos answering his own question with a crooked smile. Making small talk was not one of Conway's fortes and he knew he had to choose his words carefully. He could mention the pollution, poverty and corruption he'd been told about and ask when the government was going to do something about it, but decided to keep it light.

'Your women are not only interesting but very beautiful,' said Conway gallantly noting the appreciative looks from the other women present, particularly Lily who moved closer and squeezed his hand, a gesture not lost on the others.

'I think you will find many other things *interesting* about our country Mr Conway,' murmured the slim, grey-haired Enrile. 'Once you become accustomed to our way of life and culture I am sure you will enjoy it very much. It is so different from your country, in so many ways.' And then he asked a question which immediately changed the atmosphere from light hearted chit chat to a more serious mode.

'What do you think of the politics of our country? And,' he paused, 'especially our Mr Marcos?' said Enrile raising his voice just a little louder than necessary. Conway was immediately aware of all their eyes upon him, plus a few more in the immediate vicinity.

He was silent for a moment. It was a loaded question and he was on dangerous ground. He had no desire to become embroiled in a political discussion. In recent days the newspapers, radio and TV reports were full of the unrest and civil disobedience in Manila against the current government. Pragmatism was the order of the day.

'With respect sir,' replied Conway choosing his words carefully, 'how can a foreigner who has only been here a few weeks and with very limited knowledge of your politics give an answer which is both knowledgeable and accurate. It would be extremely arrogant of me to voice an opinion which could be taken seriously. All I can say is that I find your politics and Mr Marcos, *interesting*,' he concluded with a wide grin.

The rest except for Enrile, smiled and seemed happy to leave it at that but the Defence Minister was not going to let him off the hook so easily and continued to press him for a direct opinion.

'We have a General Election coming up soon, you must know that there is some dissent in our country, surely you must have a thought on that?' Conway parried his question again pleading ignorance until Lily intervened. 'Please Mr Enrile, excuse me, but I must take this handsome man and show him off,' she said, taking Conway's hand and leading across to the other side of the room.

'Thanks Lily, that was getting a bit heavy,' said a relieved Conway as they joined a younger, trendy group of Makati socialites where the conversation was light, friendly and stayed well away from anything controversial.

A three piece band struck up some lively rock n roll whereupon Lily grabbed Conway's hand and pulled him onto the small dance floor where they jived, twisted and boogied until they both were almost on the verge of exhaustion. Then when the music slowed into a dreamy waltz Lily came in close and laid her head on his shoulder gluing her warm, perfumed body to his.

At just after 1.00 am he disentangled himself from Lily and excused himself.

'An early start in the morning but thanks for a great night Lily.' She came to the front portico holding his hand. They kissed briefly and refusing a lift back to town with her driver, he walked through the front gates to look for a taxi. The street lighting was poor so he began to make his way toward a more major road he could see about 100 metres ahead. Rain had fallen while he was at the party and he moved cautiously trying to avoid puddles which had collected on the street and sidewalk.

What a dill I am I should have taken that ride he thought stepping around a water-filled pot hole. He had just passed a couple of parked vehicles when his foot struck a piece of steel embedded in the sidewalk which sent him stumbling face first to the ground.

It saved his life.

Two shots rang out in quick succession; heavy calibre. One came so close he felt the breeze as it whistled past and ricocheted off a concrete wall beside him. He lay still for a moment then cautiously lifted his head squinting in the darkness for any sign of movement. His heart was almost jumping out of his chest. He was defenceless. If the gunman came again he was dead meat.

Lights appeared from a house opposite, a dog barked and people came running. He heard the sound of a motor bike roar into life and take off not far from the direction of Lily's house. Half a dozen people came running to him their faces full of concern. One held a flashlight which he shone on the prone Conway. 'Are you ok sir?' he asked nervously.

Badly shaken and breathing heavily Conway was helped to his feet.

'Yes, I am ok thanks.' He stood unsteadily trying to catch his breath as the reality of what had just happened, hit him.

Someone had tried to kill him! Who and why?

# 11

Conway limped back to Lily's house where an astonished Binky let him in then rushed away to summon Lily who came hurrying down the winding staircase trying to tie a see-through white robe over a pink, silk, thigh-length nightdress.

'Darling, my God, what happened?' she cried when she saw Conway with his torn and mud stained shirt and trousers. She tried to embrace him but stopped when he stepped back and held up his hands, cut from impact on the broken concrete sidewalk.

He explained what had happened and a grim-faced Lily turned to Binky and rapped out something in Tagalog. The little maid raced away and a few minutes later returned with a basin of hot water, disinfectant and towels.

'Please take off that shirt and your pants darling,' she commanded. 'No,' she smiled wickedly, 'I just want Binky to launder them so you will have them clean in the morning.'

'*The morning*? I can't stay here Lily.'

'Yes you can,' she insisted. 'I will clean you up and you can go to work in the morning a new man, after a good rest and besides, we don't know if the person who shot at you is still out there…I will have my driver drop you off on the way to my restaurant.'

He agreed reluctantly and *sans* clothing allowed her to attend to the small cuts and abrasions. She insisted he take a shower and joined him, soaping his body all over taking great care to ensure certain parts got special attention. She was impossible to resist and it was sometime before they emerged naked, heading at pace up to Lily's bedroom where some frantic activity took place before, despite an ever eager Lily virtually welded to his body, he collapsed into a dreamless sleep.

A beautiful cloudless morning saw them sitting at breakfast in the shade of a Casuarina tree on the terrace overlooking the pool. Binky smiling, and cute as ever in her black mini skirt and hot pink blouse, served them coffee and croissants before returning to the kitchen to bring their breakfast.

Conway sipped his coffee and smiled across at Lily looking fresh and gorgeous in a canary yellow sleeveless top, and white shorts. In casual clothes with little makeup and her glossy black hair down past her shoulders, she seemed years younger than the heavily made up exquisitely dressed socialite of the previous night.

'What do you think Lily? Was that someone taking a random pot shot at me...or do you think someone really wanted me dead? I mean, what is this area like? Manila seems like a gun-happy town but I would have thought this was a quiet neighborhood?'

She frowned and shook her head.

'I know there are parts of Manila which are dangerous, but this area is very quiet and respectable Steve, things like that just don't happen here. I can only think that someone was trying to kill you. My God, why? Who would want to do that? Can you think of any reason? Is there someone you have upset? You know Filipinos are lovely people but you must also be careful, if you cross them you can find yourself in big trouble. I have seen some terrible things happen to the nicest of people in this city. They were alive and happy one day, dead the next, for the simplest of reasons.'

She was echoing Jumbo's words but he couldn't think of any incident serious enough to make someone want to knock him off. Sure, he knew Bert Groyne hated him after he had humiliated the bloated bar owner but he had seen Groyne in the hotel with his gang and they just ignored each other. No it wouldn't be him. Although it was rare, it was not unknown for foreigners to be attacked at random but usually they brought it on themselves. It was probably mistaken identity. 'I'll just put it down to that,' he said to himself.

Binky arrived with a large tray of sliced tropical fruit, juice and bacon and eggs for the Australian and fruit and a plate of Loganiza sausages and rice for Lily. They dropped the subject, began eating and chatted about other things including Lily's business and background.

She was part Chinese, French and Filipino. She had lived her early years in Paris where her father was a successful and wealthy doctor, her mother a famous Filipino Chinese model. They moved to Shanghai in her teens where she finished her education at the Jiao Tong University one of the most prestigious in Shanghai. Sent to Switzerland to attend a hotel and hospitality training course in her early twenties, she met and married another Chinese student, James "Jimmy" Chen.

After graduation they returned to his hometown of Shanghai where he became the manager of one of the best 5-Star hotels in the city. A series of appointments with the same hotel group saw them living in half a dozen countries until in his early forties Jimmy became general manager of the Philippine Regency Hotel in Manila. They took up residency in Forbes Park the swankiest address in town where they enjoyed the high life of Manila society.

Great party goers, never a weekend passed when they were not attending soirees put on by captains of industry, show business celebrities, movie stars or senior members of the government including Ferdinand Marcos himself. No doors were closed to them. Imelda Marcos and Lily became firm friends and it was said they would go to karaokes just to see who could sing the loudest and longest.

All this came to a halt one bright Sunday morning when following a particularly riotous party which carried on to the small hours, Jimmy decided not to wake up…ever! As an Australian acquaintance at the time observed, "Lily went from Old Gold chocolates to boiled lollies overnight!"

A long period of mourning followed while a devastated Lily cast around for something to do. Finally she took a lease on a derelict building on United Nations Avenue and using her innate interior decorating and culinary skill created, "Lily Li's Tea House". Employing the best chefs in Manila it had an atmosphere that both exuded opulence, elegance and style. Business boomed.

With her society and show biz connections Lily's Tea House soon became the place in which to be "seen". But although the beautiful Lily Li had a healthy libido and was never short of offers she chose celibacy mostly in honour of her late husband (she told herself). That was until Steve Conway arrived on the scene.

'Darling,' she said reaching over and placing her hand on his, 'I must change and go to my restaurant now. Please come and I will drop you off at your hotel.' Binky had laundered his clothes even patching the tear in the trousers. No one would guess he had spent a few minutes the night before lying face down on a muddy, rain swept sidewalk.

Conway waved Lily off as he strode into the "Down Under" to be met by Jumbo Keyes with a message from Susan Santos.

'Steve, Susan's back from Angeles and would like to see you as soon as possible. Don't know what it's about man,' he frowned, 'you know Susan, keeps a lot to herself. She'd make a goddam good little spy.'

'Ok, thanks Jumbo, I want to have a chat to you too later mate,' Conway said, turning and bounding up the stairs toward Susan's office. The little accountant's face lit up when he strode into her office. She hadn't seen him for a week and it made her feel good to see his friendly face smiling back at her.

'Hello sir,' she said, perhaps a little too brightly and louder than she meant, causing two of her accounting staff Nelly and Perla to smile knowingly at each other. Both women were married and they loved their little boss dearly and wanted her to find a man. Although they had never broached the subject with Susan, they both felt Conway would be an ideal partner for her.

'You wanted to see me I believe Susan? Actually, I wanted to see you too, glad you're back,' he said pulling up a chair in front of her. 'What's happening? Firstly bring me up to date with Angeles.'

Mayet, was in custody in Angeles on the *Estafa* charge. Under heavy questioning from the local police and in front of Burgess, Susan and Zeny she admitted everything.

Family financial and medical problems had prompted her actions. During the change of management Zeny had been away visiting a sick mother allowing a window of opportunity for Mayet to create her scam. There had been no internal control and it had been easy for her to put 'ghost' workers on the payroll. She should have deleted them but it had all been too easy and she became greedy. She indicated that a "blind eye" had been turned by certain people but would not name them.

A few months ago she had become engaged to an American on the airbase and they were to leave for the United States soon and it was a great chance to build a little nest egg. However instead of sunbaking on the beach at Malibu it looked like Mayet would be lying on a hard bamboo cot in Angeles City jail for the next few years.

'Jumbo said you wanted to see me about something urgent as well, what is it Susan?'

'I have been told of a bank account which I think you should know about,' she said quietly.

'What's this? another scam? tell me more.'

Susan shifted uncomfortably in her chair. A gentle girl, she hated drama of any kind. The Mayet situation had been stressful. She and Zeny had been summoned to appear in the Angeles City court and had undergone intense cross-examination by Mayet's lawyer. It was hard enough to sort out the mess the accounts were in without anything else but she had an auditor's nose and a professional attitude to her work and if there was anything suspicious she was not afraid to investigate even if it meant delving into the unpleasant areas of defalcation and theft, a common by-product of her work.

'Sir I had a call from our bank manager, she wanted to talk to me about something but said she preferred to do it in her office so I went there this morning. She asked me if I knew anything about an account which had been set up some time ago in the name of a company called Transco which is supposedly affiliated with the Down Under.

This company makes regular deposits paid in by a member of the Down Under staff. The deposits are substantial, made once a month and withdrawn once a month. She only mentioned it because the signatories to the account were Down Under staff who they knew to be of a low level and could not possibly earn the kind of money deposited. She just felt it was odd that I was not a signatory and according to her staff the person transacting the account always seemed to be quite nervous. They became suspicious and reported it to her so she felt she should talk to me about it.'

'So you know nothing about this account?'

'No sir, I do not,' replied Susan shortly. Was he questioning my integrity?

'How big were the deposits Susan?'

'At least one million pesos…sometimes more.'

Conway whistled softly.

'Who are the signatories?'

'The bank manager would not say.'

'I would like to talk to her and I want you to come with me.'

'Yes sir, when would you like to see her?'

'Immediately.'

Conway's thoughts were racing. He had been puzzled about the low profitability of the hotel although since he and Susan had arrived things seemed to have picked up and the bank account looked healthier but was that because there were now checks and internal controls Susan had put in place? Still something fishy is going on. Maybe this bank account held a clue?

Ten minutes later they were sitting in the office of the bank manager Lourdes Delarosa who had graciously agreed to see them at short notice. Attractive, slim, smartly dressed in a crisp white blouse and dark blue business suit, she greeted them with a smile and ushered them into her office and sent for coffee. Susan introduced Conway who came straight to the point.

He told Ms Delarosa that Susan had been reconstructing the accounts of the hotel since his arrival and he felt there were some suspicious circumstances surrounding their makeup. The account in question was unknown to him and his accountant and if the funds were from the Down Under he had to know from what source. Therefore he needed to know full details of the account, the names of signatories, dates and amounts of the transactions and he also wanted to speak to the bank staff handling the account.

'I view this matter as very serious Ms Delarosa and I thank you for bringing it to our attention. And,' he said, giving her what he hoped was a winning smile, 'I hope you will be kind enough to assist us in this investigation.'

'Of course,' she said, returning a winning smile of her own.

'Excuse me sir,' said Susan leaning across and speaking in Tagalog to Delarosa. The bank manager buzzed the intercom on her desk and twenty seconds later a skinny, middle-aged individual wearing a white shirt which looked like it had been ironed with a pineapple, ghastly multi-coloured tie, baggy trousers and a nervous expression, stepped cautiously into the room.

'This is our accountant Mr. Rosario. Mr. Conway you may ask him any questions you wish,' said Delarosa. Conway in English and Susan occasionally in Tagalog (she felt it easier for him to answer) questioned Rosario at length. Ms Delarosa looked on frowning occasionally at his answers, nodding sometimes in agreement. Rosario was hesitant at first, stammering over some of his answers, his voice more than once becoming almost inaudible provoking a sharp reprimand from Ms Delarosa, but by the time they finished with him, a disturbing picture had emerged.

It appeared the person bringing the deposit to the bank was a relative of Imelda Prickett. The deposits were substantially larger than those from the Down Under and sometimes were made up of mainly foreign exchange and some local pesos. Although Rosario could not say exactly why, he just felt things were not kosher with the account. The nervous almost furtive manner of the depositor; the unusually large amounts and type of currency which he would have expected to be placed in the Down Under Hotel account made him suspicious. Finally, he decided to bring it to the attention of Ms Delarosa. Conway thanked Rosario and the bank manager for their assistance and returned to the hotel with Susan, both their suspicions now fully aroused.

* * *

'Your report and remain standing,' rapped Ramon Sanchez to Roque who was about to lower himself into a chair opposite. The little policeman glowered at his unsmiling boss and stood upright still with his usual insolent mien. He cleared a throat which had seen far too many *Marlboros* and said simply, 'it's done.'

'Tell me about it,' snapped Sanchez. Roque described how he had followed Conway to Lily's house and waited outside hidden in the darkness until the Australian had left in the early hours of the morning.

'I shot twice and he fell sir,'

'Did you make sure he was dead…?'

'I couldn't, many people started to come out from their houses, I was lucky to get away,' protested Roque feeling pissed that he was not getting the thanks he deserved. He was soaked, cold and miserable by the time Conway had appeared.

To add further to his misery, many of the guests at Lily's party had left in large limousines which had roared through the puddles and drenched him constantly in his hiding place not far from her gates. No doubt if any had their windows open they would have heard a constant stream of expletives as they passed.

'Why didn't you use a silencer?'

'The three we had were stolen sir,' Roque muttered sheepishly.

Sanchez just shook his head in frustration. Typical; there were more thieves in his force than on the streets. *Manila's Finest* said the patch on the shoulder of the uniform of his men. Manila's finest what? He asked himself. He knew however, his poverty stricken force did what many men in similar circumstances do; they turn to crime to survive.

'So you are *sure* you killed him Lieutenant?' a glimmer of a smile hovered around his lips. Roque had never failed him in the past. He was a born killer and enjoyed his work.

'Yes sir, I am sure,' Roque replied, starting to relax.

Sanchez picked up his phone dialed a number then leaned back in his chair. 'Ah, Mr Prickett, *Mabuhay*, I have some good news.' He paused for a moment frowning, 'about our friend of course…the job is done.'

There was a long pause and even Roque could hear the yelling coming from the other end of Sanchez' phone.

'WHAT!' screamed Sanchez! 'WHAT ARE YOU SAYING?' Roque could not make out what was being said but he had a strange feeling that all was not well and a steadily sinking feeling that it involved him.

Sanchez dropped the phone into its cradle and looked up at Roque his eyes as cold as the grave and his lips quivering slightly. Whatever had been said, Roque knew he was in deep shit!

'So you are sure you killed him eh?' Sanchez' voice was barely above a whisper.

'Ah…er… yes, I, .I…have no reason to think otherwise, he went down…I saw him,' stammered Roque.

'You lied…you lied to me you incompetent fool!' shouted Sanchez slamming his fist on the desk which made the fat little policeman blanch and worse still, it opened his bladder. He stood there feeling the warm trickle down the inside of his jeans. He knew only too well what happened to those who fucked up instructions from Sanchez. He had an awful feeling that what his boss was going to say would open his bowels as well.

'Do you know what I was told you fool?' Sanchez was now on his feet standing over the hapless Roque who had dropped his head.

'Conway is alive and well and at the Down Under Hotel, he's been there since early this morning...so what have you got to say for yourself?'

Roque stood still with lowered head, saying nothing. He *saw* Conway go down, he was sure he hit him, what the hell happened?

'Sorry sir, I don't know what to say, I tell you I *did* see him fall, I had to presume I had go...got him,' he said, his voice shaking. 'So he is at the Down Under without any injuries at all?'

'Yes, he is working there and is obviously unharmed. He apparently has said nothing about it to Prickett who saw him with some of the staff this morning. You know what happens to people who fail me don't you Lieutenant?' gritted Sanchez.

'Er, ah, yes,' mumbled Roque nervously, he knew only too well. All false bravado had disappeared and his florid brown face was now a shade of sickly green. Sweat started to form on his brow and his shoulders slumped. He could feel his bowels about to do a duet with his bladder.

Upsetting the police chief intentionally or not was an extremely foolish thing to do. In fact it could be lethal. He had heard frightening stories of what happened to those who failed Ramon Sanchez. Roque knew personally of one individual who on bended knees swore he had "forgotten" to declare all of the proceeds of a bank heist (blamed on the NPA). This lad had been promptly fitted with a pair of "cement slippers" and dropped overboard in Manila Bay. The bullet-riddled bodies of a few other unfortunates had been found on the huge rubbish dump in Tondo. Some had been fished out of the Pasig, floating face-down; many simply disappeared never to be seen again.

Retribution was swift and final in the world of Ramon Sanchez.

'Sir give me another chance, I promise I will not fail next time?' pleaded Roque wringing his hands and squeezing his buttocks together in a desperate attempt to keep his bowels from joining his bladder in a smelly performance. Sanchez looked disdainfully at the pathetic figure in front of him and smiled thinly.

'One more chance...just one. If you fail,' he paused for effect. 'You know the consequences Lieutenant?'

'Yes, yes, sir, I do, but thank you sir, I promise I will do it and I WILL succeed! He is as good as dead! When do you want me to do it sir?' Roque started to back away toward the door because his bowels had defeated his best efforts at containment.

Sanchez nose twitched and his face contorted in distaste. 'Do not, I repeat, do **not**! do anything until I give you further orders, he will be careful now, I want it done at the right time, a time of MY choosing. Do you understand? Now go!'

Roque turned, and literally tore out the door relief flooding his face not just because he'd been given another chance but also because he was able to escape from disgracing himself completely. With one hand behind holding his backside he sprinted out into the yard looking for a toilet. Sanchez shook his head and dialed Prickett.

'Please accept my deepest apologies sir,' he said smoothly, 'I will personally take care of our little problem, do not worry, next time there will be no mistakes, yes I understand, you have my word. Oh, where are you going? How long? Ok, have a good trip.' He replaced the receiver and sat there frowning. Now I have yet another foreigner to deal with. It wasn't the first and he was sure it would not be the last.

# 12

Ada Latonga, chief cashier of the Down Under Hotel, a lumpy middle-aged woman in brown tee shirt and jeans, sat sullenly in Conway's office. Behind his desk sat her grim-faced boss and beside him an expressionless Susan Santos. Conway gave her a long hard look then pushed a bank book across the desk to her.

'Tell me all about this Ada and I want straight answers, no lies. I know more than you think, which includes the fact that you're related to Mrs Prickett.'

Ada flicked through the pages barely looking at them then looked up and stared insolently back at Conway. Why should she worry? She was Imelda's cousin, she was protected.

'Who put you up to this Ada. I know you didn't dream it up all by yourself? Where have the funds come from that make up these deposits? Why aren't they banked in our normal bank accounts? How long has this been going on?'

Ada sat sullenly, saying nothing. Suddenly to Conway's surprise, quiet, meek little Susan jumped up out of her chair and stood over Ada waving her finger under the cashier's nose blasting her with a torrent of rapid Tagalog.

It shook Ada. She sat bolt upright, her eyes like saucers. Then she seemed to cower under Susan's furious onslaught. Conway sat back and watched this exchange with interest. It occurred to him that it just might be better to leave this interrogation to his accountant because by the look on Ada's face, Susan had well and truly got her attention.

Ada nodded and shook her head, nodded again then threw her arms up and tried to stand up but Susan pushed her back down into her chair as if to say, 'you're staying here until I get answers.' This went on for several minutes until Susan stepped back and sat down, leaving Ada a pathetic figure, downcast with tears trickling down her cheeks.

'Ok Susan, what's the outcome of all that?' he asked his little tigress who continued to glare at Ada.

'She says she was told by Mr and Mrs Prickett to divert funds a couple of times a week from the foreign exchange transactions to this account,' replied Susan not taking her eyes off the crestfallen cashier.

'Yes but the forex would not make up the *whole* deposits. They're much larger than what we make as money changers. Where's the rest come from?' Conway asked, looking at a now quietly sobbing Ada.

'She says we will have to ask Mr and Mrs Prickett about that sir, she doesn't know. All she knows is that at least once a month Mr or Mrs Prickett come to her with a paper bag full of money and told her to deposit it to the Transco account.'

'Ok, I want her off the premises now. Suspend her until we know the full story. I'll take it up now with Mr Prickett.' He got to his feet indicating the meeting was over. Susan stood up and walked across to Ada still with her head down, shoulders heaving. She turned to Conway as if suddenly remembering something.

'Sir, I am sorry but I heard Mr Prickett left for overseas this morning.'

'Where to? And for how long?'

Susan motioned Ada to come with her. 'I heard he was going to Hong Kong. He usually goes there once a month for about three days.'

'Ok, I'll find out from Mrs Prickett when he'll be back and we'll discuss it with both of them then, thanks for your help.'

'You are welcome sir,' said Susan, giving Ada another earful as they left.

Conway rang Imelda Prickett and asked for a meeting in her office. Imelda and Conway usually gave each other a wide berth. They disliked each other on sight and there was mutual distrust. Conway hated the imperious way Imelda treated the staff. She ruled by fear and staff were on edge in her presence. The tension she created was palpable.

Imelda Prickett was a tough, ambitious, scheming woman. She came from a large dirt poor family in the province of Tarlac. From an early age she realized life in the province was not for her. She had bigger plans. The lure of the bright lights bought her to Manila where after being fired from several jobs in the bars, she had met Perc Prickett running a small, sleazy establishment in Ermita. He hired her as a hostess to keep the customers company and extract as many drinks out of them as possible.

For this she was paid a paltry commission but her main income was derived from offering her 'services' to those she favored. A couple of wealthy partners bought into the bar and with a few renovations and stylish interior decor, business started to pick up.

Perc always talked big but now with a bit of capital to play with, he had the chance to put some of his grandiose plans into action. Imelda decided she wanted part of the action, so using her feminine wiles she eventually married Perc giving her the opportunity to gain some control and throw her weight around, which she did with gay abandon.

Overnight the bar girl became a tyrant and later when Perc took over the Down Under she had free reign. The old saying of "never give a peasant power" most certainly applied to Imelda Prickett.

'Good morning Mr Conway, what can I do for you?' Imelda asked in her sharp, high pitched staccato tone. She couldn't bring herself to call him Steve, he was below her in the pecking order and she wanted him to know it.

Conway smiled to himself. This woman sends memos to staff on letterhead declaring "From the desk of Imelda Prickett". The pretension was laughable. Anyone would think she was the head of a multi million dollar corporation instead of the part owner of a one-star Hotel in a run-down suburb of Manila.

'Good morning Imelda.' He knew she hated him using her first name but no way was he going to call this woman Ma'am. 'I believe Perc is away for a few days, when will he be back? I have something to discuss with him.'

She was unable to hide her dislike for Conway. 'Maybe Monday, why do you want to know? Anything you have to say to him you can say to me, after all I am a co-director of this company.' Her tone was condescending and she had copied Perc's gesture of steepling her hands.

'I would rather speak to him if you don't mind Imelda,' Conway replied, failing to keep the disdain from his voice.

'It can wait.' He was going to ask her why her husband was in Hong Kong and what his business was but he knew Imelda would either lie or not tell him so he didn't waste his breath.

'Thanks Imelda,' he said and returned to his office.

As soon as he left Imelda picked up her phone and asked for Ada.

'What! When? Why?' she screeched, as the staff member on the other end advised that Ada had been suspended. She listened for another 30 seconds, her face a mask of fury and disbelief. She slammed the phone down before the other party had finished.

Conway had just made himself another enemy.

Back in his office Conway reviewed the interrogation of Ada. Perc and Imelda were up to something apart from diverting funds from the business. Where were the other funds coming from that made up those deposits?

As far as he knew Perc had no other business dealing other than the Down Under. It smelt but he had only sketchy evidence and needed more proof and even when he got it, what could he do? Of course he could report to the Australian shareholders but then what would they do? Maybe remove Perc but then who would they put in his place? All these things were running through his mind when Jumbo Keyes walked in.

'Can I see you for a minute man?' asked the big man who for once was not wearing his usual cheery expression.

'Sure take a seat mate, what's up?' said Conway, his mind still half on the Prickett problem.

Keyes lowered his bulk into a chair. 'I banned Bert Groyne and his gang from the bar last night.'

'I'm sure you had good reason, but tell me anyway.'

'Well, I've been hearing stories about a few of our guests being ripped off by some of Groyne's girls and last night a guy told me that he had been out with one of them and she had ripped him off, big time.'

It appeared that the guest had been drinking in Groyne's bar and had taken one of his dancers out for a meal. She had then suggested they visit some of her friends in Paranaque an area nearby Manila's international airport. They had finished up in a squalid little dump miles from anywhere.

There was no one else there but she assured him her "friends" would be along soon suggesting in the meantime they should have a couple of drinks. She produced a bottle of *Tanduay* rum and they proceeded to empty it. The next thing he remembered was waking up next morning in the dirty little room now alone, wearing only his underpants. Gone was everything else including his wallet containing a substantial amount of cash.

'So I went around to see that goddam Groyne and to sort it out. We can't allow this kind of thing happening to our guests, if we can help it,' growled Keyes.

'Of course not but I imagine you got no joy out of Groyne.'

'Right on, he didn't want to know. Reckoned it was the girl's first night; didn't know who she was; where she was from and too bad for the sucker who went with her, so I told him he and his scungy crew were banned from coming into our hotel, permanently!'

Conway nodded in agreement. 'As far as I'm concerned we've lost nothing. He and his mob made the place look untidy and they never spent much anyway, so good riddance.'

Keyes got up ready to leave but as he went to the door he turned with a huge grin.

'How's Lily, seen *much* of her lately?'

'Get out of here Keyes, go and annoy some of the staff.' He could hear the big American laughing as he went back downstairs to the foyer.

* * *

It was a quiet afternoon in *The Black Jack* as Sally busied herself behind the bar cleaning and polishing glasses, refilling the refrigerator with beer and soft drink and tidying up ready for the night time crowd. She normally paid no attention to the conversation between Groyne and his cohorts. It was usually made up of a great deal of swearing, dirty jokes and ribald laughter; however her ears pricked up when she heard the words *Down Under* and *Conway*.

'Yeah, I reckon that bastard Conway put the black guy up to it. Didn't have the guts to come around and front me himself. Fuck the Down Under, we don't need his poxy hotel,' raged Groyne.

'Yeah, yeah,' chorused Mullet and Biro. 'We can go to the *Wombat*, they reckon they put on a good spread and the piss's cold too,' Biro offered.

'Yeah but I don't like the atmosphere there,' moaned Mullet. 'It's not as clean as the Down Under and the Down Under staff are friendlier and prettier and more importantly the booze is a peso cheaper in the Down Under so geez, I'd still like to drink there. Who was the sheila who dudded the Down Under bloke Bert?'

'Dunno, some scrubber, she'd only just started here. You never know with these birds, some are thieves and some aren't. I'm not a fuckin' psychologist. I just sell booze and barfines. Shit, what do they think I do when they come in here lookin' for a job, ask 'em what fuckin' convent they went to?'

'Maybe you should,' smirked Biro turning to Sally. 'Hey Sally, what convent did you go to love? And give us another round here too and a dash of speed too darlin, we're thirsty.' Sally just smiled her demure smile and said nothing.

'I'm not gunna take this lyin' down boys,' scowled Groyne. 'I hate that Conway, I'm gunna make him pay!'

'Watcha gunna do mate? yer can't salvage him,' said Mullet, his eyes rolling as the whiskey, his seventh for the afternoon, started to take its toll.

'I'll think of something, no worries; a bit of physical pain never hurt anyone Mullet.' Groyne's face lit up in an evil grin. He nodded to himself as if he'd already figured out what he had in mind for Conway.

Sally's heart jumped when she heard this. Oh my God! She moved closer to the group to try and hear more but they changed the subject to horse racing so she went back up the bar to serve a rowdy group who had just stumbled in.

During her meal break she excused herself and raced up Mabini Street past bars with names like *Cane Cutter, The Other Office, Kings Cross,* weaving between slow moving jeepneys, taxis and motorbikes. She was almost skittled by a truck on the corner of United Nations Avenue finally arriving at the Down Under where, between gasps she asked the guard at the front door if she could speak to Conway.

'Sorry ma'am, he is out and won't be back for an hour or two, come back later.' She stood there heart pumping trying to regain her breath wondering what to do.

'Please, can you tell Mr Conway to meet me at *Barrio Fiesta* restaurant on United Nations Avenue at 10 pm, it's urgent, very urgent!'

'Ok ma'am,' smiled the guard, lucky Mr Conway he thought to himself as Sally turned and ran back to *The Black Jack*.

\* \* \*

'Hi Steve,' said a familiar Australian voice. Conway glanced around to see a smiling Jack Roberts accompanied by a well built, fair-haired man around the same age. Roberts as usual was smartly dressed in his well-cut dark blue suit and tie; his companion was also immaculate, sporting a tan sports coat and cream trousers set off by a pale blue shirt and tie. They stood out among the casually dressed drinkers where tee shirt, shorts and rubber thongs were de rigeur.

'Steve, meet Chuck McGaw my counterpart at the American embassy,' said Roberts as McGaw, smiling broadly, shook Conway's hand.

'Nice to meet you Steve, heard some good things about you from my friend here,' said the American in a well-modulated eastern American accent.

'How do you like Manila?'

Conway replied that he had not been in town long and was still getting used to the place but found the town and the job "different and interesting" evoking a wide smile from the American.

'Those were my feelings too when I first came here a couple of years ago Steve and the longer you stay I'm sure the more you'll like it, they're great people. What do you want to drink guys?'

Roberts and Conway settled for San Miguels, McGaw ordered a Jack Daniels and coke for himself. Roberts suggested they move away from the crowd at the bar to somewhere a little more private. They went across to a banquette by the far wall where Robert's tone became serious.

'Steve, this is confidential,' he said quietly, 'I don't want any our conversation to go outside the three of us right?'

Conway frowned, 'of course, what's the problem, it sounds ominous?'

Roberts leaned over to Conway and said quietly, 'you may, or may not know, but there is a growing *Shabu* problem in this town and…'

'Hang on Jack, what's *Shabu?*'

'It's a cheap form of heroin,' replied Roberts. 'The real stuff is too expensive for most of the addicts here so they get their charge from this stuff. It's odourless, colourless, you can smoke it, no injection needed and it gives a gradual long lasting rush; it's become the preferred drug, more so than cannabis and coke.'

'I was just telling Steve about *Shabu*,' said Roberts as McGaw arrived with their drinks.

'Yeah, it's bad shit,' McGaw said, taking a sip of his *Jack*.

'It's bad alright, bloody dangerous would be a better description,' continued the Australian detective.

'People become weird on this stuff. They lose their families; their livelihood, everything and what makes it worse, you don't even know they are on it. You could have a barmaid using it right now and you wouldn't even know,' he said looking across at the bar where the staff were laughing and chatting to their customers.

'So what's it got to do with me?' asked Conway.

'Well nothing really, except that whether you like it or not, we know there are some around you who are into trafficking this crap and we want to warn you and ask you to let us know if you see any evidence of dealing, ok?' Roberts looked at McGaw who nodded and glanced over the rim of his glass at Conway for his reaction.

Conway sipped his beer and paused before replying. 'Sure, I hate drugs too, I've seen what it does first-hand in Australia but so far as I have said before, I haven't come across it personally here; not in this hotel anyway.'

'Have you met Ramon Sanchez Steve?' asked Roberts.

'Ah, yes, I have, why?'

'What do you think of him?' said Roberts, watching Conway closely.

'To be honest, I don't much care for him, I only met him once and found him cold and unfriendly but other than that, I don't know the man, why?'

'Are you aware he is a good friend of the owner of this hotel?'

'He seems to be but so what?' asked Conway slowly putting the bottle of San Miguel down on the bar in front of him.

'As I said at the start Steve, this conversation is confidential right?'

Conway nodded and waited for Roberts to continue.

'We have reason to believe, and I must tell you, we have no proof,' said Roberts lowering his voice even more, 'but we think there is a link between the growing drug problem including *Shabu* in this area and the local constabulary and as you know, Sanchez is the boss around here.'

'How do you know Jack, what reason do you have to think he is involved?'

'Our sources,' Roberts said emptying his bottle of San Mig then abruptly, stood up and held out his hand.

'Sorry to take up your time mate, but duty calls, Chuck and I have business to attend to.' He winked, 'and I'm sure you have too. Thanks again, let us know if you see or hear anything.'

They left with Conway reflecting on their words, not noticing a pair of baleful eyes watching him from the far corner of the bar.

\* \* \*

Just after 10 pm Sally sat at a table toward the back of *Barrio Fiesta* nervously clutching a handkerchief and watching the front door praying that Conway would come. She had feigned a sudden migraine attack and asked Groyne to excuse her. He agreed, reluctantly. She was not only his best worker but good for business. Many of his customers came to ogle her rather than the dancers.

The minutes ticked by like hours. She was beginning to despair. Maybe he had not returned to the hotel; maybe the guard forgot to tell him; maybe he had better things to do than see her. Maybe he was with "that woman". Maybe he had been beaten up already and was in a hospital somewhere...or worse.

She shuddered at the thought. Please God not that. But *where* is he? She kept asking herself over and over and had almost given up when he appeared.

He stopped just inside the front door and looked around, his face breaking into a smile when he spotted her. Relief flooded over her. As he arrived at her table she jumped up and threw her arms around him and kissed him full on the lips. He was taken aback at this sudden show of public affection.

'Hey what brought all this on?' he said, his eyes twinkling.

'I'm so glad you're here sir, ah, Steve, thanks for coming I was getting so worried.'

He took a seat and became serious. 'Now, what is so urgent? The guard said you looked very worried when he saw you this evening.' Before she could reply, a waitress came and they quickly looked at the menu. Conway ordered a meal and drinks for them both then listened carefully as she told him what she had overheard in *The Black Jack*. It did concern him but he didn't want her to know.

'Sally don't worry too much, Groyne is all hot air, you know what he's like,' he smiled, reaching over and patting her arm. She continued to voice her concern and he continued trying to pacify her.

'I am afraid for you Steve,' she said, 'Sir Groyne knows some bad men…' At that moment the drinks arrived followed soon after by their meals which gave him the opportunity to change the subject.

It was his first visit to *Barrio Fiesta* and he could see why the place was so popular with Filipinos and foreigners alike. The food was delicious, the service, quick and efficient. As they ate he asked her about places of interest for tourists in the Philippines.

She told him of Baguio and the world famous rices terraces, Taal Volcano in Tagatay, the beaches of La Union, and Cebu as well as the beautiful Mindanao region then she mentioned Boracay.

'What and where is Boracay?' he asked. She explained that Boracay was the gem of the Philippines, a truly beautiful tropical island paradise just over an hour's flying time in the Visayas region of the Philippines. It had sparkling, white sandy beaches, one of which at one time had been named as the most beautiful beach in the world. Her Marine had taken her there a couple of years ago and it had left a deep and lasting impression on her and not just because of its physical beauty.

'Oh it is so romantic,' she said, her eyes lighting up, 'I love the place, I hope I can go back again one day,' she said and this time it was *her* eyes that twinkled.

'Sounds a great place for tourists, I'm sure my guests would love it; but how does one get there?' He said spooning his *sinigang*, a tasty vegetable soup.

'There are two ways,' she replied enthusiastically, 'you can either take Philippine Airlines to Kalibo a town in the Aklan region, a flight of about an hour then a bus ride to the port of Caticlan. From there, you take a 30 minute banca ride to Boracay or, fly direct to Caticlan a small town on the mainland opposite the island on one of a number of smaller airlines who service this route. The accommodation is a bit limited, with only a couple of good quality resorts. There was limited electricity which tended to be erratic at time, but that makes it all the more romantic.' She lowered her head embarrassed at her enthusiasm but what she had told him was true.

Boracay had only recently been discovered by foreigners and was said to be one of the best scuba diving sites in the entire Philippines with plenty of other water sports including parasailing and windsurfing. There was talk of a golf course being built and the Department of Tourism were making noises about bringing more power to the island and building world class resorts to attract more tourists. But if you just wanted to relax and do nothing, it was ideal. Her love for Boracay was infectious and he made a mental note to visit there as soon as he could arrange a few days off.

She yawned involuntarily and he looked at his watch. It was getting late; their meal was finished so he suggested they leave. He paid the bill and they strolled along United Nations Avenue looking for a taxi. It was a beautiful balmy Manila night and romance was in the air. As they crossed Jorge Bocobo Street a cab pulled up beside them. He held open the door for her but as she bent down to enter she stood and turned to him. 'Will you come home with me please?' she asked softly. Without a word, he got in beside her.

As the taxi rolled away in the direction of Sampaloc, another vehicle, black with tinted windows, followed.

# 13

Perc Prickett rolled over and opened his eyes. Where the fuck am I? Then the fog started to clear in his addled brain and he remembered. He was in a hotel room in Hong Kong and his phone was jangling sending bolts of pain through his skull. He rolled over to pick it up but something prevented him. There was a lump in the bedclothes beside him. He blearily pulled the sheet away to reveal the smooth white back of the Chinese 'princess' he had met in a Wanchai bar the night before.

She woke and rolled over to face him and smiled. He let out a horrified yell. 'SHEEIITT!!!' The Chinese princess had a face that would frighten a bull dog out of a butcher shop! How could this be? Last night in *Bottoms Up* bar she looked like something out of a dream. In the cold grey light of a Hong Kong morning the beady black eyes, bent nose, heavily pockmarked face and crooked yellow teeth, sent shivers down his spine. Miss Hong Kong now looked like something out of his worst nightmare.

'Geez, I'll have to give away drinkin' that fuckin' *Slivowitz* or whatever they call it,' he moaned. 'God, I'm crook! My head feels like it's about to fall off.' He took another look at the princess and shuddered. He turned his face away and picked up the phone then wished he hadn't. It was Imelda and she was *not* a happy camper.

With his head thumping he slumped back in the bed eyes closed holding the phone at arms length from his ear as Imelda screeched and yelled. It was something about Conway and Ada and how he had to get back there pronto. Then he felt soft warm lips around a part of his anatomy he hadn't used in a long time and his face became wreathed in a beatific smile.

He let the phone drop beside the bed with Imelda still screaming until she finally must have run out of breath. Something told him he was in deep shit but at that very moment he didn't care. He opened his eyes and looked down at the bobbing black head. 'I'll give you four years to stop,' he mumbled happily before almost levitating with a loud 'YAHOOOOO!!'

The princess lay still and waited until she heard Perc's loud snore before carefully, and quietly crawling out of bed. She dressed quickly and looked around the room for his trousers. There they were, in the far corner where he had flung them the night before in his haste to get into the cot where, to her surprise (and delight) he promptly passed out. She found his wallet in a back pocket, extracted the contents and blew him a kiss before tip toeing out of the room and his life.

*  *  *

A furious Imelda slammed down the phone. The fool! What is he up to there in Hong Kong? Probably with some bar girl or too drunk to do anything. He's supposed to be doing business for us, not just him! I'll have to attend to this matter myself, as usual. She gritted her teeth and picked up the phone again.

'Send me Eduardo, now!'

A few minutes later a skinny, swarthy individual with swept back hair, googly eyes, sporting earrings, a grubby white tee shirt, jeans and a shifty expression tentatively knocked on her door. Imelda brusquely beckoned him in.

'Eduardo, I want you to do something for me.'

Eduardo had no qualifications in anything, but as a relation of Imelda had been given a job in the kitchen as a cook and was known to have fucked up more meals than the rest of the chefs in Manila put together. He was one of the many relations she had employed in the Down Under.

It was more than just nepotism. She needed people around who would keep her informed of what was going on and alert her to any chicanery or mutiny among the staff. Imelda needed people who were scared of losing their job and importantly, of her. Eduardo fitted both categories perfectly. He kept his ear to the ground and had been responsible for the termination of more than a few staff. His fear of her made him the most loyal of lieutenants.

'Yes ma'am, what can I do for you, anything for you ma'am?' he said. Imelda was well aware of the effect she had on Eduardo. She knew his fawning tone was bullshit but she loved to see him grovel.

'We have had you following the movements of a certain member of our staff but now we may want you to do something else,' she said leaning back in her chair.

'Yes ma'am anything ma'am, what?'

'You may have to eliminate him.'

Eduardo's mouth dropped open like a trapdoor. 'What! ma'am, *salvage!* Are you serious?' he said, immediately regretting the temerity of questioning his boss.

Imelda's face darkened. 'Of course I'm serious,' she snapped. 'This person is giving us concern and looking into things that we are not happy about and action will have to be taken, sooner rather than later. I will give you further instructions when I think it has to be done, but in the meantime keep close to him and report anything you think I need to know…and you must not mention this to anyone, anyone! Otherwise the consequences for you will be unpleasant. Do you understand Eduardo?'

She glared at him to make sure he got the message loud and clear. Eduardo shuffled his feet uncomfortably and wasn't sure where to look or put his hands. He'd done some pretty nasty things in his time, but never murder.

'Yes, ma'am, anything you say ma'am, just tell me when,' mumbled Eduardo wishing he was back in the kitchen putting shit on some unfortunate junior or helping himself to more than his share of rice or anything else he could steal.

What Imelda wanted was not beyond him. He didn't like Conway or any of the foreigners but the magnitude of what she was asking shook him. However, he dared not think about the consequences if he failed. Imelda continued to scowl as if daring him to refuse. But Eduardo just stood there, his mind a whirl of conflicting thoughts; the main one being fear.

Neither of them noticed Susan Santos standing just outside the door.

* * *

The taxi rattled to a stop outside Sally's apartment and after an altercation about the fare, Conway paid and said testily, 'Sally, why do they call them *Golden taxis* for God sake when they're painted black and have you ever been in one where the bloody meter works?'

She began to laugh. 'Steve, this is the Philippines, things are often not as they seem. *Golden taxis* have been around since I was very young and I'm sorry,' she leaned against him still laughing, 'but I can't remember ever being in one whose meter is not broken, and you know, the drivers always like to play a game about the fare, especially with foreigners. As I said darling, this is the Philippines.'

He grimaced with the air of resignation of one who realizes, if you can't beat 'em, join 'em and followed her inside through the heavy gates which, unlike his first visit, had been left open.

The guard recognized him as they passed and gave him a smile and a salute. Conway couldn't help himself. 'Isn't it past your bedtime mate?' But it was lost on the guard who just kept smiling as they mounted the stairs.

Once inside the apartment she left the overhead light off and turned on the bedside lamp giving the room a warm, intimate glow, then asked him to take a seat at the small dining table while she set about making coffee. The door and the outside window had been repaired and the place looked even better than when he first saw it. Everything else looked much the same except for one thing: the photo of the Marine was missing.

She placed two cups of steaming coffee and some cheese crackers on the table then went to her small radiogram and spun a love song by Barry Manilow. Oh no! not Barry Manilow! He sipped his coffee and prepared to grin and bear it. 'Is it ok, the coffee?' she asked tentatively, looking as if she expected him to spit it out.

He wished he could. It was terrible, but he hadn't the heart to tell her, so he just smiled and said it was fine. She sat beside him drinking her coffee and chatting on mostly about her family. Things apparently hadn't been going so well for them in recent times.

Mom had been ill for a long time and needed an operation to repair something in her bowels. Dad was on his last legs with a kidney disease. They needed another caribou on the farm; a neighbor had leaned over the fence and shot the previous one because the old man hadn't paid a gambling debt. Her young sister was now selling herself, one of her brothers was in Muntinlupa jail for fraud and the other was about to join him on a similar charge. They had all asked Sally for money. And I thought I had problems, he mused looking down at his coffee cup. You don't know when you're well off Conway.

He finished his coffee, thankfully, (the biscuits helped kill the taste) and started checking out her record collection. It varied from Barry Manilow to Bruce Springsteen, the Beatles, Madonna, Andy Williams and a dozen Filipino artists he'd never heard of. She came over and stood beside him.

'What kind of music do you like Steve?'

'All kinds I guess, from pops, rock n roll to the classics, but I do have a leaning toward folk music of the Sixties, Woody Guthrie, The Weavers, Pete Seeger, Kingston Trio, Joan Baez, stuff like that.' Fortunately Barry had finished and she put on a slow moody song by a Filipino songstress. She came and stood beside him and he slipped one arm around her waist while reading the dust jacket of *Bruce Springsteen's Greatest Hits.*

'Please be careful darling, I could not stand it if anything happened to you, Sir Groyne has some bad friends,' she said pulling him closer. He looked down into eyes brimming with tears and kissed him lightly on the cheek. She hugged him and he kissed her again, this time with passion. She responded equally and they stumbled back and fell back onto her nearby bed the kiss unbroken: then followed a frantic grabbing at each other's clothes quickly shed and thrown in any direction across the bed and onto the floor.

He gazed at her body, slim, spectacular and golden in the in the glow of the bedlamp. Her long black hair spread out like a fan behind her head. The light danced and cast shadows off full heavy breasts tipped by large brown, now distended, nipples, sitting proudly above a concave belly below which a thick dark triangle beckoned. She came to him and unlike his encounter with the voracious Lily, this time it was lovemaking.

She threw her head back and moaned softly as he kissed her from earlobe to cheek, the breasts, belly and lower. He heard her quick intake of breath as she felt his tongue enter her most private parts.

'Oh my God, that is so wonderful,' she whispered starting to slowly arch her back, her hands now holding each side of his head, eyes closed, mouth wide open. It had been too long since a man had explored her body and she had forgotten the ecstasy, the sheer joy of being with someone she truly cared for.

For Conway, his feelings at that moment for Sally were something he had not felt for a long, long time. She was a lovely, sweet woman who genuinely cared for him and making love to her was a wonderful, exhilarating experience.

She moaned softly as his palms caressed the smooth fullness of her breasts. 'You're so big,' he whispered. 'So are you.' She giggled, her hand reaching down across his belly. She gasped as he entered her slowly, then met his thrusts in a frenzy of bucking, writhing and moaning which had him worried the guard would think she was being attacked and come to her rescue.

He held on for dear life fearing that if he let go he'd finish up on the carpet some fifteen feet away. Fortunately the guard didn't come and after a body shuddering climax they both collapsed together and stayed locked in each other's arms for many minutes, fondling, exchanging soft kisses and simply enjoying the sheer pleasure of their intimacy.

She stretched over and started to kiss his chest a few times then asked him.

'Darling, can you tell me about what happened before you came to the Philippines?' She felt him stiffen for a moment. He leaned up on one elbow and facing her.

'Sally, you know I don't want to talk about that subject, I told you before!' his voice was harsh; it spoilt the mood and her mouth opened in surprise and disbelief. His loving mood had changed in an instant to one of cold anger. At this moment she felt so much love for this man the last thing she wanted to do was cause him any pain and it seemed any mention of his past did just that. She dropped her head. 'I'm sorry, I didn't mean....' Her voice trailed away.

He immediately felt like the biggest bastard on earth. This sweet woman would never hurt anyone. She had asked an innocent question and he had jumped down her throat. He reached over and pulled her close. Her beautiful face was a picture of misery.

'Hey Sal, I'm sorry darling,' he said, kissing the nape of her neck.

'You are the first man in such a long time whose been so nice and caring to me. 'I'm so sorry for asking about your past, I'll never ask again...I promise.'

He kissed her lightly on the cheek. 'Hey look, I *promise*, I'll tell you all about it one day, but now is just not the time, ok? Come on darling cheer up,' he said kissing her again, brushing away a tear.

'Thank you my Steve, I just forgot how sensitive it is for you to talk about it.' She reached up and cupping either side of his face returned his kiss with interest, leading to more frantic activity between the sheets.

Afterwards he lay gazing at the ceiling thinking about her question. Yes, he would tell her in time but now the recollection of past events was too painful, too traumatic, the last thing he needed was to be reminded of them, but maybe one day. He glanced at his watch. Shit! It was 3.00 am! He dressed quietly trying not to disturb a sleeping Sally and used his ball point to leave her a note on the back of a used *Black Jack* cash docket he found in the kitchen.

A drowsy guard unlocked the gate and he stepped out into a stygian darkness. No lights, not a sound. It was eerie. He shivered despite the ever present humidity. Suddenly for some reason he had this premonition of danger; an overwhelming sense of foreboding.

What happened to the street lights? There were only two in the street that he had noticed and they were weak and shed little light anyway. What's going on? There had been no power cut, at least not while he'd been with Sally, so what?

The guard had locked the gate so there was no point in going back inside, he'd probably gone back to sleep and there was no way he wanted to wake Sally. He cursed himself for not bringing her home in a hotel vehicle. Jesus

Conway you never learn. Didn't the episode outside Lily's house teach you anything? He could have dropped her off and been on his way instead of groping his way in total darkness in what he knew from past experience, to be an unsafe part of Manila.

He started to walk slowly picking his way carefully, peering into the gloom and had gone no more than thirty metres when he thought he saw the glow of a cigarette quickly extinguished. It had been in front and a few metres to his right.

He froze when a voice behind him said softly, 'Sir'. He half turned toward the voice when a violent blow to the back of his head stunned him and sent him to his knees. He put his hands up to shield himself but another blow send him sprawling face first to the ground.

He desperately tried to roll away and regain his feet but a kick to his ribs doubled him up. He rolled away again groaning and grabbed at a foot as it struck him again and wrenched hard. The attacker lost his balance and fell beside him but there was more than one and another series of kicks and finally one to the side of his head knocked him senseless. One of his assailants put a foot under him, rolled him onto his back and gave him a final kick before they returned silently to a black-tinted sedan and drove off.

\* \* \*

Jumbo Keyes was beginning to get worried. It was early afternoon and he hadn't seen hide nor hair of his boss. This was most unusual. Conway was an early starter. If he was going to be delayed he never failed to phone Keyes to let him know. To add to the big man's concern was the fact that he'd phoned Conway's apartment and got no answer. Then he phoned Susan's office only to discover that she wasn't in the hotel either. A hundred things whirled around in his brain. Maybe he'd had a night with Lily and was still there but he discounted that. He would have been at work by now, an accident, maybe? Perhaps he had fallen foul of someone? It was not unknown in Ermita. Surely he wasn't with Susan?

Where the hell was he?

His phone rang. He grabbed it.

'Steve?'

The caller introduced himself as Doctor Efren Cruz from the Makati Medical Center. Did he know a Mr Steve Conway?

Keyes suddenly felt sick.

'Yes I do. What's happened to him? How is he? Is he OK?' The words poured out.

'I can't talk on the phone Mr Keyes,' said the doctor calmly. 'Can you please come to the Center now.'

'I'm on my way!' Keyes dropped the phone, charged downstairs, commandeered a hotel vehicle and sped off to Makati.

* * *

Susan Santos sat on a bench, a small, lone figure in the vastness of Luneta Park. She was worried to the point of being sick. She had only heard part of the conversation in Imelda's office and did not know to whom they were referring. All she knew was that the little she heard was shocking. Was Imelda really saying she wanted someone eliminated? Did she mean employment terminated? Maybe that was it. Surely she had misheard? It was too terrible to contemplate. She had to get away from the office somewhere and try to make sense of the turmoil in her head.

She had seen Eduardo around the hotel but did not know him personally. He looked sly and unpleasant, someone to steer clear of. She had also noticed him on occasions looking at her with undisguised lust and it frightened her.

She was at heart a simple country girl and her thoughts turned to her family down in the province of Cavite...of her dad. He was old and infirmed now and had gone down hill since her mother died. He found it hard to manage their farm even with the occasional help of Susan's brothers. But they had their own families and were busy with their lives.

She felt guilty that she had not visited him as much as she would have liked but work always seemed to take up so much of her life. She knew she was too conscientious and hated to delegate but beneath the quiet exterior was a stubborn streak which would not allow her to admit this, the only weakness in her professional makeup.

In recent times she had begun to think about her own personal situation. She had no man in her life, not even a suitor. Oh sure there had been a few when she was at university but the determination to finish her degree in those days overrode the desire for romantic relationships. They could come later but to her disappointment, "they" had not eventuated. Work and her innate shyness had been a self imposed barrier when she came to the mean streets of Manila looking for a job. She was frightened and lonely at first, but finally secured a job as an auditor with a well known accounting firm in the commercial district of Makati.

Although she enjoyed the job and the challenge which auditing brings, after a couple of years she tired of it and looked for more variety. Following more accounting jobs in Makati she came to the Down Under after being highly recommended by a friend. She found it a challenge but relished the opportunity of working in a new environment. An added bonus was the management had given her autonomy she had not found elsewhere. (What she didn't realise was her employers didn't have a clue how accounting worked and hoped she could sort out the mess). But today's event frightened her and she did not know what to do.

Who was Imelda talking about to Eduardo? She knew Imelda disliked almost as many people who disliked her but was she actually telling Eduardo he had to kill someone? I must have somehow misheard, yes that's it. Eduardo is going to arrange for someone to be fired. Employers don't go around killing their staff!

Then she started to shake. Oh my God! Was it Mr Conway! It couldn't be him could it? She had heard that Conway and the Pricketts did not exactly see eye to eye but…the bank account! Was that it? Did the uncovering of that have something to do with it?

Her stomach turned over. Mr Conway was a good man. She liked him. She knew he was doing his best to help her and sort out the problems in the hotel and improve its performance. He had won her admiration and that of many of the staff. She sat there thinking, turning over various options. She got to her feet and began to walk back to the hotel. She knew what she had to do.

\* \* \*

Jumbo Keyes rushed into the reception of the Makati Medical Center and asked to see a patient Mr Steve Conway and Doctor Efren Cruz. He was directed to a ward on the third floor where he found Doctor Cruz at the nurse's station looking at patients' records. He introduced himself, asked about Conway's condition and if he could see him.

'Ah hello Mr Keyes, nice to meet you,' said Doctor Cruz.

'How is he Doctor, what happened? He's my boss and a good friend, please tell me what's going on!' said Keyes only just stopping himself from shaking the small, white-coated medico.

'Calm down Mr Keyes,' said Doctor Cruz gently. 'Your friend will be ok. He has severe concussion, a couple of badly bruised ribs, possibly some internal injuries and lacerations. We will keep him here for a couple of days and if everything is ok we will send him home to rest. He's a tough guy, please don't worry.'

'Can I see him Doctor?' said Keyes, breathing a huge sigh of relief.

'Yes of course come this way please.' Keyes followed Doctor Cruz along a spotless white tiled corridor to a small room where Conway was the sole patient. His head was swathed in bandages, a drip was attached to his arm and, a beautiful woman was sitting by his bedside. It was not Lily Li.

'Hello buddy what've you been doing to yourself?' asked Keyes with one of his trade mark smiles. The woman turned, Keyes recognized her instantly.

'You know Sally from Groyne's bar Jumbo?'

'Of course, how are you Sally?'

'Fine sir,' said Sally shyly. She didn't know Keyes very well and his sheer size intimidated her but his easy manner and friendly smile relaxed her immediately.

'How did you get here Steve? Tell me all about it, you had us all worried buddy,' said the American taking a seat beside the bed.

It seemed that just after dawn Paolo Ruiz a neighbor of Sally had come out to relieve himself against the concrete wall not far from her front gate. As he stood there at an angle, head down both arms placed against the wall enjoying the bliss of the moment he turned his head and noticed a body lying by the side of the road.

His first reaction was to empty his bowels as well. Paolo wasn't feeling the best. He had a raging hangover from a night on Ginebra gin, a truly dreadful concotion which made Italian grappa taste like soft drink.

He slowly approached the body and noticed it was still breathing. Unable to help himself he looked around furtively and seeing no one, quickly went through the pockets and found a wallet. He extracted several 100 peso notes, left the remainder and put the wallet back. Paolo had to be the most honest thief in Manila. Sally's apartment block was the only building of significance in the street so he bashed on the gates until the guard appeared, pointed to the body then took off like a *Bondi tram* before anyone could ask him any searching questions.

The guard was horrified to discover who it was and raced back to tell Sally. She came rushing downstairs screaming at the guard to phone for an ambulance. She stayed beside Conway for what seemed an eternity before it arrived.

He had regained consciousness by then. He was placed on a stretcher and lifted carefully into the back of the ambulance. Sally climbed in after him and they sped away to the Makati Medical Center.

'I thought at first it was a random mugging but from what Sally tells me maybe it wasn't.' He told Keyes what Sally had overheard in *The Black Jack*. Keyes listened frowning at first. When Conway had finished his face became clouded and very angry.

'I'm gonna pay that motherfucker a little visit,' he said ominously.

'No wait, we don't know for sure it was him Jumbo, let Sally see what she can find out. If it was him, he'll be bragging about it. He won't be able to help himself. Then,' said Conway grimly, 'we might just give him a taste of his own medicine.'

'Beat him up?' Keyes grinned with relish.

'No, not necessarily, there are ways we can inflict more pain than a simple bashing but I'll tell you what I have in mind, when the time comes. Our girl here will find out what we need to know,' he said squeezing Sally's hand.

Keyes looked down at Sally and grinned. She sat there holding Conway's hand gazing lovingly at her hero. Conway began to squirm. The expression on his assistant manager's face said he had a few questions to ask his boss about the relationship.

'Jumbo, I'll be out of here soon then I think I'll take a few days off and have a look at Boracay. Sally tells me it's quite a place.'

'So I've heard, never been there me'self, but yeah, go for it Steve, I'll look after the ranch for you,' said Keyes with a wink. 'And?' he raised his eyebrows and looked down at Sally who had her back to him. Conway shook his head almost imperceptibly. Great girl but he wanted a few days on his own. There were quite a few things he had to think about.

# 14

Susan Santos hurried back to the hotel her heart thumping. She had to talk to Mr Conway as soon as possible. As she tried to cross TM Kalaw Street she was prevented by a huge crowd of shouting, screaming protestors waving banners and placards bearing signs *"IBAG SAK ANG ADMINISTRAYSONG MARCOS"* (Down with Marcos) and *"CORY PARA PRESIDENTE"* (Cory for President). Many of them beckoned and urged her to join in but she had more important matters on her mind. On arrival at the Down Under she hurried up the stairs to Conway's office stumbling and nearly falling on the top step in her haste. It was empty. Jumbo Keyes' office, the same. Where are they? She was in a panic. 'I have to speak to someone, my God! What am I to do?'

She rushed back downstairs to the front desk reception. 'Does anyone know where Mr Conway or Mr Keyes are?' she shouted to one of the clerks behind the counter. The desk clerk was taken aback. She had never heard quiet, gentle Susan Santos raise her voice, let alone shout.

'Mr Keyes left and said he was going to the Makati Medical Center *Ate (big sister)* we think it has something to do with Mr Conway.'

Susan paled. Fear gripped her and for a moment she had difficulty speaking.

'When…when…was this, how long ago did Mr Keyes leave?'

'Maybe an hour ago, he really was in a very big hurry. Are you ok *Ate?*'

A wave of nausea passed over her and her legs buckled slightly. Then she straightened up and without a word, pushed past incoming guests and left the hotel in such a hurry it brought curious and puzzled looks from the front desk staff and guard at the door. Out on United Nations Avenue she stood impatiently looking left and right for a taxi.

One cruised by and was about to ignore her until she jumped out in front of it and wrenched open the back door shouting at the driver she had to get to the Makati Medical Center in a BIG hurry. It would normally be at least a 30 minute journey but she said there was a tip of 100 pesos if he could get there in twenty.

One hundred pesos! The driver grinned as if he had just won the lottery. He nearly ripped the gear stick out of its housing throwing the old banger into first and with wheels spinning, took off at breakneck speed, frightening the life out of a few pedestrians, other motorists and not the least, Susan herself.

In just over twenty five minutes she stepped out of the elevator on the 3rd floor of the Makati Medical Center and walked along a white corridor to Steve Conway's room where Jumbo Keyes and a very attractive Filipina, sat by his bed. The three turned and looked at her saying nothing. She stood for a moment, embarrassed, lost for words. Keyes tried to put her at ease and explained what had happened with no reference to Sally, other than to say she was a friend whom Conway had escorted home before being mugged.

Conway smiled at his little accountant.

'Thank you for coming Susan but it's not serious, I'll be ok in a day or two and by the way, I've decided to have a few days off. We can discuss that bank matter when I get back, ok?'

Susan smiled and nodded, relieved that he seemed alright but she was still very worried. Who did this? Was it Eduardo, or just a random assault? She desperately needed to talk to him in private but this was not the time or the place. And, *who is this woman?* There was Conway lying with his head swathed in bandages being tended by a woman who obviously had feelings for him. She was surprised at her sudden twinge of jealousy.

'Ok sir, I just wanted to come to see how you are, but please, we need to speak about some other very important matters as soon as possible,' she said, trying to keep the fear out of her voice. Conway looked askance at her. He could tell there was something more than just the problem of the bank accounts on Susan's mind.

'Let's wait until I come back from Boracay, I'll be in better shape to talk about these matters then, ok?'

'Oh, ok sir,' she replied reluctantly, wishing the others weren't there. 'Please get well soon sir,' she said, then avoiding the curious look from Sally, bowed, and left. The three of them continued to discuss the previous night's events. Then Sally rose to leave.

'I have to go now too sir and I will see what I can find out about what happened to you,' she said, squeezing Conway's hand. She then kissed hers and placed it on his cheek, sent a dazzling smile to Keyes and at the door blew Conway another kiss before leaving. A bemused Jumbo Keyes grinned knowingly at Conway, but knew better than to ask questions…not now anyway.

* * *

In the Down Under, Imelda had Eduardo on the carpet. She was furious and wanted to know if he was responsible for Conway's hospitalization. 'I thought I told you I would say *when*, you fool?' she said angrily, slamming her fist on the desk making Eduardo flinch.

'Ma'am I know nothing. I did not have anything to do with it, I, I, I swear on my mother's grave,' stuttered Eduardo. Imelda knew Eduardo could not lie straight in bed but she somehow believed him. He had nothing to gain by defying her orders so, *who* did this?

'Mmmm,' she thought aloud. 'Our Mr Conway seems to have more than one set of enemies, or was it just a random attack?' She would make enquiries through her sources in the area who would know. 'When did you see him last Eduardo?' she snapped.

Eduardo shuffled his feet and looked away. This could get tricky.

'Ah, I saw him leave *Barrio Fiesta* two nights ago with a Filipina. I was on my way to buy some pork.' The part about the pork was no lie. He was on his way to pork the sister of a fellow cook named Esteban he had caught trying to steal a leg of lamb he had earmarked for himself.

Esteban knew that Eduardo had lusted after his sister Maria for years but Maria, an attractive woman in her early thirties, did not respond to Eduardo's obvious desires. In fact she felt Eduardo had slithered into this world from under a rock somewhere and she was only too well aware of his feelings toward her.

She often visited her brother at the Down Under and seen the lust in Eduardo's googly eyes. It made her shudder. However when Esteban told her what had happened and that Eduardo was about to blow the whistle on him, pragmatism took over.

They were a large family and Esteban was the only one with a job. He was the sole supporter and breadwinner and they could not afford to see him jobless. So after a long, sometimes heated discussion, Maria agreed to be 'nice' to Eduardo but insisted it would be the one and only time.

It was decided she would meet him in a short-time hotel in Malate on Sunday night and pay the 'price' for Esteban's indiscretion. That is - the indiscretion of letting another thief catch him in the act. It was on the way to his rendezvous with Maria that Eduardo had spied Conway and Sally outside *Barrio Fiesta* hailing a taxi.

'You know the girl?'

Eduardo shook his head. 'No, Ma'am, never seen her before.'

Imelda frowned. This is a new development but not surprising. There are plenty of women in this area who would want Conway, especially once they knew he had a job and was a resident.

'Find out who she is and let me know. I want to know who she is, where she works, all about her, and report back to me as soon as possible…go now…'

Eduardo left backpedalling and bowing at the same time; not an easy thing to do but he'd had plenty of practice. Outside his mind returned to the night of his assignation with Maria.

They had met at a small, dingy short-time hotel at the end of a rubbish strewn, pot-holed alley off the bottom end of Mabini Street. A skinny, balding Filipino in a black tee shirt and jeans, cigarette drooping from his lips was reading *The Tempo,* a lurid, Tagalog tabloid newspaper always full of murder and mayhem, usually with photos of the latest homicide victims splashed across the front page. Either the editor was sick or there was something in the Filipino psyche that didn't mind a daily diet of corpses.

Not one of the big spenders, Eduardo had reluctantly paid the 70 Pesos fee for the three hours and the clerk without looking up from the newspaper handed him a key and said, *'pangatlong silid'* (room three).

The room was lit by a 15 watt lamp and in semi-darkness. It was little more than a large cupboard and almost devoid of furniture, except for an old double bed in one corner with sheets that looked like they hadn't been washed since Magellan had arrived on Philippine shores. Beside the bed was a tiny shower cum toilet and an ancient TV stood on a shelf opposite the bed. It started automatically when they entered showing a grainy, black and white porno movie. This was obviously designed to get the customers in the 'mood'. To add incongruity to the scene, on the opposite wall facing the television was a po-faced photo of the Virgin Mary.

They stood looking at each other; he wearing an oily grin, she trying to hide her disgust. But her mood changed when he dropped his trousers and stood with his underpants around his skinny ankles. Eduardo possessed the smallest dick she had ever laid eyes on; and she had seen a few. She could not contain herself and began to giggle.

He looked at her in bewilderment unable to see anything funny. She continued to giggle and he continued to frown. She looked down at his dick again. Well, she consoled herself; at least he can't do much damage to me with that! He looked so ridiculous standing there; this ugly, scrawny little man with his tiny organ pointing at her, it took all her self control not to laugh out loud.

This was the first sex Eudardo had had in a very long time and he motioned impatiently to her to take off her clothes. She turned her back and undressed slowly trying to delay the inevitable. She was a little overweight but still cut a good figure, with small, pear-shaped breasts above shapely hips and nice legs. He grabbed her and they fell on the bed in a tangle of arms and legs. The old bed had seen a lot of action over the years and the springs barely supported the mattress. It began to creak and sag dangerously.

Eduardo was an eager if not expert, lover. Maria reached down and gave his little dick a tweak and he let out a yelp causing his big, googly eyes to spin like twin roulette wheels. This seemed to spur him on and he got down to business.

Maria shut her eyes and tried to think of her days in the rice paddies of La Union when life was so simple and pleasant. It was fun to take her parents their *merienda* (morning tea) and then lunch. The days were sunny and full of laughter with her seven brothers and two older sisters. Eventually she had come to Manila looking for work but with no formal qualifications and no desire to sell her body, employment was hard to come by.

Esteban followed her to Manila and found employment with the Down Under Hotel as a cook, and invited her to share a small room with him in Pasay city on the outskirts of metro Manila. She continued to look for work hoping one day she would find a good man, preferably a foreigner, who would maybe take her away from all this...maybe just a dream.

She was brought back to reality by a grunt and groan from Eduardo that signaled he had finished what he came for. He slumped back exhausted and she leapt up from the bed, showered and left while he was in the toilet.

She still felt unclean as she hurried along the dark, rain-slicked streets praying for a taxi. Please God let me find one before he comes out looking for me. She was in luck and was halfway home before he came tottering out into the street still doing up his fly. He wore a self satisfied grin which would have vanished instantly if he really knew what Maria thought of him and his performance.

\* \* \*

'Conway is in hospital! Do you know anything about this?' Sanchez said, glaring at Roque. 'I thought I told you lieutenant he was not to be touched until *I* said so. What do you have to say for yourself?'

Roque shook his head in bewilderment. 'No sir, I promise you, I had nothing to do with it. As I told you sir, I would finish the job properly when you issued the order....'

'Well, who then? Find out! I want to know lieutenant...NOW!' Roque nearly turned himself inside out in his haste to leave the building.

Out on United Nations Avenue he scratched his head for a moment then knew what he had to do. He would send word around the bars in the area via his contacts. He was feared by the locals; they were only too well aware of what he was capable of. The answer would soon come. He was more concerned with another problem...lack of funds.

He had sold the three silencers he'd told Sanchez were stolen and had taken the proceeds to Santa Anna race track to place on two "sure things" he'd been given. He bet half of his ill-gotten gains on the first "sure thing," a bag of bones with the unlikely name of *Filipino Rocket.*

Unfortunately for Roque, it didn't exactly live up to its name. If anything the *Rocket* was the slowest horse on the entire program. 'I could have run faster than that damn horse,' he moaned later to a barman in a sleazy Quezon City dive. Despite the setback, he'd been confident about his second bet because his informant told him with a sly smile that its speed was going to be "electronically enhanced".

Coming into the straight with 50 metres to go, *Mystery Mary* was in front but under pressure from a wave of horses closing in. The jockey gave the battery a belt. Unfortunately it was defective and electrocuted *Mystery Mary.* The horse dropped dead instantly, throwing the jockey over the guard rail and bringing down the rest of the field leaving horses and riders strewn all over the track.

Pandemonium reigned. A number of horses were badly injured with broken legs and had to be put down immediately while several jockeys were seriously hurt and had to be rushed to hospital. Roque watched on in disbelief. His big betting coup had come to nothing. If he hadn't hocked his gun with the silencers, he probably would have shot himself.

\* \* \*

The phone rang just as Jack Roberts walked into his office. He picked it up to hear the familiar drawl of Chuck McGaw. 'Hey Jack, what's the story with Conway?'

'What do you mean? What about, Conway?' asked Roberts slowly.

'Don't you know man? He got mugged. He's in Makati Medical Center.'

Roberts was embarrassed and furious at the same time but kept his voice calm.

'No, I didn't know Chuck.    Perhaps you could enlighten me,' he said drily.

'Well man, my sources' said McGaw emphasizing the, *my sources*, (like Jack, where are *your sources*?) tell me he was mugged in Sampaloc the other night. He'd apparently been visiting some babe and got ambushed when he left her. What do you think?  Random attack or maybe something more, after all…he was probably seen talking to us?'

Roberts paused and thought for a moment.  It was always unfortunate to hear of one of his countrymen getting mugged but it happened; it was that kind of town and nothing new.  What was new was that his usually reliable intelligence had let him down and he had to learn about it from the Americans.

Although he and the American Embassy kept in close touch and worked well together there was an element of one-upmanship when it came to their intelligence gathering and this was one of those times.  Roberts liked Conway and regarded him as one of the more reliable and sensible expats in the area. He needed to know more, much more, before he could form an opinion.

'Could be anything my friend, you know what this town is like.  Wrong place, wrong time, who knows, but thanks Chuck, this is one I owe you mate. I'll get over to the Makati Medical Center right away, we'll talk later, bye.'

\* \* \*

'I didn't realise I was so popular,' smiled Conway, glancing up from the newspaper he was reading to see Roberts give his door a cursory knock and enter without waiting for an invitation.  The big cop was still smarting over McGaw's phone call but hid it with a crooked grin.

'What happened to you cobber, the Ermita bum biter get you?'

'Something like that Jack, what're you doing here; this can't be a social call?'

Roberts affected an injured look.  'Hey mate, we like to look after our people, you know the Aussie government always has the best interests of its citizens at heart,' then seriously, 'any idea who was responsible Steve?  You been getting up someone's nose or getting out of the wrong bed mate?'

Conway ignored the jibe. 'To tell you the truth, I honestly don't know Jack.' From what Sally had told him it seemed Groyne was probably the culprit, but without proof he was keeping his suspicions to himself.  Roberts looked around the room for a moment then got up and closed the door.  No, no bugs here he concluded.  In his game you never let your guard down.  Secrecy and caution was paramount, even in a hospital room.

'This could be serious or it might be just another Ermita mugging. I'll make a few enquiries and see what we can find out,' he said quietly. 'Ermita is a small area and a rumour mill, but someone will know. Of course it could be that you were just in the wrong place at the wrong time, but something tells me that's not the case,' said Roberts chewing his bottom lip.

'Mmm…maybe.' Conway looked out the window with its view of the Makati skyline for a moment. 'I really have no idea at this stage. There was more than one but, it was dark and they came from behind, I didn't get a chance to see who they were. I'll get in touch if I find out who was responsible, but not before I've had five minutes in a room alone with the pricks. Do *you* have any thoughts?'

The big cop stroked his chin between thumb and forefinger. 'It could be a number of things. More than likely you've either upset someone, or maybe a jealous lady taking revenge,' he said, smiling at the latter, 'or as I said, maybe just a random attack. In any case, I'm sure we'll find something, in the meantime, get better. How long will you be here?'

'Another day or two, no longer.'

'Ok, I'll be in touch,' Roberts gave another of his crooked grins, and left.

A week later after leaving strict instructions he was not to be contacted by anyone unless it was the Pricketts, Jumbo or Susan, he boarded an Air Pacific flight to Caticlan where he would board a banca for his first look at the fabled island of Boracay. He never noticed the googly-eyed individual watching him as he checked in or the short, stocky guy in white tee shirt and jeans sitting in the aircraft four seats behind him.

\* \* \*

'Hello, hello, my *compadres,*' bellowed Bert Groyne to two well-built young Filipinos in tee shirt and jeans, standing just inside the door of *The Black Jack* blinking in the dim light. Sally looked up as Groyne shambled over to the two newcomers and shook each by the hand. He motioned to Sally to send over three beers then took them to a table in a far corner where they sat with heads lowered. Groyne looked around furtively then listened intently as one of the young guys began speaking in a low tone. Sally brought the drinks and tried to hover but Groyne brusquely waved her away.

From the bar she watched as her boss nodded, smiled broadly, nodded again then reached into the back pocket of his shorts and took out his wallet from which he handed a bundle of notes to each of the Filipinos. They counted the money, nodded indicating satisfaction and left without another word leaving their drinks untouched.

Groyne came back to his position at the bar and took a big slurp of his San Miguel, burped and gave all and sundry a self satisfied grin.

'What was that all about mate?' asked Biro.

'You know that little problem I had with Conway? Well the boys paid him a visit and he's now in Makati Medical Center. Doesn't pay to fuck with old Bert Groyne.'

'How bad is he Bert?' asked Mullet with a look of concern. 'You didn't do him over too badly did you mate? You know how word gets around in this place.'

'Nah, I coulda had him salvaged but as you say Mullet, word gets around. He'll live, but I think you might find we won't have too much more trouble with our Mr Steve Conway.' Sally standing nearby with her head down pretending to wash glasses heard all this. You are right Sir Groyne, word *does* get around.

'Do you mind if I take my break now sir, I want to make sure I am here for the busy period sir,' she said, leaning across the bar to Groyne.

'Huh, yeah, ok, don't be too long, you're needed here.'

She found a phone box nearby, dialed the number of the Down Under and asked for Jumbo Keyes. Aware that incoming calls are often listened in to by curious phone operators she kept her call deliberately light-hearted and innocuous. When Keyes answered she said, 'hello sir, I have something for your wife, can you meet me at McDonalds on UN Avenue in about ten minutes and I'll give it to you there…ok sir?'

Keyes recognized her voice at once. 'Ok, see you there in ten.' Ten minutes later they sat facing each other in a corner of McDonalds, well away from other customers.

'What have you got for me?' asked Keyes quietly.

Sally took a deep breath. 'Sir, it was Groyne who did it to Sir Steve. Two men came to the bar and he paid them and then boasted to his friends how he had Sir Steve hurt.' Tears welled in her eyes and began to roll down her cheeks. 'What a terrible thing to do.'

Keyes reached over and handed her a handkerchief. 'Take this babe,' he said kindly. He waited while she wiped away her tears.

'When did you hear this and are you *absolutely sure* Sally?'

'About half and hour ago, yes I am very sure sir. Sir Groyne was *so* happy. He said he would not have any more trouble from Sir Steve.'

Keyes smiled grimly. 'He is right Sally darling.'

'What do you mean sir?'

'Sir Groyne may not be troubled by Mr Conway but he sure is going to hear from me. But Sally, you know nothing, right? Nothing, Ok?'

'Yes of course sir. I would be in big, *big* trouble if Sir Groyne knew I had been speaking to you.'

'He won't know I can assure you babe, in fact you will be the least of his troubles,' said the big American with a look in his eye that made Sally nervous. 'Now you better go back to work and act as if you know nothing about Conway. I'll be in touch, and…Sally.'

'Yes sir?'

'Thanks, we owe you,' he said reaching across and touching her hand. Sally blushed and looked down. 'Oh sir, thank you but it was awful what happened to Sir Steve. He has been very kind to me and,' she hesitated for a moment as if wanting to say something else but thought better of it. 'I must go now, thank you sir.'

After she left Keyes sat for some time contemplating a course of action. What he had in mind would not have been approved by Conway but Steve old buddy…nice guys don't win in this town. He finished his Big Mac then eased his bulk from the table and strolled out into the late afternoon sunshine.

* * *

Bert Groyne was having the time of his life. The bar had been full from early evening, every one of his girls had been barfined and he was roaring. He'd moved off the San Miguel and decided to treat himself to a night on Johnnie Walker Black Label. All his stock of Scotch had been watered down except the stash he kept for himself. After drinking beer all day he was now into his second bottle of "Johnnie" and all was well with the world.

He even rang the bell and shouted the bar, something unheard of in *The Black Jack*. But he kept thinking of Conway and the drunker he got, the happier he became. Sally watched him trying to hide her disgust and wondered what Keyes had in mind. One thing she was sure of; it didn't auger too well for Sir Groyne.

Around 2.30 am Groyne decided to pay a visit to his old mate Barney Lawson in *Nightbirds*. He staggered outside into the warm night air and wobbled for a moment wondering where he was.

'Shit, that Johnnie Black has a kick,' he muttered stumbling around the corner into Mabini Street and crossed over. He stood wobbling near an alley which his addled brain told him, would bring him out somewhere near *Nightbirds*.

Normally he would never have considered walking a dark alley in Ermita in the early hours of the morning, but booze and common sense don't make good bedfellows. 'Yeah this'll do,' he said to himself. It was a mistake he was about to regret.

Half way along the alley a big hand reached out and grabbed one of the gold chains around his throat and wrenched him sideways into another tiny alley even darker than the first. He turned, struggling to free himself and never saw the large fist which crashed into his face breaking his nose, his jaw and several front teeth. He dropped face first as if pole-axed.

His attacker reached down, took his wallet from a back pocket and extracted a thick bundle of notes from there and another pocket. 'Thanks Sir Groyne, you won't be needing this,' he whispered, throwing the wallet into the darkness. No one saw the attack or the big figure leave. It would be daylight before Groyne would be found; just another assault and robbery victim in the mean streets of Ermita.

Early next morning, Father Dominic of *St Bernard's Orphanage* in Paranque had just finished prayers when he heard a loud banging on the front door. He opened it to see a taxi driver standing there with a thick brown paper envelope. The driver thrust it into his hands, jumped back to his cab and drove off. Father Dominic stood there mystified looking at the departing taxi then down at the envelope.

He walked slowly back to his vestry and placed it on a table. He cautiously ran his hands over and around the envelope squeezing it gently and satisfied it held nothing metallic, unsealed it. To his amazement it was full of crumpled peso bills of different denominations. He counted the contents and couldn't believe it…nearly fifty thousand pesos! There was also a folded, neatly written unsigned note, which read;

*A small donation, hope it helps. Keep up the good work.*

The civil unrest in Manila continued to rise.

# 15

From a hot, clear blue sky, Boracay appeared like a tropical jewel from the left side of the *Asia Pacific* twin otter as it swept low and fast along the beach on the way to landing at Caticlan, the small town on the mainland from where Conway would disembark to catch a 30 minute banca ride to the island.

At first glimpse it was the kind of picture post card paradise Sally had told him about. Dark green palm trees fringed a long beach of blinding white sand liberally sprinkled with sun worshippers. Off shore, fishermen in narrow-gutted outriggers, typical of the Philippines, leisurely plied their trade on a calm sparkling blue sea. It was a scene of such utter peace and tranquility, Manila seemed a long way away.

Climbing out of the small aircraft at Caticlan Conway had to run the gauntlet of a dozen tricycle drivers all clamouring to be the one to take him to the port to catch the *banca*. He pushed through them and chose a tall, skinny teenager with a goofy haircut, an orange tee shirt declaring *Shit Happens*, bright green, silk basketball shorts and a huge smile. When Conway nodded in his direction he eagerly grabbed the Australian's small travel bag, threw it into the trike and began to take off before his bemused passenger had clambered awkwardly into the small passenger seat.

'Ok sir?' said the boy grinning. These foreigners were usually too big for his tiny vehicle and it always made him smile to see them, knees up around their ears trying to get comfortable. Conway smiled uncertainly and the kid gunned it.

Ten minutes later after a noisy, cramped and bumpy ride along a sandy, pot-holed track they arrived at the port as a *banca* from Boracay pulled in. Conway handed 20 pesos to a woman he presumed to be the fee collector and gingerly climbed up a slippery, four inch wide board which served as a gangplank.  A boat boy threw his bag onto the flat roof of the open-sided cabin and with shoulders hunched and head down he clambered down onto a seat almost toppling into the water in the process.  Fortunately a Filipino passenger lent a helping hand to assist him board the pitching vessel.

With much yelling and hand waving among the crew, the boat backed out from the jetty, swung into the channel and with its nose pointed toward Boracay set off smoothly cresting the deep blue rolling swells until they arrived in shallow water just off Boat Station three at the northern end of the island.

A welcome breeze cooled Conway as he waded ashore in the knee-deep water to be greeted by another gaggle of shouting, jostling locals, mostly representing various resorts and places of accommodation.  These ranged from the luxurious to the basic *Nipa* hut which he was informed, consisted of one room with a glassless window, a bed, small bamboo cupboard for clothing and nothing else.

He settled for a middle range place; a solidly built bamboo offering consisting of three units. *Pacific Pearl* had seen better days but looked comfortable and came with a refrigerator, tiled bathroom, and clean sheets.  For 200 pesos a night the smiling landlady Mrs Sando promised to change the bedding daily and provide fresh drinking water.

Conway looked around his home for the next week.  It was no Taj Mahal but it was adequate and suited his purpose.  He showered and changed into a pair of speedo swim trunks, under white shorts and light blue tee shirt and headed out for a look around.  His accommodation was just a few metres from the beach which close up was as beautiful as it was from the air.  The sand, white, soft and cool beneath his feet; how wonderful it felt after the hard, cracked and broken sidewalks of Manila.

The sun was high and shone down on a sea now turquoise, giving way inshore to a beautiful emerald.  It reminded him of the Great Barrier Reef in his native Queensland.  It looked so cool, clean and inviting he couldn't resist the temptation.  Shrugging off his tee shirt and shorts he raced across the sand and hit the water in a racing dive.

The water temperature was perfect.  Cool enough to be refreshing but not cold enough to take the breath away.  It was surprisingly shallow so he had to swim for forty metres before there was any real depth.  He duck-dived, swam and carried on like a big porpoise for nearly half an hour before returning to his bungalow for yet another shower.

He stepped out of the shower refreshed and exhilarated.  This was the best he'd felt for weeks and his injuries seemed almost non-existent except for a slight twinge around his ribs.  He was a quick healer but had a long memory. His thoughts turned to Groyne for a moment but quickly dismissed them.

There was too much here to enjoy. The last thing he wanted was to spoil it with memories of that low-life.

It was time for a look around. He stepped outside and wandered along a sandy track running parallel to the beach stopping to look at the various stalls with their colourful displays of beachwear, sunglasses, handicrafts, totem bags, advertisements for diving trips, snorkelling and various other water sports on offer. There were a few small restaurants serving Filipino food and a number offering Western fare, the usual hamburgers, pizzas and pasta.

Smiling locals waved to him from small outdoor bars but it was time for lunch; the booze could come later. A few metres ahead nailed to a tree, was a simple, red printed sign which said, *English Tea House.* That'll do. He turned and walked down a narrow, sandy picketed lane to an open air *Nipa* style restaurant. He took a table which gave him a view of surrounding gardens and the beach through the palm trees.

The menu was very English indeed. *Shepherd's Pie, Toad in the Hole, Spotted Dick* as well as a variety of hamburgers, toasted sandwiches, pies and salads all to come, with *A huge pot of English tea.* He settled for a *hamburger with the lot* and the pot of tea. A few minutes later his order was brought by a bright, young Filipina waitress who's flashing smile made his day.

Trade was quiet and he sat there alone for a few minutes until Trevor the owner, an ebullient, larger-than life Englishman, came and asked to join him. Conway introduced himself and declined Trevor's offer of a beer. Trevor asked for a San Miguel and in answer to Conway's question, told how he had discovered Boracay on holidays three years before.

He fell in love with the place and the people immediately. He couldn't wait to return to London and sell his bakery in Shoreditch. He returned to his paradise where he was happy to spend his last days.

'They can bury me here Steve,' he said, his big ruddy face breaking into a contented smile.

Conway looked across at the brightly coloured tropical gardens of frangipani, sampaguita and bougainvillea, gently swaying palm trees, sparkling blue sea in the distance and the general air of peace and tranquility. No wonder Trevor was one of the happiest men Conway had ever met. He was living his dream.

Two months later the dream ended. Someone came up behind Trevor late one night and put two bullets into his head. The dark side of Boracay had emerged and rumours abounded.

Trevor was known to be something of a "ladies man". Was it the revenge of a jilted lover? A robbery gone wrong? There was more than one

Boracayan restaurateur jealous of the success of his Tea House. Maybe one less competitor? Perhaps it was a 'get square' for a previous misdeed? But the theory commonly believed but not publicly admitted, was an internal business dispute. There had been rumours of discontent among the ranks of the other shareholders. But nothing was ever proven; no one ever charged.

A month later the *English Tea House* was converted into a Filipino restaurant. But Trevor got his wish. He was buried on Boracay - without a headstone, in an unmarked grave.

Conway finished his lunch, thanked Trevor for his hospitality and set out to explore more of the island. Another track leading away from the beach took him into a small village of artisans furnishing woodcrafts and a variety of souvenirs for sale on the beach. He stood watching for a while, all the time surrounded by a giggling bunch of small children some of whom had obviously never seen a white man before. A couple of the braver ones came close and tugged at his shorts then to Conway's amusement, scuttled away giggling as if they had accomplished an act of great courage. It was then that he saw *him*...again.

Conway had noticed this short, scruffy, surly looking individual checking him out at the airport shortly after they had landed. He had obviously traveled on the same aircraft from Manila. When the Australian had casually glanced in his direction he quickly turned his head away and pretended to look at some of the items on sale at a *sari sari* stall. Then on the boat coming over he could feel the eyes of this character burning into his back but when he turned, the fellow again quickly looked down at a newspaper he was carrying. It was all too obvious and Conway was going to front him but decided against it. Instead he would play it cool and wait for this guy to make a move.

Ok, so he was being followed. Why? After the events in Manila, anything was possible. Could he be linked to the bashing, or the shooting? Maybe it's time I found out. The village consisted of a number of small alleys between the *Nipa* huts. Conway strolled slowly down one of these pretending to look into the open doors of several; just a curious foreigner taking in the daily life of a local family.

He knew the mystery man was behind him but keeping his distance. 'Ok mate, time to find out what your game is.' He changed direction suddenly, stepped around a corner and off the path into a small, darkened room of what appeared to be an unoccupied house. Through a crack in the bamboo wall he could observe his shadow looking around with a puzzled expression.

Conway flattened himself against the wall as his follower started slowly down the lane warily looking into each house. As he poked his head into the room Conway reached out and grabbed him by the collar, pulled him in and thrust him against the wall applying a painful wrist grip rendering him unable to do anything but cry out. He then placed a knee in the guy's back and placed his left arm around his throat wrenching it back causing him to emit a strangled gurgle.

'Ok you bastard, who are you? Why are you following me?' hissed Conway, releasing just enough pressure on the throat to allow him to breathe.

'Aaahhh, sir...ah....sir,...sorry sir, I am from the police and I am here to look after you and make sure you do not have any trouble, please sir, let me go,' he gasped.

'I don't believe you, you little runt.' Conway gave the wrist another twist.

'Aaaarrrgghh! Please sir, I'm telling the truth.'

'Which police? Who told you to do this?'

'Manila sir, we know you had trouble there, we are your protectors, sir, please let me go.'

Conway spun the little man around and pinned him to the wall. 'I don't know if I believe you. But I want you to tell whoever sent you that I can look after myself. I don't need your protection. Who's your boss?'

'Colonel Sanchez sir.'

'What?' Conway tightened his grip again. Sanchez! That bastard is not interested in my health. There is more to this than what he's telling me. I wonder how much this prick knows about the shooting and the mugging? This guy's no angel of mercy. He's here to spy on me, not protect me.

'What's your name?'

'Roque sir, Lieutenant Roque of the Western Police Division.'

Conway released him and hauled him outside the house. 'Ok *Lieutenant* Roque, as I said, you can go back to your boss and tell him I am doing fine here. I am quite safe and I *don't* need his *or* your protection, ok?'

Roque shrugged, his head down 'ok sir.'

'And lieutenant Roque.'

'Yes sir.'

'If I see you following me again, YOU are the one who will need protection, understand?' Roque nodded and said nothing, but the impassive expression could not hide the hate in his eyes. He limped to the end of the alley and stood looking balefully at Conway for a moment then spat into the ground at his feet. Conway ignored the gesture and waited until he was out of sight before heading in the opposite direction through the palm trees to the other side of the island.

A fifteen minute walk brought him out onto a narrow, white sandy beach where a strong, breeze was blowing whitecaps across to the province of Aklan on the mainland a couple of miles away. He'd been told the world sailboarding championships were held here each January and he could see why. The strait acted as a kind of wind tunnel perfect for windsurfing and sailboarding. He strolled along in the shallows breathing in the cool, fresh air.

Apart from the pleasant murmur of the wind it was quiet except for the occasional cry of a seagull swooping down to the waves for a meal. He walked along slowly enjoying the solitude until he came to a branch of a palm tree at right angles to the trunk and about three feet from the ground. He sat on the branch and gazed out across the sea to mountains of Aklan and began to reflect on what had brought him to this beautiful tropical island far from the place he called home.

As a young man from Christmas Creek the small country town in Queensland he had come to Brisbane, the State capital, to find work. A series of dead-end jobs finally found him as a bar manager in a South Brisbane Hotel. He enjoyed the work and the interaction with the customers and for a while it seemed he was destined to stay but the daily grind became boring and he craved something more exciting than serving drunks and breaking up their fights. The Army offered an answer.

He enlisted at Enoggera barracks and eschewed the officer training course preferring to become a 'digger' in Infantry. Initial intensive training at Puckapunyal was followed by even more rigorous training, in jungle warfare at Canungra then exercises at Shoalwater Bay. The Army turned him into a fit, skilled, infantry man. The Army also decided he needed experience, so they assigned him to 4 RAR, Fourth Battalion Royal Australian Regiment in Malaysia. Twelve months later he was transferred to 1RAR and sent to Vietnam where they were attached to the American 173rd Airborne Brigade, *The Big Red One* at Bien Hoa on Saigon's northern rim. When the Australian Task Force eventually arrived, 1RAR joined them at Nui Dat in Phuoc Tuy province located between Saigon and Vung Tau on the coast.

Somehow he survived two tours of duty, the second as a forward scout, the most dangerous position in the platoon. Many of his mates didn't. He became disillusioned on his return to Australia where he learnt not to speak of his service in Vietnam. He encountered antagonism and indifference to the war among people he once called friends. He'd been decorated but refused to wear the medal. The end result was a previously happy and carefree individual became moody and withdrawn seeking only the company of other returned soldiers with whom he served.

Despite the dangers of the job he had enjoyed being a soldier with its camaraderie and team spirit. In Vietnam many of the locals in Phuoc Tuy province, had liked and respected the efforts of the Australians as they went about their work, much to the chagrin of the enemy.

In addition to protecting the populace by stopping Viet Cong incursions and harassing them with night ambushes and frequent patrols, the Australians helped with rebuilding villages and other infrastructure destroyed by the VC. Sincere friendships had been formed between the locals and many of the soldiers. He later found it difficult to reconcile the gentle kindness of many Vietnamese he had known with the harsh, cynical attitudes of those back home.

For many months he kept to himself reliving his experiences at night, kept awake by nightmares and thoughts of mates he'd lost. His mind was a maelstrom of bitterness and despair. What had it been all about? Why did so many good men need to die? What was *his* life about now? It all just didn't make sense. He became in turn angry, moody, incredibly frustrated and began to drink heavily to drive away the demons; but that only made things worse. His parents had passed away and his only sister had married and gone to live in England.

With no one to turn to he could feel his life slipping into oblivion. His country didn't want him; his friends avoided him; no one cared. His future looked bleak. In a very low moment he considered suicide. Then something wonderful happened: He met Jane!

Jimmy, an old retired Army friend knew of Conway's condition and in an effort to try to bring his mate out of it, had convinced him to attend a barbecue. Conway went reluctantly with the intention of showing up, then leaving as soon as possible.

It was held in a large, modern brick home complete with well-tended lawns and a swimming pool in a leafy Brisbane suburb. Jimmy had been one of Conway's instructors before he went to Vietnam. They had got on well and kept in touch while he was at war. Jimmy a long serving officer had retired while Steve was overseas and was now living well on an army pension.

When Conway arrived that afternoon, he immediately felt out of place. Jimmy greeted him like a long lost friend but apart from his Army mate there was not a soul Conway knew so he found a place by the beer keg and proceeded to try and drink it dry. Fortunately, he was on only his third beer when a bright female voice beside him said, 'hey, I don't think I know you.' He turned to see a very attractive 20 something woman, slim with short dark hair and a flashing smile.

'Like to get me a beer stranger?' she grinned, handing him a glass. 'And by the way, my name's Jane.' He was taken aback by her assertiveness but her smile and cheerful manner snapped him out of his mood. He took the glass and poured her a beer. 'You look like you've done that before,' she said, as he handed her the beer. He attempted a smile but it failed and came out as a crooked grin. He was never much good at chatting to women and this good looking lady made him feel uncomfortable.

'Yeah, I've poured a few in the past. My name's Steve.'

'Jane, nice to meet you Steve, what brings you here? Who do you know? I haven't seen you at any of these soirees before.'

'Jimmy and I are old friends, we go back a long way.' He was about to mention they had met in the Army but thought better of it. They began the kind of small talk that happens between strangers who have met for the first time at a party. General stuff about the state of the weather the local sporting events skating over politics and their backgrounds. Conway kept his deliberately vague. Jane's smile was infectious, her personality warm and engaging. She was unpretentious and easy to talk to. He began to relax for the first time in many months.

Jane was a Brisbane girl working as a nurse in the intensive care unit of the Brisbane General hospital. She added that it was one of her regrets she didn't finish her training in time to serve in Vietnam. Conway said nothing in response to this, but remembered with affection the treatment given by the Australian Army nurses at their hospital in Vung Tau. He had been slightly wounded on an operation and had spent a few days there under their tender and cheerful care. Jane, with her bright, happy personality would have fitted in very well.

'Hey you two, there's a barbecue here,' called Jimmy, 'come and have some tucker. Jane, has our hero been regaling you with his adventures in Vietnam? He was decorated you know.' Jane's eyebrows shot up in surprise. 'You were there?' she exclaimed, nearly dropping the plate Jimmy had handed to her.

Conway shrugged his shoulders and became ill-at-ease. 'Yes, but I don't talk about it... most people don't want to know.'

'Hey, well I do.' She gave him another of those wonderful smiles. 'Come on Steve, let's sit over here and please tell me all about it.'

For the next hour he told her of his experiences in Phuoc Thuy but as soldiers do, tended to make light of it. She sat there hanging on ever word. For the first time he was able to talk about Vietnam without feeling guilty. Jimmy broke it up when he put on some lively music and with Jane's urging, a reluctant Conway joined her on the tiled patio by the swimming pool. Night had fallen and after some energetic jiving, couples were dancing cheek to cheek.

Conway had almost forgotten how wonderful it was to hold the soft, warm body of a woman. He breathed in the sweetness of Jane's perfume and pulled her in close...and she did not resist. He left near midnight feeling happier than he had in years.

They arranged to meet for lunch the following day and this led to many more lunches, dinners and days together at the Gold Coast where he found she was as keen on surfing as he was. Her irrepressible good humour and caring nature took him out of himself and he found himself missing her if they were apart for even one day. It seemed that she felt the same way.

Four months after they first met, they married in a quiet ceremony attended by a few close friends. Conway found a job as night manager at a top-class inner Brisbane hotel while Jane continued at the Brisbane General Hospital.

Her love had saved him and he was the happiest he had ever been; a wonderful woman, a great job and a future to look forward too. His joy knew no bounds when one day she announced she was pregnant and nine months later into the world came a gorgeous little bundle they named, Amy. Jane gave up work to care for the baby and Steve, the devoted husband, became a very doting father. Life was perfect!

Then one night at work he had a visit from two policemen.

Gently they informed him that there had been a motor vehicle accident involving his wife and daughter. They had been hit by a drunk driver as they were returning from a shopping trip. It was close to Christmas and Conway remembered that Jane had told him she was taking Amy to see the lights and Christmas decorations in the city and would buy her some new booties and baby clothes.

For a moment he couldn't comprehend what the policemen were telling him but the looks on their faces said it all. He stood there stunned, NO! IT COULD NOT BE! NOT MY BELOVED JANE AND MY BEAUTIFUL AMY. NO! NO! NO!

The next days were a blur. He walked around like a zombie. Fortunately Jimmy came to his aid and helped with funeral arrangements. The funeral was attended by the small close group of friends and a few Army mates. He couldn't stand to be in the house where there were too many memories. Everywhere he looked he saw Jane and little Amy, photos, mementos, clothing, toys, paraphernalia which reminded him of what had been the happiest days of his life, now cruelly taken from him.

He had to get away so he took off for the Outback in a four wheel drive and spent the next few years travelling and working itinerant jobs in Western Queensland and the Northern Territory. On his return to Brisbane he rented an apartment while he considered his future.

One day he noticed in *The Courier Mail*, an advertisement for a manager of a hotel in Manila. Australia held too many bad memories so he applied, got the job and here he was a few months later sitting on a beautiful island in the Philippines, a different world, but the memories were still there.

The shadows were beginning to lengthen and by now the breeze had become cooler so he walked back along the beach until he came to the track which brought him there and with vivid sights and sounds of Jane and Amy on his mind, headed back to White beach.

\* \* \*

'Geez Bert's gunna be eatin' through a straw for a while Mullet,' chuckled Biro, taking a swig of his ever-present San Mig.

'Yeah, I heard he was done over good and proper. They reckon there must have been half a dozen of 'em, the state Bert's in mate,' replied Mullet. 'But I don't think old Bert will be telling us much about it for a long time, his ugly mug is wrapped in bandages, he looks like an Egyptian mummy, ha ha ha.'

Biro scratched his head then looked at his bottle of San Mig as if waiting for Divine guidance. 'Mate, do y' reckon, it might have been some payback for what he done to Conway?' Mullet paused, his Scotch half way to his mouth, 'Ah, could be mate, but I doubt it, Conway doesn't know who bashed him, I reckon it was probably some of the local hoods. They know old Bert often carries money on him, silly bugger. It was bound to happen one day.'

Sally was nearby with her back to them washing glasses listening intently to their conversation. It gave her some comfort to know that Groyne's two closest friends didn't suspect revenge and the word would get around that it was a random mugging.

She knew only too well who was responsible and although she was no fan of Groyne, and hated what he had done to Conway, she abhorred violence and couldn't condone what had been done to him. She just hoped Conway was not aware of what had happened to Groyne. Not yet anyway. As Biro and Mullet continued to discuss Groyne's assault, Sally's thoughts turned to Conway. He was on Boracay, at least he was safe there. I wonder what he's doing now...

\* \* \*

Boracay was bathed in a magnificent sunset. A ball of orange flame drifted slowly to the horizon through crimson and magenta clouds, sending shimmering streams of gold across a sea now indigo in the fading light as

Conway stopped at a small, simple restaurant on the beach for dinner.

He looked around for a good spot and found one at a small table, not twenty metres from the water's edge. Almost immediately, another of Boracay's charming young waitresses in a rainbow coloured top and white shorts appeared and stood smiling patiently as he perused the menu.

He ordered chicken paprika with rice and a San Miguel beer. *"Malamig"* beer please miss,' he said, handing her the menu. 'Our beer is *always* cold sir,' she said with a coquettish smile taking the menu from him holding his hand a fraction too long, before heading back across the sand to the kitchen.

He sat back, kicked off his sandals and wriggled his toes in the cool sand. How good is this? He closed his eyes enjoying the sheer bliss of the moment. Locals were lighting lamps attached to palm trees along the beach adding intimacy to an already romantic atmosphere. The same waitress returned with his beer and lit the candle on his table favouring him with another beautiful smile. He smiled to himself. Have I died and gone to Heaven?

A mix of Filipino and foreign holiday makers wandered along the beach. Most were families with children, a few couples arm in arm oblivious of all but each other, a smattering of vendors and local kids squealing and chasing each other added to a carefree holiday scene. A major attraction appeared when several boatmen hauled in their day's catch and were surrounded by a crowd eager to see what bounty the sea had bestowed on the island that day.

Conway watched all this with a contented smile and wondered how he might stay there forever. His daydreaming was interrupted by the charming waitress arriving with his food.

'Enjoy your meal sir,' she smiled, 'if there is anything else you need please call me,' she said with the emphasis on *anything*. He looked up at her and their eyes held for a long moment. 'Thank you, I will,' he grinned and then suddenly realized what an edge the fresh sea air and relaxed environment had given to his appetite.

The food was delicious, the beer ice cold and he attacked both with gusto. What a life Steve old son, you could take a lot of this. He ordered another beer and thought about his next move. What to do now? Might have a look at what the night life has to offer, check out a few places and maybe have an early night, it had been a long day.

He was almost finished his beer when a voice behind him said, 'may I join you sir?' He swivelled around and nearly fell off his chair. 'Hello Lily…'

# 16

Danny Roque sat brooding over his beer. It was late afternoon. He was sitting in a small beer bar well away from the tourist strip where the booze was far too expensive for him on his meagre cop's salary.

He had lost count of the bottles he'd consumed and with each bottle his hatred for Conway increased. I will kill that *gago* (bastard) and to hell with Sanchez. I will do it without his permission. I hate that arrogant *gago* too, he treats me like a serf. Anyway he should be happy, that's what he wants. I hate that white *gago* he will pay for what he did to me. I will kill him. He won't leave this island alive.

\* \* \*

Perc and Imelda Prickett sat with Ramon Sanchez in Perc's office discussing Conway and various other activities of mutual interest. Perc had arrived back from Hong Kong the day before and copped an earbashing from Imelda for hanging up on her in Hong Kong but quickly diffused it by producing a diamond and ruby necklace of such brilliance that Imelda, who wasn't used to such largesse from her husband, was blown away and it put Perc immediately back in her good books...for now.

'What's the latest on Conway, Colonel?' asked Perc, puffing on a pipe he'd bought in Hong Kong. It had occurred to him that a pipe might add a bit of class and sophistication to his image. It didn't. He now looked a bigger goose than ever.

'I have a man on him in Boracay, one of my best officers watching his every move. We are in complete control of the situation,' smirked Sanchez.

'Yeah, you had it under control last time too, and look what happened,' grunted Perc taking a deep draw on his pipe which nearly choked him. Imelda jumped up, grabbed the pipe and pumped his back until the coughing stopped and a red-faced, gasping Perc slumped back in his chair. She threw the pipe into the trash can under Perc's desk; end of the new sophisticated image.

'As you were saying Colonel?'

The policeman had watched this little pantomime with a mixture of amusement and despair. 'How did I ever get mixed up with these two?' He said under his breath.

'Yes, we tracked Conway to Boracay and my man has had him under close surveillance ever since. He cannot go anywhere, meet anyone, do anything that we don't know about. My man is under strict instructions to report regularly and *immediately* if he moves off the island. As I said, we have everything under control…and we have…' he stopped as if he realized he had said too much, then continued, 'but what do you people want to do about him? He really is your problem.'

Perc had recovered his composure and looked at Sanchez, then Imelda, his beady eyes gleamed. 'I have an idea which will get him off our back for the time being while we decide exactly what to do with him.' Sanchez leaned closer and Imelda's penciled eyebrows shot up. What's this? Perc with an original thought?

Now it was Prickett's turn to smirk.

'Before Conway arrived, our company opened another operation in Bangkok, a bar and restaurant in partnership with a prominent Thai family. It's right in the heart of Bangkok in Patpong 1. It's a straight joint and we ain't sellin' sheilas,' he went on, 'and yeah, I admit that's a drawback, but the Aussie shareholders won't have a bar of any funny business. The problem is… it should be trading better.'

'I think the manager has been sittin' on the lap of too many of the local girls instead of doing his job and we aren't gettin' the financial reports we should be and the Aussie boys are screamin' their heads off.' 'So,' Perc paused, 'I think we should send Conway there for a few weeks to straighten the joint out and he can take Susan, the accountant to sort out the reporting. That'll get him out of our hair and allow us to do that "other thing" we've been talking about, and who knows, we might be able to pin something on him there. Whaddya reckon?' Perc sat back with a smug grin as if he had just given them a plan that would change the course of world events.

Sanchez thought for a moment mulling over Prickett's words. 'Mmmm…I think that's a good idea Mr Prickett. As you know we are about to receive a shipment of "presents" from our friends and since you told me about Conway's investigation of that bank account, it is a real cause for concern,' frowned the police chief. 'We need time to distribute the goods, launder funds and…set up something else.' He paused, nodding his head, looking at Perc then Imelda. 'With him away it would be the ideal time to do it.'

'I agree, the sooner the better,' chimed in Imelda. 'He can go as soon as he comes back from Boracay.' The meeting broke up and after Sanchez left, Imelda told Perc what she had organized with Eduardo. Perc was not impressed.

'He's a fuckin' dropkick, yeah I know he's a relative but he'll fuck it up for sure! He's not even a good thief! Couldn't you have picked someone with at least half a brain,' raged Perc, head down, waving his arms and walking around in circles.

'Where's me fuckin' pipe? He's as useful as a boil on my arse…jeez!'

Imelda watched all this unmoved. She'd seen it all before and it didn't matter what Perc said, she was going to use Eduardo anyway. He was the only one in her family who wouldn't squeal if things went wrong, he was dispensable and would be eliminated if necessary.

'Calm down and go and have a beer with your friends,' she said. It was an order rather than a request. Perc knew she wouldn't take any notice of him but he felt good just letting off steam and it gave him a thirst. He gave up looking for his pipe and headed for the bar.

\* \* \*

Conway stood up and staggered back as Lily threw her arms around him and planted a passionate kiss full on his lips. She was all smiles and cleavage and looked set for another attack when he grinned and pointed to a chair next to his. 'Hey, hey, calm down, it's great to see you but again, how did you know I was here?'

'Oh darling, I rang your hotel and they told me you had gone to Boracay for a few days so I thought I would come down here to surprise you…aren't you happy to see me darling?'

Conway frowned, but didn't say anything. I told them I was not to be disturbed, but well, it *is* Lily, so I guess there are always exceptions. Lily took his frown for displeasure.

She bridled for an instant. 'Oh, were you expecting that *other* woman?'

'I wasn't expecting anyone but yes, of course I'm happy to see you Lily, it's just a surprise, you were the last person I expected,' he said, waving a waitress over.

'What would you like to drink?'

She checked the cocktail list and ordered a frozen daiquiri. She looked across at Conway. Her smile had disappeared.

'Well, are you *really* happy to see me Steve?' There was an edge to her voice.

'Lily, I am delighted to see you,' he reached over and squeezed her hand. 'This is a wonderful surprise. I mean it,' he said sincerely.

Despite his misgivings he *was* glad to see her. She looked so bloody sexy, who wouldn't be glad to have her company on a romantic island like Boracay?

'I was just wondering what to do tonight and now you have just solved the problem. You can have dinner here with me and we can explore the night life together. What do you say?'

The smile returned. 'I would be delighted darling, do you like my outfit?' she asked standing and pirouetting.

Her long coal black hair hung unfettered just below her shoulders. She was wearing a white, cross-halter top which was simply two strips of silk split to the waist only partly covering her big breasts, allowing them to spill out a little from each side of the material. Her nipples were large round shadows beneath the silk. There was very little at the front and nothing at the back. Designed for maximum effect, it was set off by skin-tight pink capris and sandals.

She looked very, very, sexy...and knew it. She had become the centre of more than a few admiring and lusting eyes from other male diners, all envious of Conway.

He looked up and smiled appreciatively. 'You are as sensational as ever Lily darling. Now, what is *your* pleasure?' he said, handing her the menu.

'You know what *my* pleasure is darling,' she laughed. He ordered another beer from the same waitress whose radiant smile was now missing. Lily perused the menu for an age, finally settling for pork adobo, crispy pata and rice to go with her frozen daiquiri.

He studied her as she ate; daintily as a woman of refinement does, carefully choosing each morsel before placing it in her mouth. She was indeed a beautiful woman and in the soft glow of lamps from nearby palm trees she was as desirable as any woman he had ever seen.

The shoulder length, onyx hair framing the high cheekbones of her face with the huge black eyes beneath delicate long lashes all set off by the bright, cherry of her lipstick, and that body! To hell with the night life! He wanted to take her back to his little room immediately she had finished her meal but decorum demanded (he told himself) he should at least make some effort to show her what a Boracay evening had to offer.

He had several more beers, she matched him with daiquiris. By the time they left the restaurant both had a warm glow. They strolled along the beach hand in hand before heading up to the sandy track where most of the bars, accommodation, restaurants and a couple of discos were located.

They stopped at a small open bar with a thatched roof and sipped drinks watching the passing parade. It was not high season but there was still a big enough crowd to keep the local restaurants and bar owners happy.

They struck up a conversation with a good looking French doctor probably mid forties named Jacques and his beautiful blonde wife Claudine, a petite, voluptuous Brigitte Bardot lookalike. They were both bronzed and looked as if they had spent all their life in the sun. It was their first visit to Boracay and were blown away its beauty.

A bedazzled Jacques spoke of trying to buy property there.

'I have seen many islands similar to zis throughout the world,' he enthused, 'but zis is zee best I have seen, it is zee way I always imagined a tropical island to be.' Claudine was just as enthusiastic. She and Lily hit it off at once and chatted animatedly as if they had known each other for years. They made quite a contrast, Lily, the busty brunette Asian goddess, well matched, Conway noted, in the chest department, by the deeply tanned, blonde French bombshell. The way Claudine held Jacques hand and kept gazing lovingly at him indicated they hadn't been married long.

'You both look so tanned and healthy,' said Conway, 'you must spend a lot of your time in the sun?'

'Ah yes,' replied Jacques, 'we are what you would call, sun worshippers, non?' we love zee sun and beach. We sunbathe every chance we get and -'

'We love to go *au naturel,*' interrupted Claudine with a cheeky smile directed at Lily. 'Perhaps you would like to join us one day but,' she paused, 'maybe you do not like to sunbathe naked Lily?' There was no mistaking the inherent challenge in the sexy French woman's question.

'What do you think Lily?' grinned Conway. 'Are we game?'

'Of course, I love the sun on my body too. I have a pool at my home and we love to swim and sunbake nude don't we darling?'

'Huh...er yes we do,' replied Conway, a little taken aback. He was well aware, like most Asian women, Lily went to great lengths to protect her skin from the sun but a competitive woman, she was not about to reject the challenge.

'I would love to sunbake *au naturel* with you Claudine, I think it would be...interesting,' said Lily, her smile now a little forced. For a few seconds the atmosphere became a little tense between the two beautiful women as they looked each other up and down. The competition was unmistakable.

'Oo la la, my *cherie* and your Lily sunbathing nude would be quite a sight to see don't you think *mon ami?*'

'Please my Jacques, you may be a doctor but I think seeing Lily and I naked might be too much for your blood pressure.' They all laughed...except Lily.

'We can do this but we will have to find a remote beach otherwise we will offend the locals. Their culture forbids nude bathing.'

'Ah,' replied the Frenchman, 'I am sure we can find somewhere on zis beautiful island and not disturb zee locals. What do you say? Will tomorrow be ok at this bar, at say 10.00 am?'

'Sure,' agreed Conway. Jacques was right. The thought of Claudine and Lily naked engendered all kinds of visions, every one of them, lustful. They ordered champagne and after several glasses, Lily and Claudine relaxed again, gave each other hugs and resumed their friendly chat. Jacques and Conway discussed world events and each other's respective jobs then with final raucous toasts to each other, the Philippines, and undying friendship, the French couple left arm in arm back to their accommodation.

Conway and Lily continued their tour until drawn to Latin music blasting out of a disco just off the beach track.

'Darling, it sounds wonderful. I'm in the mood to dance,' she laughed, pulling Conway into the disco. It was a simple open-sided place about twenty metres square with a dark tiled floor, a simple thatched bar in one corner and a skinny young guy in a Hawaiian shirt too big for him, controlling the music from a small stage opposite. There were several couples bopping and jiving to the booming beat of a South American group with maracas, bongos, congas, panpipes and guitars belting out a hot rhythm. Lily sashayed onto the dance floor and immediately all eyes were upon her.

The daiquiris had taken effect and to say she danced with "wild abandon" was an understatement. She swayed, shimmied and pirouetted, her arms sometimes above her head thrusting her body in overt, wanton sexual abandon, to the delight of the watching males and the chagrin of the females. Her body gleamed in the soft disco lights adding to the eroticism of her performance. There wasn't a man in that disco who didn't wish Conway would disappear so they could try their luck with this exotic creature.

Finally, breasts heaving, body bathed in sweat, she stopped and threw her arms around Conway and planted a kiss full on his lips which pissed the watching males off even more. But there was one male standing in the dark at the back who never took his eyes off Conway.

It was after midnight when they decided to leave. Arm in arm they walked back to Conway's humble abode but one look was enough for her to insist he come to where she was staying at a resort called *Crystal Sands*.

'It's within easy walking distance darling,' she assured him.

*Crystal Sands* was one of the few on the island with its own generator and by Boracay's standards was luxurious. It consisted of ten villas fronting a kidney shaped swimming pool glowing emerald in the darkness from underwater lamps. She had difficulty opening her door and passed him the key. They entered a room of white marble floors, soft mood lighting and dark narra furniture. It was a veritable palace compared to Conway's modest dwelling.

A floor to ceiling bay window faced the ocean. Heavy pink drapes closed off the rest of the world if necessary. The cream walls were hung with original oils by Filipino artists, and the *piece de resistance was* king-size bed dominating the centre of the room beside a refrigerator, TV and telephone and curiously, a mirror in the ceiling above the bed.

'Make yourself comfortable darling, while I have a shower. There's beer and spirits in the ref.'

The refrigerator was well stocked with a variety of beers, whisky, brandy, vodka and small bottles of liqueurs but he selected a can of ice cold San Miguel and sat by the window looking out into the inky blackness broken only by the winking lights of a number of fishing vessels far out at sea.

She finished her shower and ten minutes later, (how come it takes women so long to actually come out of the bathroom once they've finished?) she emerged in an outfit that made him nearly swallow the can. It was designed to shock and excite. It did an admirable job of both. She *nearly* had on a white, thigh length, see-through low cut silk negligee which made him wonder why she bothered to wear it at all.

'You like?' she grinned evilly.

'My God Lily!' was all he could come up with, well not all...there were other things rising too.

'Ah...er... I'm going to have a shower too.' He cursed under his breath. 'Why didn't I have one with her? I could have killed two birds with one stone.' It was one of the quickest showers he had ever taken. He nearly ripped the bathroom door off its hinges in his haste to join her.

She had turned off the main light and the room was now lit only by the pink glow of the bedside lamp. He rubbed his hands in anticipation. Lily lay on her back, arms behind her head offering her body to him. The only problem was...her eyes were closed, her mouth was wide open, and she was snoring...loudly.

He stood there aghast, his heart and other things dropped immediately. The daiquiris and the dancing had taken their toll. He kept looking at her as he slowly dressed wishing her to wake, but nothing would have brought her round; she was completely out of it. He bent down and gave her a peck on the cheek, turned off the light and left, closing the door quietly behind him.

\* \* \*

Roque had shadowed them all night. From the time Conway ordered his first beer at the beachside restaurant until they left the disco. It had been easy under the cover of darkness and he had allowed himself a few libations along the way. He watched from behind a palm tree as they went into her room at *Crystal Sands.*

He took another sip from his bottle of beer and pondered his next move. Should he wait or should he leave? He had seen them stop for a couple of minutes outside Conway's room then move on to *Crystal Sands.* He decided to wait. He sat down and lay against a palm tree with his beer in one hand and an evil looking switchblade in the other. Conway never noticed the short, fat figure asleep at the foot of a palm tree as he went past on the way back to his room.

\* \* \*

Jack Roberts sat gazing out of his window in the Australian embassy high above the tower blocks and high rise buildings of Makati, the commercial hub of Manila. The discordant jangle of his telephone brought him out of his reverie.

'Yeah, Robert's here whose this?' he asked crankily when there was no immediate response from the other end. It was Nonoy a local informant. A nervous guy when it came to talking to policemen. He had a lot to lose, like his life, if certain individuals knew of his association with Roberts.

'G'day Nonoy, whaddya got for me mate? What? Really? Ah, Yeah, What! Who told you? When? Where? Yeah, you're sweet. Yeah, I know, don't worry, I forgive you for not getting to me first on the Conway bashing but you've redeemed yourself me old China. Yeah, ok, see me at the usual place at five o'clock and I'll fix you up, yeah, thanks, ok see you later, bye.'

The big detective leaned back in his chair thinking about what Nonoy had told him. Ah, so Mr Conway had run foul of a local bar owner. I warned you Steve my boy you have to be very careful in these parts, but it seems the guy responsible is in hospital. Bit of a coincidence that…must ask Conway what he knows about it next time I see him.

The other piece of news he'd been given was of more interest to Roberts.

There was a suspicion of a drug shipment coming through the port soon, thought to be on a Panamanian freighter. Apparently little else was known at this stage but the word around was that Sanchez or someone close to him could be involved. He leant over and picked up his phone.

'G'day Chuck, how are you mate? Won't waste your time mate, but just got word about a possible big drug bust coming off soon through the port. Know anything about it?' There was a long pause before McGaw replied.

'Well…ah…as a matter of fact, we hadn't heard about that one but, you know this town, rumours abound. Could be just scuttlebutt and as you know,' McGaw couldn't resist a dig. 'We usually hear these things first if they are legit.'

'Not this time champ,' said Roberts triumphantly. 'I'm sure my source is right on the money. When I get the details I'll let you know and we can collaborate on this one, might just help your promotion, ha ha ha…'

'Yeah, very funny Jack, but seriously, please let me know and sure, we'll be only too happy to get involved, How about we have a beer tonight and you can fill me in with what you know and in the meantime I'll have my spies check things out…ok?'

'Sure Chuck, see you at our usual meeting place at 6 o'clock.'

* * *

Lily had not long been awake when Conway knocked on her door the next morning. She let him in with a tired and embarrassed smile.

'I'm so sorry darling for last night, will you forgive me?' she said embracing him. Her body felt soft and warm. She felt sensational.

'Darling, I haven't showered yet, care to join me?'

He needed no second bidding. Seconds later, they stood glued together under a cold refreshing stream in her white tiled shower wrapped in a passionate embrace. It lasted so long when they broke away; she slumped against him almost exhausted. She lifted her arms and he began to soap her body from head to toe, stopping on the way down to pay particular attention to parts of her anatomy which caused her to stiffen with intakes of breath. 'Naughty boy,' she giggled, tapping him lightly on the head. She let the strong jet wash the soap from her body then, giving him that evil little grin, it was her turn.

She soaped him also starting at his head also stopping on the way down using her mouth to administer some joy, popular with men for centuries. He leaned back against the wall with a wide grin letting the shower wash over him as Lily went about her work.

When they had washed every part of each other's body sufficiently there was only one thing left to do...so they did it...till early afternoon. They lay there sated and exhausted until suddenly he sat bolt upright startling her.

'What's up darling?' she cried in alarm.

'Hey! We were supposed to meet the Frenchies on the beach this morning!'

'Oh darling, don't worry,' she said drowsily, 'from what I saw of them they're probably still in bed too, let's have a nap. Then I'll call room service.'

'Sounds good,' he turned to give her a kiss but she was already asleep. He looked at her, so peaceful and a wave of affection he hadn't felt for her before swept over him.

*You sure are something else Lily, they broke the mould when they made you and aren't I a lucky guy? Here I am on a beautiful tropical island with a gorgeous woman for company, and not a care in the world, well not at the moment anyway. As they used to say in Australia, you wouldn't be dead for quids.*

Meanwhile, Roque sat in a bar having a 'hair of the dog' and cursing himself for falling asleep. *But I still have time to kill him and this time there'll be no mistake* he muttered to himself.

* * *

'Sawasdee krup, Khun Somchai, Prickett here, how are things in sunny Bangkok?' Perc leaned back in his chair and put his feet up on the desk. Imelda hated him doing that but she was in Makati spending his money so he knew he was safe. He listened while Somchai the Thai partner in the Bangkok enterprise, brought him up to date with the latest goings on in *The City of Angels*. Somchai was *very* displeased with *Rusty* Gates the manager Perc had sent to run the Thai operation.

'He is never in the place Khun Percy,' moaned Somchai in his clipped Harvard-educated English. 'I am very sorry but I don't think we can keep him here. He spends all his time in the bars of Patpong II when he should be at work. I would not mind Khun Percy if he went at night occasionally, but he is there from when they open at 10 o'clock in the morning. I am not paying him to do that! Where did you get this guy from? He is useless, and all the staff are very upset. I am losing face Khun Percy. You have to do something about this and do it quickly!' he pleaded.

'Khun Somchai don't worry, I will solve the problem for you. You know me, I always come up with the answers don't I?' There was a long silence. 'Well,' spluttered Perc, 'most of the time anyway.' 'Look Khun Somchai (why do I have to call him bloody Khun all the time?) I have the answer for you,' said Perc soothingly.

'What do you propose Khun Percy apart from kicking this guy out?'

'I am going to send one of our senior managers over to sort things out for you. He is an Australian named Conway. He is very efficient and knows the business. I am sure you will find him excellent and I am positive he will do the job.'

'He's another Australian? I hope he doesn't drink as much as Gates. His bar tab is *more* than our best customer. In fact he *IS* our best customer, on the rare occasion he does come in, except he doesn't pay for anything! I hope you're right about this Conway, Khun Percy,' said Somchai doubtfully.

'No worries I promise you. He'll be over in about a week. And I'm gonna send our accountant Susan Santos to straighten your books out too. I'll phone you just before they leave. Put them up in the Montien Hotel for a few days then downgrade 'em to some flea pit ok?'

'Ok, Khun Percy,' replied Somchai, his tone indicating he was not convinced that Perc had the answer. Past experience had shown the Thai that Perc Prickett was unpredictable, unreliable and something Thais abhorred…an extremely untidy individual; a trait which to Thais, meant an untidy mind.

Perc leaned back in his chair with a self-satisfied smile. Well, that gets rid of Conway for a while and with a bit of luck he won't make it back from Bangkok.

# 17

Conway and Lily caught up with the French couple at the same bar they had met the night before and there were kisses and hugs all round although Steve balked a little when Jacques planted a couple on him.

'Sorry we missed you on the beach this morning, we were looking forward to that but we ah, kind of got involved in 'other things',' said Conway with a huge grin. Jacques looked at Lily and smiled knowingly. 'Ah, with zis beautiful creature I can understand you not wanting to waste time on a little sunbathing,' he replied, his eyes roaming over Lily's abundant body spilling out of a low cut, pale pink silk blouse and thigh-length hot pink mini skirt.

'My friends, zis is our last night in Boracay,' exclaimed Jacques holding Lily a tad too long, 'and we would like to invite you to be our guests at dinner... oui?'

'Thank you Jacques, that is most generous of you, we'd be honoured wouldn't we Lily?'

'Of course, that's lovely thank you,' beamed Lily, giving Jacques another kiss while the tanned, sexy Claudine, stunning in a brief, body hugging all white outfit, not to be outdone by Lily, took the opportunity to do the same to Conway. With Jacques leading the way, they strolled down a sandy track lit by oil lamps toward boat station two until they came to another beachside restaurant called *Neptune*.

'I hope you like seafood my friends, because here it is *magnifique*,' smiled Jacques as they were welcomed by the *Maitre D*, a handsome, middle-aged Filipino named Manny, wearing the traditional *Barong*.

*Neptunes* befitting its name was decorated in a nautical theme. Tables were set with cloths showing King Neptune sitting on a throne with all manner of sea creatures including whales, fish, turtles, octopi and a shark or two at his feet. The waitresses were dressed accordingly in skimpy bras and short skirts featuring tropical motifs of red, green, blue and yellow. It seemed they were *Neptune's* mermaids.

It was agreed that champagne again was appropriate for this auspicious occasion, to be followed by the seafood platter, which Jacques assured them would be more than enough for all of them. He ordered a magnum of Krug, promptly served by the ever-smiling Manny in a gleaming, stainless steel ice bucket. They sat chatting, laughing and toasting each other beneath a sky ablaze with a million stars while Boracay worked its magic on a beautiful, balmy night. Lily leaned against Conway and squeezed his hand.

'This is so romantic darling I am soooo glad I came to Boracay,' she said leaning into Conway. He put his arm around her, 'not half as glad as I am Lily.'

The seafood platter arrived and Jacques had not been exaggerating. It looked and tasted magnificent! Piled high with succulent, freshly caught prawns, crabs, oysters and bugs, it had as a centrepiece, a huge steamed lobster in lemon butter sauce. Conway couldn't remember a better seafood meal even back in his native Queensland which prided itself on the quality of its cuisine from the sea. When the platter was a forlorn heap of bones and shells Conway got to his feet and raised his glass of champagne.

'Jacques and Claudine, you have done us proud, may you have a safe journey back to France and thank you again for this wonderful meal and your great company. I sincerely hope that we stay in touch. My dear friends, I toast you and I salute you.'

The French couple beamed and Jacques responded in kind promising to maintain the friendship and inviting them both to France.

'We have some beautiful beaches in France Lily my dear where you and Claudine can sunbathe *au naturel* without zee problem,' he said with a twinkle in his eye. This time Lily joined in the laughter. Then with more hugs and kisses, Conway and Lily reluctantly said their goodbyes and headed back along the lamp lit track toward her accommodation. Both now had a pleasant glow from the champagne and were determined that *this* night would be different. They stopped for an occasional quick kiss, oblivious of the figure in the shadows some distance behind.

Without warning, Lily pulled Conway into the darkness away from the lamp-lit track.

'I want you to fuck me darling,' she breathed into his ear. 'I've always wanted to be taken on the beach darling, please do it to me now.' Her body was glued to his and he could feel her breasts heaving against his chest. He bent to kiss her when he heard a twig snap. He sobered up immediately. His training as a forward scout in Vietnam kicked in. He froze and remained perfectly still for a few seconds then silently stepped away from Lily.

'Darling, what's wrong?' she cried. Bewildered and half drunk, she staggered backward and fell heavily. Her head hit a thick branch as she went down leaving her spreadeagled on her back stunned and unmoving.

Conway remained motionless. Someone was close, very close. He could hear the rasping breathing of someone creeping in his direction now only a few metres away. He knew whoever it was could not be sure exactly where *he* was. He moved silently to his left stepping slowly. He could see the dark outline now facing away from him. It stopped and bent forward as if listening.

Conway tapped the shadowy figure on the shoulder. It whirled around and Conway saw the gleam of a blade. He ducked to his left as the knife flashed past his right shoulder. He kicked out and caught his assailant between the legs as he made another lunge.

His assailant screamed and doubled up. Conway kicked him under the jaw but did not connect properly. The attacker stumbled and came again but slower. This time Conway was able to step to one side grab the wrist and twist it and at the same time sweep the guy's legs from under him. He continued to apply great pressure to the wrist and twisted the fingers back and the guy screamed dropping the knife as two fingers snapped with a sickening crack.

He dropped onto the chest and smashed his adversary's jaw from side to side repeatedly until there was no movement. Satisfied it was over, he stood up gasping for breath, his heart pumping so fast it threatened to burst from his chest. He staggered back and leaned against a palm tree. It was a few minutes before his emotions settled and his breath returned to normal. He picked up the knife and hurled it into the darkness and looked back again at his attacker.

The figure remained motionless on the ground. Conway's eyes had become accustomed to the darkness so he bent down and had a closer look. It was Roque! You bastard! You came to protect me, my arse! Then he remembered Lily. He scrambled over to where she lay now moaning softly.

'Stay there darling don't move, I'll be right back,' he whispered

He could see lights through the trees. He checked the still unconscious Roque then raced over to find several Filipinos having a drink at a small bar. He quickly explained the situation and while one took off to find a doctor, and a policeman, the other two hurried back with him bringing a thin rope, water and towels. Roque remained where he fell and woke screaming in pain when they tied his hands and feet. Conway sat Lily up, wiped her brow with a damp towel, gave her water and told her to sit still for the moment.

Fifteen minutes later the other Filipino arrived with a nurse. The local doctor she said, was on Aklan attending to patients. She checked Lily and told Conway all she needed was an aspirin and a good night's sleep. The police apparently were nowhere to be found but the Filipino guys assured Conway they would take care of Roque.

Conway thanked them and promised to buy them a beer the following day. They smiled their flashing Filipino smiles, shook Conway's hand and offered to escort him back to Lily's accommodation but Conway said it would not be necessary, and with a limping Lily holding his arm, walked her back to her room.

Once inside she showered, but the booze, excitement and drama of the night was too much for her. 'I'm so tired darling,' she said climbing into bed. She was asleep almost instantly. Conway gave her another peck on the cheek and left with the words *de javu* ringing in his ears.

Lily woke early next morning yawned, stretched and looked to find no Conway. She lay for a few minutes thinking, then picked up her bedside phone and dialed a Manila number.

* * *

Conway was awakened by loud banging on his door. He yawned, blinked and staggered to the door. He opened it to find two uniformed policemen.

'May we speak to you sir? It's about the incident last night,' said the older one, who by his bearing was obviously the senior of the two. Conway invited them in and while the junior officer took out a notebook and recorded the interview the senior asked a series of questions about the incident. Did he know his assailant? Did he know the assailant was a police officer? Was he aware this person was trying to protect him? Had he done anything to cause this attack? What was the reason for this attack and who caused it?

Conway told them all he knew and described in detail of the confrontation with Roque the day he arrived and observed that it was a funny way to protect someone by coming at them with a knife. The policeman was non-committal but said he would be sending a full report to Manila. Then he smiled, 'Enjoy the rest of your stay on our island Mr Conway, I hope your lady friend is ok now, good day to you sir.'

Conway breathed a sigh of relief. I wonder what they will do with Roque? Nasty little bugger. I hope he's out of my life now. He looked out the window to see another bright blue, Boracay day. Mmmm, time to have a shower and go to check on the delectable Lily.

\* \* \*

Ramon Sanchez slammed down the phone. That fool Roque, can he not do anything right? He defied me and went against my orders, he will pay for this! Sanchez leaned back in his chair and looked at the ceiling. Apart from being angry, he was also a worried man. The Roque fiasco was not the only thing on his mind.

He was being pressured by certain parties in the Port Authority for more money to allow the drug shipment in under threat of exposure and he had also heard a whisper that the Australian Federal police and American authorities had got wind of it.

The ship was almost in harbour, impossible to stop it now. There was a lot at stake. This was to be his last shipment before he retired and joined his family in the United States. It was vital that everything went smoothly, this one last time. But right now I had better find out more about this Roque incident. He picked up his phone and told the operator to put him through to a number on Boracay.

\* \* \*

Susan Santos looked up from her desk to see Eduardo standing at her door. She shivered involuntarily. 'What can I do for you Eduardo?' she said, trying to keep her voice level. Eduardo grinned showing yellowed, broken teeth which made her shiver again. From behind his back he produced a few sheets of A5 paper. 'Our time sheets from the kitchen *Ate*, I thought I would bring them to you this month, Esteban is busy, and,' he leaned over her desk and covered her small right hand with his left, 'it gives me the chance to see you *Ate* because I think you are very *maganda.*(beautiful).' Susan withdrew her hand immediately, unable to hide her look of disdain. His touch made her skin crawl.

He looked down at her first with surprise then scarcely concealed rage. Who does she think she is? Just because she is the accountant, does she think she is better than me, one day I will show her! My relatives are her boss I can have her sacked like I have others. He turned to leave then stopped and said, 'do you know when Mr Conway will be back *Ate?*'

'No I do not Eduardo, why do you ask?' replied Susan, her tone brisk and businesslike. What business was it of Eduardo's? The little cook controlled his temper and gave her one of his wheedling smiles. 'Oh, it's just that I like Mr Conway and miss him,' he lied. The truth was he hoped Conway would drown on Boracay or some other misfortune would befall him so he would not be given the job of killing him.

Susan pretended she didn't hear the last comment and put her head down and continued her work. She wished Conway would come back, soon. She needed to tell him what she knew...urgently! Eduardo got the hint and slunk off.

\* \* \*

'Darling, I am sorry but this is my last day, I can't leave my restaurant for too long. You know what happens when the cat's away,' said Lily.

'Well, we better make this a day to remember?' Conway replied, his lips roaming across her naked body.

'I thought we were already doing that darling,' she giggled.

'This is just a start sexy one,' he grinned, his tongue drawing circles around a large pink, distended nipple. She started to writhe and moan as his tongue continued to journey between her breasts, teasing one then the other. She took his head in her hands and forced it between her legs. Her body erupted as she felt his tongue enter her most private part.

'Oh God! That's so wonderful!' She moaned, 'please stay there darling,' and he did. They continued to rock and roll for another couple of hours then, deciding it was time for some sustenance, rang room service.

A handsome young man in a gaily coloured tropical shirt, snow white shorts and a cheeky smile, wheeled in a trolley with a large silver pot of coffee and a huge bowl of fruit containing mangoes, pineapple, bananas, strawberries and grapes. Conway had ordered a hamburger and chips while Lily settled for chicken adobo and rice.

'Making love always gives me an appetite darling,' she cooed, tucking into the adobo as if it was to be her last meal on earth.

Gone was the refined Lily of the beachside restaurant. Here was a very hungry, very naked lady who had sated one appetite and was about to sate another. She devoured her lunch then lay back on the bed arms behind her head with a smile too inviting to refuse. Another frantic session of fun and frolic followed before they showered and strolled to a beach bathed in glorious sunshine. On the spur of the moment they hired a catamaran to sail around the entire island.

Lily had been to Boracay before but never seen it from the sea. On this clear, cloudless day she marvelled at its serene beauty; the hidden coves, verdant vegetation, lush with loaded coconut palms, wild bananas, tropical flowers in bright profusion and forests divided by glittering streams, sweeping down to sparkling white sand beaches fronting an emerald sea.

'It's breathtaking darling, I never knew it was so beautiful,' she murmured, standing with her arm around Conway as their boatman guided them expertly from the calm waters of White beach out into the chop of the open sea and back again into the safe haven on the other side of the island. After an early dinner at an Italian restaurant they walked for more than an hour at sunset along the beach kissing and splashing each other like a couple of kids.

He stayed with her that night and next morning stood on the beach waving as her *banca* glided slowly seaward then wheeled around and gathered speed toward Caticlan. She was still on deck waving as it disappeared into the distance.

Now completely recovered from his injuries, he stayed for another three days, swimming, snorkelling, eating at delightful little restaurants; exploring more of the island; walking alone along deserted beaches. He sat for hours watching the great variety of birds wheeling in the bright blue sky and the fishermen at evening bringing in their catch. It was like an 'end of the earth' experience. He had never felt such peace.

One day he sat on the sand of one of the hidden coves and reflected about Boracay. It was indeed a tropical paradise and with proposed changes in the wind maybe a paradise that would one day be lost. There was talk of bringing more electricity to the island and with that further development was sure to take place. Then, the Boracay he knew and had come to love would never be the same. The next morning he caught a *banca* to Caticlan and boarded a flight to Manila, arriving back at The Down Under on a hot, humid afternoon.

# 18

'Steve, can you come to my office for a moment please mate?' Perc's tone was polite. Conway looked askance at his phone. What's with Perc and the smarmy voice, something's up!

'Take a seat mate, got a job I think you might like,' said Prickett. His oily grin made Conway even more suspicious.

'How would you like a trip to Bangkok? Have a look at our operation and pull the local manager into line. I've had word he's been dragging the chain a bit. You can take Susan and she can sort out their books. We're not gettin' any reports and we dunno what's going on. Keyes can look after the place while you're away, ok mate?'

Conway thought quickly. He wanted to front Perc and get to the bottom of that account he and Susan had found but he'd not had a chance to talk it over with her because on his return from Boracay he'd learnt she was in Cavite attending to some family matter. There is some funny business going on in this hotel and I have to somehow find out what it is and I need Susan to help me.

And then there was the situation with Groyne, and what about Sanchez? I have to talk to Jumbo about that also. I've been shot at, bashed and attacked with a knife by one of his men. Is he the one? And if so why? Someone or some people want me out of the way. There's got to be a common thread to all of this.

'Yes ok Perc,' he heard himself telling Prickett. 'Give me a day or two to organize a few things here and we'll be on our way. How long do you think we need to be there?'

'Up to you, play it by ear, you can stay as long as you like, but I don't want

Susan away too long and I want those financials pronto,' replied Perc. 'But yeah, I reckon a couple of weeks at least, maybe longer. I'll tell them you'll be there Saturday, ok?'

'Sure, that's fine, I'll let you know what I think after I've sized up the place and had a good look at this manager, what's his name?'

'Gates, Rusty Gates, thanks mate,' said Perc, getting to his feet and leaning over his desk to shake Conway's hand. 'I know I can count on you.' Steve left Perc's office bemused. I wonder what's brought on all this bonhomie? Bit out of character for our Perc. There's got to be an angle?

Keyes was waiting for him when he got back to his office.

'Hey, you look like a new man, I think I better go to Boracay m'self...and take Ang of course,' he grinned. 'So how was it...what you expected?'

'Yes and more.' Conway told him about the Roque incident but made no mention of Lily's presence.

'Jumbo this guy was one of Sanchez's men, what do you make of that?'

'That sounds bad man,' said Keyes uneasily. 'I wonder if Sanchez put him up to it or if he was just wanted revenge after what you did to him?'

'Hard to say, but either way it's not good. But why would Sanchez want *me* out of the way? I know he doesn't like me but I haven't done anything to spike any of his little games,' frowned Conway, shaking his head. 'Weird!'

Keyes thought for a moment. 'Maybe you have. Remember, he and Prickett are thick as thieves, and everyone around here knows you're not happy with the way things are and the sacking of Ada wouldn't exactly have endeared you to them.'

'Mmmmm, it's really getting strange now. Perc just treated me like a long lost brother and wants me to go to Bangkok to sort out the manager there. I can't understand his change in attitude. Mate, there's something going on in this hotel which I haven't figured out yet but of one thing I *am* certain. Imelda hates my guts, so go figure,' he turned to look out his window.

'Steve, something tells me it's a good thing you're off to Bangkok for a while.'

'Kind of a coincidence don't you think?'

'Yeah, seems like it, how long will you be there?'

'Don't know yet, could be a few weeks, Perc doesn't seem to want me back in a hurry. Kinda funny that.' He couldn't suppress a grin. 'It's not all bad, I'm taking Susan with me apparently the financials there are also in a mess.'

'Well, at least you'll have some pleasant company.'

'Yeah, now about Groyne, heard anything yet?'

Keyes shuffled his feet and looked around the room for a moment.

'Ah, yes I have, he *was* the one responsible for your bashing, well, not him personally, but guys hired by him.'

'You sure about this? How come?'

'Sally confirmed it, she saw Groyne handing over the payoff.'

'Right, I'll attend to Mr Groyne when I come back from Bangkok.'

'No need,' said Keyes quietly, 'it's taken care of.'

Conway frowned, 'Ok, I won't ask you how, but you can fill me in on the gory details later. When is Susan coming back?' Before Keyes could reply Conway's phone rang.

'Hi Susan, speak of the devil, how are things there, when are you back? Tomorrow, good, yes I need to talk to you urgently too. See you tomorrow and, oh by the way, we're going to Bangkok, bye.'

'Hope that cheers our little accountant up,' grinned Conway.

'Another piece of news you might be interested in Steve,' said Keyes, producing a newspaper from his back pocket. 'Have a look at this.'

It was a front page story in the *Manila Bulletin* about the impending arrival of an Australian TV crew coming to investigate the "sordid bar scene of Manila" and interview someone from the Philippine government about an extradition treaty that had recently been ratified between the Australian and Philippine authorities.

Conway read the story then looked up at Keyes. 'Not exactly good news for Mr Groyne and our friend Barney Lawson is it?'

'And a few others who'll be heading for the hills when these guys arrive,' said the big man turning to leave. 'Catch you later, nice to see you back guy, I will-' his voice was drowned out by a sudden explosion of noise from outside Conway's window. Another protest march was in progress. Drums boomed, cymbals crashed and an out of tune trumpet ripped the quiet morning asunder. Added to this pandemonium was the periodic discordant shriek of a loud hailer firing up the crowd in Tagalog.

Both men went to the window and looked down to see the street choked with a sea of protestors holding brightly painted banners, some in Tagalog, some in English, all calling for the downfall of President Marcos.

'This joint is going to blow any day now,' said Keyes grimly.

'They're getting noisier and more frequent aren't they?' Conway leant out the window to get a better look. 'What do you think's going to happen?'

'Hard to say, but I know that Ver the army chief is a hard head. There could be blood in the streets.'

The long procession of protesters finally wound its way out of sight and peace returned. Keyes went back to his office and Conway got stuck into a pile of paperwork.  He kept at it until 7.00 pm when he figured he'd had enough and decided to call on Sally.

* * *

Eduardo stood nervously in front of Imelda waiting for her to finish her phone call.  She finally put down the phone and glared at him. 'Well!  What did you find out about Conway?'

'Ah,' began Eduardo, 'I am told he was bashed by two local guys who they say, were hired by a Bert Groyne, the owner of *The Black Jack* bar near here.  I couldn't find anything more, but it seems Conway somehow must have upset Groyne.'

'Are you sure about this, is that all it was?'  She looked up at him with hard eyes.  Her expression was enough to cause his bowels to spring to life.

'Yes, ma'am, I'm sure, just a minor thing, part of what happens here, you know that,' he ventured a little too boldly.  Imelda looked at him sharply.  She did not care for underlings speaking above their station.

'And the girl, who is she?'

'She works for Groyne ma'am'

'Ah hah, that's interesting,' said Imelda, leaning back steepling her fingers. 'So our Mr Conway is consorting with bar girls now,' she said aloud, but thinking how she might use it against the Australian.  'Ok, you can go.'

The little cook was relieved and almost ran from her office.  Thank God she didn't mention anything about killing Conway.  He went back to the kitchen in a much better frame of mind and looked around for something to steal.

* * *

Sally was bending down putting an empty beer bottle into a crate when a familiar voice said, 'any chance of some service around here?'  She looked up and nearly dropped the bottle.  A smiling Conway stood with both hands spread on the bar.  He looked tanned, fit, handsome and so damn desirable she wanted to rush around the bar and give him a huge hug, but Mullet and Biro were drinking nearby.  Although both, especially Biro, were almost *non compos*, she didn't want to make a big show and give them any ideas.  Groyne was due out of hospital and back any day.

'Hello sir, nice to see you again, where have you been?' she said in an impersonal tone, loud enough for Groyne's friends to hear.

'Spent a week on Boracay, you were...' he was about to say, 'right about

- 160 -

Boracay' when he noticed Biro and Mullet scowling at him. Conway looked around the bar.

'Bert not here?'

'No sir,' replied Sally deadpan, 'Mr Groyne had…an accident.'

'Nothing serious I hope,' said Conway, keeping a straight face.

'Some bastards ambushed him,' growled Biro looking accusingly at Conway. 'He's been in hospital all week. You wouldn't know anything about it would yer?'

'I don't go around bashing people mate,' Conway replied, picking up the beer Sally had placed on the bar. 'Actually the reason I came tonight was to tell Bert that I have lifted the ban on him coming into the Down Under.'

'How come?' asked Mullet suspiciously.

'Well, Bert can't be held responsible for the actions of his staff out of hours can he boys,' said Conway smoothly. Banning Groyne effectively stopped him from coming to see Sally and she was worth more than some petty incident between one of Groyne's girls and a guy who should have known better. Turning to Sally, Conway told her to give the two roughheads whatever they were drinking and then walked to the far end of the bar out of earshot. He finished his beer and signaled to Sally for another.

'What time do you finish?' he asked quietly as she handed him another San Miguel. She glanced back up the bar checking to make sure Biro and Mullet couldn't hear her answer.

'Eight o'clock, I'm on early shift, why?' she answered lowering her voice.

'Would you like to have dinner with me at some place of your choosing in Sampaloc?'

'Sure, there is a good place I know, you will like it. It's small and cosy.' She scribbled the address on a small piece of paper and concealing it in her hand passed it across pretending to wipe the bar in front of him. He finished his beer, paid Sally and as he was leaving Mullet called out,

'Thanks Steve, see you in the Down Under…mate!' Conway smiled to himself. Looks like we're friends again. It was a typical Manila night, humid with little breeze as he walked quickly up Mabini Street toward UN Avenue.

On the spur of the moment he stopped and went into *Kings Cross* a bar, a little larger than *The Black Jack*, just as sleazy and full of avaricious girls. Several of them danced tiredly on the stage which ran the length of the right hand side, while half a dozen lounged around in alcoves waiting to pounce on the next punter who ventured in. Normally Conway would give it a miss but he liked the manager Charlie Horne, a knockabout bloke from Sydney, who was always good for a laugh but more importantly, had a good ear for what was happening in Ermita.

'G'day Steve, long time no see mate, what'y havin?' Charlie said, lifting his glass of vodka in recognition.

'San Mig's fine Charlie, what's new?'

'Nothin' much, you hear about Groyne?' asked Charlie, taking a long swallow of his vodka. Charlie's capacity for vodka was legendary. It was said his daily intake was at least two bottles and then some.

'Yes, just been in *The Black Jack*. Any idea who did it Charlie, what's the word?'

'Nah, silly bastard was drunk n carrying money around here in the early hours, some guys *never* learn. Dunno who did it but reckon there must have been a few of 'em. They did him over good and proper. Want a girl mate?'

Before Conway had a chance to reply, two of Charlie's denizens descended on him. The one on his right was probably older than Steve and the other on his left had a few years on her. They reminded him of an old Aussie TV show called *Aggie and Flo*. Aggie who was wearing some ghastly perfume had him around the neck in a death grip trying to kiss him while Flo bent down trying to unzip his fly.

Somehow extricating himself from Aggie's grip of steel, he brought his legs together nearly strangling Flo. 'Ah, no thanks Charlie, got to be on my way mate, just thought I'd touch base for a quickie, a drink that is,' he laughed.

'Yeah no worries mate, good to see y' again Steve,' grinned Charlie, as Aggie stood disconsolately and Flo rubbed her ears and neck. Conway downed his beer and put a hundred peso bill on the bar. 'Give the girls a drink on me.' He shook Charlie's hand and made a beeline for the door and safety.

\* \* \*

Just on 8.30 pm Conway strolled into *Margie's Lechon* in Sampaloc. As Sally described, it was small and intimate with a bar to the left and a scattering of small tables and chairs around a slightly upraised stage where a garishly printed sign boldly declared, *"Live Music, EVERY night!* Sally had not yet arrived so he took a table near the door. She came a few minutes later looking beautiful and a little out of breath.

'Sorry Si…ah Steve darling, the traffic, it's just *so bad* tonight.'

'Situation normal, you look great,' and she did. She had changed from her work clothes and now wore an off the shoulder pink dress with a slim white choker and her long dark hair caught in a pink bandeau. Her bright red lipstick and the white choker contrasted beautifully on her bronze skin. These women know how to dress, thought Conway. She looked more than great; she looked, sensational!

He ordered a beer for himself and an orange juice for Sally. She immediately wanted to know all about his Boracay sojourn. He told her how right she was about the island and how much he enjoyed its beauty and the relaxed atmosphere. He never mentioned Roque and certainly not Lily. He was only too well aware of Sally's attitude toward the sexy restaurant owner.

She sat there never taking her eyes off him for a moment, all the while giving him that delicious smile. She looked so beautiful he found it hard to keep his mind on what he was saying and nearly put his foot in it a couple of times letting Lily's name slip when he mentioned the dinner with the French couple and the trip on the catamaran. He ordered their meal and as he spooned his Kare Kare, he noticed her just picking at her chicken adobo.

'What's up, something's on your mind isn't it?' he asked. She tried to avoid his question saying it was nothing important, but he persisted until she finally opened up.

'Steve, darling, there is something I want to ask you,' she said, putting down her fork and looking at him with an expression he could not read. He wasn't sure if she was sad, or happy, but he detected a tear in her eyes. 'Ok what is it?' he said a little too sharply.

'First of all, Sir Groyne, he is in hospital and was badly hurt and I think you got Mr Keyes or someone to do it…did you?'

Conway reached over and placed his hand on hers. 'Sally, I swear I did not! I had no knowledge of what happened to Groyne until I came back to Manila, and that is the truth. Yes, Mr Keyes and I did discuss some retribution but we didn't decide on anything. I was going to take the matter further but while I was away decided not too, and you know why?'

'No, why?' she asked, her head bowed.

'Because,' he said slowly, 'sooner or later Groyne will pay for his sins one way or another but more importantly, I wanted to be able to come to see you and, *that's why* I lifted the ban on him coming to The Down Under.'

'Thank you,' she said, breathing a sigh of relief. 'I should have known you would not do such a thing, but I wonder who?'

'It could've been anyone. Apparently he was carrying a lot of cash on him that night, not a very smart thing to do wandering around Ermita at night, wouldn't you agree?'

'Yes, of course, poor Sir Groyne.' She was satisfied with Conway's explanation and began to attack her meal with some vigour. Conway changed the subject to the growing unrest in Manila.

'Jumbo…Mr Keyes and I, saw a big demonstration this morning, they seem to be getting larger and more frequent and the crowds seem, to me anyway, to be angrier. What do you think?'

'I agree, the mood here is becoming more worrying day by day. We want Mr Marcos to step down but he refuses. Steve, I'm scared about what might happen.'

'Yes, it's starting to look bad. Do you think there might be a civil war?'

She stopped eating and looked at him for a moment. 'I don't think so. Of course, there are many Marcos supporters but I don't believe Filipinos will turn on each other. I am just very worried what the army might do. General Ver who is head of the army is a very dangerous man. If Mr Marcos orders him to use violence to stop all this I am very afraid for our people.'

They continued to discuss the pros and cons of the outcome of the unrest then, he told her of his mission to Bangkok. Her face fell.

'You have been away and now you are going again, how long for this time?' she said miserably. 'Maybe only a week or two,' he said trying to reassure her. 'Hey, I'll be back in no time, but there are problems there and I just have to go. Don't worry I'll be back before you know it.' She bit her bottom lip and said nothing.

Three young men in tee shirts and black jeans carrying guitars, accompanied by an attractive woman in a long sequined gown arrived...the evening's entertainment. They stepped up onto the small stage and began to set up their instruments and do sound checks. That was enough for Conway. He was not in the mood for a loud, late night so with Sally's agreement he paid the bill and they left. At her apartment he accepted her invitation to come in for coffee but remembering the last time, asked if she had anything else to drink.

'I hoped you would come again so I put some beer in the ref,' she smiled, unlocking the door of her apartment. Once inside it was all systems go. She handed him an ice cold San Mig and turned on some soft mood music.

'Excuse me for a moment darling,' she said, disappearing into the bathroom. He looked at his watch and sipped his beer. Nearly 11.00 pm. Mmmm, ok, I better not stay long, too many things to catch up on in the morning.

He had nearly finished the beer when she emerged from the bathroom. He took one look and nearly dropped the bottle. It was some kind of cream frilly satin creation that began at the slopes of her full, tempting breasts and finished abruptly mid-thigh. It was held up by two wispy shoulder straps. She was still wearing the bandeau and choker, and *he* nearly choked as she glided across the carpet toward him. Two in one week! This only happens in the movies doesn't it? he said to himself as he placed the bottle on her bedside table.

'Darling you have no idea how much I have missed you,' she whispered, taking his hands and placing them around her. He tried to say 'me too' but her lips mashed his, making speech impossible. He felt the velvet smoothness of her back and drew her closer in a long passionate kiss which only ended when he led her to the bed. She dropped the straps of her negligee, stepped out of it as it fell to the floor, then climbed on to the bed and lay on her back gloriously naked, her arms reaching up to him. 'Darling, I want you so much.' He was in such a hurry to get his gear off he tripped and fell face first onto the bed in a tangle of shirt, trousers, underpants and socks.

She giggled and pulled off his pants and what remained of his clothes. Now naked, he went to work enthusiastically and she was soon writhing and moaning with pleasure as his tongue roamed over her from head to toe and back again.

They kept at it groping, caressing, thrusting, seemingly unable to get enough of each other until it ended in a shuddering, leg stiffening climax. They lay kissing and cuddling until Conway reluctantly called it a night.

This time there was to be no walk in a darkened street. They dressed and went downstairs where Sally asked the guard to find a cab. He came back in ten minutes with a Golden taxi. He gave Sally a lingering kiss, checked the taxi meter worked, and headed off into the night.

* * *

'Come in Susan, nice to see you,' said Conway smiling broadly. He was genuinely glad to see her. Her professionalism gave him confidence. She shyly returned his smile but it was fleeting and quickly replaced by a worried frown. Susan had something on her mind and he sensed it had nothing to do with accounting. He invited her to sit down and tried to get her to relax.

'Hello sir, you look much better now,' she said sitting down rather primly, placing her hands in her lap.

'I'm fine thanks Susan, now what can I do for you.' She sat for a few moments collecting her thoughts. Sir, there is something I must tell you. I'm not sure if what I am going to tell you is about you - but you need to know.'

He listened intently as she related that part of the conversation she had overheard in Imelda's office and said nothing until she finished. Not wanting to alarm her he tried to pass it off lightly.

'You didn't hear the whole conversation did you?'

'No sir.'

'And my name wasn't mentioned was it?'

'No sir, but sir I heard the word "salvage", you know what that means in this country don't you?'

'Yes I do Susan, but do you *really* believe Imelda would try something like that?'

'I can only tell you what I heard sir.'

'And you say she asked that little guy in the kitchen Eduardo, to do the job?'

He began to laugh. 'Susan, if Eduardo is the assassin I don't think I have too much to worry about.' He looked past her to his door then leaned forward keeping his voice low. 'By the way, as for that bank account, we'll have to wait until we come back from Bangkok but in the meantime get one of your most trusted girls to keep an eye on the new cashier. She seems ok but I don't know who's who in this place anymore, she could be another Imelda spy. I want to know if there are any more movements to that account, now, about this Bangkok trip...'

He briefed her on the staff problems but concentrated mainly on her accounting responsibilities and what he hoped they would achieve in Bangkok. She listened carefully nodding a few times and said she hoped she would not be away too long because she was starting to make good progress with the Manila accounts.

'It's a much smaller operation there, you might only be needed for a week, ten days at the most,' he assured her. 'Of course it depends on the situation we find, but I don't see you away for longer than that.'

'Do they have an accountant there?'

'A bookkeeper I believe, the final accounts are prepared by a local accounting firm.'

Susan nodded. 'I see, well, if I have any major questions I will contact them. When do we leave?'

'We fly out Saturday at noon. Have you been to Bangkok before?'

'No sir,' she smiled for the first time. 'I am looking forward to it.'

'So am I,' he replied, 'this could be a very interesting interlude.'

As they sat and chatted in the departure lounge of Manila's International airport waiting for their boarding call they were unaware of being observed by two men, each unaware of the other, but both sharing a great deal of interest in the two from the Down Under Hotel.

# 19

Steve and Susan checked into the Montien Hotel just after 4 pm to be met by Somchai, a pleasant, rotund man in his early fifties and Wanthip, an accountant in his twenties, hired by Somchai to keep the books.

The four of them sat in the spacious lobby served drinks by a beautiful young Thai waitress in scarlet and gold traditional dress. She smiled, and knelt as she placed each of their drinks on the table in front of them. It was not subservience, but a delightful Thai tradition, one of many that was to capture the hearts of both Conway and Susan.

Somchai brought Conway up to date with the current situation. To say he was a very unhappy, exasperated man, was an understatement. 'This Gates, I do not know where Khun Percy got this guy but he has to go, Khun Steve, I cannot afford him. He just does not do anything! My God! He spends most of his time in *Spitfire*, a bar in Patpong II.'

'Do you have a phone number for this guy? Where does he live?' asked Conway. 'I'll pay him a visit today Khun Somchai.'

The Thai partner shook his head. 'I'm sorry I don't know where he lives. He was in a flat near Victory Monument but I've been informed he had left and was living in the Sukhumvit area somewhere.'

While Conway chatted to Somchai, Susan questioned Wanthip about the financial reporting situation. There was a bookkeeper but she had been away on family matters for some weeks and had only recently returned. The paperwork was well in arrears and needed to be updated. Wanthip had recently been too busy with his own practice to call and had hoped Gates would have provided some assistance, a forlorn hope. It seemed the so-called "manager" was more interested in figures of a different kind.

For the next hour the four of them discussed what could and should be done. Somchai then excused himself with apologies saying he had another appointment but would like to invite them to dinner on the following evening. Wanthip also had to leave telling them his wife had just given birth to their first child and he needed to go home.

'I will call you tomorrow,' he said to Susan.

Both Thais left after standing with palms together and a slight bow of their heads giving the newcomers a *wai*, the traditional Thai prayer-like gesture of respect. Susan said she was tired and retired to her room. Conway sat in the lobby finishing his drink pondering his next move.

The Montien Hotel was located in Suriwong road in the Silom district, the heart of Bangkok's commercial and entertainment area. It sat at one end of Patpong 1 a small *soi* (street) notorious for being the 'red light area' of Bangkok. The "girlie" bars and its flea markets made it a magnet for tourists. Patpong was in fact, two parallel streets owned by a Chinese immigrant family, the Patpongpanich family, since 1946.

Over the years nightclubs begun to sprout there and it became popular with the military on leave during the Vietnam War. By the 70's and 80's Patpong with its raunchy and illegal sex shows in upstairs bars, became the centre of the adult entertainment industry in Bangkok. The Down Under bar and restaurant was located in Patpong 1. With Susan in her room, Conway decided to pay a visit, incognito.

He crossed Suriwong Road and began walking down Patpong 1 coming alive with vendors erecting their stalls for the night market. He shouldered his way past wide-eyed tourists wandering up and down looking at the garish signs of the various go-go bars and strip clubs with evocative names like *Firecat, Lipstick, Pussy Galore, Kings Castle, Champagne, Grand Prix* and even a *Kangaroo Club.* Squeezed in between all this were restaurants offering cuisines from various countries including Indian, Italian, Japanese and the ubiquitous Thai.

He stopped outside a large green and gold sign featuring a kangaroo logo which boldly declared, *The Down Under Bar and Restaurant.* Immediately he could see why trade was not flourishing. For a start, the large floor to ceiling windows and front door were covered entirely by dark grey curtains keeping out the bright afternoon sunshine. It was impossible to tell whether the place was open for business or not. He pushed open the heavy glass door and stood for a moment surveying the scene.

It was a large square room and dominated by a circular bar in the centre with a stainless steel top, around which three bored male customers sat in the gloom staring into their drinks. It was well designed and tastefully furnished with a number of small square and circular tables set with green and gold checked cloths and white china crockery. The walnut wall panels on the right were adorned with prints of kangaroos and koalas from the Australian Tourist Commission together with large framed, coloured photos of rugby league and Australian Rules football matches. An advertising poster for *Fosters Lager* held a place of prominence and on the far wall to his left was a huge poster of a Qantas jumbo jet advertising cheap flights to Sydney.

The whole operation represented a substantial financial investment by the Down Under shareholders. Here it was in the heart of the wild nightclub district of Bangkok yet there was no atmosphere, no chat, no laughter, no noise...nothing.

A bored looking bar attendant gazed wistfully at the blank screen of a large television on the wall. Why didn't she turn the damn thing on? Conway could see why Somchai was so concerned. He was one of the major investors and he was definitely not getting any return on this investment.

Conway cleared his throat causing the bar attendant to look around, startled as if she was not expecting anyone else that day. She was a pleasantly plump girl and her face lit up as she took his order. She seemed pleased to be able to relieve the boredom by serving someone. He introduced himself and she held out a plump little hand.

'I am very pleased to meet you Khun Steve,' she beamed, my name is Porn. He smiled, an interesting name for someone working in Patpong. Porn read his thoughts.

'Oh sir,' she giggled, 'it's short for Siriporn.' This girl had worked in bars before, he mused, and after all, this *was* Patpong!

'Who's the boss here?' asked Conway as she handed him a bottle of *Singha* beer. Her face clouded for an instant.

'Khun Rusty sir, but he isn't here at the moment,' replied Porn quietly.

'Any idea when or where I can find Khun Rusty? I'm an old friend.'

Porn looked decidedly uncomfortable.

'Sorry sir, I am not sure, maybe tonight, maybe tomorrow. Can I have your name and contact number. I will tell him to get in touch with you when he comes in.'

Conway gave her what he hoped was an ingratiating smile.

'Thank you Porn, now can you tell me where the *Spitfire* bar is? I've been told it's a good place to have a drink?' Her eyebrows shot up and her mouth fell open. For a moment she was lost for words. This guy knew more than he was letting on.

'Sir if you go out of here and turn left at the next soi, it is a passage between here and Patpong II, then turn right, you will see it down on your left, you can't miss it.'

'Thanks Porn.' He downed his beer, threw a 100 baht note on the bar and told Porn to keep the change. The *Spitfire* wasn't hard to find. Within three minutes he was in Patpong II standing outside a typical Patpong bar with its lurid photos of scantily clad girls pasted either side of a narrow front door.

He went in pushing through yet another heavy dark curtain. The place was narrow, dark and reeked of stale beer. Suspended by wires from the ceiling was a large papier mache replica of a World War II spitfire and to Conway's left was an upraised stage with the obligatory chrome poles and four or five girls in multi coloured bikinis shuffling to some obscure disco band.

His prey was the only customer in the bar. He fitted the description Conway had been given in Manila; a skinny individual, in his late thirties, medium height, with fair thinning hair. He was sitting on a stool against the right hand wall with an attractive long-haired bikini clad girl on his lap and another two similarly dressed either side of him.

Conway ordered a beer and stood looking at Gates from the corner of his eye. He was wearing navy shorts and a white tee shirt emblazoned with *I Love Thailand.* To a casual observer he was just another tourist enjoying the pleasures of the flesh in Patpong. In his right hand he held a bottle of *Singha* beer while the other encircled the girl on his left. He was laughing and talking bullshit to the one on his lap stopping occasionally to kiss one of the other girls. Each girl held a drink and there was a line of empty *Singha* bottles on a shelf beside Gates indicating he'd been in the *Spitfire* for a few hours. He was having the time of his life but the festivities were about to come to an abrupt halt.

Conway put his beer on the bar and sauntered over to the happy little group. The girl on Gates' right looked at Conway quizzically with a half smile as he approached. The one on the left was being smothered with a kiss while the lady on his lap was having her right boob squeezed.

'G'day mate,' smiled Conway, 'you're having a top time aren't you?'

Gates ignored him.

'Gates, isn't it Rusty Gates?' Conway said, raising his voice. This time Gates turned, looked at him and scowled.

'Yeah, who're you? Piss off, can't y' see I'm busy?'

Conway saw red. 'My name's Conway, Steve Conway, I've just come from Manila to see you…arsehole!'

Gates squinted at Conway for a moment then the penny dropped. He was only half drunk and he *had* heard of Conway. His eyes widened and his mouth dropped open. Gone was the happy bullshit artist of a second ago.

'Fuck!' The smart arse smile on Gates' face was replaced with one of trepidation.

'Excuse me,' said Conway, reaching over and easing the dancer off Gates' lap. Then he grabbed the Bangkok manager by the scruff of the neck.

'Pay the fucking bill and come with me you little shit!' he growled, hauling Gates off the stool. There was frantic movement behind the bar as the bill was added. Conway then marched a protesting, stumbling Gates from the bar.

The dancers on stage barely took any notice of the commotion. Gates hadn't bought *them* any drinks, so who cares? The lovelies he'd been taken from climbed back on the stage not bothering to look as Conway dragged their boozy playmate away. They'd earned a few ladies drinks commission from him and they knew he'd be back, and if he didn't, there was always another punter willing to play games and pay for their "services".

Out in the street Conway dragged the hapless Gates to a small outdoor café, sat him down and ordered coffee for both of them. Gates sat there still scowling. What's with this bastard? I was just having a drink and a good time. Shit this is Patpong! Is this joker some kind of killjoy?

'You want to keep your job pal?' said Conway, pushing the cup of coffee toward him.

'Yeah, I reckon,' came the surly reply.

'Then *do it!* And stop spending all your time in that bloody bar! You aren't paid to sit on your arse all day in that place. You've had your first and last warning. I'll be here for a couple of weeks and will decide if you are going to remain as manager. Smarten up arsehole or you're out...got it?'

'Yeah,' mumbled Gates, looking down at his coffee.

'Ok, go and sober up and I'll see you at eight o'clock sharp tomorrow morning.'

Gates looked like he was going to protest but thought better of it. He looked again at his coffee then back at Conway. 'Ok, you're right, I fucked up. I....'

Conway interrupted him. 'I want you there ON time! Washed, shaved and dressed accordingly. No tee shirt and shorts. Long trousers, clean polo shirt and shoes, you're going to look like a manager and bloody well act like one, understand?'

'Yeah ok mate, sorry mate....'

'Don't be sorry just do the job you're being paid for. I'm here to fix the operation and to pull it out of the shit and you either shape up or ship out! Got it?'

'Yeah, ok.'

He finished his coffee and sheepishly offered his hand. They shook hands and the little manager wiped his mouth, gave a crooked grin, and walked away weaving slightly, toward the Silom Road entrance to Patpong II. Conway watched him till he was out of sight then slowly walked back to the Montien Hotel. Tomorrow he hoped would be the start of a new day and new beginning for the Bangkok Down Under.

* * *

The phone nearly jumped off the desk as Ramon Sanchez entered his office.

He picked it up and uttered an abrupt 'Yes! Oh, it's you, what have you got for me?'

He listened, intently nodding, giving monosyllabic answers to his caller. 'When? Where? How long? Yes.' His face creased in a rare smile as he replaced the receiver. Things were starting to fall into place. Soon his time in this town would be over and he would retire in comfort to his ranch in the San Fernando Valley of California, a rich and contented man.

His mood changed when he looked up and saw Roque standing hesitantly at his door, plaster over his left eye, the right eye still a nice shade of yellow and black, his mouth swollen and his right arm in a sling.

Sanchez began to shake with rage. 'What have you got to say for yourself you incompetent fool? You defied my orders and look what happened! Now not only have you failed and disregarded my orders, you with your stupid actions may have led this Conway back to me! He is no fool, he knows you are one of my officers and he will put two and two together.' He deliberately looked at Roque's feet and back up again his eyes cold. 'I should put you in the Pasig!'

Roque felt his bowels about to move. My God is he checking my foot size? Visions of a one-way trip to the bottom of the Pasig River flashed into his head.

'Get out of here you idiot, I'll get someone else to do the job. GO!'

Roque stumbled from Sanchez' office and almost collided with a beautiful, smartly dressed woman about to enter.

* * *

'Ang, would you like to have dinner out tonight my little *sampaguita*?' asked Keyes, leaning over the cot tickling little Joey's tummy.

'Sure, why not, my big *sampaguita*,' laughed Ang, 'we haven't been out for ages, where did you have in mind?'

'How about *The Kamayan*? Your sister will babysit Joey right?'

'Sure, I'll get her over, what time?'

'Seven thirty, ok with you dear?'

It was true, they hadn't been out for a few weeks and she enjoyed *The Kamayan,* a restaurant noted for its excellent Filipino food. Located in Padre Faura Street it was within walking distance of their apartment.

'Can't wait you big fat pudding,' laughed Ang giving Keyes a hug. Little Joey looked on gurgling happily, kicking his tiny legs.

At 7.30 pm they entered the *Kamayan* ready to enjoy a quiet dinner together.

For a midweek night it was unusually busy and they had trouble finding a table until one became vacant in the far corner well away from the front door. They settled down to order when Keyes glanced across to the other side of the restaurant to a series of alcoves which gave diners some privacy.

All alcoves were occupied with business types and their spouses or girlfriends and young mooning couples. But there was one in particular which startled him because of the occupants. Facing him he could see the grim features of Ramon Sanchez. And to his left looking glamorous in a black off the shoulder gown was...Lily Li!

Sanchez stern and unsmiling listened as Lily chatted animatedly between mouthfuls of food. It was possible that Sanchez was a customer of Lily's restaurant and as police chief and a prominent citizen, it would be prudent for Lily to nurture the relationship but Keyes a regular customer at Lily's restaurant, had never seen him there. What concerned him was her manner. She was chatting and laughing like they were old friends. Somehow I don't think Steve would be too impressed if he saw this cosy little tete-a-tete, thought Keyes.

He said nothing to Ang. She was enjoying her night out so there was no way he was going to spoil her mood. He kept the conversation light hearted and told her how beautiful she was. She blushed and giggled, told him how much she loved him and asked, 'where is that nice Mr Steve?'

'He's in Bangkok, be back in a week or two,' replied Keyes offhandedly, looking across at the far alcove.

'He should get himself a nice girl,' she opined, 'he'd be a good catch for someone,' she said tucking into a steaming bowl of lechon.

Keyes looked over at Lily and shrugged. 'I think he's met a few already but not sure if he's found the right one yet.'

They finished their meal and as they were leaving Keyes deliberately steered Ang near to the alcove of Lily and Sanchez. Walking past Keyes looked and caught Lily's eye. She stopped in mid conversation. The smile vanished and was replaced by one of embarrassment or was it guilt? What had she to be embarrassed or even guilty about? Did she know about the feeling between Conway and Sanchez? Keyes covered his curiosity, waved to her and received one in return. As Keyes left, Lily said something to Sanchez and pointed to the back of the big American. Sanchez frowned and nodded in agreement.

* * *

Conway showered and was about to climb into bed when he received a phone call from Susan. She could not sleep and asked if they could meet in the lobby; she had something to tell him. There was an edge to her voice which left him with an uneasy feeling. A few minutes later they sat in the same comfortable chairs they had occupied earlier that day. She was wearing a simple white blouse and jeans, no makeup and looked more like a schoolgirl than a 30 year old woman. She also looked innocent and quite beautiful.

'Well Susan, what's this all about?' asked Conway, ordering tea for both of them from a hovering waitress.

Susan was unusually nervous. 'Sir,' she hesitated, then taking a deep breath said, 'I don't know how to tell you this but I think…' another deep breath, 'I have to leave the employ of the Down Under.'

He felt as if he'd been kicked in the stomach. That premonition of unease was correct. 'What! Why?' he said, groping for words.

'I, I, I have been offered another job,' she stammered, 'in Makati… there is an increase in salary and it's with a very prestigious accounting firm, the conditions are very good.' The words poured out. She stopped for a few seconds, took another deep breath and continued. 'But it's more than that sir,' she said, her voice now barely above a whisper.

'Well, what is it? I will see if I can get you an increase, I don't want to lose you Susan, your help is vital to me doing my job.' He didn't try to hide his desperation.

'I feel frightened sir, and I am worried about you. I am worried about the job, it is a big mess and there is something else…'

Just then the waitress appeared with their tea, pouring each a cup and gently placing the teapot to one side of the table before gliding away across to her station on the other side of the vast lobby.

'Don't worry about me, I can look after myself. And as for the job, I know it's a bit of a mess but we can beat it, I know we can and I need you to help me beat it. So what else is there for God's sake?'

'I'm in love with you.'

He dropped his cup and stared at her, dumbfounded.

She hung her head and twisted a small handkerchief in her hands then looked up at him. There were tears in her eyes.

Susan was a complete professional. She had never before let her personal feelings interfere with her job and to her the only way out was to resign her position. But everything she told him was the truth. She had been offered a position of senior accountant with a leading international accounting firm in Makati. She was afraid for Conway and although the job in the Down Under was confronting, she knew in her heart she was capable of handling it. Her feelings for him had been growing in recent times and when he had been hospitalized, she knew that what was in her heart was more than just concern for his welfare.

He was lost for words. It took him a full minute to regain his composure. He leaned over and took her small hand in his.

'Susan, those are the nicest words I have heard in a very long time.' His face broke into a broad grin. 'Hey! What am I going to do without you? You are, one of the sweetest human beings I have ever met, and'... he said sincerely, 'the most intelligent, and I just can't, and don't want to work without you. Please don't leave Susan.' He paused, and looked her straight in the eye. 'I don't want to compromise our working relationship but I can tell you that I *do* have very strong feelings for you too.'

She shook her head. 'No, I'm sorry sir, please forget what I said, I will never mention it again.' She got up to leave but he took her arm and stopped her. He put his arms around her but she did not respond and stood with her arms at her side. He looked down at her and smiled. The top of her head was level with his chest.

'I need you,' he said quietly kissing the top of her head. 'Let's get this job done here and go back and clean up Manila.'

'Yes sir,' she whispered, putting her arms around him for a moment then disengaged herself and stepped back. 'Please excuse me,' she said softly. 'I will return to my room now.' He watched her walked across to the elevators, a beautiful, petite, elegant Filipina. Why couldn't I see it before? The best woman I have met since Jane died and here she has been under my nose the whole time. God, I hope she doesn't leave...I'd be stuffed without her. He yawned and finished his tea...time for bed. Back in his room he cleaned his teeth and was still thinking about her when sleep came.

\* \* \*

Ramon Sanchez perused the previous day's police blotter checking the arrests and other statistics when his phone rang. He grimaced when he heard who it was.

'Yeah, g'day Ramon, how they hangin' mate?' Sanchez ignored Perc's puerile attempt at humour. These foreigners are so crude. What does he want now?

'Mate, I've got another good idea, I think you might go for this one too,' said Perc confidently.

'What is it Mr Prickett?'

'Why don't you send one of your men or maybe two over to Bangkok and knock Conway off there. It's away from us, we'll be clean, I'm sure your boys could do the job. Drop him in the Chao Praya River and he would float out to the gulf of Thailand or maybe fit him with "cement slippers". On second thoughts, that might be a better idea, whaddya think mate?'

Sanchez grimaced again. He hated being called 'mate'.

'I don't think that's a good idea Mr Prickett for a couple of reasons.'

'Why mate?'

Sanchez gritted his teeth. 'For a start, who's going to pay for this? The airfare, accommodation, the cost of doing the job, it won't be cheap. Will you foot the bill Mr Prickett?'

'Ah,' replied Perc backing off. 'I thought you might be able to arrange all that mate.'

'I cannot afford such a thing. You know my budget is very small everyone knows that Mr Prickett.'

Well how come you're a fucking millionaire Sanchez? thought Perc, everyone knows that too.

'What's the other reason Ramon?'

'Even if we did send someone I think it would be too risky; too many chances of things going wrong there. None of my men are familiar with Bangkok. Of course we could get a local hitman but here we can control everything, we know what's going on. I would feel much more confident doing it in our backyard.'

Perc thought about it for a few moments. 'Yeah, I guess you're right but we better do something about him when he comes back.'

'Yes, alright Mr Prickett, I'm glad you see things my way.'

'When are the "presents" arriving?' asked Perc changing the subject.

'Any day now. I will keep you informed,' replied Sanchez curtly.

'Ok, thanks mate, see ya later,' said Perc. He replaced the phone and mouthed, 'pompous prick'.

\* \* \*

Sally unlocked her apartment door and without changing fell onto her bed. It had been a long tiring day. Groyne had returned and was his usual grumpy self, abusing the staff, Sally in particular. He had lost a lot of weight. His face was thin and drawn and he walked with a limp. Bert Groyne was a different man physically but the bad temper and mean spirit remained. 'What am I to do?' she sighed. Sleep was almost upon her when the phone at her bedside rang. Startled, she reached over and picked it up then slumped back on her bed.

'Hello…yes,' she said wearily, then sat bolt upright.

# 20

Rusty Gates arrived at the Down Under the next morning at exactly 8.00 am looking like a new man, well, almost a new man. He was clean-shaven, his hair combed and apart from blood shot eyes and a nice set of black bags beneath them, he looked presentable in an olive green and white striped polo shirt and cream slacks.

He introduced Steve to the six staff present. All, Conway noted, were casually dressed in jeans and tee shirts. First up was Malee, the cashier now very much wide awake, fear in her eyes. Standing beside her Sumalee the cook, a dumpy woman of indeterminate age, and two waitresses, Porn from the day before, who now looked at him with more than a little anxiety. Holding her hand was Pie, a cute young lady in her teens. Also nervous was Oy the resident clerk, a woman in her late thirties and finally, a handsome young man, early twenties with a long unpronounceable Thai name shortened to "Tommy".

Steve gave a little speech in which he said he was there to help them and Khun Rusty improve the trade and bring more customers thus possibly increasing their pay packets. The last bit brought smiles all round.

Turning to Gates he pointed to the curtains. 'The first thing we'll do is open those and *keep* them open at all times so passers-by can see we are actually open for business. The television must remain on turned to news, current affairs and sports channels. Let's put the girls in some nice bright uniforms, you can organize that right? Get their consensus on what they want ok?'

Gates nodded in agreement. Maybe this Conway was not so bad after all?

'And Rusty, I want you to put a blackboard out the front and each day write up the daily "specials" from the menu, liaise with Sumalee on that. We need to let the public know what major sporting events are on television so write that up on the board as well, got it?'

'Got it Steve, will be done,' replied Gates, 'anything else?'

'I'll have a look at your menu and a few other things as well a little later, but first I want to introduce you all to Miss Santos.' Conway turned to Susan standing quietly beside him.

'Susan is my chief accountant in Manila. She is here to look at the accounting system, bring the books up to date and improve the system where necessary.' His words elicited a nod of approval from all present, particularly Oy, who visibly relaxed as if a huge weight had been lifted off her shoulders. Help had arrived at last? She offered Susan a quick smile, which was immediately returned.

Conway signaled that the meeting was over and with Gates in tow retired to the manager's ground floor office for further discussion while Oy showed Susan upstairs to her office. The bookkeeper had been away in Chiang Mai for ten days visiting her terminally ill father and the daily record keeping and updating had not been done. She came back to find on her desk a pile of untidy day sheets, sales records, bank statements, creditors accounts and sundry items of paperwork and other correspondence. This was grist to Susan's mill. She put down her handbag, took off her jacket and sat down with Oy to sort it out.

In the following days, business began to improve dramatically. With the curtains opened, the television switched on, the blackboard outside highlighting in brightly coloured chalk, the daily specials and the latest upcoming sports events, the Down Under started to take on a whole new look and draw customers.

Gates consulted the staff about a uniform and without Conway's involvement came up with something in keeping with the Patpong scene; racy but tasteful. Their choice featured gold, off the shoulder blouses, bottle green mini skirts, black fishnet stockings and white shoes. It got a big tick from both Gates and Conway; overnight the attitude of the staff changed.

The bored detachment was replaced by smiling, eager-to-please faces. The effect on turnover was almost immediate. Sales increased and the cash register began to sing. The industrious Susan quickly brought the records up to date and designed new internal control procedures. Wanthip couldn't believe his eyes. He had as promised, called on Susan that first morning and looked in dismay at the mess on Oy's desk. Now, what a difference! Susan had created new daily recording procedures for both sales and expenses, tightened up the internal control of the stocktaking and cash. Bank statements well in arrears, had been reconciled, an assets register had been created and she and Oy were now in the process of producing a full set of accounts.

'Khun Susan has worked wonders Khun Steve. I am amazed she has done so much in such a short time,' he said, shaking his head.

Conway nodded 'she's special all right,' replied Conway with pride.

Gates was the biggest surprise of all. Almost overnight he had risen to the challenge and become a responsible and motivated manager. He now took a great interest in all aspects of the operation, even sitting with Oy and Susan to learn the intricacies of the daily recording and updating of the accounting system. His drinking had dropped dramatically and his enthusiasm galvanized the rest of the staff.

Somchai could not believe his eyes.

'You are a miracle worker Khun Steve, this is a different man. How did you do it?' he asked, both happy and bewildered at the same time. Conway's eyes twinkled. 'He just needed a bit of motivation, some direction and…a good kick in the backside. It often works wonders Khun Somchai.'

A happy Somchai reported the improved progress of the operation to Perc who grudgingly admitted Conway had done reasonably well but then quickly took credit for sending him and Susan to Bangkok.

'I told you I would fix it for you Khun Somchai, you can always rely on Percy Prickett!'

On the other end of the phone Somchai rolled his eyes. 'Thank you Khun Percy, can I keep them for another week?'

'As long as you like,' replied Perc expansively, 'where are they staying mate, got 'em in something nice and cheap now?'

'No, they are still in the Montien. I think it is better they stay there. The Montien is close to the operation, they are doing a good job and I want them to be content Khun Percy. If I put them in some down market place I think they will take it as an insult, especially after the good work they have done.'

'Ah,' said Perc. There was a long pause. He did a quick calculation of the daily accommodation and other costs at the Montien. 'In that case Khun Somchai I think one more week will be enough then send them back, I need them both here.'

'Oh, that is a pity,' exclaimed a disappointed Somchai. 'Ok I will let them know, *Kawp Khun krup* (thank you) Khun Percy.'

Trading figures continued to rise with families flocking in for lunch and dinner. Here in the middle of Patpong they had found a haven of peace which offered good value for food and drink in clean, comfortable surroundings. At night there was an ever-growing number of expats sitting around the bar eating, drinking and watching the latest international sporting events on television.

The relationship between Conway and Gates had changed markedly to the extent that on a couple of occasions they went out together to explore what Patpong had to offer although the *Spitfire* was still off limits. One night Gates took Conway to *Firecat*, an upstairs bar in Patpong 1.

At the top of a steep set of stairs they turned left into a dimly lit bar with tiered seats on the right overlooking a stage where a fat naked German was having sex with an equally bored Thai girl. This apparently was part of the "entertainment" the spruiker downstairs was referring to.

The next "act" on the program was something that reminded Conway of *The Eagles Nest* in Angeles City. It consisted of a girl (considerably younger than the "entertainer" in *The Eagles Nest*) lying on her back shooting darts from her vagina at balloons floating about above her. The object was to see if she could hit them all and if so, the punter who bought the balloons would then pay her a suitably increased fee. She never missed one. As one after the other exploded with a loud "pop" a grinning Gates turned to Conway and said, 'She'd play William Tell off a break doncha reckon mate?'

Conway didn't hear him because apart from the head banging music, his attention was taken by a stunning nude dancer who had appeared out of the darkness and stood in front of him smiling suggestively saying what appeared to be, "bacloom, bacloom." He turned to Gates and looked askance. Gates looked at him with an expression which said, "I know all about Patpong".

'Mate she is asking you to go with her to the "back room" for a quick "boom boom" they have trouble pronouncing their "r's",' he laughed.

Conway declined but as the dancer flounced off he couldn't help thinking what a sensational body she had. A body that would put many a Paris or New York model to shame.

Such was the female "talent" in Patpong 1.

Things were certainly falling into place in the Bangkok Down Under. Apart from the increased trade, the books were now up to date and a full set of accounts including a Balance Sheet had been produced. The transformation was virtually complete.

Susan and Conway had become closer and shared several candle lit meals in a number of Bangkok's finest restaurants in towers high above the city providing the spectacular panorama that was Bangkok at night. Despite the romantic temptation, apart from a quick peck on the cheek, there had been no further intimacy.

To show his appreciation of their efforts Somchai took them both on a tour of Bangkok and for quiet, reclusive Susan it was simply magic. She marvelled at the magnificent architecture and grandeur of The Grand Palace and the Wats with their gleaming gilded *chedis,* polished orange and green roof tiles, mosaic-encrusted pillars and rich marble pediments and murals.

The mysterious Emerald Buddha took her breath away and Somchai proudly related the colourful history of the small image from when it first appeared in 15th century Chiang Rai. It was believed to have originated in India then transported to Ceylon then to Thailand, taken by raiders to Laos in the 16th century but won back by the Thais in a war 200 years later and has remained in Bangkok ever since.

They were taken to the huge Chatuchuk market said to be not only the largest open-air market in Asia but some say, the world. Susan's eyes popped at the head-spinning array of goods on display of top quality clothing, exquisite handicraft art and antiques, music, videos, CDs and flowers, much at unbelievably low prices.

After a day doing the rounds of the wonderful sights of Bangkok Somchai hosted them on a night dinner cruise in a converted teak junk on the mighty Chao Praya River. As they cruised beneath the stars Susan gazed in wonder at the twinkling shoreline of Bangkok. The night was alive with the sounds and smells of this magical city. The sheer romance of the moment enveloped Susan and she did not refuse when Conway finally reached over and took her hand.

A week later the three of them met again at Don Muang, Bangkok's international airport. Conway and Susan were about to board a flight back to Manila. There had been a farewell party in the Down Under the night before with hugs and kisses from the staff and a genuine handshake from Gates. Conway and Susan left with some misgivings and a hope in their hearts that the work they had begun would be continued.

They stood in the departure lounge, the final boarding call for their flight echoing in their ears. Somchai looked at them and smiled. Was that a tear in his eye?

'I hope you both will come back one day,' he said sincerely. 'You have not been here long but you have done a wonderful job for me and our shareholders and I...we...all of us here thank you, very, very much...we will miss you.'

'We will come back Khun Somchai,' replied Conway, feeling a bit emotional himself. He had grown to enjoy the hurly burly and bustle of Bangkok. Its traffic was mad, everything was going at a million miles an hour but, he'd enjoyed the job, the sights, the food...and what great people?

'Susan and I need to return to see that what we have started was not in vain and continues to produce the results you, your shareholders…and me, expect. Sure, we can monitor it by regular reports but there is nothing like being here on the spot.'

Somchai nodded, 'Yes that is true Khun Steve.' Then with a wide grin he stepped forward, put his arms around Susan and gave her a big hug.

'Make sure you bring this lovely little lady back with you ok?'

'Sure,' smiled Conway as they shook hands, 'I wouldn't come back without her.'

As their Philippine Airlines flight lifted off on that Saturday evening, at a secret rendezvous somewhere in Manila, the Minister of Defence, Juan Ponce Enrile and Vice Chief of Staff of the Armed forces, Lt. General Fidel Ramos held a meeting which would change the course of Philippine history.

\* \* \*

Sally replaced the receiver and slumped back onto her pillow. The call had taken her completely by surprise. Her mind was in turmoil. She was going to have to make a decision, a big one, which could change her whole life. She tossed and turned and it wasn't until the early hours did she drift off into a dreamless sleep.

\* \* \*

Jumbo Keyes was also unable to sleep. He was still thinking about what he had seen in the restaurant. Why was Lily with Sanchez? Was it just an innocent dinner date? What had she in common with someone like him? They looked pretty friendly. There was a familiarity which bespoke a deeper relationship. I wish Steve was back here, he really needs to know about this little episode. Something is going on between those two and my gut feeling tells me it involves Mr Steve Conway…But what? Ang usually a deep sleeper was still awake, aware of her husband's restlessness. She reached out in the darkness and touched his hand.

'Darling, what is it? You've been tossing and turning all night, what's on your mind?'

Keyes rolled over and faced her. 'Nothing for you to worry about my little Filipino treasure, come here,' he said pulling her to him.

\* \* \*

Keyes and Sally were not the only ones having trouble sleeping. In Malacanang Palace President Ferdinand Marcos was also having trouble dropping off. He was a very worried man. He was receiving daily reports of the growing unrest and protests in the streets. His health was deteriorating and he knew only too well, so was his grip on power. He had gone on television and given a long, rambling speech trying to calm the populace but to no effect and the damn Americans were badgering him on the phone every day to step down.

COMELEC (the Commission on Elections) had declared him the winner of the recent general election, so why couldn't the people accept the decision? They had always stood behind him in the past. And now the Catholic Bishops Conference had condemned the election result and to make matters worse the United States Senate had passed a similar resolution.

His beside phone rang. It was General Fabian Ver, Chief of the Philippine Armed Forces.

'Excellency, we have trouble,'

'I know that!' snapped Marcos.

'I mean *real* trouble,' said Ver anxiously.

'What is it now General? The way things are it can't get much worse,' said Marcos wearily.

'Ponce Enrile and Ramos have held a press conference withdrawing their support for you and...' he paused, 'they are saying that you cheated in the recent elections and that Aquino is the rightful president.'

Marcos was now fully awake and alert. The Minister of Defence and Ramos, Ver's deputy, had turned against him and were no doubt trying to persuade the army as well as the people to join them.

'Traitors, I will crush them!' fumed Marcos. 'Arrest them!...now!... immediately! I want them behind bars before morning!'

'Yes Excellency, it will be done,' replied Ver, wincing as Marcos slammed down the phone.

\* \* \*

Conway and Susan sat in a coffee shop in Remedios Circle well away from the Down Under discussing the Bangkok interlude and the problem of the secret bank account.

'Bangkok was wonderful wasn't it sir,' smiled Susan, now much more relaxed in Conway's company.

'Susan,' grinned Conway, 'you can call me sir at work, because we should keep our relationship there professional but outside of work please, call me Steve, ok?'

'Ok Si...Steve,' she laughed, 'I will try to remember.'

'Yes, Bangkok was wonderful and as I told Somchai I hope we go back one day but, we do have some urgent matters to attend to here, like that bank account for example. I'm going to front Mr Prickett in the morning to sort it out.'

'Oh,' said Susan. She bit her lip, her relaxed manner disappearing instantly.

'Do you want me to be there with you?' She asked reaching over covering his hand with hers.

'No, I can handle it, I just want an explanation and if everything is kosher we can get on with our work. If not, well, I am not sure what happens from there.'

'Darling, I am worried, I am also not sure this is a good idea,' she murmured.

He smiled to himself. This is probably the first time in her life this shy, reserved woman has ever called a man "darling". It sounded so genuine and loving coming from her and reminded him of his beloved Jane.

'Susan I have to get to the bottom of it one way or another.'

'Yes, but I am afraid of the consequences for you. And maybe for me too,' she said nervously.

'Don't worry, I will protect you whatever happens, I promise,' he said, leaning over and kissing her on the cheek.

\* \* \*

'Come in Steve, what can I do for you mate? Take a seat,' said Perc still with the oily unconvincing grin.

Since their return from Bangkok he had barely acknowledged the efforts of Conway and Susan in the Thai capital. Imelda had completely ignored them. Conway couldn't care less but the fact that they had not even bothered to offer a word of thanks to Susan burned him; time to light a fire under these two.

Conway threw a bank book on the desk. 'What's this Perc?'

'Huh,' grunted Perc leaning over and squinting disinterestedly at the book for a few seconds then his expression changed. His eyes widened and he looked at the book as if it was a land mine about to explode.

'Do you want to tell me what this book is all about or do you want *me* to tell you?' said Conway. There was no mistaking the accusatory tone in his voice. Perc flinched and opened the book.

'Where the fuck did you get this?' he said, leafing through the pages slowly shaking his head as if he had never seen it before…or suddenly wishing he hadn't.

'I don't like your tone Conway and I have no idea what the fuck it is, come on, where'd you get it?' replied Perc angrily, feeling attack was the best form of defence.

Conway leaned over the desk his face a few inches from Pricketts.

'It came from the desk of our cashier, or former cashier, Ada Latonga. She told me some very interesting things about you and your sweet wife. This book contains a substantial amount of the foreign exchange transacted in this hotel that should have been deposited in the company's account. I have a statement signed *under oath* to say that this was done under explicit instructions from you and Imelda. These deposits also include funds from your, shall we say, other "extraneous" activities.'

Conway was bluffing because he had no idea where the surplus funds making up the deposits came from and he had no statement, signed or otherwise, but it was worth throwing out a line to see if Perc would take the bait.

Perc's ruddy booze induced jowls turned the colour of a pale stool. How much did this bastard know? Why didn't Sanchez bump him off when he had the chance, the useless bludger.

'Dunno what the fuck yer talkin' about. Never seen that bloody book before in my life, you're goin' the right way to gettin' the sack pal!' yelled Perc, the colour returning to his cheeks, his blood pressure soaring.

Conway's blood pressure was also rising.

'Listen to me pal! You're going the right way to getting kicked out of this rathole and into the local immigration jail! I'm sure the Australian shareholders would just love to know about this little book and these other rorts you've been up to.'

Fuck, thought Perc, I've got to get rid of this joker before he blows the whistle. He definitely knows more than is good for him…or me.

'Look Steve, mate,' said Perc, attempting conciliation. 'Calm down, it's not what you think. That book is like what you might call, a Christmas Club! Yeah that's it, a Christmas Club! Imelda and I thought it would be a good idea to put some of the funds away so that we could give the staff a huge party at Christmas and surprise them with double their 13 month pay. You know mate, like a special Christmas bonus. I had it ok'd by the Australian shareholders ages ago, long before you came on the scene. Mate believe me, I didn't know that was the book they were using. There's nothin' to worry about, don't get your knickers in a knot, everything's above board, I promise you,' said Perc hoping against hope Conway would swallow his bullshit.

Conway shook his head.

'No go Perc. You expect me to swallow that crap? With the amount of money in this book you could put on a party for all of Manila! It'd be the biggest bloody party in Philippine history. What about the rest of the funds? There's a lot more than the foreign exchange in this book, where did they come from?' asked Conway grabbing the book from Prickett.

'Hey fuck...' cried Prickett reaching for the book but was pushed back in his chair.

I'm gonna have this bastard salvaged tonight so help me God raged Prickett inwardly but somehow maintaining a calm exterior he said, 'look mate,' the tone now more wheedling than ever. 'Imelda and I have a few "investments" in Hong Kong. That's why I was up there recently. It's the proceeds from those. It's our...let's say, "retirement fund".'

'What investments Perc.?'

'That's my business, nothing to do with this hotel or you or anyone else,' snapped Perc.

'I can check out your story...mate! If it doesn't fit, I will be filing a full report,' said Conway pocketing the book and turning to leave.

'Do what you fuckin' like,' ranted Perc getting to his feet. 'Get out of my fucking office, I'm gunna have you fired, shareholders or no fucking shareholders!'

Conway returned to his office and phoned Susan

'What happened, how did it go?' she asked nervously.

'As I expected, he thinks I know where the surplus funds came from so there could be some more fireworks. He's going to fire me for sure. There's some bad stuff been going on here Susan. I don't know where those extra funds have come from but I have a pretty good idea.'

'Where?'

'Sorry, I can't tell you right now.'

'Oh my God! I am afraid! What do you think will happen now?'

'Don't worry,' he said, trying to calm her. 'I'll contact the major shareholders in Australia and tell them the story. They can decide what to do. In the meantime I will play it by ear. If you see Jumbo around send him to my office please. Forget it Susan, he's just walked in.'

* * *

Perc sat in his office still seething. 'I'll fix that Conway bastard,' he said to himself grabbing his phone and calling Imelda. 'Come here now!' Then he dialed the number of Ramon Sanchez.

Imelda frowned, as she put down the phone. What's wrong now? She was used to Perc and his tantrums. It was usually shit on his liver caused by a raging hangover but this time there was panic in his voice. She got up from behind her desk, gazed admiringly at her image in the long mirror on a wall to her left, applied some lipstick, touched her hair and left to find out what was worrying her husband.

A furious Perc described his conversation with Conway to her.

'I've had enough of this guy. We have to do something about him, and fast!'

'You know what I wanted to do with him my dear husband.'

'Well do it! I don't give a fuck now *who* does it, *how* and *when*. Just fucking do it, shit!' Perc had inhaled too deeply and again nearly choked himself.

'Your wish as usual, is my command my little bowl of *lechon*,' she said, sweeping from his office in a whirl of taffeta and expensive perfume, leaving Perc still spluttering and gasping for breath. Back in her office she summoned Eduardo. He stood before her, hands behind his back, dreading what she might be about to tell him. His heart sank as he heard her words.

'I now order you to carry out the instructions I indicated when we first spoke, you know what I mean don't you?' she said, coal black eyes boring into him.

'Yes, ma'am,' he muttered.

'Do it. Now go!' She commanded. His shoulders slumped. He stood for a moment about to say something but changed his mind and left.

\* \* \*

Ramon Sanchez picked up his phone to hear the voice of Perc Prickett; a very different Perc Prickett. Gone were the weak attempts at humour and pretentious bullshit. The tone was businesslike and serious.

'Hello Ramon, I'll come straight to the point. When is that shipment arriving, and on what vessel?'

Sanchez paused before answering. Although they had done a lot of deals, he always tried to dominate where possible and let Perc in on any plans only when it suited him; and usually at the last moment. He was the one to ask the questions and not the one to give answers, however this time he demurred.

'The ship is *The Asian Explorer* and it will be in port by the end of the week. Please do not worry Mr Prickett, I will keep you informed,' said Sanchez smoothly.

'Yeah, and make sure you do. This operation's gotta go without a hitch, right?'

'Yes, it will Mr Prickett and…'

Perc cut in, 'There's somethin' else. Bloody Conway has to be taken care of and this time, for keeps and no fuckups right?'

'I assure you there will be no mistake this time. I have a plan to get rid of Conway. Your worries will be over very soon Mr Prickett.'

'Whaddya got in mind?'

'You will find out all in good time Mr Prickett, just leave it to me.'

'Yeah, righto,' said Perc hanging up.

* * *

Susan and Conway sat at dinner discussing the day's events, she still very worried. He felt the same but did not want to add to her concern so attempted to play down the seriousness of the situation with a calm, unworried tone.

'I don't believe that story about the funds being used for a staff party at Christmas do you?' asked Susan, sipping an orange juice.

'No, of course not, it's rubbish and I guarantee the shareholders in Australia know nothing about it. It's just a slush fund for Perc and Imelda. I'm going to phone Australia in the morning and ask them.'

'Oh dear, I do hope this works out, I hate this intrigue darling, it's worrying me so much I can't sleep.'

'Hey, don't worry, I'll sort it out,' he said lightly, hoping his eyes did not reveal his true feelings.

Susan looked at her watch. 'It's getting late. I had better be going home now.'

'Where do you live Susan, I've never thought to ask you?'

'Las Pinas. It's an area south of here. It takes me an hour sometimes to get to work, depending on the traffic.'

'How do you normally go home? What route?'

'I usually take a jeepney to Baclaran, then another which takes me along the coastal road through Zapote and then to Las Pinas. Darling, I better hurry or I will miss my jeep.'

'I'd take you home but I want to think about things and try to figure out what to do if things turn pear shape which I think they will. I hope you don't mind love?'

'No, of course not,' she said leaning over to peck him on the cheek.

He stood and waited with her on MH Del Pilar Street until her jeepney arrived. When it was lost in the heavy evening traffic he began to walk along Flores Street back to his apartment. On the spur of the moment he turned left into a narrow lane he often used as a shortcut. Deep in thought, trying to ignore the ear-splitting music of a rock band blasting out of a bar nearby, he was unaware of the figure creeping up behind him in the darkness.

# 21

Peter Richardson from Australian television barged into *Nightbirds* with his cameraman, sound man and a posse of plain clothes police in tow causing instant pandemonium!  Dancers, cashiers and other female staff scattered, running in all directions, heading for the toilet, dressing rooms, even some for the front door while their bemused male customers wondered what the hell was going on.

The police often raided the bars usually around Christmas and Easter not for moral reasons, but to line their pockets with fines they imposed on the girls and the occasional customer they arrested.  Foreigners were generally left alone but if any of them decided to object, they were hauled away to spend the night in a cell often with their "girlfriend", and usually released the following morning after payment of a hefty fine.

The advent of a TV crew meant the cops could strut their stuff and pretend they were serious about cracking down on prostitution.  It was laughable. *Nightbirds* was literally metres away from the local Catholic Church and had been in operation for several years.

This raid however was different from those in the past.

The signing of the extradition treaty between the Philippines and Australia meant that the Australian Federal police could take a more pro-active role against the activities of the Australian criminal expats.  Thus on this particular raid, the police contingent included several members of the Australian Feds.  Ignoring the fleeing dancers the Australians made a beeline for the office of Barney Lawson and dragged him protesting to a waiting van parked immediately outside the front door of *Nightbirds*.  Then they took off around the corner to *The Black Jack*, where a few minutes later they wheeled Bert Groyne out to join his compatriot.

Sally late for work, hurried around the corner from Mabini Street and saw Groyne hauled out of *The Black Jack* and bundled into the back of a van parked outside. Two things became immediately obvious. Bert Groyne would not be returning to *The Black Jack* and her days there were over. The decision she had wrestled with all night had now been made for her.

* * *

Conway was halfway along the alley when he thought he heard a slight noise behind him. He stopped and looked back. A tingle up his spine told him someone was there but in the pitch blackness it was impossible to see anything. He walked on a few more paces and stopped again cocking his ear but the rock band drowned out all other sound. He shook his head, probably just rats among the rubble. He quickened his pace toward the lights of United Nations Avenue. He didn't hear the figure creep silently toward him holding a long bladed knife in his upraised hand or the almost silent 'plop' causing the figure to stagger and fall.

In his apartment he made coffee and was considering his options in the bank account affair when his phone rang. It was Sally and her voice sounded strange, unsettled; there was something wrong. What now?

'Hi Sally, this is a pleasant surprise, I was going to come to see you but...' she cut him short.

'Si...Steve can I come to see you please, there is something I need to talk to you about.'

'Sure, you sound upset, what is it?'

'I'll tell you when we meet, can I come now?'

'Sure.' He had no sooner given her his address when the phone rang again. This time it was Jumbo Keyes.

'Yes Jumbo,' he said wearily.

'Steve I have to come and talk to you man. It may be nothing but I think you should know about it,' said Keyes, his voice also sounded different. What's going on tonight? Everyone wants to tell me something and it all sounds mysterious and dramatic.

'Can't it wait till morning? I've got someone coming to see me.'

'It's not Lily is it?' asked Keyes, his tone hardening.

Conway frowned, 'no, it's not. Why?'

'Ok I'll tell you in the morning. As I said, it's probably nothing.'

'For God sake Keyes what the hell do you want to tell me?'

'It's Lily man, I saw her having dinner with Sanchez, and they looked pretty pally to me.'

A light came on in Conway's head.

'Where are you now?'

'In the hotel, why?'

Conway explained how Lily had appeared out of the blue on Boracay saying she had been advised by someone on the Down Under staff of his whereabouts.

'Remember, I left strict instructions that my trip to Boracay was to be kept secret and that no one, like no one, was to be told where I was. So I want you to check with all the switchboard staff, front desk or anyone else who may have been likely to take an incoming call. Find out if anyone remembers a woman phoning wanting to speak to me. And more importantly, did they let on where I was…ok?'

'Got it man. With three shifts it might take a day but I'll get onto it right away.'

'Thanks, because from what you just told me, our Lily might just be in cahoots with Sanchez and it could explain her sudden appearance and other things which happened on Boracay…and before.'

'Yes it could. They looked pretty friendly in that restaurant. *Too* friendly if you ask me.'

'I don't like the sound of it either and to make matters worse I fronted Perc today about that mysterious bank book. He was not a very happy little chap. He threatened to fire me so I'm going to lay low for a few days. When you find out about Lily, phone me and we can meet somewhere and try and figure out what to do from there.'

'Sure thing,' said Keyes hanging up. Conway finished his coffee and started to read the *Manila Bulletin* with its banner headlines about the defection of Enrile and Ramos when his door bell rang. Standing there with an uncustomary serious expression was Sally. She was carrying a yellow leather shoulder bag and looked as ravishing as ever in a low-cut maroon top and white mini skirt. He ushered her in and went to embrace her. To his surprise she put both hands up to his chest and prevented him from doing so.

'Sally, what?' he said, for a moment lost for words.

Her face was a picture of misery. 'Steve there is something I must tell you.'

'Please do,' he said ushering her in. He looked at her forlorn figure and wondered what the hell was going on? These days there seem to be one surprise after another and they were usually unpleasant.

'Would you like a drink?'

'No thank you,' she said quietly. 'He's back!' she blurted.

'Who's back?'

'Marvin'

'Who the hell is Marvin?'

'He's the Marine I told you about. The one who left.'

'So, why the sad face?'

She looked at him as if to say; how insensitive are you? Don't you care? Don't I mean anything to you?

'Ok, sit down and tell me all about it,' said Conway leading her to a sofa. 'When did you hear, and what are you going to do?'

She told him about the phone call. It was Marvin calling from the United States. He had married but it hadn't worked out. He realized she was the one he really loved and wanted her back, if she would have him.

'And will you? Remember what he did to you Sally?'

'I guess so,' she shrugged, 'but it will be a way out of here and it's better than serving drunks in *The Black Jack*. He is offering me a new life, why would I not consider him?' she said with a hint of defiance, her tone begging the question. Why haven't you asked me?

'But then again,' she sighed, 'I don't really know if I should…you know how I feel about you,' she reached over and took both his hands in hers. She was impossible to resist. He brought her to her feet and kissed her long and lovingly until she pushed him away.

'I shouldn't,' she said stepping away from him. Tears rolled down her cheeks.

He stood bewildered, wanting to comfort her but not knowing what to say.

'Well, when will he come for you?'

'As soon as he can get a furlough which he thinks will be in about a month. Then, if things work out between us he will take me back to America.'

He took a handkerchief from his pocket and handed it to her. 'You should be very happy now you've found a way out of here.'

She wiped away the tears and closed her eyes for a few seconds. You stupid man, can't you see I am in love with you?

'Oh, I must tell you,' she said suddenly changing the subject, handing him back the handkerchief. 'Sir Groyne has been taken away.'

'Oh really, when? And who by?'

'It was the police. They have raided before but never taken Sir Groyne away in the past. I don't know what is wrong but I think this time it is serious. I heard them talking in the bar about some treaty between Australia and the Philippines where bad Australian guys here can be deported. Anyway, I don't want to go back there.' She picked up her shoulder bag she had left on a sofa. 'I think I had better go.' She walked to the door but he took her arm and stopped her.

'Sally, I…' was all he said before they flung their arms around each other.

'I will miss you *so* much. You've been so kind to me. I loved you but I knew in my heart you never loved me,' she said brokenly. He couldn't speak, the lump in his throat threatened to choke him. He stood softly stroking the long dark hair, her head buried in his chest.

I don't want to lose her, but she deserves happiness and she needs to get away from here. Her words had shocked and hurt but he knew in his heart her decision to go with the Marine was the right one. They stood holding each other for many minutes until she suddenly kissed him quickly on the cheek and left without another word.

\* \* \*

Early next morning, two small boys running along a narrow alley between Flores Street and United Nations Avenue discovered the body of a man lying face down with a long-bladed knife in the dirt near his right hand. A closer look revealed a bullet hole in the back of his head. They ran away in panic. Five minutes later one brought his father back to the scene. The father gingerly put his foot under the body and turned it over. There staring back at him was a pair of sightless googly eyes.

\* \* \*

James Sinclair the managing director of the Down Under's Australian operation was about to reach for his phone when it rang. He picked it up and heard a familiar voice.

'Hey g'day Steve, just the man I wanted to talk to. I've had Perc on the phone abusing me for sending you to Manila…what? Ok, go ahead.'

Sinclair listened in silence for a few minutes. 'No Steve, we have no knowledge of any Christmas Club fund. Perc Prickett and a Christmas Club? You've got to be joking! No, I repeat we know nothing about it and we certainly gave no approval of *any* company funds to be diverted to another account. I think maybe I better come up there and see for myself what's going on. Don't worry, we have seen the results since you've been there and we have no problem with you, we're very happy. That new accountant has sent us a couple of financials and they are a bloody big improvement on the past. Yes, ok mate. Thank you for the call, see you soon.' Sinclair replaced the phone and spoke into an intercom to his secretary. 'Get me on the next flight to Manila.'

* * *

Conway sat at the far end of the bar in the Manila Yacht Club. Normally he would be looking out at the wide expanse of Manila bay marvelling at the sunset which blessed the Philippines capital every evening, but not on this occasion.

'What did you find out about Lily, did anyone remember her calling?' asked Conway dispensing with any pleasantries as Keyes arrived, slumping down on a stool beside him. The American shook his head. Conway ordered two beers and suggested they move to a small table well away from the bar and out of earshot of the other customers.

'So, no one remembers her calling and no one remembers telling anyone I was in Boracay? Do you believe them? Maybe someone did and they're too afraid to admit it?'

'I don't think so man. I know the staff on duty at that time very well and I believe them. There's no way they would have disobeyed my orders. I made it *very* clear that anyone breaching this order would be fired on the spot. No Steve, no one in the Down Under told Lily you were in Boracay. I'd stake my life on it.'

Conway banged his fist on the table. 'Then it must have been bloody Sanchez who told her!'

'Looks like it. Otherwise who else Steve? It seems we have a nigger in the woodpile.' Realising what he had just said, Keyes roared with laughter, causing everyone in the bar to turn and look for the joke. They had a few more drinks then under cover of darkness left to find a taxi. Driving up Roxas Boulevard they were stopped by a motor bike cop and moved to the side of the road to allow six police outriders and a convoy of trucks carrying heavily armed troops to roar past.

Roxas Boulevard was not only choked with its usual rush hour traffic but the sidewalks on either side were a sea of slow moving people shouting and thrusting their arms in the air. Many were carrying the usual banners telling Marcos to step down and *LONG LIVE CORY.*

Finally after an interminably slow journey, Keyes dropped Conway off at his apartment and returned to the Down Under. Conway walked out onto the balcony and gazed out over Manila Bay for a few minutes trying to get his head around things before going back inside and making coffee. He took it into the lounge and sat down wondering what his next move should be. He drained his coffee and decided to have a shower. Maybe that would clear his head and give him some inspiration. He grabbed a clean towel from a pile of washing the maid had left on the lounge and was about to step into the bathroom when his phone rang. He picked it up to hear a familiar voice...'hello darling.'

*  *  *

'Having your usual Chuck?'

'Sure Jack,' smiled McGaw easing himself into a seat beside Roberts. 'Now, what's on your mind my friend? What's this big news?' It was mid afternoon in an almost deserted bar at the lower end of Mabini street. The drinks came and the Australian leaned closer and lowered his voice.

'I've had a tip about a certain ship about to arrive in port with a cargo you and I should take some interest in old son.'

McGaw smiled crookedly, 'another scoop Jack?'

Roberts ignored the barb. 'Dunno, but my source is good. Never let me down in the past.'

'Oh yeah, you've got a short memory old buddy,' McGaw reminded him.

'Don't get too cocky pal, you guys have been left holding the bag on more than one occasion,' Roberts shot back. The American glanced around to see if anyone could hear them. The only other customers were two Filipinos at the far end of the bar deep in conversation. They were well out of earshot.

'Ok Jack...shoot!'

'A freighter, Liberian or Panamanian registered carrying dope among other things,' said Roberts his voice now barely above a whisper. 'Don't know what kind. My source believes it's uncut heroin.' We also don't know how much or how it's concealed but it's thought to be from Khun Sa the Burmese war lord; the stuff's been trekked over through Laos into Vietnam and loaded in Hai Phong.'

'You can confirm this?'

'Shit no, but we better get organized and make sure we're ready when and if it does arrive, just in case. I'll be given the name of the vessel either tonight or tomorrow for sure, then we can liaise with the local NBI and make our plans for a joint operation, ok?'

'Sure, let me know immediately you find out the ship's name and arrival, this sounds like it could be big. Now if I remember rightly, it's your turn to buy dinner.'

'You never forget do you McGaw,' grinned Roberts. 'Ok finish drinking that rubbish and I'll take you somewhere decent.'

*  *  *

Imelda walked into Perc's office just as he took a call from Sanchez.

'G'day Ramon, yeah, huh! I dunno.' He put his hand over the mouthpiece and turned to Imelda.

'Have we got someone called Eduardo Garcia working here?'

Imelda stared at him and said slowly, 'yes, why?'

'Yeah we have, why?' said Perc into the phone, holding up his finger to Imelda. 'Where? Ok, I'll get someone to come and identify him, now, about that shipment.

What's the latest? Ok, got it thanks,' said Perc with a self-satisfied smirk, replacing the receiver.

'What's this about Eduardo?' snapped Imelda. She hated being the third party in her husband's dealings with Sanchez. She was always the last to know and it pissed her off no end. 'Huh, oh he's dead,' replied Perc without a hint of concern for his employee. 'He was found with a bullet wound in the back of his head in that lane between Flores and United Nations Avenue; better get someone around to the morgue to officially identify him.' He looked quizzically at Imelda. 'You wouldn't know anything about it would you?'

'Don't be stupid,' she said angrily, 'was he robbed?'

'Dunno,' replied Perc disinterestedly. 'You better organize identification. Who was he anyway, where did he work?'

Imelda gritted her teeth. How did I ever get mixed up with this guy?

'He was a relative of mine, he worked in the kitchen.'

'Oh,' said Perc, 'uh' sorry, better organize that...'

'I know, I will do that now.'

Back in her office she sat and wondered. Who could have done this? Not Conway, I doubt if he would have a gun, he's not the type, and besides he wouldn't know Eduardo was after him. It must have been a random hit from a local thug. Now I'll have to find someone else.

* * *

'Darling, I want to see you again,' cooed Lily, 'when can we meet again, I've missed you so much.'

'Oh really,' replied Conway coldly. 'I've been meaning to contact you too...there was something I wanted to talk to you about.'

'Well maybe we can meet and you can ask me then darling. When would you like to meet and where?'

'Tonight at your place, 8.00 pm.'

'That would be lovely darling. I will have my chef prepare dinner for us.'

'That won't be necessary, I won't be staying long.'

'Oh,' she said warily, 'darling what's wrong, you sound upset, what is it?'

He ignored her question. 'I'll see you at 8 o'clock this evening.'

On the dot of 8.00 pm, he arrived in a taxi at Lily's mansion and told the driver to wait. Binky greeted Conway like a long lost friend and ushered him into the small ante room of his first visit and said Lily would be along in a few minutes. It was more than a few minutes and Conway's short fuse became a good deal shorter.

'Hello darling, how wonderful to see you,' gushed Lily when she finally appeared arms outstretched. She kissed him on both cheeks then led him by the hand to another larger room overlooking the swimming pool where Binky was waiting holding a silver tray containing goblets of French champagne. Conway reluctantly accepted one and stood unsmiling waiting for Binky to leave. As she left, Lily flashed him that familiar coquettish smile and clinked her glass on his.

'Darling, she pouted, 'you seemed so short on the phone today. Don't you like my outfit? You haven't said a word about it,' she said, putting down her glass and doing a slow pirouette giving him the full treatment.

'Yeah, yeah, you look sensational,' he said shortly. He was in no mood to boost her ego but there was no denying, as usual, she did look terrific. The tight, full length pink and white silk creation was sleeveless and caught at the neck. It did a beautiful job of emphasizing her honeyed skin and hour glass figure. Her glossy black hair was worn up and held by a couple of silver clips emphasizing the swan-like length of her neck. The high cheekbones were dusted with the hint of some exotic peach makeup and her eyes were illuminated by pink khol matched with a cherry lipstick. She could have been an elegant Russian countess straight out of *War and Peace*. In different circumstances he would have been dazzled - but not this time.

She continued to smile, so sure of herself, only too well aware the effect she had on men.

'I want you to tell me again how you knew I was in Boracay,' he said sharply.

She suddenly realized this was not a social call. Something had brought about this change in him, but what? She was bewildered and hurt. Her smile vanished and her tone changed.

'I told you,' she replied defensively. 'Someone at your hotel told me you had gone to Boracay.'

'Bullshit Lily!'

She flinched and stepped back as if he had slapped her.

'I left *strict* instructions before I left that *no one* was to be told of my whereabouts…*no one!*' The colour drained from her face and she became flustered.

'I…I…I, well, don't you believe me?' she said desperately. She stepped closer and took a long swallow of her champagne and tried to embrace him but he held up his hands to prevent her.

'Please darling don't do this…does it really matter who told me?'

'Bloody oath it does! You lied to me Lily. Sanchez told you didn't he? He sent you there to report on me and as a back-up to one of his men, the guy who attacked me the night we had dinner with the French couple. Didn't he? Lily, what is it with you and Sanchez?'

'Steve please, please, he is just an old friend. I have known him for years. He was a close friend of my late husband and I…' He cut her short.

'Lily,' he said very slowly, 'did Ramon Sanchez ask you to keep an eye on me?'

'Yes, yes he did. I admit that. Is that a crime?' She tossed her head defiantly and stalked over to where Binky had left the bottle of champagne on a small ornate round table, and refilled her goblet. She turned and faced him, her eyes blazing.

'Listen to me Steve Conway, I was worried about you since that attack outside my home and I wanted to see you again. Colonel Sanchez rang and told me you were on Boracay and said he also knew about the attack on you and was concerned for your safety.' She stopped for a moment and took a huge gulp of her champagne. 'He suggested that since I never seemed to have holidays I should take a short break, go to Boracay and keep an eye on you and let him know if you had any trouble there. I thought it was a great idea because I needed a holiday and would be killing two birds with one stone. But I swear on my father's grave, I did *not know* about that other man! Sanchez never mentioned anything about him. I am sorry I lied to you about Boracay, but what I am telling you now *is* the truth! Believe it or not, I don't care anymore!'

She was either telling the truth or was an Oscar winning actress. Only time would tell. Jumbo's words of how chummy she and Sanchez were in the restaurant came back to him but for the moment he had no way of disproving her story.

'Ok Lily, I believe you…for now. I have only met Sanchez once and we disliked each other on sight so it's passing strange that he should be worried about my welfare.'

'Darling please, I promise you, I had *no knowledge* of your relations with Colonel Sanchez but again, I thought he was just concerned, like I was.'

I don't know if I really believe all this but I'll give her the benefit of the doubt. Many in Manila's political, military and police circles frequented her restaurant so it's not beyond the realm of possibility that she and Sanchez would be friends and if he was a buddy of her late husband her story could be true....only time will tell.

'Ok Lily.'

She sighed with relief taking his hands and placing them on her breasts. 'Darling, let's not talk about Colonel Sanchez right now. I think we have better things to do don't you?'

Now he was dazzled.

'Lily, I don't know if I believe you, but you have a way about you that's hard to resist. Just a moment,' he said placing his goblet on the small table beside them and striding away toward her front door.

'Darling, where are you going?' She cried in dismay. In the driveway the taxi waited, the driver asleep. Conway reached in through the window and shook him awake.

'I won't need you now,' he said tossing a 100 Peso note into the driver's lap. He raced back up the steps to a puzzled Lily who greeted his return with relief and a 100 megawatt smile.

\* \* \*

General Fabian Ver, a hard-eyed individual in his mid sixties, wearing the full uniform of Chief of the Philippine Armed Forces, bedecked with medals, stood ramrod straight in front of his president. The two men made quite a contrast; the strong, tough military man and the Philippines President a pale, drawn, shadow of his former self.

Ferdinand Marcos looked up from the ornate chair in which he was sitting and asked for an update on the unrest in the streets.

'Your Excellency, we were unable to arrest them. Enrile has barricaded himself in Camp Aguinaldo and Ramos in Camp Crame,' said Ver staring straight ahead.

'Are there any troops with them?' asked Marcos grimly.

'Only a few hundred at the most Excellency, what do you want me to do?'

Just then an aide came into the room and bowed to Marcos. 'Your Excellency, Radio *Veritas* are replaying the press conference of Enrile and Ramos, I think you should hear it.' Marcos switched on the radio beside his bed and he and Ver listened intently. When it was over Marcos strode around the room wringing his hands then turned to the aid. 'I am going to give a news conference of my own now! Call the press immediately!'

Shortly afterwards before a huge gathering of local and international press Marcos called on the rebels to surrender urging them to "stop this stupidity".

It fell on deaf ears. To make matters worse at 9 pm that night Radio *Veritas* aired a message from the highly influential Catholic Archbishop of Manila, Cardinal Jaime Sin, exhorting Filipinos to come to the aid of the rebels by giving emotional support and taking food and other supplies to EDSA the Boulevard separating Camp Aguinaldo and Camp Crame.

Marcos summoned General Ver.

'What do you want me to do Excellency?'

'Send the troops immediately and destroy the transmitter of Radio *Veritas*.'

'It will be done Excellency,' said Ver snapping a smart salute.

Marcos continued to watch the unfolding events on television. He was sick, and tired, and now more worried than ever. Events were moving too quickly. He knew his grip on power was slipping but he would fight them. I am the Father of this country they cannot do this to me.

# 22

The *Asian Explorer* dropped anchor in Manila Bay near the island of Corrigedor just after midday. That evening the captain, Juan Suarez went ashore and met two men in a restaurant on Roxas Boulevard.

The three had a meal and stayed for some hours chatting over many bottles of San Miguel beer and several bottles of French wine. By the time they left the restaurant all three were very drunk. To any observer it was obvious that by the way they clapped each other on the back, laughed and hugged, a happy event had taken place or perhaps some big deal had been finalized. Captain Suarez staggered off to find a taxi back to his ship while Perc Prickett and Ramon Sanchez took off toward the entertainment strip of P. Burgos Street in Makati to celebrate.

* * *

The sun blazed down on a bright blue Manila morning as Conway and Lily sat once more at breakfast by her swimming pool. Binky brought out the usual hearty meal for Conway and something light for her boss then skipped away inside. Lily sipped her orange juice and smiled across at Conway.

'What are you thinking lover? You seem preoccupied this morning? I hope you are not thinking about our conversation last night darling?'

'Huh,' said Conway snapping out of it.

He *was* still thinking about what Lily had told him of her relationship with Sanchez and wondered whether it tied in with everything that had been happening to him. She seemed quite genuine in her concern and her story made sense but he couldn't dismiss those nagging doubts.

'Sorry,' he said, buttering a piece of toast. Taking a sip of Lily's excellent Brazilian coffee, he leaned back and yawned. 'Actually, it was nothing too world shaking, just a few little problems at work but nothing I can't handle. By the way, I've been meaning to ask you, how are things with your restaurant. You seem to be doing very well, any thoughts of expanding?' She was about to take another sip of orange juice but stopped with the glass half way to her lips.

'It's a coincidence you should ask such a question Steve because,' she put the glass down. 'I have something important to tell you.'

Not you too, he thought. 'Ok, what revelation do you have for me Lily? Don't tell me you're the illegitimate daughter of President Marcos or that Sanchez is really your brother? Or even worse, you're actually a man?' he grinned.

She stood up and smiled wickedly.

'Do I look like a man darling?' she sucked in her belly and thrust out her pouter-pigeon breasts.

'Ok, ok, I believe you, whoops,' he laughed, nearly spilling his coffee. 'So what is this "important news"?'

She sat down and toyed with her glass. Gone was the playful Lily, her expression now serious. 'Steve, we both know this country is in turmoil and I am not sure what is going to happen. Do you know that our Minister of Defence, Mr Ponce Enrile and the Vice Chief of the Armed Forces Lt. General Ramos whom you met at my party, have turned against President Marcos and have barricaded themselves in military camps opposite each other in EDSA?'

He nodded, 'yes, I saw that in the newspapers. Things are beginning to look bad, could be bloodshed if it's not handled properly.'

'I agree, and I tell you Steve…I am frightened. I have foreseen something like this happening since Aquino was murdered.' She shook her head, despair in her eyes.

'This country is heading down a very dangerous path,' she continued, 'I can see civil war and much bloodshed. Steve, I don't want to be around for all that. I am seriously considering selling my restaurant and moving back to Shanghai. My late husband's family phoned me recently and suggested I return there. It sounds fantastic in Shanghai these days and I want to check it out. Steve, they are sure there are great prospects for me there. The economy is booming, and I believe now that when the Chinese Government take back Hong Kong, which they will in 1997, Shanghai will become the most prosperous city in all of Asia. Darling it appeals to the entrepreneur in me,' she leaned across the table and placed her hand over his. 'I believe I have a future there because only God knows what will happen to this country!'

'You're not going to leave a sinking ship are you Lily?' he chided, only half in jest.

She bridled.

'I am a single woman. I have no one. My first responsibility is to *me*!' she said angrily.

'Hey, calm down,' Conway said, raising his hands defensively. 'I was not entirely serious Lily and I do see your point. You have to look after number one, especially in these current circumstances. To tell you the truth, I feel exactly the same as you. I am not sure if I want to stay in this country after what has happened to me since I've been here.'

He squeezed her hand. 'You know Lily, you are one of a kind. I will miss you if you go.' There was undeniable sincerity in his tone. She put down her coffee cup, and came around to his side and threw her arms around him.

'Then come to Shanghai with me darling. We would make a great team.'

'It's a tempting offer and thanks for the invitation. I'm sure if anyone can make a go of it there, you can Lily, but I have a job to do here. Whether I stay or not remains to be seen, but there are a few things I need to sort out before I decide where my future lies. Shanghai sounds like it could be a whole new challenge. Maybe we can talk about it when the picture becomes clearer in this country. It's in a state of flux at the moment and anything could happen. Frankly, I don't really know if I will have a job this time next week. So let's just wait and see ok?' He disengaged himself and stood up. 'And now I'm sorry, but I have to leave.'

'You're always leaving me darling,' she pouted. 'But what you say sounds fair, kiss me and I will take you wherever you want.' She looked at her watch. 'I must go to my restaurant now anyway.' They shared a long lingering kiss and twenty minutes later she dropped him at his apartment.

He phoned Keyes to be told James Sinclair the managing director had arrived from Australia, and was looking for him.

'Ok. Where are the Pricketts?'

'They've hightailed it to Angeles city. Methinks they're not too keen on speaking to James Sinclair. What do you want me to do?'

'Ask Sinclair to phone me, tell him I'm playing it cool after Prickett's threats.' Within ten minutes Sinclair was on the line. James Sinclair, an ebullient Scotsman, came straight to the point.

'What the hell is going on Steve? Where are the Pricketts? This bloody hotel is running on auto pilot, I am *not* happy with what I see here,' said the Scot, his voice rising.

'I understand completely James but don't worry the Down Under is in good hands with Jumbo Keyes. As for the Pricketts, I believe they are in Angeles

City right now. Let's meet for lunch and I'll bring you up to speed.' Sinclair calmed down and they arranged to meet at a restaurant in the Greenhills area of Makati's commercial hub.

* * *

'Nice to see you again Steve sorry about this morning,' smiled Sinclair, as they shook hands. 'No worries James, you had every right and believe me, I am very pleased to see you too,' said Conway as they were taken to a table.

'First of all, I think we better have a drink,' smiled the Scotsman. '*Royal Salute* for me and whatever you're having. Don't worry Steve today's on me,' said Sinclair at Conway's raised eyebrows. *Royal Salute* was top of the range whisky and outside his budget. Conway ordered the Scotch and a San Mig for himself then wasted no time bringing the MD up to date with recent events.

Sinclair listened in silence nodding occasionally then said, 'bashings, attempts on your life, secret bank accounts! You must have wondered what the bloody hell you'd got yourself into?'

'That's an f'ing understatement James.'

Sinclair drained his Scotch and signaled for another round of drinks. 'Yeah, and on top of all that,' continued Sinclair, 'this country seems about to implode. Steve, these attempts on your life and the bashing, it seems to be too coincidental to be random doesn't it? What do you think? What else have you been up to?'

'Well,' began Conway, but Sinclair interrupted and looked him in the eye.

'Come clean Steve, have you upset one of the local femmes because that can be a *very* dangerous thing to do? More than one foreigner has come to grief here getting on the wrong side of one of the local ladies who has just happened to have a jealous boyfriend.'

'No way was it random and no, I have *not* upset, as far as I know, any of the local women in fact quite the opposite,' replied Conway, trying unsuccessfully to suppress a grin. 'Sure I've trod on a couple of toes but nothing to warrant any of the crap that has happened. All I will say, is, I have my suspicions but can't prove anything.'

'What about the cops, what do they say?'

'Jack Roberts from the Australian Federal Police is looking into it but so far no result. Nothing from the local police either.' Better to leave the local constabulary out of it, thought Conway.

Their drinks arrived and both men sat in silence for a minute or two with their thoughts. Sinclair was the first to speak. 'Ok, now this bank account you found? What's all that about, give me the story again.' Conway repeated what he'd told Sinclair in their phone call about the discovery of the secret bank account, how he and Susan had interviewed bank staff and the former head cashier Ada Latonga, and how Perc had tried to pass it off as a special account for the staff's Christmas party and annual leave payments.

'It's bullshit James.'

'Ok,' replied the MD thoughtfully, 'I'll have a word to the Pricketts, when they come back to Manila. Don't worry, I'll sort this out one way or another, then get back to you. Under the circumstances I think you should lay low for the moment.'

Sinclair, a solidly built 50 year old with a great capacity for alcohol, turned out to be great company and they stayed on after the meal drinking and exchanging experiences, pleasant and otherwise, in the Philippines. With the sun well over the yardarm they called it quits. Sinclair paid the substantial bill and they took a taxi back to Ermita, unaware they were being followed by a black sedan.

\* \* \*

Things continued to hot up in Manila. The capital was now gripped in the fever of revolution. Troops loyal to Marcos had destroyed the transmitter of Radio *Veritas* but the station simply switched to a standby transmitter. In the meantime hundreds of thousands continued to flock to EDSA armed only with prayers and rosaries.

Despite the seriousness of events the atmosphere was actually festive, indicative of the basically happy nature of Filipinos. Performers entertained the crowd, nuns and priests set up prayer vigils while others set up barricades of sandbags and trees and blocked EDSA and several intersecting streets with motor vehicles. Everywhere supporters of Cory flashed the *LABAN* (fight) sign, an "L" formed with their thumb and index finger.

In a further show of solidarity Enrile left Camp Aguinaldo and crossed over EDSA to join Ramos in Camp Crame to the cheers of the crowd. But reports filtered through of Marines massing near the camps to the east and tanks approaching from the north and south.

Things were looking grim for the rebels.

Then armoured vehicles under the control of Brigadier General Tadiar advancing on the camps along Ortigas Avenue were stopped by tens of thousands of people. Nuns praying and holding rosaries knelt in front of the tanks while men and women, old and young, linked arms in an attempt to block the troops. Tadiar threatened to shoot but the crowd stood resolute. The troops were forced to retreat but it was obvious that this standoff could not continue, but who would win; Marcos with his heavily armed troops, or, "People Power"?

* * *

Two of *Manila's Finest* stood stiffly at attention in the office of Colonel Ramon Sanchez. Sergeant Roy Martinez and patrolman class 1 Artemio Reyes had been selected by Sanchez for a special mission. Sanchez told them to relax then showed them a photo.

'This is the man I have been telling you about. I want him detained and taken care of. He has been a thorn in my side and that of my friends. You know what to do with him. If he is not at the Down Under Hotel he will be at his apartment and here is the address of both,' he said handing addresses and a photo to Martinez.

Sanchez lowered his voice, his tone chilling. 'Just a reminder to you both, you know what happens to those who fail me.' Both men looked at each other. Lieutenant Danny Roque had disappeared, and there were rumours...

'It will be done sir,' said Martinez, 'we will take care of this Conway for you. We will not fail sir.'

Both men saluted briskly then turned on their heels and marched from the office. Sanchez leaned back in his chair with a contented smile. Goodbye Mr Conway.

* * *

In the streets there was more action and events seemed to be turning even more against the rebels. There was no doubt the forces of Marcos were gaining control of the situation. Marines approaching from the east lobbed tear gas grenades at the demonstrators as 3,000 more Marines entered the east side of Camp Aguinaldo. Helicopters of the 15th Air Force Strike Wing under the command of M/Gen Antonio Sotelo were ordered to neutralize Camp Crame.

To the shock and dismay of President Marcos and his supporters, Sotelo suddenly defected and landed his helicopters in Camp Crame and joined Enrile and Ramos.

Things were now more evenly balanced. The situation was on a knife edge. It could go either way. The ailing President decided to act.

He went on television telling the nation he would not step down but during a broadcast the station went off air. It had been captured by a contingent of rebel soldiers. It came back on later with a voice declaring; "This is Channel 4, serving the people again". On EDSA the crowd had swelled to over one million. Rebel helicopters attacked Villamor Air Base and one helicopter fired a rocket into Malacanang Palace. It caused only minor damage and was simply an act of contempt. Most of the officers who had graduated from the Philippines Military Academy defected and now most of the Armed Forces had changed sides.

It seemed the tables were turning. But was it really the end for the dictator?

\* \* \*

Perc Prickett smacked his lips and wiped the gravy from his chin. He was feeling extremely pleased with himself. He'd received a phone call from Ramon Sanchez to advise that the "presents" would soon be unloaded. In addition, the small matter of Steve Conway was being taken care of. He would be eliminated and this time there would be no hitches. 'Relax Mr Prickett,' said a confident Ramon Sanchez, all was going according to plan.

'What are you looking so pleased about?' asked Imelda suspiciously. They were dining in the poolside restaurant at the Billabong and Perc had been like a cat with two tails ever since he'd taken that phone call ten minutes ago but until now, had not disclosed the details. He could be a real pain in the butt.

Perc had also heard about the arrival of James Sinclair and was pissed off. What was bloody Sinclair doing here? And why didn't he tell me he was coming? He had never done that before. He would be sure to ask a few rather tricky questions about the events that had been taking place in the Down Under and Perc knew he didn't have the answers, truthful ones that is: Time to leave town for a few days old son.

'Darling, our worries will soon be over. Mr Conway will not be troubling us any further and you and I my petal, will soon be living in the manner to which we will both quickly become accustomed. That was Ramon Sanchez and he had good news…for the three of us.' He gave her the details of his conversation with the police chief and her smile grew wider…and wider.

'Where's Conway, and what about Sinclair?' she asked.

'Dunno where Conway is, don't care. All I know he won't be in our hair much longer. As for Sinclair, no worries, with Conway out of the way I will simply give him the usual bullshit. He won't be able to prove or disprove anything and will go back to Australia and leave us alone. I think this calls for a celebration my love. Would *Verve Cliquot* suit Madame? Garcon!'

'I never really doubted you my fat little *lechon*,' beamed Imelda, 'I sometimes underestimate you but you always surprise me. No one can beat my Perc,' she gushed. A waiter brought the champagne and filled their glasses.

Perc lifted his glass and said in his best James Cagney voice. 'Damn right baby! As they say in the classics, *tonight let's drink and be merry, for tomorrow...*'

\* \* \*

Lily Li stepped from her limousine and walked quickly across the compound into the Western Police District building. She smiled at the desk sergeant who nodded and went back to his newspaper. No need to ask what she wanted, he'd seen her with Sanchez before. It seemed they were close friends. A short corridor took her to the office of Sanchez. The door was slightly ajar and she raised her hand to knock. Then she heard Sanchez say the name, *Conway.*

She stood listening and as Sanchez continued her blood ran cold. She stood rooted to the spot for a few seconds then began to shake. She looked back, thankfully the corridor was empty but someone could come around that corner at any moment and she would have some very difficult questions to answer. Slowly, she stepped backwards toward the front office, almost tip toeing, her heart in her mouth, praying no one would come from Sanchez' office. It was a short distance to the police chief's office on her arrival but now the front entrance seemed the longest and most frightening walk of her life.

Luck was with her. The sergeant was not at his desk; probably in the comfort room. She breathed a silent prayer, thank you God. She made it to the front entrance and was about to step outside when she collided with two uniformed officers entering the building. Her heart jumped into her mouth. They stopped and apologized, but the older one looked at her suspiciously and took her by the arm.

'What are you doing ma'am, walking backwards from our offices, that is a very odd thing to do ma'am?' he asked, looking at her closely, noticing the pale face and trembling hands. She thought desperately of something plausible to say. Sanchez could come out of his door at any moment! He would immediately wonder what was happening and why she was so upset. He might just put two and two together...

'I have just heard some bad news, I am very upset now please let me go,' she pleaded. The lust of the younger office saved her.

'Sexy,' he said with a leer, looking her up and down. 'Do you have a boy friend ma'am?'

She ignored his question. Tears began to roll down her cheeks. 'Please! I have to go, I've just heard the news my husband has been killed,' she cried, trying to keep her voice low but grief stricken. Wrenching her arm from the other cop's grip she ran to her waiting limousine. She ripped open the rear door and yelled to her driver, 'Take me to the Down Under Hotel now! Fast!'

The two cops were still watching bemused then began to laugh as the limousine roared out of the compound causing an incoming motor cycle cop to swerve suddenly and hit a concrete pylon sending him sprawling onto the bitumen.

* * *

Susan finished her day's work. She was tired; it had been a long day. She put away her files, locked her desk drawers and walked out along United Nations Avenue, then turned left into MH Del Pilar. When she reached Padre Faura she stopped and looked around. Where was he? She jumped as she felt a tap on her shoulder and heard a familiar voice.

'Hi Susan.'

'Oh, you startled me darling, where have you been I have been so worried about you?' she said, throwing her arms around him.

'Tell you later,' he said kissing her on the cheek. He hailed a passing taxi. 'Where are we going?' she asked as the cab glided to a stop in front of them.

'I've read about a nice, cosy restaurant well away from here. I need to stay away from this area as much as possible for the moment,' he said handing the driver a written address.

The traffic as usual was a nightmare, especially excruciating as they crawled slowly down Aurora Boulevard and crossed EDSA choked with protestors. It was nearly an hour before they finally turned into a narrow ill-lit lane brightened only by a circular fluorescent sign which said *Casa Ramada.*

The narrow frontage opened out into a small open-air garden style restaurant the centrepiece of which was a small white marble fountain. Stars twinkled above on a beautiful night and the air was heavy with the sweet fragrance of sampaguita and roses.

'This is a lovely place, how did you find it?' asked Susan looking around as an attractive Filipina led them to a table beside the fountain.

'I saw it advertised in the newspaper apparently it's a hangout for movie stars and media types. I believe it's one of *Erap's* favourite restaurants.'

'Joseph Estrada, wow! He's one of my favourite movie stars,' she exclaimed, looking around again to see if the famous Filipino action star was present. Conway grinned to himself. Filipinos loved action movies, the more murder and mayhem the better.

Joseph Estrada known as *Erap*, was a particular favourite with all Filipinos. He epitomized the macho image visualized by many Filipino men and was adored by the women. Conway had taken Susan to a movie called *Laban Kung*

*Laban* and had been amazed how excited and enraptured this gentle, reserved woman had become watching the violence on screen.

They ordered their meal and ate in silence for a while. Susan had let her hair grow longer and it framed her beautiful face as she ate. She looked so sweet and innocent. I can't let anything happen to her he thought as she daintily brought a morsel of pork adobo to her mouth.

'Have you spoken to Mr Prickett again?' she asked tentatively.

'No, but I had lunch with Mr Sinclair. He's taken on board what I have told him and he is going to speak to the Pricketts. At this point I am just waiting to see what will happen.'She put down her fork and spoon and looked hard at him.

'There is something I must tell you Steve.' She paused for effect. 'Eduardo was found dead. He had been shot.'

'What? Where did this happen and when?'

'Yesterday…he was found in an alley not far from the Down Under, the one that joins Flores Street with United Nations Avenue. You know…nothing of this?' she asked slowly. He looked at her incredulously then carefully, deliberately, put down his knife and fork.

'I cannot believe you said that Susan. Why the hell would I know anything about it? Is that the kind of man you think I am, a man capable of murder?'

'Well?'

She lowered her head. 'No, it's just that…'

'Then why did you ask the question?' he said interrupting her. 'Of course I know nothing about it! And you say he was shot. I don't even have a bloody gun!'

'Well, I know he was trying to kill you and I thought…'

'I have no idea who killed him. I had *nothing, I repeat, nothing*, to do with his death. But I guess I can't blame you for thinking I was involved I've had good reason to want to kill someone because Jesus, there's been enough attempts to rub me out,' he said angrily.

'I'm so sorry, please, please forgive me, how could I think such a thing, but I just *had* to ask you,' she said, her beautiful face a picture of misery. His heart melted and he leant over and touched her cheek. 'It's ok sweetheart. Come on, finish your meal and let's see if we can catch a movie starring *Erap.*'

\* \* \*

Lily leapt from her limousine and rushed into the Down Under Hotel past the guard to the reception desk where Judy the front desk clerk looked up in surprise, as this distraught, fashionably dressed woman banged the desk in front of her.

'Where is Mr Conway? Mr Conway! I need to see him now! Is he here?'

Judy shook her head and looked fearfully at the wild-eyed woman in front of her. 'I, I, I, am sorry Ma'am,' she stuttered. 'I don't know where Mr Conway is, I haven't seen him for days, maybe he is at his apartment, you can...' She didn't finish because Lily was already running for the front door. 'Oh please God, let him be there,' she prayed as her vehicle sped to Conway's apartment.

She was out of the vehicle before it had come to a complete stop and accosted a guard lounging on a chair in front of the large glass front doors. He gave her Conway's apartment number and she waited impatiently for the elevator to come to ground level. She thumped the door of Conway's apartment so loudly it brought the neighbour opposite out into the hallway.

'What is all this noise for? You'll wake the dead!' he said testily.

There was no response from within the apartment. She turned to the neighbour. 'Mr Conway, do you know where he is? I have to speak to him urgently!'

He shook his head. 'I do not know,' he grunted, stepping back into his apartment slamming the door behind him.

Lily stood there defeated. She leaned up against the door of Conway's apartment and began to cry.

* * *

They left the restaurant and stood waiting outside for a taxi. The street was remote and Conway was beginning to think they might be in for a long wait. As he looked to his left he didn't notice a large black Toyota sedan with blacked out windows roll to a halt in front of Susan.

He heard her scream and wheeled around to see her being bundled into the back of the Toyota by a tall, black-clad figure.

'What the fuck?'

Black clad attempted to backhand him but the Australian ducked and smashed a left hook into the hooded jaw sending him sprawling to the pavement. He lunged for the back door and tried to rip it open but was belted across the head from behind and slumped half conscious against the side of the vehicle. His legs buckled as he was hit again and hauled into the back seat falling on top of a still screaming Susan. A few in the restaurant heard the commotion and came running but all they saw was a large black sedan speeding off into the night.

# 23

General Fabian Ver roared into Malacanang Palace leapt from his armoured jeep and hurried up the front steps ignoring the salutes of the Presidential Security Command guards. He was ushered into the Presidential chamber where Ferdinand Marcos sat waiting, wearing his traditional white *Barong*. Ver looked at his president in despair. The *Barong* hung on a body once robust and full of life, now frail and thin; the presidential face gaunt and ashen, the eyes bloodshot from booze and lack of sleep. Ferdinand Marcos was a very sick man. A desperately worried Ver informed him of the defection of the PMA graduates.

'Excellency, we must immobilize Sotelo's helicopters. We have two fighter planes ready to destroy them the moment your order is given!' An exhausted Marcos sighed and considered his options. Long minutes passed before he looked up at his General. To Ver, his expression seemed one of resignation and defeat.

'My order is not to attack,' he said quietly.

'But Excellency the civilians are massing near our troops, we cannot keep withdrawing…' implored the General, but Marcos interrupted him.

'My order General is to disperse (them) without shooting.'

A frustrated Ver glared at his Commander in Chief.

'Fuck! We cannot withdraw all the time…'

'No, no, no! Hold on. You disperse the crowds without shooting them. You may use any other weapon.' Marcos dismissed him with a salute. An angry, dispirited General Ver left Malacanang palace knowing in his heart that all was lost.

He was right. Later that morning, the Filipino people spoke and Corazon Aquino was sworn in as President of the Philippine Republic.

* * *

Back at home a frantic Lily Li picked up the phone and dialed the Down Under Hotel.

'I must speak to Mr Keyes…it's urgent!'

'Sorry ma'am,' said the operator, 'My Keyes is not on duty.'

'Can I have his phone number it's a matter of life and death!' she cried, 'please hurry.'

'Just a moment please,' replied the operator languidly, ignoring Lily's desperate tone. The next twenty seconds waiting for the number seemed like an eternity. *Where is that stupid girl?* She sighed with relief when the operator finally returned and read out the number.

'Thank you. Now are you sure that is the correct number? Ok.'

She slammed down the phone and dialed Keyes' number. No answer.

'Shit! Where is this man?' She was about to hang up when she heard, 'hello Keyes here.'

Lily blurted out what she had heard at the police station.

'Mr Keyes, Mr Conway is in mortal danger, you must find him quickly and tell him what I have told you…please Mr Keyes…'

'I'll phone him right away, he's probably at his apartment.'

'No, he's not there, I've already been. Do you know where else he might be?'

Keyes thought for a few moments before answering. This was bad, very bloody bad. After what Conway had told him, all kinds of scenarios entered his head. One thing however *was* clear. Lily was on side.

'He could be anywhere.' Then he said the words Lily was too frightened to even allow herself to think, let alone say.

'I just hope they haven't got to him already. Lily are you *sure*, that what you heard was an attempt to kill Steve Conway? There is no mistake?' Keyes asked, trying to remain calm.

'What do you think the words "Conway" and "eliminate" mean Mr Keyes?' she snapped.

'Ok, sorry, thank you. I'll phone the Australian Embassy immediately and get back to you later.' He dialed the embassy and asked for Roberts, telling the operator it was a matter of the utmost urgency.

'I'm sorry, Mr Roberts is not here, please leave your name and phone number and I will have him contact you when he is available.'

'For God sake do you know *when* he will be available?  Please…this *is* a very urgent matter, it could be life and death.  I must talk to Mr Roberts now!'

'No, I am very sorry sir, but leave your name and number and I will make sure he gets your message,' the operator replied in her mechanical, public service voice.

He left his details slamming the phone down in frustration and growing alarm.

* * *

In the darkness of the back seat of the Toyota, Conway struggled with his assailant until he felt the cold steel of a pistol barrel shoved against his temple.

'I will shoot you and her now if you do not stop struggling,' hissed his captor.

Susan, could barely move with Conway squashed against her and the Filipino gunman hard against him but somehow she was able to slip one arm around Conway.  Then she began to sob.

'It's ok,' said Conway unconvincingly.  His words had little effect.  Her small body continued to tremble.  'Susan, it's probably mistaken identity.  Once they know who we are I'm sure they'll let us go.'  She knew he was lying and shivered involuntarily.  Who are these people and why have they taken us?

The darkened windows made it impossible to see in which direction they were being taken.  All he could hear was the noise of the beeps and horns of the heavy traffic beyond those windows.  The front seat was blocked from his view by a blacked out glass panel.  He could not tell how many were in the vehicle as few words had been exchanged but in a vehicle of this size he estimated there were probably four including the driver.

'Be quiet,' ordered the gunman, thrusting the revolver against his head harder this time.  He glanced at his watch as the Toyota finally came to a halt.  They had been travelling a little over half an hour and were probably still within metro Manila.  They were ordered out and told to stand facing the vehicle with their feet apart, hands outstretched onto the roof.

Conway's stomach knotted fearing the worst.  After surviving the horror of Vietnam am I going to be shot down like a dog?  He tried to put his arm around a still sobbing Susan but it was roughly pulled away.  Suddenly, fear left him to be replaced by a burning rage.  If the fucking VC couldn't kill me, these bastards aren't going to either.

His eyes swept quickly from left to right trying to get his bearings.  They were in a storage yard on the Manila docks partly filled with shipping containers.  In the dim lighting beyond them to the left he could just make out what appeared to be a line of warehouses. A number of ships lay at anchor beside the dock, freighters, container vessels and a large cruise liner.

So there were only three of them including the driver who remained in the car. They were now searched. (why the hell would they search little Susan?) One of the gunmen was tall, the other stocky and considerably shorter. Both clad in black.

Conway had no idea what was to come next but if they were to get out of this he had to do something…now! He moved slightly toward Susan's left and with his lips hardly moving, from the corner of his mouth he whispered, 'scream.'

She made no move and for a second he thought she had not heard him. Then she screamed. Even Conway jumped. It was high-pitched and in the still night air it sounded like the shriek of terror from a wild animal.

The gunman behind him grunted in surprise. At that moment Conway made his move. He elbowed him sharply in the belly and followed it with a vicious backhander sending the guy sprawling onto his back. The taller of the two stood staring open-mouthed for a second then raised his pistol to fire but Conway was too quick. He kicked him between the legs…hard. He stood for a moment frozen with shock then dropped to the ground clutching his groin in agony.

The first gunman had dropped his pistol and was scrabbling around on the ground trying to find it when Conway karate kicked him beneath the ear knocking him out. The driver seeing what was happening opened the door to join the fray…Bad idea. Conway slammed the door breaking his arm leaving him trapped against the cab screaming. Tall guy had reached his knees in a valiant effort to regain his feet. Conway whirled around and kicked him under the chin hurling him onto his back, out cold. Grabbing Susan's hand they ran, weaving in and out of the containers toward the darkened warehouses.

\* \* \*

'Hello, Jack Roberts? Hi, this is Jumbo Keyes, the assistant manager of the Down Under Hotel. I want to report a missing person.'

'Yeah, who is it…an Australian?' asked Roberts wearily. It had been a very long day and he was in the middle of an important meeting and did not want to be disturbed. The bloody woman on the switch needs her bum kicked. I told her no phone calls. Bloody Consular should be handling this not me I'll get the details and pass it on.

'Yes it's Steve Conway.'

'Conway!' Roberts disinterested tone changed instantly. 'Steve's a mate of mine, tell me more Mr Keyes. When did he go missing? Tell me everything you know…everything! When and where did you last see him? Do you suspect foul play?'

'Absolutely Mr Roberts,' replied Keyes to the last question.

Keyes outlined the details of his last meeting with Steve and the attack on Boracay by a member of the Western Police Division which followed his bashing in Sampaloc and the shooting outside Lily's residence.

'Mr Roberts, I heard there was to be another attempt on his life and now he's disappeared.'

Roberts listened in silence taking notes. When Keyes had finished, Roberts questioned him further. The American did not reveal the source of this latest rumour indicating it could be hearsay, but since he hadn't heard from Conway in the past couple of days, he feared the worst. Roberts was non-committal, thanked Keyes for his information and said he would look into the matter as soon as possible.

'Thank you sir…and Mr Roberts,' Keyes voice betrayed his fear. 'I am *very* worried given what has happened to Mr Conway in recent times. Without being too melodramatic sir, I believe this could be a matter of life and death. *Please* will you look into this matter…now!'

Roberts a cop for over thirty years, hated any member of the public telling him how and when to do his job.

'Mr Keyes, I am *extremely* busy, have very limited resources, but I *assure* you I will give this matter my top priority thank you,' replied Roberts abruptly ending the call.

'You better pal,' said Keyes to himself, 'otherwise you will be less one countryman if you aren't already.' He phoned Lily and related his conversation with the Australian detective.

'All we can do is hope for the best now I am sorry to say Lily. I will go and scout around the area and make a few enquiries, I have a photo of him so that might help. *The Black Jack* might be a good starting point.' Lily thanked him and said she would ask among her customers and let him know if she heard anything.

* * *

At Club Filipino following the inauguration of Corazon Aquino there were great celebrations. The new President of the Republic smiled and gave her famous *LABAN* sign and looked with pride at those gathered around her. There was a proud Aurora Aquino, the mother of her assassinated husband

Ninoy, holding the bible upon which Cory swore her oath of allegiance. Beside her stood a smiling Juan Ponce Enrile, Fidel Ramos and many other leading politicians, church leaders including Cardinal Jaime Sin, head of the Philippine Catholic church, together with high ranking businessmen and women.

Outside Club Filipino all the way to EDSA a crowd of two million people cheered and many wore yellow, the colour of Aquino's campaign for the presidency and sang *Bayon Ko* (My Country) a popular folk song which had become the unofficial national anthem.

At Malacanang Palace Marcos conducted his own inauguration taking an oath of President of the Philippines on a balcony above hundreds of shouting loyalist supporters. He had invited many foreign dignitaries but none attended, although Moscow sent a message of congratulations.

Some likened it to a Shakespearian tragedy, with the king shorn of his power yet still taking the oath. His wife, Imelda Marcos had to get in on the act and tearfully sang *Dahil Sa Iyo* (Because of You) the couple's theme song. The television broadcast to the remaining government channel was cut off by rebel troops who had captured the station.

When the ceremony ended Marcos and his family, with a few close associates, remained confined in the Palace as tens of thousands gathered at Mendiola Bridge just one hundred metres away. The mood was angry but priests pacified them and warned them not to become violent.

Desperately Marcos cast around for advice finally phoning US Senator, Paul Laxalt who advised him to "cut and cut cleanly". There was a long pause. Marcos clenched his teeth and expressed his disappointment then said…'I agree.' That afternoon he spoke to Ponce Enrile requesting safe passage for him and his family. It was granted and at 9 pm that night the Marcos family was transported to Clark Air Base before flying to Guam and on to Hawaii where they had been accepted in exile. The nation cheered as their yoke was finally lifted.

The long reign of Ferdinand Emmanuel Edralin Marcos was over.

* * *

The noise of the heavy calibre bullets smashing into the concrete wall just above their heads was deafening. Susan ducked and clutched his arm as splinters stung Conway's cheek. He immediately felt a warm trickle of blood. They crouched low stumbling on in the darkness. Conway's breath was coming in short, ragged gasps. His heart felt as if it was about to burst through his chest.

'*Saan sila nagpunta?*' (Where did they go?) '*Nandoon sila*' (I think they're over there),' yelled their pursuers, now within a few metres of their prey, cursing and shouting as they crashed and blundered into things unseen.

Conway pulled Susan down and wrapped his arms around her. They huddled together trying to quieten their breathing which seemed to shout their presence. If they were captured again, there would be no mercy. He was convinced they would be executed immediately. How did I get into this? I took this hotel job in the Philippines to start a new life and find peace. Here I am in the Port area of Manila being chased by people hell bent on salvaging me. *Salvage.* Where I come from it means resurrect. Here it's termination with extreme prejudice. How the hell are we going to get out of this?

He froze, the hair on the back of his neck tingled as footsteps came nearer and he felt Susan grip his arm fearfully. The beam of a flashlight shone back and forth and up and down only metres from where they lay. His breathing seemed harsh and loud in the still, foetid night air. The footsteps were almost upon them. They could see the shadowy outline of one of their pursuers. In a moment they would be discovered.

His hand found a small rectangular object. It was heavy and felt like half a brick. Holding his breath he drew back and hurled it as far as possible. In his awkward prone position it was difficult to throw any distance but he heard it crash against something well away from the dark figure in front of him.

Flashlight swung around and shouting in his native tongue stumbled away in the direction of the noise. Conway waited for a few seconds then slowly and silently rose to a position just above a crouch then together they moved away step by silent step. It would be dawn soon and they needed to put space between themselves and their pursuers. The danger was one false step, one stumble, one noise and they would be discovered.

They crept past shipping containers, large cartons, pallets of oil drums and bales of what appeared to be cotton, each step taking them further from danger. But these guys were determined and still too close for comfort, shouting and cursing in frustration. A weak shaft from a street light outside filtered through a broken window. Conway stood with his back to the wall and squinted out onto the dock. There was no movement in the gloom. His eyes began to become accustomed to the light revealing a door twenty metres to his right.

He motioned to Susan to drop to the floor and they crawled toward it. Sweat poured down his face and spine. He breathed out slowly trying to stifle a cough which would have brought them undone.

Below the door they lay for a moment. Slowly he reached up his fingers closed around the door's handle. He turned it a quarter inch at a time. It was locked. He lay back down and swore under his breath. What now? He could hear them getting closer again. Then he remembered glimpsing another exit further back down the warehouse on the same side as they were now. If they could make it there, they might still have a chance.

He had no idea of how many were looking for them but it was now more than two; probably at least half a dozen. Maybe there were more outside but that exit was their only hope. He glanced down at his luminous watch, 4.45, dawn would break soon; even now the first light seemed to be filtering through the darkness. Time was running out.

Every step was slow, careful and silent as they got closer to that door. Every three paces they stopped and stood like statues, listening. Slowly, very slowly they approached the exit. His muscles were screaming with tension, their breathing harsh. Surely they must be heard. Just inside the exit he half rose and carefully peered around the door. There was no movement, nothing but an eerie silence.

They eased their way around the door and moved outside in a crouch. In the first grey streaks of dawn they slowly stood with backs pressed to the wall. They made their way cautiously along the wall until they came to a corner which faced on to an exit gate about thirty metres away. Between them and the gate was a small shed, probably a watchman's office. This cut the open space to the gate in half. If they could get to the other side of the shed they could see any pursuer coming from the warehouse without being seen themselves.

Bent low they crept quietly toward the shed. They made it and breathed a collective sight of relief, so far, so good. They could not hear their pursuers. There was still this silence. He took a deep breath and heard Susan behind him sigh with relief. They moved around the little shed toward the gate.

'*Magandang amaga*' (good morning) Mr Conway, I've been waiting for you!'

They froze. Standing two metres to their left was Ramon Sanchez and in his right hand he held a squat .45 Glock pistol pointing at Conway's head. From behind a shipping container to Sanchez' right emerged six other figures in jeans and tee shirts, all pointing revolvers in their direction.

Game over!

# 24

Susan gripped Conway's hand. She was almost hyperventilating with fear. Conway looked at Sanchez with a mixture of hate and bewilderment.

'You! Why? Sanchez, why?'

'You don't have to know why, you white monkey,' sneered Sanchez, 'but I *can* tell you this, your employer and I will not miss your passing.'

'Oh my God,' cried a white-faced Susan, 'what do you mean? Who are you?'

'This is Ramon Sanchez, the Chief of Police of the Western Division. You know of him don't you, Susan, he's the keeper of the peace, the protector of the public, one of Manila's finest,' said Conway. 'But in reality he's just a cheap punk, a common criminal, no better than the people he throws in the slammer, and probably worse than most. He's also a drug trafficker and those extra funds in that account is drug money he and Prickett have been laundering. I'm right aren't I?'

Sanchez mouth twisted in an ugly smile which didn't reach his eyes.

'You have been meddling in things which do not concern you Conway. We could not allow you to continue, you and your little friend I am afraid...will have to disappear.'

'Yeah, you're good at making people disappear aren't you Sanchez? But for a cop you're dumb! This time you have gone too far. The Australian Federal police and the Americans are on to you. My employers in Australia have already been alerted and will ask all kinds of embarrassing questions if anything happens to us.'

'You are the fool Conway. Your police and the Americans cannot touch me. As for your Australian employers if they ask questions they will be told you and this woman, have disappeared with a large sum of money from the hotel bank account. Foreigners disappear in this country all the time, in a week you and your friend will be forgotten.'

'You're a fucking disgrace to your uniform and your country. This is what I think of you arsehole,' said Conway, spitting at the police chief's feet.

Sanchez' eyes dilated and his pale face reddened. He took a step forward and pistol whipped Conway across the face opening a gash across his cheek sending him staggering backward losing his grip on Susan.

He glared back at Sanchez, blood streaming down his cheek. 'You're a big man with a gun and a few mates; not so good if there was just you and me, you piece of shit!'

Sanchez took another step forward to repeat the dose but thought better of it and turned to his men. 'Tie them up and take them to the *Asian Explorer*,' he snapped pointing to a rust bucket moored half way along the dock. 'I want them on board and out of sight. Quickly, it's getting light.'

Conway went to put his arm around Susan but was roughly dragged away. Two held him while another tied his hands doing the same to Susan who looked ready to faint. They were hustled along the wharf and up a gangplank onto the *Asian Explorer* where a solidly built bearded man greeted Sanchez with a smile and a handshake.

'So these are my two new passengers?' asked the bearded one.

'Yes, they both love the sea and requested a voyage on your fine ship captain. They have also declared a fondness for swimming, I hope you can accommodate them my friend,' Sanchez said with a knowing smile.

'I am sure I can sir, they will have a nice long swim where I am taking them,' laughed Suarez mirthlessly.

Conway watched this exchange in a daze. The whole thing was surreal. It's like a fucking b-grade movie starring two ugly bad guys and Susan and I. But it *was* real and these bastards are going to kill us. Obviously they are going to drop us overboard somewhere out in the deep. Poor bloody Susan, a gentle, innocent girl who has never hurt anyone or anything in her life and, it's *all my fault.*

'You know where to take them,' said Suarez to a couple of the crew. Two burly seamen took hold of each of their arms and pushed and prodded both along narrow, ill-lit companionways, down steel ladders, through small doors in bulkheads down deep into the dark, foul smelling bowels of the ship.

They were pushed through a low door into a tiny, damp, unlit, evil-smelling chamber with a ceiling so low Conway was barely able to stand upright. The door was closed and sealed, leaving them in total darkness.

Susan began to sob uncontrollably and because his hands were still bound he could not hold her and could think of no words of comfort. They were in deep trouble and all he could do was hope and pray that someone realized they were missing.

* * *

Jumbo Keyes burst into *The Black Jack* and looked around wild-eyed. Biro and Mullet were in their usual spot at the bar doing their usual thing. Mullet was closest so Keyes walked up to him and grabbed him by the shoulder and spun him around, spilling his Scotch into his lap in the process.

'Hey what the fuck!' yelled Mullet angrily as a dark stain spread across his cream shorts.

'Either of you bastards seen Conway?' growled Keyes ignoring Mullet's howls of indignation, 'or you?' he said turning on Biro who paled when he saw the expression on the black giant's face. A look he'd never seen before… it frightened him.

'Nu..nu..no!' They both stammered in unison.

'Where's Groyne?' demanded Keyes.

'He's…ah… in boob mate,' stammered Biro, 'the cops took him away a couple of days ago, think he's in the Immigration jail,' and anticipating Keyes next question, 'Bert's girlfriend runs the joint now, she's fallen on her…' but Keyes was already charging back out the front door. He stood on the sidewalk wracking his brains. Where to now? Then he took off in the direction of *Nightbirds*.

It was the same story there. No Conway, and Lawson was also in custody. Ok, only one thing for it, the Western Police District and a certain police colonel. But before I do, I better phone Lily. He went to the office of Barney Lawson. It was empty so he used the bar owner's phone.

'Any luck Lily?' asked Keyes hopefully.

'No, no one has seen him, I am really worried now Mr Keyes, I think something awful has happened to him,' she said panic-stricken.

'I am going to beard the lion in his den right now.'

'What do you mean Mr Keyes?' Then she realized…

'Oh no! *Please, please,* don't go to see Sanchez,' she pleaded, 'it is too dangerous!' But Keyes had already hung up.

A slightly built desk sergeant glanced up and then did a double take when he saw the big black American burst into the station.

'Can I help you sir?'

'I want to see Colonel Ramon Sanchez, and it's very urgent!' bellowed Keyes, fixing the little desk sergeant with a fierce stare.

'I am very sorry sir, but I am afraid Colonel Sanchez is not here at the moment,' replied the policeman shaking his head.

'Where's his office?'

'Down the corridor on the right sir, but as I told you…' Keyes was halfway down the corridor before he had finished his sentence.

Ramon Sanchez was on the phone to Captain Suarez organizing the time to unload the "presents" when Keyes stormed into his office.

'Who are you? What do you want? Get out!' shouted Sanchez. Keyes leant over the desk and grabbed Sanchez by the shirt front and lifted him effortlessly from his chair.

'Where's Conway, asshole?' snarled Keyes.

'Let go of me, I will have you arrested,' gasped Sanchez. 'I know nothing about Conway. Arrest this man!' screamed Sanchez as three cops, guns drawn, rushed into the room. Keyes released Sanchez who slumped back into his chair his eyes blazing.

'You goddam motherfucker, I *know* you know where Conway is!' yelled Keyes as more police piled into the office. The big American belted the first one, backhanded a second and thumped a third before going down under a kicking, punching pile of brown uniforms. Bodies where hurled back and forth across the room banging into wall and overturning chairs until finally Keyes was subdued, handcuffed and carried off to the cells.

Sanchez had cowered in the corner while the mayhem took place. With his office empty again, he picked up the phone he'd dropped onto his desk when Keyes grabbed him.

'Ah, ah, are you still there Captain? Oh, no…no…just a minor problem,' gasped Sanchez, 'nothing…to worry about.'

'Now, about the unloading of my "goods"; when are you due to sail? on the high tide just after midnight? Good! I want to leave the unloading till the last moment. I feel it will be safer then. So I will be there to supervise and take delivery at around 11.30 pm Captain. Good, thank you.' Sanchez replaced the receiver with a satisfied smile and leaned back in his chair humming 'California, here I come.'

\* \* \*

Keyes was thrown into a small, windowless cell with several other prisoners. Their eyes widened as this large black foreigner was pushed in among them. They stepped back to give him room watching him warily. What had this man done? Obviously something very bad?

I've really fouled it up for you this time Steve old buddy, thought Keyes ruefully as he stood gripping the bars. Why couldn't I have been smarter and kept my temper. I might have got something out of that piece of garbage instead of landing in this shithole. The look on that guy's face told me he knows something but now I'm no use to you at all buddy. You really fucked it up this time didn't you Keyes?

\* \* \*

Outside in the streets millions of Filipinos cheered wildly and celebrated the arrival of their new President as she drove that evening in a motorcade up Roxas Boulevard. At the Port of Manila, a freighter had almost finished loading its cargo in readiness for imminent departure.

\* \* \*

The foul air in their little dungeon was suffocating, the heat almost unbearable. The humidity must have been bordering on 100%. Conway's eyes were blinded with sweat and his shirt was glued to his body. Susan was praying quietly. He could not see and her words in the darkness seemed eerily disembodied, as if they were coming from the Spirit World. She continued to pray for sometime then stopped and remained silent.

It was impossible to tell how long they had been held. Time seemed to have stood still. The only sound was the occasional slap of water against the thin rusty hull. They were on the bottom of the vessel with virtually nothing between them and the murky waters of Manila Bay.

'I can't tell you how sorry I am for getting you into this Susan,' he said, realizing how hollow his words must have sounded. Then she surprised him.

'We must have faith,' she said, her voice suddenly quite strong. 'Whatever happens to us is God's will. If we are meant to die it means God is calling us.'

'I can't hear him, and I'm not ready to meet him just yet Susan and I think…' he was interrupted by the harsh, drawn out clank of metal on metal from just outside their prison.

'My God, what's that,' cried Susan.

'That's the anchor chain, they're pulling it in,' replied Conway grimly.

'This ship is about to set sail.'

# 25

Ramon Sanchez stopped in front of the cell holding Jumbo Keyes, his smile, supercilious, confident.

'I'm going to charge you with assault Mr Keyes, and I am sure I can think of a few other things to charge you with as well. You, my American friend, are going to be behind bars for a long, long time, so you better get used to it.'

Why, didn't I mention this motherfucker's name to Roberts, thought Keyes glaring at the gloating police chief. If nothing else I can put the shits up him.

'I wouldn't be too cocky Sanchez. Your name has been given to certain people in other law enforcement agencies in this town. Your days are numbered, asshole.'

'These are the words of a desperate man Keyes,' sneered Sanchez. 'Otherwise you would not have come alone. No one, not even foreign lawmen in this town can touch me. I know too many people in high places. Now I must go, I have an important appointment to keep. Goodbye Mr Keyes, you won't be seeing me again.'

'I wouldn't be too sure about that asshole,' whispered Keyes.

* * *

The hawsers of the *Asian Explorer* were lifted from the bollards and splashed into the waters of Manila Bay as the old freighter prepared to ease away from the dock; next stop Singapore. Below, deep in their tiny prison Conway and Susan nearly lost their footing as the huge turbines slowly rumbled into life.

'Susan,' Conway tried to keep his voice level and make himself heard above the creaking of the hull and thunder of the engines. 'I haven't the words to express my true feelings for you and how horrible I feel about getting you into this mess.'

'You don't have to apologize darling, you are a good man. You were only trying to do your best and I am so glad we found each other.' Her voice began to break. 'I will always love you and I will…' she was interrupted by movement outside their door. 'Oh my god!, she cried, as a commotion erupted outside their door. The scrape of metal on metal, then the door was thrust open and their eyes blinded by a flashlight being shone in their faces.

Conway's heart sank. This is it! He looked across at Susan. She seemed resigned to their fate. Oh God, you never even gave me a chance to kiss her goodbye. Two armed, black-clad, masked men pulled them out into the narrow companionway and quickly untied them. Nothing was said and one motioned with his pistol toward a steel ladder leading to an upper deck. They must be going to keep us on deck until we are out at sea then chuck us overboard, thought Conway, helping Susan on to the ladder. At least we'll have our hands free, not that it's going to be much help.

They climbed to the next deck and stumbled along darkened passages to another series of stairs which brought them onto the brightly-lit top deck crowded with more armed men in black. They stood disoriented and blinking in the glare of the lights when one of the black-clad men, larger than most, stepped forward.

'G'day Steve,' grinned Jack Roberts extending his hand. 'Geez, you get yourself into some strife don't you mate? Who's the little lady?'

They stared in disbelief; then Susan fainted.

Several pairs of hands quickly picked her up and whisked her away. Conway suddenly noticed the engines had stopped. The ship was still docked.

A million questions raced through his mind. His emotions were all over the place the main one being relief. My God, we've been rescued but, who are all these guys? How had Roberts come to be on board? How had they been found?

'We've had a big result tonight mate and caught a rather big fish,' said Roberts, 'but I'll fill you in later. First we'll take you both ashore, clean you up, give you a good feed and let you rest.'

'Jack, I don't think I could sleep but I *would* love some water and I want to see Susan, please.' Conway suddenly felt his legs turning to jelly as the impact of their rescue hit home and the adrenalin in his system began to slow down.

He was taken to the sick bay where Susan lay pale and exhausted. Her face lit up when he entered. She held up her arms as he bent to kiss her. He carefully laid her back on the bed. The trauma of the events kicked in and she again burst into tears. He sat down and held her hands waiting for her to regain her composure. It was many minutes before her small body stopped heaving and the tears subsided.

'I told you God would look after us darling,' she smiled.

Roberts allowed them another half an hour together before he took them ashore and under police escort raced them to Manila Doctors hospital where they underwent a medical check which cleared them of any serious injuries though the mental effect they were advised, was likely to last for some time.

'Got a surprise for you two,' said a smiling Roberts after the check up.

'Not another one Jack, we've had enough surprises to last us a lifetime, haven't we Susan?'

'This is a pleasant one mate. I am taking you to the 5-star Manila Peninsula Hotel in Makati to recover. Courtesy of the Australian government,' winked Roberts. 'Get a good night's sleep and I'll come and see you in the morning.' He shook Conway's hand again and pecked Susan on the cheek before closing the door behind him.

They stood looking at each other still trying to comprehend the fact that their ordeal was over.

An hour later they gazed lovingly at each other in a suite of the Manila Peninsula.

'Come here Miss,' said Conway. They hugged and kissed for many minutes until she disengaged herself and stepped back.

'I have to have a shower darling, will you wait for me please,' she said with a cheeky grin.

'Go go, you little devil,' he laughed, patting her on the backside. She took a couple of towels from the bed blowing him a kiss before closing the bathroom door behind her. Twenty minutes later she emerged enveloped in one of the huge white towel and another around her head. She looked like a little girl and he told her so. She smiled prettily and poked her tongue out at him.

'Don't be long darling, I'll be waiting,' she said in a tone so full of carnal promise and out of character for Susan, he stopped at the bathroom door to check her expression to make sure he'd heard correctly.

After the luxury of a long warm shower, he came out vigorously drying his hair, tossed the towel away and went over to the bed. She had turned off the main bedroom light leaving the room lit by the soft, golden glow of a bedside lamp. He looked down at her laying there, the covers pulled up to her throat. She was smiling, innocent and angelic. Then he roared with laughter...not again! She was in a deep sleep.

* * *

'How are you both this morning?' asked Roberts cheerily, joining them for the buffet breakfast. Conway assured him they were both on top of the world, the bloom in Susan's cheeks confirming his statement. They looked refreshed and rested; a far cry from the dishevelled, tired and scared couple he had rescued the night before.

'Ok, I know you are both dying to know what went on last night so here's the story.'

They sat hanging on every word as Roberts told them of the tip off about the *Asian Explorer* and how he had mounted an operation with the assistance of the American Embassy and the Philippine National Bureau of Investigation. The "Big Fish" he had referred to was Colonel Ramon Sanchez, Chief of the Western Police District.

'We caught him red-handed taking a delivery of a pretty sizeable shipment of heroin, and weapons,' said Roberts, slicing a succulent piece of pink papaya.

'As you know Steve, we've had our suspicions for quite a while about this guy and the drug scene, but had never been able to pin him...until now. What we didn't know, was that he was supplying the NPA with guns and other military hardware. Anyway, he's going for a long stretch in Muntinlupa jail and who knows; being a cop he'll have a lot of enemies in there. He'll be lucky to come out alive.'

'And guess what? When we hinted at a possible reduction in sentence and perhaps even something better, he sang like a canary, spilling the beans on one, Mr Percival Prickett, his wife and a number of politicians who were close to Marcos. The NBI will take care of the locals and we'll look after the Pricketts who unsurprisingly, have denied any involvement, blaming Sanchez for everything. They claim he coerced them. There sure ain't any "honour among thieves". We know now,' he went on, 'the Pricketts have been in this caper with Sanchez for years, and were laundering the money from these deals through a secret bank account in the Down Under Hotel...' he paused, looking at them with raised eyebrows.

Conway and Susan looked at each other.

'Jack, Susan and I have been investigating that account and it's one of the reasons we got into that mess. When Sanchez captured us I told him we knew he and the Pricketts were laundering drug money. I was bluffing but after what you had told me and the extra funds in that account, it wasn't hard to put two and two together. Now it's confirmed what will happened to the Pricketts?'

'We arrested them in Angeles City last night. Perc will be extradited to Australia to face a series of crimes involving fraud and other matters including murder. We have reason to believe that they were involved in the disappearance of a number of locals and an Australian, one George Wallace Coleman.'

'My predecessor Jack, what do you know about him? I asked in the hotel but no one seems to know what happened. He was here one day, gone the next, very fishy indeed; especially as no one wanted to talk about it.'

Roberts nodded and held up his cup for a waitress to refill his coffee. 'Yes, that's because in this town loose lips can lead to cement shoes. It seems he got wind of what the Pricketts were up to. An NBI informant in the drug scene apparently spilled the beans naming names to a friend of his working in the Down Under Hotel, a certain Efren, a driver, who was very friendly with Coleman. He tells Coleman the Pricketts were trafficking drugs. Coleman reports it to the police and guess what…they both disappear. Imelda was involved so will be charged as an accessory to murder as well. You will also be interested to know my friends,' said Roberts, his craggy face breaking into a broad smile. 'Perc will be accompanied to Australia by Messrs, Groyne, Lawson and several other fine examples of Australian manhood.'

Conway shook his head in admiration. 'That was some operation Jack, but how did you know Susan and I were on board that ship?'

'We didn't. What happened was, when we boarded and rounded up the Captain, who by the way, also faces a long jail term, a young Filipino crew member alerted us and told of two foreigners, a male and female who had been brought aboard as prisoners. The kid nearly crapped himself when he saw us charge on board and couldn't wait to tell us he had nothing to do with you two. Luckily, he worked on the deck near where you were held so he led us to you. And you know what Conway?' grinned the big cop. 'I wasn't at all that surprised when your ugly mug appeared. Trouble seems to follow you around my friend.'

'Conway smiled ruefully. It certainly does, ever since I came to this city, there's been one thing after another; shootings, bashings, even on Boracay someone tried to knock me off.'

'Yeah, Keyes rang me and gave me the story. You've certainly kept me and my boys on their toes Steve, even the other night they tried again but we…ah, it doesn't matter, shouldn't have mentioned it, now let's…' Roberts stopped as if he had said too much, but Conway pressed him.

'Ok Steve, it won't hurt you to know this. Remember taking a short cut between Flores Street and United Nations Avenue a few nights ago?'

'Yes…I do. Hey! Wait a minute!' Conway put down the spoonful of cereal he was about to eat and looked hard at Roberts. 'That's where they found Eduardo! You didn't…'

Roberts smiled crookedly and held out his hands, palms upturned in a gesture of innocence. 'Of course not, what do you think we are? Probably some local hood got him; look what happened to Groyne?'

They stared at each other for a few seconds and Conway decided to drop it.

'Yeah, maybe…this Ermita can be a dangerous place at night can't it Jack?'

They finished their breakfast and again thanked Roberts profusely. Conway shook his hand while Susan stood on tiptoes, put her arms around him and kissed him on the cheek, causing the big tough cop to blush.

'Don't leave town you guys, I'll need statements from both of you but I can wait a day or two,' he grinned. 'Just get yourself together again ok?' He gave them a brief wave and ambled out into the sunshine of a bright Manila morning.

* * *

With Perc and Imelda in custody, James Sinclair met with Conway and advised him a majority vote of the shareholders at an Extraordinary General Meeting had agreed to offer him a shareholding in the company and control of the Asian operations. A delighted Conway accepted immediately.

Although the overthrow of Marcos dominated the front pages of all Manila metropolitan newspapers, the arrest of Sanchez, the successful drug bust and the rescue of an Australian Steve Conway and Filipino Susan Santos was also given prominent coverage.

This resulted in an immediate phone call from an 'over the moon' Lily Li who's delight was tempered by her concern for Keyes whom she hadn't heard from since he had told her he was going to visit Sanchez.

'And darling,' she paused, 'I have decided to lease my restaurant and check out the opportunities in Shanghai but I will keep in touch and I want you to promise me you will do the same, ok?'

'Sure, when will you leave Lily?'

'In two days time darling, I have a lessee already. I am so busy finalizing things I won't have time to see you, bye bye my lover. *Please*, don't forget. Keep in touch, I don't want to lose you,' she said, blowing him a kiss down the phone.

Jumbo Keyes was released from the Western Police District jail soon after following another raid by Roberts, McGaw and the NBI.

To Conway's shock and dismay, Susan returned from Las Pinas a week later to announce that after much thought and soul searching, she had decided to accept the position with the accounting firm, and had been appointed to head up their Hong Kong operation. Zeny Diaz would come from Angeles to take her position in Manila.

Conway tried to talk her out of it but she was adamant. As much as she cared for him, the recent events both politically and personally were enough to convince her she needed both a change of job, scene and country and this offer was simply too good to refuse.

On the night before she left for Hong Kong they had dinner together in a Filipino restaurant on United Nations Avenue. It was not a happy occasion. Their conversation was awkward and punctuated by long pauses. Neither knew how to express what was in their hearts.

Conway thanked her for her loyalty and love and said how much he would miss her.

'Susan I came here to find peace and start a new life. At first what I found was something completely different, but now I see a new beginning. I have also come to love and respect the Filipino people. They have taken me into their hearts and I could not ask for more. Your country has turned the page and like me, is beginning a new chapter. From what I have seen of their courage, determination and strength they will forge a great new era in the history of this country.'

'Thank you darling, as a Filipino I am so proud and happy to hear your words. I love you and will never forget you and I hope one day…' tears welled in her eyes. She was unable to finish the sentence.

It was late when they walked back to MH Del Pilar where she would catch her jeepney to Baclaran on the first leg to Las Pinas. As they waited, Conway thought about the times he had stood with her on that very spot waiting for the jeep to take her home and tonight…it would be for the last time. She gripped his hand tightly. He looked down to see tears rolling down her cheeks.

A few minutes later from the direction of TM Kalaw Street along came a typical, brightly coloured jeepney which she reluctantly waved down. As it pulled up beside them, they looked into each other's eyes for a long moment.

Her took her in his arms and kissed her long and lovingly. The ever romantic Filipino passengers in the jeep began to cheer. The cheers would have turned to tears had those watching, known they were witnessing the last act of a love affair. Finally, reluctantly, Conway stepped back still holding her hands. She looked up at him, her cheeks wet. It was a look he would never forget.

'Goodbye darling, I love you,' she said softly. Then she climbed into the back of the crowded vehicle, sitting on the end so she could still see him and wave. The lump in his throat threatened to choke him as the jeepney slowly rumbled off down MH Del Pilar. They waved frantically to each other until she was out of sight…

He stood like a statue for many minutes staring down Del Pilar to where he had last seen her. Tears blurred his vision. Images of their sweet times together flashed through his head. Is this the end? Will she ever come back to me? Will I ever see her again? With shoulders slumped, he turned and walked slowly back toward the Down Under. Rounding the corner into United Nations Avenue, he glanced down at his watch.

She had caught the last jeep to Baclaran.

# The Last Cyclo to Thanh da

## John J Pullinger

*Life, Love, Death 'n Fate.*

Manila hotelier Steve Conway returns to Vietnam to look for an old wartime friend and falls in love with a local girl. But the relationship is threatened by cross-cultural differences, family resistance, and an insanely jealous, dangerous ex suitor.

Conway persuades his employers to allow him to look at expanding their operation in Saigon. He realizes he has found the love of his life and the relationship blossoms but behind the scenes he is unaware that moves are taking place to bring about its destruction.

He also does not realise he is being stalked by a crazed ex marine intent on killing him.

What started out as a short holiday becomes a turning point in Steve Conway's life leading to a roller coaster ride of love, hate, murder and ultimate tragedy.

9 781921 787218